The Playgroup

Nelsie Spencer

The Playgroup

St. Martin's Press
≈ New York

www.stmartins.com

Design by Kathryn Parise

LIBRARY OF CONGRESS CATALOGING-IN-PUBLICATION DATA

Spencer, Nelsie.
    The playgroup / Nelsie Spencer.— 1st ed.
       p. cm.
    ISBN 0-312-31172-9
    1. Upper East Side (New York, N.Y.)—Fiction. 2. Mother and
child—Fiction. 3. Women comedians—Fiction. 4. Married
women—Fiction. 5. Play groups—Fiction. 6. Adultery—Fiction.
I. Title.

PS3619.P644P57 2003
813'.6—dc21

                         2003053048

First Edition: September 2003

10 9 8 7 6 5 4 3 2 1

For Doug

Acknowledgments

Since I'm an ex-actor and *way* past my ingénue phase, this is probably as close as I'm going to get to that Oscars speech, so bear with me.

First of all, if you could picture me in something slinky, yet age appropriate, at the Dorothy Chandler Pavilion standing behind the podium clutching a big, golden statue, I would appreciate it. Take a moment to check my jacket photo and get the mental image—Okay!

"This is so exciting, really! I never expected . . ." Now my Miracle Bra–enhanced breasts are heaving in my low-cut evening gown as I gain my composure. I smile humbly, gazing out at the cheering audience.

"There are two people without whom I couldn't have written this book; first of all, my wonderful husband, Doug. Thank you for waking me every morning at five A.M. (even though I always growled at you) with a hot cup of coffee, and encouraging me to get up and write.

"And my brilliant teacher, Lou W. Stanek; from the minute we met you totally 'got' me and never, for a minute, tried to take me away from *my* voice. Thank you for your wisdom about the craft, for your love of story, and for your insight, humor, and expertise.

"I owe a huge debt to my early readers: Tracey Grimaldi, Ally Sheedy, Kate Long, Patience Moore, Carty Spencer, and especially Dennis Drake. Your support kept me writing. And thank you, Charlotte Sheedy, Ellen Pall, and Mary Wowk, for your suggestions and expertise in navigating the world of publishing. Thank you, Regina Scott and Ally, for some great insights at the eleventh hour."

The music has begun to play, my cue to wrap it up. I lean into the microphone, showing off my cleavage and my Harry Winston gems.

"And thank you to Gretchen and Susan and all the women at Madison Playgroup," I yell over the orchestra. "And Andy at 3 Guys Coffee Shop. And, of course, thank you, Katherine Tegen, my wonderful friend and agent who took this book when no one else would, and my editor, Jennifer Weis, whose notes really *did* make it a stronger, tighter book. And special thanks to Eliza Shallcross, my anal-retentive (thank God!) copy editor— a woman I never met but a woman whose knowledge, patience, and attention to detail made a huge difference to me and my book."

The music is so loud now that I am shouting, waving my statuette in the air. "And, most of all, thank you to Rayna and Malcolm." My voice catches here and my eyes fill with tears. "You are my biggest teachers and your presence in my life keeps me humble. Your arrival on the planet inspired the whole thing."

I am dragged away from the podium by Billy Crystal. Cut to commercial.

To the Reader

Though many of the places mentioned in *The Playgroup* are real, all of the characters and situations are from my imagination.

As far as Park Avenue Playgroup is concerned, the characters and events that occur there are also fictitious. Though the book was inspired by my treks to the East Side when both my children attended The Madison Playgroup, both they and I had a wonderful experience there. In fact, the co-directors of The Madison Playgroup—Gretchen Lengyel and Susan Beatus—are two of the most caring and knowledgeable women that I have ever met in Manhattan's private school arena.

The Playgroup

Chapter One

"Have you ever noticed how there are no whorehouses for women?" The slim, fit comic looked at the audience as if waiting for an answer. "Well, I have, and I've decided to open one. I have. It'll be similar to the male version; there will be all these different rooms where women can receive a variety of services and choose from a stable of handsome men. But"—she thrust her index finger into the air—"the services that we offer will be a little . . . different.

"For instance—for fifty dollars the man of your dreams will make out with you, just make out—for an entire hour." She raised her eyebrows at the crowd. "Even if you ask him to go further, even if you *beg* him—he will stop, look you deep in the eyes, and say, 'I don't want to rush things. It's too perfect between us. I'm—just—not—ready.'" She brushed her highlighted blond bob from her face, enjoying the laughter from the crowd, then, "Or for twenty-five dollars you can pick out your dream stud and for half an hour he will act like he's really interested in whatever you're talking about." Ellie hit *pause* on the VCR. The lithe image of the comic froze on the TV. "Wow, I'd completely forgotten about this bit." She picked up the video case.

"Caroline's—December '97," she read aloud to the empty living room. She grabbed the remote, took a sip of coffee, then pressed *play*. Her frozen image came back to life.

"I don't find homosexuality weird. Not at all. The fact that God expects men and women to couple—for life—that's the one I'm still trying to fathom. Don't get me wrong, I love men. It's just men and women are *so* different; we think differently, we communicate differently, sexually we're *so-o-o* different. Right? I mean, why would women pay for sex? Men love sex; they hate to snuggle. Of course my whorehouse will offer snuggling. I think it'll be a big seller, don't you? It's going to be a little pricey, I'm afraid. I mean, I know we're paying these guys, but they're still men, right? And I think men feel the same way about snuggling as women feel about anal sex. It's just not natural." The video Ellie nodded and waited for the laughter to subside. "So, for snuggling we might have to offer a package deal—y'know, intercourse followed by fifteen minutes of snuggling will be—say two hundred bucks. But just snuggling—fifteen minutes of snuggling only? That'll be two hundred and *fifty* bucks." A loud whoop of familiar laughter rose above the rest. The sound of it made Ellie's stomach leap; she hit *pause*.

"Oh, my God, Robbie." She pressed the power button and the TV went blank. She felt suddenly lost as she took another sip of coffee and looked out the window. The morning sky over Seventy-sixth Street had turned from gray to white.

She was a shitty friend, move on. The words from last night echoed in her head.

RING!!!

"Shit, shit, shit!" She dropped the remote on the tomato red sofa and sprinted to find the cordless.

She looked on the phone cradle in the hallway, empty. "Of course!"

She ran to the kitchen, scanning the scene; counters, butcher block, microwave—no phone.

RINNGG!!

"Where the heck did I . . ." She darted for the bathroom, threw back the batik shower curtain. There it sat, tubside, just waiting for her. She grabbed it and hit the *talk* button just before it rang again.

"Hello," she said in a breathless whisper.

"What are you wearing?" a raspy male voice asked.

She stopped short, sat on the edge of the tub, and looked down at her boxer shorts and T-shirt.

"Black fishnet stockings, three-inch heels, a red garter belt and matching bustier," she purred into the phone.

"Panties?" asked the caller.

"Who needs panties?" She smiled as she slipped into the cool, empty tub.

"That's quite an outfit for six thirty in the morning."

She leaned back, resting her head on the bath pillow. "I'm quite a woman."

"Aaahhh!" An ear-piercing scream jolted Ellie upright in the tub.

"I gotta go." She scrambled out of the tub.

"But I want to tell you how I'm going to peel those fishnets off your delicious legs then bury my face in your . . ."

"Peter, I gotta go!"

There was another, longer, more urgent scream. Ellie ran into the bedroom.

"Angus is awake, bye." She threw the cordless on the bed, scooped up her five-month-old, whipped up her T-shirt, unsnapped her nursing bra, and popped her nipple into his gaping mouth with the speed and ease of a pit mechanic. He sucked hungrily, his wide blue eyes darting around the room, then locking with Ellie's. "Hello, cutie cakes. Happy now?"

He closed his baby blues and sucked blissfully in response. Calm had been restored. Ellie lay down and situated Angus so he could nurse and, hopefully, go back to sleep. She caressed his perfect little head and gently fingered the soft spot on the top. She could feel her pulse slowing, her milk letting down, a heavy tingling in her breasts, and all those delicious, nursing hormones being released into her bloodstream. She watched Angus nurse. He had definitely reached nirvana. She looked across the expanse of their king-sized bed to her daughter, sleeping, motionless, wondrous. My life is perfect, she thought, now all I want to know is, what's gonna fuck it up?

The night before, after the children were happily snoozing in their family bed, Ellie had once again summoned the energy to get up and suit up. After three years of marriage and two kids very close together she and Peter were still totally attracted to each other and fucking all the time. Part of it was due to Peter's unfailing libido and his unending attraction to her. The rest was thanks to Ellie's philosophy about sex after kids: "Sex is like working out. I rarely *want* to do it, but I just put on the outfit and show up. And afterwards I'm always glad I did."

So, true to her creed, Ellie had put in her diaphragm, slipped into her lavender see-through nightie (with the matching thong), and slinked into the living room. Peter's thick, blond hair had glowed in the TV light. He was reclined on the opened sofa bed, engrossed in yet another show about the building of the Sphinx. Without looking up he patted an empty space on the sofa bed. She sat next to his handsome, naked body and placed a hand on his strong, broad back. He grabbed her foot, pulled it to him and held it tight. As always this gesture filled her with love for him.

It had been their first Christmas together. They had had three dates and no sex, yet. Peter had invited Ellie to spend the holidays with his mom and dad in New Jersey. At first Ellie had been on cloud nine at that prospect. After all, Peter *was* the first nice guy she had dated—ever. But the closer Christmas came the stronger her desire for flight had become. The night before they were supposed to leave for Christmas with Peter and his nice, normal, blue-collar family the phone rang.

"Hi, it's me," Peter's voice sang through the phone.

"Hi," Ellie replied. The sound of his sweet voice filled her with dread. "Peter, listen." Her brain began to scramble. "I hate to say this but I can't go to New Jersey."

Silence from his end.

"I just got a call about a catering gig," she lied. "It's on Christmas Eve and it pays double time and I really need the money, so . . ."

"Fine," was all he said and the line went dead.

Ellie held the silent receiver in her hand, and a sweet breeze of relief blew through her. Well, that's that, she thought, hung up the phone and went to the kitchen.

An hour later the doorbell rang. Ellie opened the door to the smell of pine and a huge potted Christmas tree filling her dim hallway.

"Merry Christmas!" Peter's head popped out from the side of the tree. "I figured if you couldn't come to Christmas, I'd bring Christmas to you." Then he pulled out a box of lights from behind his back.

Ellie stood paralyzed, filled with a mixture of fear, annoyance, and love for this man that she barely knew. "Come in," she said finally.

The two of them strung the lights wordlessly. Now what? Ellie wondered as she kicked off her slippers and plopped down on her thrift store sofa.

"Check it out," Peter said, as he turned off the floor lamp and plugged in the lights. They began to blink on and off as a tinny version of "O Tannenbaum" filled the room. "They're musical, too." He turned to Ellie, beaming, then sat down next to her and grabbed one of her bare feet. Then he settled in next to her and put her foot in his lap, holding it tightly.

No one's ever held my foot before, Ellie thought, blissfully. Her foot in his hand gave her an inexplicable feeling of safety and belonging that she had never before experienced. I think I love this man, she had thought as the two of them sat silently and her foot melted in his wonderful hand.

*B*ack in their living room in the blue glow of the TV, Ellie put her hand to her breast and felt wetness. "Shit! Remind me to get breast pads," she told Peter when she saw the small circle of breast milk on her nightgown.

"Mm-hmm," Peter said, riveted by the bearded archaeologist who was droning on and on about rainfall and limestone erosion.

"And I'm thinking of changing diaper services. Someone at the gym said that Tidy Didy was . . ." She stopped, found the remote amongst the crumpled sheets on the sofa bed, and muted the TV.

"Hey! That was interesting."

"Do you remember when *I* used to be interesting?"

"You're still interesting," he said, still watching the muted TV. "Don't I follow you around all the time with a hard-on?"

"Peter, your hard-ons for me have nothing to do with how interesting I might or might not be. If I ever, God forbid, was in an accident and ended up brain dead you would be in the ICU, looking at my lifeless body, about to shut off life support, see the outline of my breast through the sheet, and get a hard-on. Am I right?" She looked at him, waiting for the truth.

"Okay, okay!" He grinned. "I want to fuck my wife. So shoot me."

"You want me, but you don't want to talk to me. Face it, I'm boring. My life is all about breast pads and diaper services."

"You're not boring, you're a stand-up comic."

"Peter, I haven't done a set-since Angus was born. And only about ten sets since Ahnika was born."

"Well, you're pitching your series idea to HBO."

"What idea? I haven't come up with an idea to pitch yet and it's less than four weeks away."

"Mm-hmm." She had lost him to a muted Sphinx show. She turned off the TV with an angry gesture of the remote.

"Really, I bore myself. I haven't watched the news since Angus was born. We could be at war and I wouldn't even know it. Arlene's always talking about this novel or that novel that she's read. She's even in a book club. I just smile and nod, pretending that I've read something besides *Curious George* or *The Runaway Bunny* in the last two years." She jumped off the sofa bed and started to pace.

"I don't have any friends. I'm so sleep deprived I can barely finish a sentence, let alone be funny or original."

"You have friends. What about Arlene?"

"Yeah, she's fun."

"Now, is she the one with the lawyer husband?"

"They all have lawyer husbands. She's the one with the breasts and the curly hair, green eyes?"

"Kinda curvy?"

"Right. She's great. But she probably already *has* a best friend. Most women in their early forties do. I still miss Robbie. I wish I didn't but I do."

"She was a shitty friend. Move on."

"I have moved on. It's just—I need new lipsticks."

"What?"

"Well, who am I supposed to go to buy lipsticks with? You? A girl is supposed to have a best friend. Otherwise, God would've made men better at chatting on the phone and more willing to go to Meg Ryan movies."

"Two beautiful kids, a rent controlled two-bedroom apartment in a doorman building, a fantastic husband." He patted his chest and raised his eyebrows at her. "What's the problem?"

"I know." She stopped pacing and looked at him, petrified. "Its perfect." She sat down on the edge of the sofa bed as her eyes brimmed with tears.

"Honey." He turned her toward him. "What's up?"

"My mother called today."

"And?"

"You know what she said when I told her about pitching my idea to HBO? She said *I* was following in *her* footsteps! Can you believe that? I've been writing since I was in eighth grade. I was always writing—poetry, journals, short stories. And *I've* been getting paid to write since 1994. . . ."

"El, what if she never does it?"

"Does what?" she asked, turning to him.

"That step thing. The nine step."

"It's not the *nine* step. It's the *Ninth* Step." She smiled at his ignorance in the world of Twelve Step lingo. "Making amends to persons we had harmed. You make it sound like some elaborate dance she has to do, 'the nine step.'"

"Well . . ."

"Oh, you are . . ." She grabbed a chenille throw pillow and hit him on the head.

"Hey!" He laughed grabbing the pillow from her. "But isn't that what you want? You want her to perform some elaborate dance."

"No. That's not it. One word is all I'm waiting for—sorry."

"Well, what if she never says it? You're driving *yourself* crazy waiting for it."

"You are talking yourself right out of a blow job, mister." She turned away from him.

"But really, what if she never says it?"

She whipped around to face him. "But shouldn't she? Shouldn't she say she's sorry?"

"I think you have to let go and let God here, El." He leaned in and kissed her on the neck.

"You're evil," she said softly, not resisting. "But you're right. Oh! Get this: she's got a fucking book tour."

"Really?" He kissed her on the mouth, lips parted, his tongue just skimming her teeth.

"Yeah." She kissed him back. "A book tour that's coming to New York."

He reached around beneath her nightie and started stroking her bare ass.

"Oh, God. I can't think when you do that." She went limp.

"That's the idea." He was nibbling her neck as he maneuvered her onto her stomach. "We're happy, get used to it."

"That's the problem. I'm not used to this . . . this . . ." she was struggling to stay focused ". . . bliss."

"Uh-huh." He began massaging her neck with his lips and teeth as he continued to delicately explore her inviting ass. She had started to drift into space as he moved down her back to her ass and started artfully biting and licking her. Then Ellie had finally surrendered to Peter's velvet fingers and gone to another place; to that place where she just floats on the sea of arousal.

Angus was now softly snoring, his jaw slack on Ellie's nipple. She gently slipped it out of his mouth, kissed his pink cheek, retrieved the cordless from the sheets, and sneaked out of the bedroom.

Back in the living room, she sank down into the sofa and reached for her coffee. She took a sip.

"Uh!" she said to the empty room. "Kids and hot coffee just don't go together."

She auto-dialed Peter and headed back to the kitchen and the microwave. "What're you wearing?" she asked when he answered.

"Hi, sweetie, how's my boy?"

"Sleeping, thank God." She put the coffee back in the microwave and hit *start*. "So what time did you get to the office this morning?"

"Quarter to six."

"You're insane. Honey, you need your sleep."

"I know, but I've got this big deadline on Tuesday."

Beep! She retrieved her coffee from the microwave.

"Now, listen. I have a wardrobe question."

"Oh, right, today's Ahnika's first day at Park Avenue Playgroup. What time does she have to be there?"

"It's eleven to eleven-twenty."

"You're kidding? Twenty minutes for five grand?"

"No, no. They do this thing called 'phasing-in' so the kids don't freak out. They start off in small groups, too. Then the groups get bigger and the sessions get longer until it's everybody together for the whole two hours."

"Two hours for five grand?"

"Hey, it was *your* idea to send Ahnika there."

"How long does this phasing in stuff take?"

"She should be done around Thanksgiving."

"Your kidding me!"

"I'm kidding."

"Wait a minute. What's she wearing?"

"I'm not worried about what Ahnika's wearing. Between your mother and my mother she's wardrobed into her fifth year. What am *I* wearing?" she asked, heading back for the sofa.

"Are you serious? Didn't you just buy all those clothes in Soho?"

"Peter, I'm going to the East Side. I don't have any headbands or loafers. These are not my people! I-I-I don't know the secret handshake." She had decided against the sofa and opted for pacing.

"Don't tell me you're intimidated by some silly women with family money? You had family money."

"'Had' being the operative word. Past tense. Anyway, I'm not intimidated. I just don't belong there. All that WASPy, Ivy League shit gives me a twitch. I know those people. They're my mother's people." She caught her reflection in the hall mirror. Her inch-long, white blond hair was sticking up all over. In vain she tried to mat it down into something a little less punk looking. "And my hair."

"I love your hair. I'll never forget that first night after you cut it."

"That was some night. If I'd known it would've made you the animal you are today, I would've cut and bleached my hair before our first date." She tugged at her spiky hair. "Oh, Peter, what could we have been thinking?"

"We were thinking that it's a good stepping stone for a prestigious nursery school."

"Do you hear how crazy that sounds? You and I went to public schools and we turned out fine."

"Ellie, this is Manhattan in the year 2000, not the suburbs we grew up in the sixties. And I did fine because I worked my butt off. Look, I'm proud that I'm a fire captain's son and all that. But, I've built the business, and now we're making all this money. Why not give our kids an easier road?"

"But five thousand dollars to have people we don't know play blocks with our two-and-a-half-year-old? That's insane, right?" She was moving into the playroom.

"We thought you could make some new friends there. Remember? Other mothers who don't feel resentful that you and I are happy and fertile."

"Peter, how am I going to make friends with these women?" Ellie began frantically throwing wooden blocks into a plastic bin. "We have nothing in common. While they were furnishing their country homes, I was probably passing puffed pastry at their Christmas parties, for Christ sake!"

"So you didn't go to Smith. So what? None of them ever had their own TV show."

"Honey, it was public access." She smiled as she put the last block away and snapped the plastic lid in place.

"Yeah, but you had a development deal with Comedy Central."

"Peter, *you* could get a development deal with Comedy Central." She was calmer now as she rearranged Ahnika's stuffed animals.

"Look, just go and check it out. At the very least it's material. Maybe the TV show could be about the mothering rituals of the American WASP."

"Mothering and WASPs? There's an oxymoron in there somewhere." She walked into the bedroom and stared into her closet.

"So, do I rush to Brooks Brothers and buy some sexless yet appropriate outfit, or do I just wear my motorcycle boots, hip-huggers, and a baby tee to show off my belly button ring?"

"Yeah! Maybe you'll meet some lipstick lesbian there who wants to have a three-way with us."

"At Park Avenue Playgroup? I'm sure the place is just crawling with lesbians."

"Seriously, El, you're always telling me how isolating it is being a mother. Maybe you'll meet some nice moms there."

"Maybe. Who knows? Stranger things have happened."

"Hi, Mommy!" Ellie looked down to see her sleepy and smiling two-and-a-half-year-old. She was instantly bathed in wonder and joy.

"Morning, snuggle bug. Peter," she said into the phone, "Ahnika's up. I gotta go."

"Give her a kiss for me. I love you. Bye."

"Bye." She tossed the cordless on the bed. "Climb on, cutie." Ellie sat on the edge of the bed and patted her shoulders. Ahnika struggled to her feet as she rubbed the sleep from her eyes and climbed on for a piggyback ride. "Let's pick out some great outfit for your first day of school."

"Oh, boy!" yelled Ahnika. "School!"

Angus rolled over and blinked his eyes at his mother. Ellie's day was about to start in earnest.

Chapter Two

Central Park was lush after a summer of thunder showers, the leaves shining and fat in the midmorning sun. Angus was dead asleep in the Snuggli; his head slumped into Ellie's chest. Ahnika was happily waving at doggies and chatting to herself in the stroller. She looked like the poster child for the funky, West Side toddler: black leggings, little red zippered boots, a tie-dyed swing top, and her blue jean jacket.

Ellie, after about five costume changes, had gone with the boots and hip-huggers but a slightly longer T-shirt. No belly button ring showing. Maybe later in the school year.

When they exited the park at Seventy-second Street on the dreaded East Side, Ellie rubbed her lower back and scanned the area for signs of any border patrol. I hope I'm not stopped and checked for ID she mused; I don't have a Bergdorf's credit card.

The buildings lining Fifth Avenue were proud and solid. Several nannies (one in a nurse's uniform) pushed their charges in Emmaljungas (the Rolls-Royces of baby carriages) up and down the park side of Fifth. Ellie headed for Madison Avenue. If I'm going to be on the East Side, she thought, I might as well be in the thick of it.

A pack of designer-suited shoppers passed her as she turned north on Madison.

Accessories! Ellie thought as she gave them the once-over. *That's* the big difference between the East and West Sides—accessories; jewelry and scarves and puffy headbands. Everyone over here is perfectly, obnoxiously accessorized. Just check out their earrings: Chanel, Reinstein/Ross, pearls. Mine were ten bucks on the street. The pack of women disappeared into Pierre Deux.

Shop, shop, shop, Ellie mocked them silently as she watched them eyeing the overpriced home furnishings. Okay, El, cut it out. *This* is why I hate the East Side; I'm so busy in my head feeling both superior and intimidated all at the same time. It's exhausting! Look at these babes, they just ooze confidence, Ellie thought as she watched them through the front window. But really, Ellie, would you *want* to be them? They're so shallow and materialistic.

The ladies who lunch were shopping and chatting, oblivious of their voyeur.

But, Ellie, if you're deciding what kind of people they are based on their earrings, then who's shallow? Ellie shook her head and looked to the heavens. God, help me out, could you? I'm doing it again. It's so like Dad I hate it.

𝒴ears ago, Ellie and Jack, her first cousin and best friend, had driven the ninety miles to see her dad and take him out to dinner. Paul, Ellie's dad, had been serving his fourth year on his first conviction and had been granted a four-hour pass. Ellie was sixteen and, in the face of a mountain of evidence to the contrary, still thought her jailbird dad was the coolest and the smartest. After all, it was the early seventies and Angela Davis was in jail, right? And *she* was super cool. (Of course, she wasn't in jail for trying to buy a bank with its own money, but that's a minor detail.) They had gone to The Jolly Roger, where all the families of the inmates went. A very pretty, redheaded waitress shuffled up to their table.

"Can I take your drink order?" she asked, tugging at her short, tight, petticoated uniform.

"That uniform's ridiculous," Paul said, instead of placing his drink order.

"I beg your pardon?" the waitress asked, then looked down at her uniform as if considering it for the first time. It looked like the mini version of something Lana Turner might have worn in *The Three Musketeers*, with puffed sleeves and a low neck accentuated by a crisscross tie underneath her breasts.

"It's sexist and demeaning that they make you wear that outfit," he told her in a protective tone.

Ellie beamed with pride that her father was a feminist and coming to the aid of this poor exploited worker.

The waitress took a deep breath, closed her eyes, and yelled, "Andy!"

A fat yet muscled man in his mid-forties walked swiftly from the cash register to the table. His polyester shirt was open to the middle of his chest to reveal a plethora of blond chest hair and a couple of big pecs. He was wearing brand-new Lee jeans and his silver belt buckle was a big coiled snake. He smacked the waitress playfully on the butt; she smiled at him lovingly.

"Is there a problem?" Andy asked the group, all innocent and friendly like.

Ellie knew a threat when she heard one. Her father didn't say a word. The waitress looked at Andy and then looked at Paul to let him know who the troublemaker was.

"No problem at all, sir. But I'd love a Seven-Up with lots of ice, please," Ellie said taking her voice up an octave.

"Make that two," Jack chimed in.

The waitress and Andy turned to Paul, waiting. He was looking down, studying the grinning pirate on his place mat. Ellie found herself eye to eye with the snake on Andy's belt buckle, her face hot with embarrassment for her father. Would he have the balls to say what he felt about the poor exploited waitress or not? Ellie wasn't sure which one she was hoping for.

"Gin and tonic with lime," he said finally, looking up, tossing his sandy blond hair and giving his best country club grin. The waitress met his gaze, then wrote down his order and walked away without a word. Andy put his big pink hand on Paul's shoulder and gave it a good squeeze.

"You folks enjoy your dinner, now." And he walked back to the cash register.

Ellie started talking cheerily about the trip up. Paul didn't look up from his pirate. Didn't say a word. When the waitress came with the drink order, Ellie's chatter got louder and more animated. When the waitress walked away she stopped talking and looked to see her dad's response. He took a long sip of his G&T as he watched her ruffled ass bounce across the room.

"Frigid," he announced with all the authority of Sigmund Freud.

Since his incarceration, Ellie's dad had been reading everything in the prison library about psychoanalysis—Freud, Jung, Erikson—and now considered himself an expert. At the time, Ellie had thought her dad was brilliant, able to diagnose this poor, sick woman in less than ten minutes. What a guy!

$\mathcal{A}$s Ellie watched one of the shoppers in Pierre Deux examining a throw pillow, she shook her head at the memory. And hoped to God she wasn't like her father.

"Go, Mommy! Go!" Ahnika bellowed from her stroller. "We going to school."

"Alright, sweetie. You're right. Mommy was just a little lost for a moment." They continued up Madison and Ahnika went back to talking to herself and looking for doggies. They passed a dandy of a man in a gray suit. His blue-striped shirt had a contrasting white collar and he wore a tiepin and cuff links. More accessories, Ellie thought. Yes, she had entered a new world, a world of cuff links and buffed fingernails, of puffy headbands and Ferragamo loafers. And she was scared.

Park Avenue Presbyterian had an impressive flight of stone stairs leading to two huge wooden doors. Ellie stopped and sighed.

"Ahnika, honey, can you get out of the stroller? Mommy needs to . . ." She felt a tap on her shoulder.

"Need some help?" Ellie turned to see a gorgeous, leggy woman in her mid-thirties, with a darling, dark-haired boy holding her hand.

"Uh, yeah. Thanks. You going to the playgroup?" Ellie asked. She looks familiar, Ellie thought.

"Yes we are!" Leggy said in that overly cheery voice that inexplicably afflicts all mothers. Her hazel eyes seemed to sparkle as she lifted the stroller. "Mason, c'mon, sweetie. Up the stairs." Mason marched up the stairs, scowling.

"Oh, she can get out. I . . ." Ellie called as she and Angus hurried to hold the door open.

"Thank you," Leggy said as the four of them left the bright sunshine and entered a huge, dark anteroom. Leggy put down the stroller. "There you go."

The ceilings were at least twenty feet high with two huge chandeliers. An enormous stone fireplace was against the far wall. King Arthur's court, Ellie thought.

Leggy turned to Ellie and thrust out her hand. "Missy Hanover."

Missy Hanover reeked of confidence. She was tan. She was thin. And she was very tall (maybe six feet). Her shiny, chin-length, golden brown hair was swept off her patrician face with, yes, a tortoiseshell headband. Though Missy Hanover was wearing leggings, running shoes, and a T-shirt, everything about her screamed money—old money.

Well, I can't imagine *how* I would know her. She must just look like someone famous, Ellie decided as she took note of Missy's accessories: pearl earrings, a Tag Heuer watch, and a big fucking diamond engagement ring with lots of baguettes and guard rings, all platinum, of course.

"Ellie Fuller. Nice to meet you." She gave Missy a nice firm handshake that her mother would've been proud of.

"Mommy! Mommy!" Ahnika was straining against the stroller straps, her eyes fixed on Mason who was crawling under a dark green sofa at the far end of the room.

"Okay, okay." Ellie stooped and unbuckled Ahnika. She hopped out of the stroller. It tipped over backward and crashed on the dark brown tiles thanks to the numerous bags hanging on the handles. "And that's Ahnika," Ellie said as Ahnika sprinted to join Mason.

"And who's this sleeping angel?" Missy asked, stroking Angus's fuzzy head.

"That's Angus."

Missy gently tipped his head back and peeked at his sleeping face. "Oh, my God! He's delicious!"

"Thank you. I thought for sure we'd be the first ones here," Ellie said as she bent to pick up the stroller, then put her gym bag in the seat for ballast. "I didn't know how long it would take to walk across the park."

"Oh, you're a West Sider?" Missy asked.

"Yep," Ellie said trying to sound confident. But she felt suddenly as if Missy were studying her. Jesus, she thought. You'd think I just told her that I was a contortionist or a talk show host.

"Mason, sofas are not for jumping," Missy called across the cavernous room, using the parenting book lingo. Mason, with Ahnika watching from the floor, continued to bounce.

"Mason, sweetie, we're guests here. I'm going to count to five. If you don't stop jumping by then you're going to get a time out."

Mason hopped off the sofa, still scowling, and started crawling under it. Ahnika bent down and peeked at him. Mason roared loudly.

"He's in his lion phase. I'm sure its testosterone driven. Harper, my daughter, never roared."

As if on cue, Ahnika gave out a nice loud roar. Ellie felt proud. I think I like this one, she thought. Any woman who uses the word "testosterone" five minutes after meeting you can't be half bad.

Missy settled into a large oxblood leather armchair. This place looks exactly like Granddad's study looked thirty years ago, Ellie mused as she sat in a dark green leather wing-backed chair next to her.

"Look at those two," Missy said, tilting her head toward the kids. They had abandoned the sofa and were crawling on hands and knees around the area rug, still roaring.

"Well, I'm shocked. Ahnika's usually very shy in new situations. I thought she'd be clinging to me." Ellie watched the kids play, wondering if Missy could somehow sense that Ellie was not part of the club and that she didn't belong at this WASPy school. Or did the fact that her mother had gone to Smith and her grandfather had been a bigwig in the auto industry somehow shine through? Yes, Ellie had met the Fords and the heads of GM. She'd gone to big family reunions at her grandparents' sprawling house in Grosse Pointe. But she had *always* felt like the weird one, the hippie cousin from California. The only grandchild who didn't go to boarding school.

One Christmas, Ellie and her mom had taken a last minute trip to visit her grandparents. Ellie's dad had just been indicted for fraud and leaving town seemed like the logical thing to do. All her preppie aunts, uncles, and cousins still lived in Grosse Pointe and everyone had been invited to a Christmas party at the Ford mansion. It was 1970 and Ellie wore her new striped velveteen bell-bottoms and a matching lavender blouse with a big collar and puffy sleeves. She felt so cool. So groovy. When she arrived at the party she discovered that all the other girl cousins were wearing little matching kilts with big brass safety pins, white blouses with Peter Pan collars, and navy cardigans. What a bunch of kissy assholes, Ellie thought. But she had spent the entire party hiding in the Ford's pool house, hoovering a huge bowl of mixed nuts and chain-smoking Parliaments that she'd stolen from her mother.

So, that 'time-out' thing really worked," Ellie said, trying to shake off a sudden urge for a cigarette and a big bowl of mixed nuts. "I've never tried it."

"You're kidding?"

"No. I'm not tough enough."

"I can't believe you've never used a time-out."

"Neither can my mother." Ahnika sprinted for the double doors with Mason in hot pursuit. "No running, guys."

"Oh, my mother thinks I'm way too easy on Mason, that I baby him."

"Well, he *is* a baby. He's two for God's sake. *My* mother wrote a best-selling book on family dynamics. So you can imagine."

"You're kidding. A bestseller? What's the title?"

"Oh, I'm sure you've never . . ."

"No, tell me. I'm a big reader."

"*The Family Dance.*"

"Oh, my God! I love that book!"

"I know," Ellie said flatly. "Everybody does." There was a long silence.

Ellie didn't want to have yet *another* conversation with someone about how her mother's book had changed their lives.

One of the huge doors opened and sunshine spilled into the dim room. A jumble of mothers, nannies, strollers, and children, all in silhouette, piled into the room. Missy jumped up and ran to hug one of the mothers. Mason abandoned Ahnika as a chunky, sailor-suited little boy called him over.

Perfect, Ellie said to herself. They're all buddies.

Ahnika ran over to the group and roared her best roar yet, then ran back to the safety of her sofa. That's my girl, Ellie thought. Mason followed Ahnika, roaring all the way. The little sailor and a little angel dressed like Caroline at JFK's funeral followed, laughing and screaming.

"Camille! *Fais attention au divan! Sois sage*," called a dark-haired, petite woman wearing an Hermès scarf and a simple red dress.

Ellie was rethinking her outfit.

Great, they all know each other *and* they all speak French. I might as well have ex-waitress tattooed on my forehead. The next hour stretched out in front of her like a jail sentence. What will I do? What can I say? Two years of high school French twenty-five years ago. I'm doomed.

"Ellie Fuller—" Ellie looked up to see Missy standing over her with the perfectly coifed Frenchy "—this is Marie-Claire Chevalier."

"Ahlow. Nice to meet you," Marie-Claire said in a thick French accent as she held out her hand, red nails gleaming.

"*Bonjour*," Ellie said.

Marie-Claire patted Angus gently on the head and began speaking to Ellie in French. She said something about *petit bébé* and *très* something or other.

"*Non, non. C'est tout*," Ellie interrupted her. "That's it. *Bonjour, au revoir, ou est la bibliothèque?* That's the end of my French. *C'est tout*."

Marie-Claire looked confused. Missy laughed, then began jabbering to Marie-Claire in French. Ellie was smiling and nodding, pretending to follow. Missy's probably explaining to Frenchy that I'm a culturally challenged biker from the West Side, she mused, eyeing the exit.

There was a thud and a scream. Camille had tumbled off the green sofa and was sobbing in a ball.

Thank God, thought Ellie as Marie-Claire jumped up and ran to her aid.

"She thinks I'm looking for the library, doesn't she?" Ellie asked her newfound friend and translator.

"I'm afraid she missed the joke." Missy said, smiling.

"Hello, my wonderful playgroupers!" said a loud voice from the far end of the room. All eyes turned to a short, sturdy woman standing next to the elevators.

Veronica Leeds, the cofounder and codirector of Park Avenue Playgroup, was standing with her arms outstretched, looking like a grandmother greeting her grandchildren at the airport. She wore a long denim apron that was covered with appliquéd flowers, frogs, Elmo, etc. Several colorful papier-mâché bracelets clanked on both wrists. Her thick salt-and-pepper hair was in a short, confident cut.

Lizzie Daniels, her other half, stood behind Veronica, towering over her by a good six inches. Lizzie's denim apron was crisply ironed (*sans* appliqués) and her thin, sandy blond hair was chin length and pulled off her long, narrow face with a puffy madras headband. She was trying hard to not look dour and disappointed.

"Well, what's everyone waiting for?" Lizzie said as she gestured toward the waiting elevator.

Missy leaned in to Ellie and whispered, "The Cagney and Lacey of preschools."

Ellie tried not to laugh. "Did you make that up?" she asked. Missy nodded proudly. "That's a good one."

Everyone marched obediently into the elevator. Marie-Claire began retying the bow on Camille's dress as she spoke softly to her (in French, naturally) and Mason and Ahnika were playing peekaboo between Ellie's legs. The chunky sailor's brown eyes filled with tears as he squeezed the hand of his tall, handsome, dark-skinned nanny. When the elevator doors closed, Lizzie and Veronica began to sing softly:

> *"The elevator is a quiet place*
> *A quiet place, a quiet place . . ."*

Like magic, all noise and movement stopped, and the children listened to their new teachers dutifully. The little sailor forgot about being sad and even Marie-Claire and Camille, despite the language barrier, were sucked in.

". . . It floats us gently up in space
Up in space, up in space
The elevator is a quiet place
Hush, hush, hush."

The elevator doors opened precisely as the song ended. Ellie and Missy exchanged a *these guys are good* look. Maybe this *is* worth it, Ellie thought as she watched the children race out of the elevator to descend upon their newfound utopia. Ahnika headed straight for the water table, grabbing a funnel and a sieve. Ellie pictured Ahnika's cute little swing top getting soaked in about two seconds. But in an instant yet another woman in a denim apron appeared out of nowhere, plastic smock in hand, and slipped it on Ahnika without her noticing. Ellie took a look around the large sunny room. Sailor boy was playing with a mountain of blocks, with his towering nanny close by. Camille and Marie-Claire were in the doll/dress-up area (surprise, surprise). Missy was watching Mason standing at one of the five easels, slathering paint all over his paper with every color available. Ahnika's water table, just the right height for two-year-olds, was loaded with funnels, sieves, cups, etc., and stood right next to a play kitchen bursting with plastic food of every description, miniature pans and dishes, a microwave, the works.

Angus stirred in the Snuggli and made a delicious baby sound. Ellie looked at her watch. Shit! She thought, he's going to wake up any minute and I'm going to have to nurse him in front of all these people that probably don't even *have* nipples!

"Go. Go, go, go." Ellie looked up to see Veronica flicking her hands toward Ellie in a shooing motion.

Whatta ya mean "go," Ellie thought, but found herself unable to resist Veronica's directive. She gave Ahnika one more glance, then reluctantly headed out of the play area and into a little waiting room.

I guess we're not supposed to be in there, Ellie thought as she eased herself onto a striped love seat. When she looked up Veronica was mysteriously gone. Ahnika's being so independent, she thought. I'm glad she's happy. I *think* she's happy. The waiting room didn't allow for spying. "Out of sight, out of mind," Veronica had explained when Ellie toured the place last spring.

"Honey, this is the Kids' Room," Ellie could hear Missy explaining to

Mason. "I'm not allowed in here. I'm going into the Mommy Room. You just . . ."

"*Nooo!*" Mason wailed.

Angus stirred. He's hungry, Ellie realized, a chill going through her. She checked her watch. Only fifteen minutes, thank God, for phasing in.

"You can go." Ellie looked up to see Lizzie's long face peering down at her.

"Go where?" Ellie asked, confused.

"Go wait downstairs. Didn't you read the packet we sent?" Lizzie asked with a tone she might use on a naughty preschooler.

"Of course," she lied. She feared a time-out might be in her future if she didn't watch out. "But—" Lizzie bent down and gently took Ellie by the arm and helped her to her feet "—aren't we phasing in?" Angus was stirring in earnest. If Long Face doesn't let go of my arm I'm gonna belt her, Ellie thought.

"She's happy as a lark!" Veronica chirped as she bounded into the room.

"Go ahead and go. She's fine." Lizzie wasn't even trying to mask her impatience now. She handed Ellie her purse, and the Cagney and Lacey of preschools succeeded in shooing Ellie into the elevator and away from her baby daughter.

"But it's only fifteen more minutes and . . ." You two are the Antichrists, she thought. Why do I suddenly feel like Mia Farrow in *Rosemary's Baby*?

"Trust us."

Is that tannis root I smell, Ellie wondered?

"Have a cuppa coffee, relax," Veronica said, reaching into the elevator and pressing *one*. There was a loud pounding in Ellie's ears and she was feeling lightheaded. The last thing she saw as the elevator doors closed was Lizzie's hard, smiling face. The elevator click-clicked as it descended. Her whole torso felt hollow and tinny.

"This doesn't feel right." She spoke to the empty elevator. "Nope, nope. I don't like it."

Click-click . . . click-click . . .

"I didn't say good-bye to her. What is that? If she comes out and looks for me she'll feel like I've abandoned her."

The elevator stopped with a thud. The doors opened on the lobby. Ellie didn't move.

"I *have* abandoned her!" Her mind raced. "Do I go back up?" She tapped her foot, looked at her watch. "Oh God, I hate this." The elevator doors closed; it sat still. "I'm going to have to go back up there and challenge Long Face." But she didn't move. She stroked Angus's head, it calmed her. She gave it a kiss. "Am I irreparably damaging your sister? Is she up there freaking out?" She bit her lip, touched his head again for luck, and pushed *eight*.

"We're going back!" she told Angus, feeling like John Wayne deciding to return to the battlefield to save a wounded buddy. Angus's little head tilted back, away from her chest. His eyes opened, he looked up and smiled.

"Hi, handsome. Did you have a nice nap?" He yawned, stretching open his pouty mouth, showing off his two tiny bottom teeth. "We're going back upstairs to rescue your big sister from the evil preschool teachers." He blinked twice and craned his chubby neck, checking out his surroundings. The elevator stopped on eight. His chin began to quiver. As the elevator doors opened he started to wail.

"Angus, Angus! Okay! Okay!" Ellie sprinted for the Mommy Room, unsnapping the Snuggli as she went.

"Willaby wallaby wamille,
An elephant sat on Camille."

The troops were singing, seemingly happy. Ellie stole a look through the open door as she passed. Ahnika was sitting on Lizzie's lap, smiling and doing her best to sing along.

"Waaahhh!"

"Okay, big guy, I'm trying." Ellie started to tilt Angus sideways toward her nipple. She stopped. Which breast did I use this morning? She squeezed her right one, then her left. It was plump and full.

"Willaby wallaby Wason
An elephant sat on Mason."

Ellie thought she heard the rustling of paper over the singing. Yep, there was Missy sitting in a corner reading *Town & Country*. She looked up from her magazine and smiled. Ellie smiled back, trying to act casual with her breast in her hand and a screaming child on her lap. How come *she* got to stay in the Mommy Room and I was banished to the lobby? Ellie wondered.

"Mom's getting you lunch ASAP." Thank God the singing is loud, Ellie thought. If Ahnika hears Angus, I'm sunk. She pulled up her T-shirt, unsnapped her nursing bra, and . . . Angus was happy again.

"Willaby wallaby we
Singa sing along a-with me!"

Ellie closed her eyes and tried to relax.

So, here I am, my worst fears realized; nursing Angus in front of Miss WASP U.S.A. in the middle of Park Avenue Playgroup. Perfect! Ellie could feel Missy's eyes on her. She's watching me, thinking I'm some sort of a savage for nursing my child in public?

"Good for you."

"What?" Ellie opened her eyes. Missy *was* watching her nurse Angus.

"Good for you for nursing."

"Oh, yeah. Thanks." Ellie smiled, feeling awkward as hell. Is she staring at my breast or am I nuts?

The singing stopped followed by screaming and wild applause. Angus spun his head toward the hubbub, not bothering to release his suction on Ellie's nipple.

"Ow!" She grabbed her stinging breast. "Angus, honey—" she took a deep breath "—try to stay focused. Okay?" In an instant, he was back on, sucking away. Ellie stroked his head and tried to look maternal.

"Get Angus off your breast or I will shoot you!" Ellie looked up to see Ahnika standing in the doorway, tears brimming in her eyes.

You couldn't follow directions, Ellie chided herself silently. You couldn't just stay downstairs like the nice ladies told you to.

Ahnika started to cry—loud. Oh, this is good, Ellie thought. Now *everyone* will come out and watch me nurse Angus while I emotionally torture his sister. Ellie felt a chasm in her chest open up.

No one had warned her about this—not the books or the well-meaning friends or the annoying relatives. No. They'd all talked about sleep deprivation and exhaustion and the older sibling being furious about the new baby. But this feeling in her chest, this feeling of being torn between her two babies, no one had mentioned that. A feeling that her love for Angus was somehow a betrayal of her love for Ahnika and vice versa. These feelings had been a complete surprise. Part of her wanted to tear Angus off her breast, toss him on the love seat, run to Ahnika, and hold her forever. The other part wanted to snap her fingers and—*POOF!*—make Ahnika disappear, then find a quiet secret place where she could nurse and snuggle with her precious baby boy forever.

The ever-chipper Veronica stooped down next to Ahnika, "Ahnika, let's go make a collage. Doesn't that sound fun?"

Ahnika cried louder.

"C'mon, pickle face." Veronica gently held her by the shoulders.

"NNNOOO!!!" Ahnika arched her back like someone possessed, fell to the floor, and screamed as if she were being tortured.

Ellie's mommy instincts finally kicked in, and she sprang to action. In an instant, she was on the floor next to Ahnika. With one hand, she held Angus on her breast. (Miraculously, he was still nursing throughout the melee.)

"Ahnika, Ahnika sweetheart. Look here. Look what Mommy's got. Mommy's got a lap for you." With her free arm, she peeled her baby girl off the floor and onto her half-vacant lap. Ellie rocked her sobbing daughter with one arm and held her nursing son with the other. "Okay, okay." She closed her eyes and cooed to her babies, her mission clear as the rest of the playgroupers watched in silence.

As they trudged down Park Avenue, Angus was back in his Snuggli, facing out and kicking his feet like a madman, and Ahnika was in the stroller, happily eating the biggest cinnamon bun on the East Side. Missy, carrying Mason, was doing her best to keep up.

"Where's your stroller?" Ellie asked Missy.

"I'm trying to wean him off it."

"Looks like it's going really well."

"I know, I know. But we live so close, I just thought . . ."

"I swear I feel like I've been through a war. At these prices, you'd think they'd supply the Valium. At least for the phasing in period."

Missy gave her a look.

"I'm kidding. Valium wouldn't cut it. I need heroin."

"But look at all the artwork you get," Missy said, gesturing to the roll of paintings shoved under Ellie's stroller.

"Yeah, three paintings in twenty minutes; she's one prolific girl. Do I have to save them all?"

"Don't ask me. I have an entire closet devoted to his big sister's masterpieces. Every time I try to thin them out, I get a stomachache."

"We're going to have to get a bigger apartment." They both chuckled.

" 'Get Angus off your breast or I will shoot you.' I can't believe she said that." Missy switched Mason to her other hip.

"Well, it's been tough on her. She wasn't even two when Angus was born," Ellie said defensively.

"No, I mean, she's so advanced verbally. Her vocabulary, her sentence structure is perfect. She's brilliant."

Y'know, I'm liking this woman more and more. "She's always been really verbal."

"Face it, she's a genius." Missy produced a lipstick out of nowhere and, while holding the soon-to-be-napping Mason over her shoulder with one hand, she freshened up with her free hand.

"Great color. What is it?"

"Malt Shimmer by Bobbi Brown. Try it." Missy handed the lipstick to Ellie.

"You're kidding. Malt Shimmer? That's the color my ex-best friend always wore." Ellie tried it on, checking out her reflection in the rearview mirror of a parked car.

"Ex-best friend? That's intriguing."

"It's a long story. I used to always say Robbie is a single girl's best friend. I got married and had kids. She didn't even have a boyfriend. I wasn't single and miserable anymore. She didn't want to be friends anymore." Ellie could feel a catch in her throat. It took her by surprise. She took a deep breath.

"What do you think?" She turned to Missy and pursed her lips slightly.

"Yeah, it works. It's a good color for you."

"Bobbi Brown, Malt Shimmer. Who knew? Well, I'm desperate for some new lipsticks." She handed it back to Missy.

"Keep it."

"No, I'm not going to keep your lipstick. That's crazy."

"I'm serious. I have about five of them because I always forget to take one with me and then I have to dash into Bergdorf's and buy another one."

"Thanks." Ellie smiled at Missy and put her new lipstick in her purse.

26

"I just love getting a new lipstick. Every time I put it on for the next two, three weeks it cheers me up. Gives me a little lift. Really. Robbie used to say 'When I'm depressed I buy a new lipstick. When I'm suicidal I buy a Chanel lipstick.' Don't you love lipstick?" Ellie asked, wondering if she'd alienated Miss WASP with her post-feminist ode to lipstick.

"I do. I do." Missy smiled as she shifted the now-napping Mason to her other shoulder and the two women continued down Park Avenue.

Chapter Three

"She gave you her lipstick?" Peter, in boxer shorts and a polo shirt, was leaning over the ancient pedestal sink in the tiny bathroom, brushing his teeth, toothpaste foaming out of his mouth.

"Yeah, isn't that wild?" Ellie was expertly applying contraceptive gel around the edge of her diaphragm.

"That's like a kiss." He spat and rinsed. "She wants you."

"You just don't understand women. Men bond over sports, women bond over lipsticks."

"But she just met you and she's giving you her lipstick? Isn't that a little much? Admit that she wants you."

"Peter, if you could see Missy Hanover you would know how absurd that is. She's like a different species than I am. I mean, next to her I feel like a bucked-toothed hillbilly." Ellie's hand disappeared between her legs as she inserted her diaphragm.

"So, she's really rich?"

"The woman has polo ponies, okay? I think she's pretty fucking rich."

"Do you think she has a riding crop?" he asked as he kissed her neck, pressing his pelvis into her.

"You are relentless." Ellie smiled and shook her head. "Thank God I love the way you fuck me or you'd drive me crazy."

"Is she a babe?" He stood behind her and cupped her breasts in his hands.

"A babe? No way. She's so WASPy that I would be surprised if she even *had* a vagina. If you stripped her there wouldn't be anything there. No nipples, no vagina, just smooth, flesh-colored plastic, like Barbie."

"But Barbie's a babe. You've gotta admit that."

"I'll admit nothing." She turned and kissed him.

"You are so delicious. I've been thinking about you all day."

"Good." She gave him another kiss, deep and long. Ellie loved the fact that Peter spent his days longing for her. She even loved that he sounded like he was reading aloud from *Penthouse* "Forum" when he spoke to her.

"If she wanted you, would that turn you on?"

"Oh, yes. But what I'd really like is if you watched us make love." Ellie knew what he wanted to hear and was perfectly happy to say it.

"Oh, God! You are the best. Now go put on something enticing." Ellie buried her face in Peter's chest, bit him gently, then disappeared into the dark bedroom.

In less than five minutes, they were on the sofa bed with Peter's head between Ellie's legs. He was eating her, as always, with passion, his magical tongue deftly caressing her clit. Ellie's gold bikini bottoms lay in a ball on the floor and the top (two gold triangles with string) was still holding in her milk-swelled breasts.

The paint's already peeling, Ellie thought as she stared at the ceiling. What the heck is that? We just had this place painted after Ahnika was born. . . .

Peter made a yummy sound.

Oops. Get in the game, El, she chastised herself then closed her eyes and searched her mind for a good fantasy.

Ellie had a little trove of sexual fantasies stored in her brain ready to pluck if she had trouble coming with Peter. They were lined up in her head like *Let's Make a Deal*.

Behind curtain #1 was an old faithful. The setting: the Jack Kramer Tennis Club. The star: Manny Gonzalez, tennis pro and Moondoggie look-alike. Ellie, age twelve, wearing her virginal white tennis dress, socks with pom-poms, and pristine white tennis shoes, stands at the baseline, clutching her Dunlop. Over the club PA system, the seventies' band Bread sings their hit song *I Wanna Make It with You*.

Manny smiles at Ellie from across the court. His black hair glistens in the California sun. His tanned thighs flex and relax as he approaches her, lip-syncing all the way.

He stands behind her and puts his arms around her. The smell of his High Karate envelops her. His strong, callused hands cover hers as he gently adjusts her grip. His forearms are thick and veiny. Ellie, weak with desire, falls back into him. She feels Manny's cock stiffen in his tennis shorts against the small of her back.

He sings softly in her ear, "*I wanna make it with you . . .*" She turns to him, their eyes meet . . .

In the pre-adolescent version, they made out passionately and then Manny asked her to go steady. Over the years, the ending has had many different variations. The latest involves wild sex in the back of the pro shop.

Curtain #2 stars Jeff Bridges. (In Ellie's mind, the sexiest man on the planet.) Jeff has just seen Ellie's critically acclaimed, touching, yet hilarious one-woman show and thinks there's a movie in it. After several meetings with Ellie, Jeff must go to Prague to start filming his latest movie. He starts making intercontinental calls to Ellie—supposedly to discuss script ideas, etc. But his calls start coming later and later and become more and more intimate. Eventually, he's calling at midnight and begging Ellie to fly to Prague to be with him. She refuses but doesn't hang up. In desperation, Jeff begins to describe to Ellie, in deep, sexy tones, exactly what he wants to do to her.

. . .

Curtain #3 is quick and a surefire winner. Ellie, looking sexy as hell and, miraculously, ten years younger, is at the star-studded party celebrating the opening of her touching yet hilarious movie (based on the one-woman show, of course). From across the room she sees George Clooney. Is he staring at her? Later, as she stands at the food table nibbling on some flat bread and goat cheese, she feels someone's breath on her neck. She's too aroused to move. The mystery man whispers in her ear, "All I can think about is eating your pussy." She is wet in an instant but tries to act casual as she reaches for a marinated shrimp. When she finally gets the courage to look, he is gone. She hurries out a door where she thinks he's gone and finds herself in a hallway with another door at the far end. She walks to the door and opens it. The room is dark.

"Close the door," a soft, sexy voice tells her. She obeys. George emerges from the shadows and kisses every part of her as he slowly undresses her.

Peter was still between Ellie's legs, working his magic, when she opted for George and the cocktail party. She skipped ahead. Behind the door, as scripted, George was waiting, hungry for her, wanting her so much he could barely speak. He grabbed her, opened her chiffon blouse, and began nibbling on her breast as Peter continued his expert tongue action on her swelling clit. Suddenly, in the corner of the darkened room where George was ravishing her, Ellie saw the faint outline of a woman. George moved down to her pussy. Who is this woman, Ellie wondered? Peter/George was now swirling his tongue on her. Perfectly swirling her clit. Ellie was close, so close. The woman stepped closer. She was watching them. Ellie's back arched, she moaned. The mystery woman was now standing over Ellie. It was Missy. She smiled at Ellie and stroked her hair as she came. Ellie pulled Peter/George into her. "Oh, God! Oh, God!" Pulling his face deep inside her. She was writhing, squirming. It was too much, too intense. She pushed him away. Peter put his damp mouth on hers and entered her wetness. They made love for what seemed like only a moment. It was perfect.

Chapter Four

Ellie raced past the trendy boutiques on Columbus Avenue pushing the double stroller like a pro toward Reebok Sports Club, New York, the largest and fanciest health club in the city. The Millennium Building, an angular, charmless high-rise, which housed the club, loomed large in the distance. It was Wednesday, and Ellie had a standing 10 A.M. appointment with Arlene on the Transformer machine. It was her favorite workout day. Chatting and laughing with Arlene on the Transformer made the otherwise gruelingly boring forty minutes of cardio fly by. Ellie and Arlene had been gym buddies for a year. Arlene had two darling daughters; Natalie was four and Janey was two. Arlene's dad was in the shoe business and Arlene had given up a high-level job at Sketchers to be a stay-at-home mom. Arlene and Ellie had met in a body-sculpting class over a year ago and since that time had spent plenty of time chatting in the whirlpool and steam room. But they had yet to go to a movie together, though they had been saying "next week" for the last three months. Between ear infections, interviews for preschool, and life, it just kept getting put off. Ellie glanced at her watch—9:55. She picked up the pace.

"Oh my God!" She stopped in her tracks. She was face-to-face with Robbie.

It was easy to spot Arlene's curly brown hair amongst the row of huffing and puffing gym members. Arlene was already programming her Transformer machine by the time Ellie climbed onto the machine next to her. "Did you leave the kids downstairs?"

"Yes. It's only Angus's third time."

"Was he freaking out?"

"Not at all. He loves it as much as Ahnika. Thank God."

"Really. If it weren't for the childcare here I'd just be a fat shit. Did you see my girls?"

Ellie nodded, "Happy as could be; Natalie was climbing up the slide and Janie was hiding under it." She began to program her machine.

"Did Ahnika survive her first week at Park Avenue Playgroup?"

"*She's* loving it. The question is, will I survive it?"

"That bad, huh?" Arlene punched a few buttons on her machine. "I hate it when it asks my weight. It's so invasive."

"Arlene, it's a machine. It won't tell anybody."

"Easy for you to say. You're so fucking tiny, you make me sick," Arlene said, then started pumping her arms and legs.

"Is that a compliment? Am I supposed to say thank you to that?"

"Of course it's a compliment. You're perfect! Hey, are you okay?"

"I just saw my old writing partner." Ellie started pushing buttons on her machine. "How much time did you program?"

"Wait a minute. That friend you had a falling out with? What's her name, Bobbie?"

"Robbie, Robbie Boots." Ellie set the resistance on her machine for four. She was ready to sweat.

"Whatever her name is, tell me what happened."

"What happened today—or when she pissed all over our twelve years of friendship six months ago?" The mountainous terrain of Ellie's virtual trek appeared on her readout screen in little red triangles.

"Both. I mean, I remember when you guys had the big fight but you've never really told me the story." Ellie hit *enter* and began her workout.

"Well, I'm on my way to meet you and I look up from the stroller and there she is. Her huge face smiling inanely, right at me."

"Did you speak to her?"

"No, it wasn't her. It was her *face* on the side of this bus. A three-foot-tall close-up of her face was plastered on the side of the M11. I couldn't believe it. There she was: Robbie Boots, feminist, activist, holding up some big fluorescent green fuzzy thing next to her face. Underneath it said: *The Miracle Duster! Available only on the Home Shopping Network.*"

"Oh my God. She's the Miracle Duster lady!" Arlene's arms and legs were pumping, her breath labored.

"What do you mean? You've heard of this thing?"

"I *have* one. I'm a Home Shopping Network junkie." Arlene was leaning into Ellie, whispering. "I watch it late at night. When the kids and Scott are asleep. I got these earrings from HSN." She pointed to her diamond studs. At least Ellie had always *thought* they were diamonds.

"Zircon?"

"You bet. Don't they look real?"

"You had me fooled."

"What does she look like? Wavy red hair? Big white teeth?"

"That's her."

"She sold me my duster. It really works! It's got positive ions or something. Everything sticks to it. Even popcorn."

"You're scaring me. I don't know what's more upsetting. The fact that a smart, articulate woman has been reduced to hawking some stupid household product, or that you are wasting your time and money watching the Home Shopping Network when you should be writing comedy."

"So she got a job—What's the big deal?"

"No, you have to know Robbie to understand how disturbing this is. This is a woman who refused to use the word 'penetration' when she talked about sex, said it was too passive. She would say 'engulfment' instead."

Arlene's mouth dropped open.

"Do you see what I'm saying? This is *not* a woman who would be selling some fluorescent duster that preys on the insecurities of anal-retentive women."

"Hey, you get the duster, with an attachable long handle for those hard to reach places, *and* a little pocket calculator for only twenty-nine, ninety-five."

"You actually use this thing?"

"I used it a couple of times. Last time I saw it, Janie was pretending Natalie was her puppy and she was brushing her with it."

"That's worth twenty-nine, ninety five."

"So, you met Robbie when you were at Juilliard, right?" Both women were beginning to sweat, getting into a groove.

"Right. Just before I dropped out to become a comic. Brilliant career move. Anyway, me and a bunch of other dancers went to this comedy club because some guy from the acting program was doing open mike there. So, we're in the audience, waiting for him to go on and one of the other dancers tells me that I'm funnier than this guy and that *I* should go up and do five minutes. So, I'm a little drunk. I think, what the fuck. So, I borrow a cigarette from somebody, go up onstage, and do an imitation of this totally neurotic ballerina in our class, who used to smoke constantly and only talk about food, calories, and Balanchine."

"Were you any good?" Arlene wiped her brow.

"Well, everyone at the Juilliard table howled because they got the joke. I don't know what anyone else thought. Except Robbie; she went on right after me."

"Was she funny?"

"Wait, listen. She gets up there and starts ad-libbing about dancers. Does like three minutes on me, well, on dancers and how they give everyone else B.I.D."

"B.I.D.?" Arlene looked confused.

"Body Image Distortion. Y'know."

"Yeah, I know. Next to you I feel like a whale." Arlene smacked herself on her ample hip.

"When you compare, you despair," Ellie said.

"Are you saying that you despair when you compare yourself with me?" Arlene wiped sweat off her upper lip and looked at Ellie in disbelief.

"Of course. You have perfect breasts. You went to Columbia, for Christ's sake.

"Yeah, but so what? I used my fancy degree to work in the shoe business. Being a stand-up comic is much more interesting than . . ."

"The point is," Ellie said, cutting her off, "everyone glamorizes everyone else's life. You want straight hair like mine. I want curly hair like yours. You think it's fun and interesting that I was a comic. I'm envious that you have a real education and can perhaps name the capital of North Dakota."

"Bismarck." Arlene flashed Ellie a smart-aleck grin.

"See?"

"Okay, okay. You're right. Can we get back to the Miracle Duster Lady?"

"So, she does this great set, then she comes over to our table to make sure nobody was mad."

"Were they?"

"Well, some of the other dancers were a little pissy. Dancers get a lot of flak, you can imagine. They are envied and despised a lot by other women because other women think that because they're thin that they have these perfect lives. Which is so ironic, since dancers, next to comics, are *the* most insecure group of people I've ever met. Not to make a sweeping generalization."

"Were you pissy?"

"No, because I'd always felt like an outsider at Juilliard. I mean, I was ancient when I auditioned."

"How old were you?"

"Twenty-seven."

Arlene rolled her eyes.

"Believe me, for a dancer that's old. So, I always felt like it was some fluke, some big mistake that I'd even gotten in."

"That's how I felt at Columbia."

"Really?"

"Really."

"There you go. See, I didn't have the training that most of them did. And I didn't have the same reverence for dance that they all did. Well, a year later I dropped out and became a comic. I think that says it all."

"So, she comes to your table to make nice with the perfect, yet snippy dancers and . . . ?"

"I told her that I loved the bit about body image distortion and that I thought that men have B.I.D. in reverse; how they think they're *thinner* than they are."

"God, isn't that the truth."

"And I told her about this guy that I had seen at a Giants' game. He had no muscle tone, was about thirty pounds overweight, all he was wearing were these spandex bike shorts, and he had written GIANTS on his chest in Magic Marker. And I thought—honey, if I wanted to see that much of your body I'd be dating you."

"I *have* dated guys like that," Arlene said, laughing.

"You have not." Ellie punched Arlene in the arm. "Anyway, I tell her that story and I was expecting her to laugh."

"She didn't laugh?"

"No. She just looks at me stone faced and says 'Can I use that?' and starts to write it down on this little pad.

"She was stealing your material?"

"Thanks to Robbie I realized I *had* material. That moment was the beginning of my comedy career and the beginning of our friendship. Three weeks later, I dropped out of Juilliard."

"That took a lot of guts."

"Yeah, well, I guess so." Ellie cranked up the resistance on her machine and pumped like a madwoman.

You're skipping a part, a voice came in Ellie's head. A big, important part.

"How did your parents feel about you dropping out?" Arlene asked panting.

"I gotta get some water." Ellie paused her machine, grabbed her water bottle, and went to fill it at the drinking fountain.

Should I tell her, she wondered. I mean, what am I waiting for? We've known each other for almost a year now. I've gotta tell her. But she's going to think I'm nuts.

"I think it's full."

Ellie jumped. Arlene was standing right behind Ellie, watching her water bottle overflow.

"I'm a bulimic," Ellie blurted out as she turned to Arlene, her water bottle dripping in her hand.

"What?" She stepped away from Ellie.

"I'm a bulimic. Y'know, a barfer. Or at least I was. *That's* why I left

Juilliard. I fainted in dance class. I was so malnourished and dehydrated from purging and starving myself that I ended up in the hospital." She was talking as fast as she could. "And I was too embarrassed to go back to school. Isn't that silly? At the time I told myself I hated Juilliard and I was happy to get out, to be free to be a comic, my true calling. Anyway, I wasn't sure I wanted to tell you that part. I mean, I don't really talk about it that much. It was a long time ago. I'm abstinent twelve years now." She finally took a breath.

"Abstinent?" Arlene looked frightened.

"It's the bulimic version of what sober is for the alcoholic. It means I haven't thrown up or used laxatives in twelve years."

"Wow," was all Arlene said.

I've totally freaked her out, Ellie thought. Shit! I've done it again. I've said too much. She looked around the room. Is everyone looking at me? Of course they are, Ellie answered herself inside her swimming head. You just announced to the entire training floor at Reebok Sports Club New York that you're a fucking bulimic. This is great. I've alienated Arlene *and* I'm gonna lose my membership. I'll be friendless and flabby.

Ellie was about to drop her water bottle and bolt for the nearest exit when Arlene stepped toward her and gave her a long, sweet hug. Ellie's eyes filled with tears. Arlene put her arm around her, and the two women walked to the bathroom.

*A*ren't you glad you asked me about the Robbie story?" They were peeing in separate stalls, their voices echoing off the gray and purple tiles. "You didn't think it would be this sordid, did you?"

"Nothing surprises me anymore. My sister used to be gay; now she's married to a Republican." They flushed simultaneously. The two women emerged from their stalls, laughing, and headed back to their machines to finish their workout.

"So, you left Juilliard . . ." Arlene prompted Ellie as she climbed on her machine.

"I left Juilliard, spent thirty days in bulimia rehab, then Robbie and I became joined at the hip. She was my stand-up mentor; thanks to her, I had a spot at Caroline's in less than a year."

"I think it might also have had something to do with the fact that you're hilarious."

"Yes, yes. That helped," Ellie said, climbing back onto her machine and pressing the restart button.

"So we started doing this cable show on public access."

"*Muffy and Shari's Beauty Tips.* I loved that show. When I first saw you in step class I thought, Oh my God, it's Muffy from that wacky cable show."

"We were pretty wacky. And that show, if you can believe it, got us a development deal with Comedy Central, and the writing gig for *Women Aloud.*

"Then Peter came along and in less than six months I was pregnant. I went to *Robbie* to tell her the good news." Ellie gave Arlene a *guess what?* look.

"What?"

"She tried to talk me *out* of marrying Peter and *into* an abortion.

"Really?"

Ellie nodded.

Boop! The timer on Arlene's machine was sounding.

"That was quick." Arlene's Transformer slowed to a crawl. She grabbed her water bottle and took a long drink.

"Time flies when you're hearing family secrets. Especially someone else's," Ellie said.

"Good point. Whirlpool?"

Ellie glanced at her timer. "I'm there. I've got thirty-six more seconds."

Arlene was stretching out her calves on her now motionless machine. "Check it out. Action at three o'clock."

Ellie took a beat trying to figure out just where three o'clock was. She glanced to the right and saw Steve, a tall, muscled personal trainer with a boyish face, flirting wildly with one of his clients, a silicone-breasted redhead with zero percent body fat.

"He's trouble, but cute," Ellie said.

"Please! I was always a sucker for those big corn-fed boys. Married one."

"How many of his private clients do you think he's had?"

"How many *hasn't* he had?" Arlene was blatantly watching the duo.

BOOP!

"We're outta here." The two women grabbed their water bottles and headed for the elevators. As they passed the flirting couple, Steve was adjusting Big Red's grip, reaching around her from behind in a tight hug.

"Hey, Steve." Ellie waved and gave him a sly smile. "Tough job, huh?"

Arlene elbowed Ellie in the ribs, and the two of them burst into laughter as they rounded the corner.

$\mathcal{A}$rlene was still blushing as she slowly lowered herself into the empty whirlpool.

"I can't believe you said that."

"Oh, he loved it." Ellie positioned her calves right in front of her favorite water jet.

"How about busty? She's a piece of work." Arlene was kneeling in the water facing the side of the whirlpool, bubbles crashing against her thighs.

"Does she love her breasts or what?"

"She'd better love them. I'm sure they cost her a pretty penny."

"Her or her husband. Did you see the rock on her finger?" Ellie took a deep breath and closed her eyes.

"Hey, don't doze off. I'm not leaving this whirlpool till I hear the whole *Robbie* story."

"Okay. Where was I?"

"You were pregnant . . ."

"Right, right. So, obviously, I *didn't* get an abortion and I *did* marry Peter." Ellie could feel a soothing stream of hot water surrounding her toes. She spoke slowly, with her eyes still closed.

"Well, Robbie might be the most ambitious person I've ever met. And I was pretty darned ambitious *before* I had a kid. Once Ahnika was born it was like—development deal, Letterman audition, who cares? I just wanna stay home and gaze into my infant's eyes."

"It's pathetic. I have a friend—no kids—and after Natalie was born she used to say to me, 'Where's my smart, interesting friend Arlene? Where did she go?'"

"They think we've been body snatched."

"They're right."

"Oh, this was the last nail in the coffin. Get this; Ahnika's only a few weeks old and we have this meeting at Comedy Central and my sitter cancels at the last minute."

"Perfect!"

"So, I *bring* Ahnika to the meeting."

"No!"

"What was I gonna do? Robbie screamed at me afterward because I nursed Ahnika during the meeting."

"You did?"

"It was nurse her or try to talk over her wails. After that we fought all the time; all of my sketch ideas involved pregnant or lactating women and she nixed every one. Get this: when I left a message on her machine that I was pregnant *again*, she didn't call me back for two weeks, even though we had a deadline. It was a nightmare. Long story short, we finished the pilot—which sucked, by the way—Angus was born and *Robbie* wouldn't return my calls from the hospital. I come home from the hospital to find a five-page, single-spaced letter from her (which included a contract) that basically said, *You're a shitty friend, no more collaboration, good-bye.*"

"She sent you a contract?"

"A contract that officially ended the collaboration."

"Whoa!"

Ellie shook her head. "I felt like I'd been punched in the stomach. I mean, I knew that things were bad, but I always thought the friendship would survive.

"I mean, I don't recognize my life. Five minutes ago I was this marginally happy single woman. I have a very promising comedy career, a best friend, who's also my collaborator, so our lives are *totally* entwined. So, I'm without a man, big deal. History has proved I have incredibly bad luck in that department, anyway. Then BAM! Peter finds me and everything changes. In less than three years I'm a housewife and a mother of two."

"What do you mean Peter finds you? I thought you two met at Juilliard?"

"Oh boy! That is a whole *other* story for another Wednesday."

"Forget Wednesday. What are you doing Friday? I'm dying to see *Meet the Parents.* Do you wanna go to a matinee? Unless you and Peter were planning on seeing it together."

"Are you kidding? Peter wouldn't go to a stupid comedy like that with a gun to his head. I'll get a sitter."

"So you want to see it? You just said it was a stupid romantic comedy."

"It is. I *love* stupid comedies!"

"Great! There's a 12:30 show at Sony."

Ellie couldn't believe it. She was going to see a movie in the middle of the day with a girlfriend. Since her split with Robbie, Ellie had thought that she was destined to go to movies like *Meet the Parents* by herself for the rest of her life. She beamed like a schoolgirl as she kicked her feet in the churning water, counting the minutes till Friday.

Chapter Five

"Two for *Meet the Parents*." Ellie scanned the nearly empty lobby; no Arlene. She checked her watch. She's five minutes late, she thought as she situated herself next to the escalator, where she could watch the trickle of matinee theatergoers enter from both sets of revolving doors.

Ten minutes . . . fifteen minutes. Still no Arlene. Ellie took out her cell phone and checked her machine.

"Shit!" she said out loud as she listened to Arlene's message. Arlene couldn't make the movies because Natalie was sick. Ellie was beyond disappointed. Fuck it. I give up, she thought. I just won't have any girlfriends. God, is it too much to ask to spend two hours sitting in the dark with a friend watching mindless entertainment? What is the problem? She stood at the bottom of the escalator totally unmoored. She toyed briefly with the idea of seeing the movie by herself, but it somehow seemed incredibly pathetic.

She longed for the idle days before parenthood and the split with Robbie. The two of them used to go to every stupid comedy that came out and, because they were comedy writers, they could call it research and deduct it.

She had a sudden impulse to call her ex-best friend and see what she was doing. Yeah, Ellie thought. I'll just call and say, Hi, it's me. What are you doing? Want to see *Meet the Parents* with me? Meet me at Sony; I'll save you a seat. Ellie's palms started to sweat; her mouth felt dry. She dialed the number. She's probably not home. If I get the machine, I'm hanging up, that's for sure. I'm not leaving her another message that she can just ignore.

"The number you have called, 212-555-7787, is no longer in service. There is no new number."

Ellie took the cell phone from her ear and stared at it. She could faintly hear the message repeating. There was finality to the recording that hit Ellie hard in her chest. Her eyes filled with tears that spilled onto her cheeks. She couldn't stop looking at the receiver, couldn't seem to move.

Even though they hadn't spoken in months, Ellie still knew where Robbie was, or *thought* she knew. She still thought reconciliation could be a phone call away. But now Robbie's number was no more. A number Ellie had dialed literally hundreds of times—a number that had kept her sane and abstinent in rehab—was gone, meaningless. And why had Robbie changed it? When had she changed it? After Ellie's last message?

"Excuse me." A teenage girl in a seventies-style Ultrasuede peacoat wanted to get on the escalator, and Ellie was in the way.

"Oh, sorry." Ellie stepped aside, turned off her cell phone, and headed out the door.

EIGHT MORE, SEVEN MORE, SEEX MORE . . ." Jorge, the body-sculpting teacher, cheered on the room full of sweaty bodies over the din of unbearable house music. About twenty women were struggling through crunches. "COME ON, YOU CEN DO EET!"

Jorge had the face of a five-year-old boy and the body of the Michelin

Man. He was somewhat legendary at Reebok for his relentless classes and sexy Spanish accent.

"...TREE MORE, TWO MORE, ONE MORE, OKAY! YOU DEED EET!"

Ellie let out an audible groan. I can't go on, she thought as she pulled her knees into her chest, giving her abs a rest. She was hating the class, but loving the distraction. After leaving the Sony building, she had headed to the gym like a lemming. Working hard and sweating to music was like an old friend.

Ellie had been ten years old when her mother enrolled her at Rosalie and Alva's Dance Studio and she had fallen in love with the world of dedication and discipline. A world far removed from a con man father and a drunken mother, a world where all that mattered was the alignment of your hips and the height of your leg. And Ellie had been instantly good at it. She had the body, the bones, and the determination.

Ellie went back to her crunches. "JUS TREE MORE, TWO MORE, AND ONE. YOU—ARE—FINISH!"

She rolled off her bench and onto her mat. Jorge walked to the back of the class and dimmed the lights. The sadness and disappointment of the day rushed over her.

She counted the classes she'd taken that week as Jorge walked to the stereo in the front of the room—Sunday, Monday, Tuesday, Wednesday, Friday. Shit, that's five, she thought. I'm only allowed four a week. Was this a slip?

Maybe I should call Melanie, Ellie thought, and tell her I took an extra class. Melanie had been Ellie's sponsor for seven years but Ellie hadn't spoken to her since Angus was an infant.

How many miles a day do you run?" Melanie had asked Ellie the first time they had gone shopping together. The two women made their way through the throngs of shoppers at Fairway, the Upper West Side's always congested, farmer-style market.

"I don't really keep track," Ellie said, steering the shopping cart toward the towering produce section.

"Don't you lie to me, girl!" Melanie, an ex-fashion model who looked like the child of Sidney Poitier and Audrey Hepburn, had grown up in the Bronx and spent her teenage years modeling and barfing her way across Europe. Ellie had chosen her as a sponsor because there was no bullshit about her. "There's not a bulimic on this planet that doesn't know how many miles they've run and how many calories they've consumed."

"Okay. About three to five miles a day."

Melanie had stopped walking and was furrowing her perfect eyebrows at Ellie. "Did you ask me to take you grocery shopping because you don't have a clue what kind of food a normal person has in their kitchen?"

"Yes."

"Do you want me to be your sponsor?"

"Yes."

"Then, let me try again; how—many—miles—a—day—are—you—running?" Melanie's perfectly lined lips formed each word slowly and clearly.

"Six to nine."

"Thank you." She picked up a dark green avocado from a pile. "Do you like avocados?"

Ellie shook her head. "Too fattening," she said, swerving the grocery cart to avoid an ancient woman with a walker.

"When was the last time you had a period?"

"I don't know."

Melanie picked up two more avocados and put them in the cart. "I want you to eat one of these a day."

"A whole avocado *every day*!"

"Listen, sweet pea, do you want to bear children one day?"

"Look! I'm not throwing up anymore. What's the big deal?"

"When was the last time you used laxatives?"

Ellie's face flushed and she stared at the sawdust-strewn floor. "Last week," she said, then looked up. "But I used Herblax from the health food store. That's okay, isn't it?" Melanie gave her a *you know better than that* look. "Okay, you're right, but it was the first time since rehab, and I went right to a meeting and . . ."

"Girl." Melanie put one of her slim hands on Ellie's shoulder. "In AA an alcoholic has a slip when he or she drinks. It's very clear, very simple. As an anorexic/bulimic, there are lots of ways you can slip—" she counted them out on her fingers "—you can binge, you can overexercise, you can skip a meal, you can use laxatives, and you can vomit."

"Look. I haven't purged since before rehab. I'll *never* do that again."

"Never say never," Melanie had said as she took the helm of the shopping cart. "Remember, sweet pea, there is no cure for this disease; just a daily reprieve based on a spiritual surrender." And Melanie had headed down the narrow aisle, filling Ellie's cart as she went.

Alright, my gorgeous ladies, jus' relax. We are done," Jorge told the class.

Maybe I should get my butt to a meeting, Ellie thought. I haven't been to one in ages. But Jesus, haven't I been to enough meetings?

Ellie had spent years in daily meetings, feeling all the feelings she had been avoiding with her addictions. Mostly she had cried. For the first three years, she had gone to a meeting a day and had cried in every one.

"Time for to cool down. You are fabulous!" Jorge pushed *play* on the stereo and the tones of a mournful string section swelled and filled the room. Ellie stretched her arms up and her toes down. So I took an extra class after a shitty morning. Big deal. It could be worse. I could have my head in the toilet, for Christ's sake.

"Deep breath in, an' as you breathe out jus let everythin' go. No more problem, no more worry. You are right here, safe and happy with Jorge."

Ellie followed Jorge's directives as an instrumental version of the theme to *Born Free* filled the studio. She had a flash of sitting on her father's lap in a dark movie theater watching Elsa the lion frolic on the plains of Africa as the credits rolled. Her eyes swelled with tears. She let them spill out and roll into her ears.

Oh, God! Too many feelings for one day, she thought. Maybe I *do* need a meeting. At least there I could cry. She pulled her right leg toward her nose, stretching her hamstring. But I don't *want* to go to a meeting. I don't have *time* for a meeting.

That's what I need: time. Just a little extra time—for me—to cry.

Chapter Six

Ellie hated the commute to the East Side almost as much as the place itself. Her plans of strolling through the park and enjoying the changing of the leaves had become nothing but a fantasy. The daily struggle with Ahnika over her absolute refusal to wear anything but her Darth Vader costume (a Halloween gift from Jack, Ellie's cousin) contributed to their tardiness. As did Angus's habit of wanting to nurse just as they were walking out the door. Wouldn't you know it?

She had become what was a common sight on the Upper West Side in the A.M.—a harried mother. You could see them in the mornings on almost every corner, desperately trying to hail taxis as they struggled to fold double strollers while trying to keep their children from running into traffic, overloaded with lunch boxes and diaper bags that inevitably fell to the sidewalk, spilling their contents everywhere.

This morning, thanks to a livery cab that took pity on them, Ellie and the kids had actually made it to the lobby of Park Avenue Presbyterian before the teachers had arrived. Ellie was taking a moment to put on lipstick (Malt Shimmer, of course) as she took a look around the cavernous lobby.

Where's Missy, she wondered? Since that first day of PAPG, Missy and Ellie had continued to pursue their unlikely friendship. They had spent almost every playgroup day for the past five weeks at the Seventy-sixth Street playground or eating and chatting (while Angus nursed or napped) at Three Brothers, the local coffee shop.

Maybe Mason's sick, Ellie thought. She scanned the room; Nanny, nanny, everywhere a nanny. All those concerned mothers disappeared after phase-in, didn't they?

"Hi, Ellie," Libby Merrill and Faith Roberts sang in unison from across the room.

"Morning," Ellie said, screwing down her lipstick. "What's up?"

"Faith and I were just discussing the wonderful job we think they're doing here. Don't you think?" Libby asked. Libby (mother of Caitlin) was an anorexic blonde with a slight southern accent and a penchant for dressing monochromatically. Today she was sporting burgundy—burgundy shoes, burgundy skirt, burgundy blouse, cape, and pocketbook.

"I think they're doing a great job," Ellie said, marveling at Libby's outfit. She is committed to that look, God bless her.

"I think Caitlin's vocabulary has really taken off since the beginning of the year," Faith said.

"Really?" Ellie said, feigning interest.

Faith Roberts (mother of Devin) was some sort of communications heiress and a little on the chubby side. Faith and Libby continued to sing the praises of Park Avenue Playgroup as Ellie smiled and nodded and silently did her Margaret Mead thing: Yep, Faith's wearing those silly loafers with the tiny bows again. They're definitely an East Side thing. I've never seen them west of Fifth Avenue. And she must have them in *every* color. And the two of them always look like they've just had a make-over at the Lancôme counter. It's another one of these East Side phenomenons. And Libby with the hose, again. Who wears hose anymore? And Faith's earrings match her pin. I don't even *own* a pin.

Ellie looked down at her own clothes—jeans, thermal tee, and hiking boots. Oh, my God! I look like a lumberjack. On the West Side this is a perfectly acceptable outfit. I cross the park and suddenly I look like I'm suffering from gender confusion.

And look at that little Camille in yet another precious dress and a bow in her hair the size of a bagel. Doesn't *she* ever want to come to school dressed like Darth Vader? Or maybe even like a fairy princess? Camille sat quietly next to Sophie, her French nanny. Sophie is very French and very sexy, Ellie observed. I think that's redundant. Even *she's* better dressed than I am. Ellie tried in vain to brush a yogurt stain off her jeans.

Just then Missy, dressed in her usual running clothes, thank God, breezed in with Mason in tow. Ahnika, hair uncombed and, yes, wearing her Darth Vader costume, jumped out of her stroller and ran to meet Mason, her huge plastic mask clacking all the way. Angus, sitting propped up in the corner of the sofa, was happily gnawing on a teething biscuit. Ahnika and Mason scrambled under their favorite chair and began to wrestle.

"Gentle, Mason," Missy called, as she bent to air-kiss Ellie. "Did you get my message?" She settled on the sofa between Ellie and Angus and began playing with Angus's feet. Ellie answered her with a blank look.

"You must've been asleep. Anyway, I'm in charge of drinks for the cocktail party. Can you bring three bottles of white wine—?"

"AAAHHH!" Caitlin's scream pierced the air. Devin was standing over her and had her by the hair.

"Devin, use your words," Faith said calmly from her seat.

"Mommy! Mommy, make him stop!" Caitlin pleaded.

"Devin, sweetheart, let go of Caitlin's hair. I don't think she likes that," Libby said, looking alarmed.

"He's very physical," Faith said with pride.

"Stop! Stop it, Devin! Mommy!" Caitlin was now swinging her arms and kicking her feet in vain.

"Devin! *Stop!*" Ellie stood and shouted, over Caitlin's cries. Devin dropped Caitlin's hair and she ran to her mother screaming. Libby shot Ellie a *thank you* smile. Devin sank slowly to the floor and crumpled into tears.

"Did I cross a line?" Ellie whispered to Missy as she sat back down.

"Maybe. But I think you saved Caitlin's life."

"Well, I certainly saved her hair. That kid's out of control."

"I told you about the teeth marks he left on Mason."

"And while Mason was writhing in pain, Faith probably turned to you and said—" Ellie cocked her head and gave Missy a proud smile "—Devin's very expressive with his teeth."

Missy chuckled quietly. "I heard he gets time-outs every day."

"Thank God! Okay, back to the party. What am I bringing and when is it?" Ellie had a vague memory of some piece of mail from PAPG that mentioned a "Get Acquainted Night."

"It's tonight. Don't tell me you're not coming. You *must* come. It will be *such* a bore without you. I've told Tony all about you. He's dying to meet you, of course. And *I* can't wait to meet this Peter of yours."

"No, we're coming. We're coming." Ellie hoped she could find a sitter and that Peter didn't have a late meeting. "We'll be there. Three bottles of white. No problem."

What are you wearing? That's what Ellie *wanted* to say next. That's certainly what she would've asked Robbie in a similar situation, or any other girlfriend she had ever had. But not to Missy. No. Missy Hanover, Ellie was certain, had never uttered the words "What are you wearing?" in a moment of insecurity. Missy, Ellie was convinced, had been someone's hated and envied cousin with the Peter Pan collar and the perfect little kilt. Missy, most certainly, had never arrived *anywhere* in the wrong outfit.

And this woman, who didn't seem to have suffered a single moment of self-doubt, this woman who used expressions like "dash into Bergdorf's" had decided, for reasons that Ellie couldn't fathom, that Ellie and she should be friends.

"It's at six o'clock, here, in the basement. They have a very nice meeting room down there. It'll be fun."

Ellie gave her a *What are you nuts?* look.

Missy leaned into her. "Oh come on. I'm simply dying to get a look at some of these husbands. What do you suppose Libby's husband is like? He's a shipping magnate, you know."

"Oh, that's all a cover," Ellie whispered back. "I heard he's really some sort of religious cult leader."

"Are you serious?" Missy's eyes widened as she stole a look at Libby, in her burgundy ensemble, chatting with Faith.

"Absolutely. Faith told me. *That's* the reason for Libby's fashion eccentricity. It's some bizarre rule of his. Like not being allowed to pee at est seminars. He only allows his followers to wear one color at a time." Ellie found herself making up stories out of the blue just to see if Missy would bite.

"Oh my God. Poor little Devin."

"Missy." Missy looked at Ellie with a furrowed brow. "I'm kidding."

"You are horrible." She gave Ellie a smack on the shoulder and tried not to laugh.

"You are *so* easy."

"How do you even think of these wild stories? You're amazing."

She thinks I'm amazing, my daughter's brilliant. It's damn hard not to like her. Ellie looked at her new bud and smiled. But what, dear God, am I gonna wear to this fucking party?

Chapter Seven

"For Kids Only," the Child Care Center at Reebok Sports Club, was bustling with toddlers when Ellie, Angus, and Ahnika arrived. The big, bright, open room housed a small red plastic slide, a block area, a wooden playhouse, and lots of toys. Ahnika ran immediately to the red plastic slide. The minute Angus saw Ruth, an athletic black woman with short cornrows, he was struggling to get at her.

"Here's my big boy," Ruth said when Ellie handed him over. Her big teeth shone bright against her dark brown skin.

"Bye, cuties!" Ellie said, then signed the two of them in, grabbed one of the "For Kids Only" beepers (in case of emergencies) and headed out. As she waited for the elevator, she could see through the glass wall that Ahnika, sliding down the slide for the umpteenth time, had barely noticed her exit. And Angus was truly indifferent to her absence as he and Ruth played patty-cake. Why can't leaving them always be so easy? she wondered as the elevator doors closed.

But instead of pushing *2* and going up to the gym for her regular Boot Camp class, she pushed *L* and headed back down to street level and hopped in a cab.

Leaving the premises while your children were in the childcare was, of course, strictly forbidden. Ellie had never done it before, but this was an emergency.

Ellie raced through the revolving doors at Saks and checked her watch. Twenty minutes to get here. It's gonna take twenty minutes to get back. She did the math in her head. Okay. I've got less than an hour to find and buy the perfect outfit to wear to this stupid cocktail party. She searched her pocket for the beeper they'd given her. She was praying it wouldn't go off as she hustled past the bright, fragrant cosmetics area, dodging mannequin faced women in lab coats hawking the perfume of the moment.

"Somewhere, the new fragrance by Paul Laredo. You never know where it might take you." A fifty-something woman with Kabuki white skin and a black helmet of a hairdo approached Ellie with her perfume sprayer poised.

"No thanks," Ellie said with a smile as she hopped on the escalator.

Ellie had a love/hate relationship with Saks. She hated it because it's where her mother always used to take her shopping when she came to town. Ellie had dreaded those visits because it had always been such a charade to show Mom how good she was doing. And she hated the trips to Saks because they had always been about—guess who—her mother. In those days, what Ellie really needed was rent money, or a couple of pairs of jeans, or new toe shoes; she had always needed toe shoes. But what her mother *wanted* to give her was something like a navy blazer or a nice pair of khaki pants. Something classic. Something that could've been plucked right out of Sara Fuller's closet. Whatever it was, it always ended up hanging untouched in Ellie's closet until she gave them to a friend or the Goodwill.

And she loved Saks because it was near the Modern and St. Patrick's. She loved seeing all the artists selling their wares on the street. She loved it because it had that old New York feeling. But most of all, she loved Saks because it held one of the few good memories that Ellie had of time spent with her father.

. . .

It was 1969 and Ellie was ten. Sara and Paul (Ellie's mom and dad) had still been madly in love. They were a golden couple that other people envied. She was the beautiful, petite debutante from the East and he was the handsome charmer from the other side of the tracks who had snagged himself a debutante. It was back when everyone was still "buying your father's act," as Ellie's mother used to put it. Before countless disappointments over big deals that had never come through.

To this day Ellie is not sure just what her father did for a living in those days. It wasn't a normal job, that's for sure. He didn't go to an office, but he wore a suit every day. He slept late and came home even later. But there was always food on the table and presents under the tree on Christmas morning. And there was always a lot of talk about the big money that was coming, the pony Ellie would get and the swimming pool they would dig in the backyard.

Then, one night when Ellie was fast asleep, her bedroom door burst open. She woke with a start and saw her daddy's silhouette in the doorway.

"Daddy? What's happening? What's wrong?"

"Nothing's wrong, sweetie. Things couldn't be more right." He bent down his wiry six-foot frame and swept the sleepy Ellie up in his arms.

"What are you doing, Daddy?" She wrapped her arms around his neck and put her head on his shoulder. "I'm sleepy." He kissed her ear and ruffled her hair with his free hand. He smelled like cigarettes and liquor.

"I know, Ellie Bellie Bella Bellou," he whispered in her ear, brushing her brown shoulder-length hair from her face. "But I've got big news! Big, big news that I have to tell you and Mommy." They marched into the master bedroom and turned on the lamp next to the king-sized bed. Ellie's mother sat up in bed squinting, with a look of terror on her face.

"What? What is it, Paul? What's happened?"

"It's happened. The big 'it.' The 'it' I've been waiting for all my life."

Ellie climbed out of her father's arms and onto her mother's lap. The two of them snuggled together, looking at Paul expectantly.

He took a deep breath, paused, leaned into the two of them and whispered, "We're gonna be millionaires!"

The next morning they left for New York City, all three of them, just took Ellie out of school and went. The "big deal" involved a bank in Manhattan and some life insurance company. It was spring and New York was picture postcard perfect for the four days they were there. They stayed at the Waldorf and, while Paul was having meetings with the bigwigs, Ellie and her mom lunched at the 21 Club, ice-skated at Rockefeller Center, and even saw Nureyev dance. But, the clearest and dearest memory of that trip in Ellie's mind is shopping at Saks Fifth Avenue with her daddy. On the last day, when Paul had supposedly sewn up the "big deal" and Sara was at the beauty parlor, Ellie and her dad were planning an outing together, just the two of them.

"Well, Ellie Bellie Bella Bellou, what shall we do? It's your call?" Paul was straightening his tie in the bathroom mirror.

Ellie couldn't believe it! She knew *exactly* what she wanted to do. But would she have the guts to tell him?

"Anything you want." He moved to the bed and started polishing his shoes with one of those cloths that hotels give you along with a travel sewing kit. "The Metropolitan Museum of Art is one of the best museums in the world."

Ellie sat silent on the dresser, picking at a hangnail.

"We could take the ferry to the Statue of Liberty." He wadded the shine cloth into a ball, tossed it in the air, then bounced it into the trash can off his knee. "It's a gorgeous day."

Ellie didn't want to do anything cultural like that. No. She wanted the lime green swinger jumper that she had seen in the window at Saks on their very first day. It had a long thin hip belt that tied with tassels on the end. The mannequin in the window had worn white fishnets and a white poor boy underneath. Her brown suede shoes flopped off her little mannequin feet but laced like ice skates and were cooler than anything Ellie had ever seen at Miraleste Elementary School.

"C'mon, missy, time's a-wasting." Paul was double brushing his wavy, sandy blond hair with his two precious silver-backed brushes that had belonged to his father.

Ellie was still working on that hangnail. It started to bleed. She wasn't sure, but she thought this was the first time she and her dad had spent time alone together. It felt odd. Who is this guy? Doesn't *he* think this is weird, she wondered?

Suddenly, he whisked her off the dresser by her shoulders and swung her around, landing her on the bed. She landed with a bounce, giggling.

"Let's go, beautiful! Your date is ready." He bowed and held out his hand, waiting. Ellie jumped off the bed and they headed out the door, hand in hand. As they marched down the opulent hallways of the Waldorf, arms swinging, Paul began to whistle the theme to *The Bridge on the River Kwai*. Ellie loved it. She felt like they were in some wonderful New York musical like *On the Town* or *Mame*. When they entered the crowded elevator, Paul was still whistling, glancing at Ellie conspiratorially. Ellie, caught up in his fun, joined in. Suddenly, she felt safe and comfortable with him. Suddenly it felt perfectly normal to be spending the day with this dapper stranger who was her father. All talk in the elevator quieted, then stopped. Then, one by one, the other passengers began to whistle. By the time the elevator stopped almost everyone had joined in the fun.

As the doors opened on the staid Waldorf lobby, Ellie half expected an orchestra with horns and a string section to start playing *The Bridge on the River Kwai*. Then guests, bellboys, and doormen would all whistle and dance together in a huge production number.

Many of the whistlers continued the song as they made their way into the lobby, then waved to Ellie and her dad as they went their separate ways.

Ellie and Paul, still whistling, ended up standing on Park Avenue in the taxi line. When it was their turn, they scrambled into the roomy backseat of a Checker cab.

"Where to, madam?" the cab driver asked ceremoniously.

"Saks Fifth Avenue," Ellie replied with all the confidence and savvy of a native New Yorker. Her father didn't bat an eyelash.

"That's right, sir. We've got some shopping to do." Paul looked at his beaming daughter and gave her a wink like they were sharing a secret.

Less than an hour later Ellie skipped out of Saks Fifth Avenue wearing her dream outfit. And in one of the display windows at Saks there stood a naked, shivering mannequin.

The "big deal" in New York had turned out to be the beginning of Paul's downfall. INDICTED FOR FRAUD was the headline when he had been arrested the following winter. The pony never arrived, the swimming pool was never dug, and Ellie never went on another outing with her dapper father.

Now, more than three decades later, Ellie was back in Saks, once again in search of her dream outfit (sort of). After making a quick sweep of all the floors, she hurried into an empty fitting room with an odd assortment of choices: a black, beaded, spaghetti-strapped Bill Blass cocktail dress; a red boat neck minidress with a low back; and a navy suit with knife pleats and a short, boxy jacket. She reached in her coat pocket and looked at the beeper. "No pages" the readout told her. "Thank God."

Ellie scrutinized herself in the beaded number in the three-way mirror. She stood on tiptoes trying in vain to create the effect of high heels. She turned around and looked over her shoulder at her butt; the size four hugged her ass just right.

"It's a great dress, no doubt about it," she said to her reflection, "but I think it's a bit much for a preschool cocktail party.

"How's everything going?" a twentyish, Hispanic salesgirl called from behind the dressing room door. "I brought you these." She waved a pair of tired-looking black pumps under the door.

"You're a doll." Ellie slipped on the too-big pumps and took another look at the fancy dress. "I don't know who's wearing these dresses or where they're going."

"It's a Bill Blass. His things are classic. You could wear it for years." She had a thick Bronx accent.

"I *could* wear it for years, but where? I just don't think it's me." Ellie opened the fitting room door and gave the salesgirl a look.

"Oh, my God. It fits you perfect! Really. I've seen this dress on a lot of women. You look great in it." She seemed truly impressed. Ellie looked in the three-way again and reconsidered the dress.

"God, I hate this. I'm going to a fucking cocktail party, pardon my French, and I don't know what to wear."

"This *is* a cocktail dress. This would definitely work. And you would turn some heads, girl."

Ellie checked the time. "Shit!" She looked at her new confidante, who wore a gold necklace proclaiming her name in swirling letters. "Listen, Hermosa?"

She nodded.

"Hi, I'm Ellie." They shook hands. "Listen. I've got twelve minutes to buy a dress and some shoes to wear to this snooty cocktail party for my daughter's preschool. Ya gotta help me."

"No problem, Ellie. We can do it." Hermosa twirled her finger; Ellie did a slow turn. "Too much."

"I thought so." She turned her back to Hermosa who unzipped the beaded outfit like a pro. "It's this WASPy school where everybody is always accessorized and perfect-looking. You know the type?"

"Please. I wait on those women all day." She took Ellie's two remaining choices off the dressing room hook and handed the suit to Ellie. "Put that on. The red is great but too much for these WASPy women. I'll get you a blouse." And she was gone.

Ellie left the Bill Blass in a heap and scrambled into the skirt. It fit. She looked at her reflection. "It's a little long and a little boring." She turned to get the back view. "Nope, nothing sexy about it. This just might work."

"Ellie?" A white silk blouse sailed over the top of the door. "Put that on, I'll be right back."

"Don't go far. I'm down to nine minutes." She wiggled into the blouse (much like one her mother had bought her several years back) and tucked it in, in record time. Next came the jacket: short and boxy with square gold buttons. Ellie turn slowly to the mirror. "I look like an anchor woman that got scalped. If only I had a nice Jackie O.–type wig I might be able to pull this off." She looked at her watch. "Seven minutes!" She looked back at her reflection, closed her eyes, and sank down onto the corner chair.

What am I doing? she wondered. What's happened to me? I don't even have anyone to go shopping with. I've put the future of my social standing in the hands of a twenty-year-old Hispanic girl.

If Robbie were here, Ellie thought, she'd say, "Fuck 'em. Get the red dress and blow their minds. Show off that body of yours, for fuck's sake. Give all those WASPy boys something to dream about." Ellie put her head in her hands and stared at the beige carpet. "God, I miss her," she said softly to the empty dressing room. "When am I going to stop missing her?"

"Everything all right?"

"Uh, yeah. I'm fine." Ellie jumped up and took a deep breath. "We're down to six minutes."

"Here." Some chunky gold jewelry jangled over the top of the door. "Same designer. They perfectly complement the buttons."

Ellie held them up to her neck and ears. "I hate them. They look like something my mother would wear. So we must be on the right track." She opened the door and gave Hermosa the full effect. "Well, am I boring? Am I WASPy? Huh? Huh? What d'ya think?"

Hermosa suppressed a smile. "For this style I think you look great. Really."

"Okay. Listen, Hermosa, here's what I want you to do." She handed her the jewelry and started stripping. Off came the jacket, the skirt. She tossed them to Hermosa, who caught them like a major leaguer. "Take this stuff, I'm going to give you my credit card, and ring it up." Off came the blouse, underhand to Hermosa. "Forge my signature, then meet me in the shoe department on the third floor."

"I can't forge your signature. No, no. I can't do that."

"You can and you must! I'm begging you." Ellie was struggling to get her jog bra over her breasts as Hermosa stood stunned in the doorway. "Go, go! I'll meet you on three." Hermosa hesitated, then disappeared. "I'll name my next child after you!" Ellie called as she stepped into her aerobic shoes.

Thanks to Hermosa's forgery and daring, Ellie skipped out of Saks Fifth Avenue with—well, not exactly *her* dream outfit. More like her *mother's* dream outfit *for* her. Then she hailed a cab and headed for Reebok.

Well, I did it, Ellie mused as she signed the kids out of "For Kids Only" and returned her beeper.

"Mommy! Mommy!" Ahnika yelled when she saw Ellie. Ahnika bounded across the floor with Angus doing his Vietnam crawl slowly but surely behind her.

"Hi, my cuties!" She sat on the floor; Ahnika climbed into her lap. The kids are happy, my beeper never went off, and nobody was the wiser.

Chapter Eight

Ellie, hair wet and wrapped in a towel, peeked into the living room. Angus was fast asleep in his swing, and Ahnika sat on the arm of the sofa while Kimmie painted her toenails with glow-in-the-dark polish.

Happy as clams, Ellie thought as she sneaked away.

Back in her bedroom she dumped the Saks bags on her bed and surveyed her new ensemble. She wrestled to get the nude hose up her thighs. She felt two hands gently cup her naked ass. She froze.

"Ricardo, stop. My husband will be home any minute." The hands moved up and caressed her breasts. He pressed his pelvis into her. She turned.

"Oh! Hi, honey. I thought you were someone else." She kissed Peter on the lips.

"Very funny." He pulled her to him and started nibbling her neck.

"Listen." She stepped back, panty hose straddling her thighs. "We've gotta be out of here in fifteen minutes."

"Do we have to go to this thing?"

"Hey, you were the one who got me into this." She stretched the panty hose up over her butt. "We are going. You look great in your suit and I have a new outfit."

Peter picked up the empty Saks bag. "I thought your mother wasn't coming till *next* month."

"Just shut up, sit on the bed, and close your eyes."

"Daddy!" Ahnika called. They exchanged a *we never get a moment alone* look.

"Go. But don't come back in till I tell you to."

"Here I come, sweetie." He gave Ellie one last kiss and was gone.

Ellie, suddenly excited about the "costume" she was going to wear and the evening ahead, went into overdrive and was dressed and mascara-ed in less than ten minutes. She stepped onto the bed and wobbled in her new pumps as she inspected her persona in the dresser mirror. As usual, her image was headless. The only full-length mirror in the apartment was built into the closet door in the playroom, and she wasn't about to leave the safety of her bedroom.

"Not bad." She bent down so she could see her face. "It really is not horrible. Peter! Can I see you a minute?"

He appeared in the doorway in no time and Ellie, still slightly wobbly, tried her best to look sophisticated and confident. His face was blank. "Like I said, I thought your mother wasn't coming till next month."

Ellie jumped off the bed, closed the door, and kicked off her pumps. They shot across the bedroom, one bouncing off the window with a clang.

"No. Keep the shoes on. I like the shoes." He ran to retrieve them.

"Damn you, Peter. Damn you! You put me in this WASPy environment that you know I can't stand, then you won't support me when I try to fit in." She tore off the jacket and threw it at him. He caught it.

"If I thought Ahnika going to Park Avenue Playgroup would make you dress like your mother I would've reconsidered." He was trying to suppress a smile.

"Why do you find this so funny?" She was stepping out of the skirt. "It's easy for men." She stuffed the skirt into the Saks bag. "They don't have to make *any* aesthetic choices. You just wear jeans and a flannel shirt or a suit if it's fancy. So you have to pick out a tie. Big fucking deal."

Peter was largely ignoring her as he rummaged in her closet. She sat on the bed in her stockings and the blouse and fell back, defeated.

"Was it really bad? Did I really look like my mother?" She began slowly unbuttoning the blouse.

"Wait. I think the blouse could work." He stood over her displaying a black leather skirt. "This looks great on you."

"I am *not* going to wear a black leather miniskirt to Park Avenue Playgroup's cocktail party. No! No, no, no!"

"Come on. Show those uptight women what you're made of. You want to look tasty for Missy, don't you?" He unzipped it, bottom to top. It made a long rectangle.

"You never give up." She was now grinning from ear to ear.

"Okay. Then do it for Missy's husband. I'm sure he hasn't gotten laid in years."

"Yeah. Poor guy. He's probably one of those nerdy preppies with the loafers, no socks, and in bad need of a haircut."

"Try it. I think the blouse will dress it up. And it'll look great with those new shoes."

"Suddenly you're Mr. Blackwell?" She smiled at him as he straddled her and eased the skirt under her hips. "All that diaper changing is coming in handy, huh?" They were face to face. She kissed him. He rubbed her mound through the smooth, silky panty hose. It sent a shiver through her crotch, then heat and wetness.

"I like these. They're shimmery." He had abandoned dressing her and caressed her inner thighs with both hands. Like a reflex, her pelvis reached up to him. Her breath quickened. She rubbed his growing cock through his suit pants.

"God! I want you inside me right now!" They kissed, long and wet. Peter struggled his hand down her tight hose and eased his finger inside her.

"Oh, my God! You're dripping." He reached for his zipper with his other hand. Ahnika screamed with delight in the other room. Ellie put her hand over his.

"No! Honey, the kids are in the other room. We can't."

"We can. Kimmie's with them." His eyes pleaded with her.

"Listen—" she kissed him sweetly and reached down into her panty hose, gently taking his hand by the wrist "—I'm a mother first, your love slave second."

He dropped his head in exaggerated disappointment and didn't resist her pull on his hand. "You just drive me crazy."

"I'll make a deal with you." She looked him steadily in the eyes, took his finger that had been inside her, and put it in his mouth. He moaned and sucked hungrily. "I'll wear the slutty skirt to the party and let you play with me in the cab on the way there if you'll get off me." She gave him a playful shove. He didn't budge. Just then the door banged open.

"Can I watch the Franklin video?" Ahnika waited in the doorway, oblivious of their compromising position.

"Sure!" they said in unison.

"Thanks!" She slammed the door and the sound of her footsteps faded into the living room. Ellie and Peter looked at each other and started to laugh.

When they arrived at Park Avenue Presbyterian, Ellie was weak-kneed from all the foreplay in the cab. She took a moment to steady herself as Peter paid the driver.

"Shit!"

"What?" Peter asked.

"I should've worn the suit."

"You look great!"

"I look like an overdressed waitress." She fussed with her pearls and buttoned another button on the blouse. Peter unbuttoned it and gave her a kiss on the cheek.

"Really. It looks very classy. The pearls, the shoes . . ."

"The leather mini up to my crotch." She tugged on her skirt in vain.

"You have much shorter skirts than this. What's the big deal?" He put his arm around her and they headed into the church.

"Trust me, in mere moments you'll understand *exactly* what I'm talking about." They found their way to the large meeting room and stopped in the doorway.

"This is going to be a nightmare," Ellie whispered to Peter as they scanned the room.

"Unbelievable," Peter said, wide-eyed.

Libby Merrill, sipping a glass of white wine and dressed head to toe in beige, was standing next to a tall, stoop-shouldered man with glasses and very little hair. Marie-Claire, wearing a red pants suit with yet another Hermès scarf, huddled with a short dark-haired man sporting a bow tie. Faith, wearing the same outfit from the morning (only with heels instead of the tiny bow shoes) was standing at the food table, chewing and nodding at a sandy-haired preppy prototype that was chatting away.

"And where the hell is Missy?" Ellie asked, then looked down at her seemingly endless legs. "I swear, I'm Bette Davis in *Jezebel*."

"You look great," he said and kissed her on the cheek.

"I'm the only one in the room who looks like she has reproductive organs."

"But that's a good thing."

"What do we do now? We don't have to mingle, do we?"

Peter held up the bag of wine. "We have a mission. Follow me." He took her arm. "Kitchen?"

"Kitchen," she agreed. "If we're lucky, this wine thing could keep us busy for the whole party."

When they pushed their way into the large, stainless steel kitchen, they found Missy, in a navy sheath, matching headband, and a beautiful enameled butterfly pin, taking plastic wrap off a sumptuous-looking cheese platter. A tall, swarthy man stood behind her nuzzling her neck. Ellie and Peter exchanged a quick look. The swarthy one stopped abruptly when the door banged shut.

"Ellie! You made it!" Missy ran to her and air-kissed her.

"I was a little panicked that you weren't here," Ellie said, air-kissing her back. "You look fantastic! I love that pin. Have I seen it before?"

"I don't think so." She stepped back and gave Ellie the once-over. "You look smashing! Tony, *this* is Ellie!" Missy presented Ellie to the swarthy one. "Ellie, this is Antonio." Antonio took Ellie by the shoulders and studied her.

"So, *this* is my Missy's little Ellie." He sounded like Ricardo Montalban. He kissed Ellie on both cheeks, then went back to gazing at her.

"So, *you* are Missy's Tony." Ellie smiled and tried to keep her knees from buckling.

His light green eyes were penetrating her and she felt rubbery all over.

So Tony is really Antonio, she thought. Who knew? Who knew that *Missy* would be with someone so—sexy and so—sexy!

"Hi. Peter Moore." Peter thrust his hand toward Antonio in an almost hostile gesture. "I'm Ellie's husband."

"Peter," Antonio said warmly as he grabbed Peter's hand. "We have been anxiously awaiting your arrival."

Ellie jumped in. "Peter, this is Missy."

"Peter!" Missy took his outstretched hand, leaned into him, and kissed him square on the lips. He briefly lost his footing. They both giggled.

"Missy, I'm glad to meet you, as well," Peter told her, blushing like a teen. They all looked at each other, grinning.

"Corkscrew," Ellie finally said. "Peter and I are in search of a corkscrew." Missy took one from a drawer and handed it to her. Antonio put his hand over Ellie's and eased the corkscrew away from her.

"Wine is my specialty." He took the bottles from Ellie, put his arm around her, and walked her out of the kitchen and back to the drink table.

He *is* sexy. Mmm, mmm, mmm, Ellie thought, trying to act casual.

"Back in Argentina, my father has a huge wine cellar. I opened my first bottle of wine when I was less than ten."

Ellie watched him open the wine—competently. Antonio, I've got news for you, she wanted to say, women can open wine bottles, too. We've been doing it for decades. In fact, I once opened forty-seven bottles of wine in a row. I'd tell him that story, she mused, but then I'd have to admit *I* was tending bar at a party of two hundred for Mayor Koch at the time.

Antonio poured a glass and handed it to Ellie. She started to protest that she was still nursing. Then she thought, what the heck, even the gyno said one glass is okay. She took a sip. It was the first taste of liquor she'd had since before she was pregnant with Ahnika, over three years ago. Not that she missed it. She had never been much of a drinker. "Food is my drug," she was fond of saying. But the wine was pretty darn good. She had to admit it. It was cool and warm in her throat at the same time. She took another sip and smiled to herself. The cool/warm feeling sank into her chest. She felt like she was being bad, in a fun way. Antonio pulled the last cork out with flair.

The kitchen door swung open with a bang. Peter and Missy walked into the party, laughing and laden with platters. Ellie was surprised and pleased to see them getting along so well. God, I love that Peter. He is sweet and sexy. She took another sip. I love his smile, his full lips, his big white teeth. Those teeth and lips are mine, all mine. The cool/warm feeling shot to her crotch like an arrow.

"Señor Azcurra, so glad you could make it." Veronica, dressed in a bright pink and orange Lilly Pulitzer dress from another decade, appeared out of nowhere. Her signature bracelets clanked as she kissed and hugged Antonio with obvious familiarity. They began to talk in Spanish. Missy joined them.

Okay, here it comes again, Ellie thought; Spanish, French, I'm fucked. She watched Missy smile, laugh, and talk. She is the definition of polish. She speaks at least three languages, has a staff, plays polo. What else can she do? I'm just happy that I haven't stuck my finger down my throat lately. Could I ever really be friends with this woman? Would she ever want to sit on the sofa with me and read our *Vogue* horoscopes aloud?

She gave her skirt another tug and took a gulp of wine.

"Hi, sexy." Peter was suddenly behind her. He reached under her skirt and caressed her thigh.

"Can we leave now?" She ushered him toward the food table. "I'll give you a blow job in the cab if we can go now." She smiled and raised her eyebrows as she took a bite of a gleaming red strawberry.

"That's a hell of an offer, but I think I'll have to pass. Unless you faint or fake a seizure, we have to stay for at least twenty more minutes. Besides, I wanna get my money's worth here. This party is probably costing us at least a couple of hundred." He popped a raspberry into his mouth.

"Find a pay phone and call my cell," she whispered. "I'll feign a babysitter emergency."

"Ellie! Ellie Fuller!" Lizzie Daniels was approaching; Ellie froze. "And Peter! So glad you could make it."

"Fuck," Ellie said under her breath, then emptied her glass.

Peter whispered, "Do I know this woman?"

"Yes!" She hissed back through a big, fake smile. "That's Lizzie Daniels, she and Veronica are the codirectors of the playgroup. You met them at Ahnika's interview, remember?"

"Right, right."

"I was talking with Missy earlier. You never told me your mother was Sara Fuller." Lizzie Daniels's nasal voice had its usual accusatory tone.

She was wearing a madras headband, of course, this time with a subtle gold thread woven through. No doubt, Ellie thought, to match the buttons on that hideous suit.

"Hi, Lizzie. Good to see you again." Peter saved the day, shaking hands with Lizzie as Ellie stood dazed, empty wineglass in hand. "What a lovely suit that is." He stole a glance at Ellie. Oh, my God! It's the navy suit I bought today, Ellie realized. The one I almost wore!

"I didn't know you had a writer in the family." Lizzie was almost flirting as she shook Peter's hand.

"Two. Two writers. Actually, Sara followed in *Ellie's* footsteps."

God bless that wonderful husband of mine. He's like my press agent. Now if he could just wave his magic wand and turn Old Long Face to stone.

"Really?" Lizzie said, not a drop of interest in her voice.

"Yes. She's been writing comedy for years."

"Since *before* my mother started writing self-help books," Ellie said before she could censor herself.

"In fact, she's got a big meeting with HBO next week," Peter said beaming as Missy, Antonio, and Veronica joined them. Ellie gave him a wide-eyed look which she hoped said *Shut the fuck up*. He shrugged his shoulders at her, as if to say *What?*

"Ellie!" Missy said. "Why didn't you tell me? Your own TV show on HBO? How exciting!"

"Well, I don't know about my own show. I've got an appointment to pitch an idea, that's all."

"What's the idea," Veronica asked. "Are you going to star in it?"

"Well . . . I . . . it's . . ." Ellie was suddenly craving another glass of wine and a vat of mixed nuts.

"She's very closemouthed about these things," Peter told them, putting an arm around her. "She hasn't even told me."

"Did you know Ellie's mother wrote *The Family Dance*?" Lizzie asked Veronica.

"*The Family Dance*? I loved it!" Veronica was even more gregarious than usual. "I recommend the book *all the time*!" She grabbed a Carr's wafer and smothered it in Brie.

"Even Tony read it and he never reads anything but fiction." Missy patted Antonio's shoulder maternally. I hate them all, Ellie thought.

"Well, she's such an easy read," Antonio said as he popped a slice of kiwi in his mouth and washed it down with some wine. "So accessible. Not dogmatic."

Ha! Try being her daughter, Ellie thought. She had barely moved or breathed since her mother's name was first mentioned. Thanks to the wine, she felt slightly removed from the buzz around her. Between the gushing about her mother and the questions about her nonexistent TV show the idea of faking a seizure was sounding more and more appealing.

"And she's a Smith girl, am I right?" Lizzie was addressing Ellie. All eyes were on her now.

"Oh, yes."

Veronica thumped her chest. "Class of '66." She smiled proudly.

"Class of '64." Lizzie piped in.

"Smith and Madeira. That's my mom." Ellie smiled and raised her empty glass in a mock toast. God, help me! Please, get me out of this. Please don't make me stand here in this miniskirt with all these East Coast, boarding school, old money types and talk about how *fabulous* my mother is.

"To Smith girls." Antonio raised his glass toward his wife. She gave him a sly smile and kissed him on the cheek. Everybody drank.

"What year?" Lizzie said stepping closer to Ellie.

"What?"

"When did you graduate?"

"Oh, *I* didn't go to Smith."

"Ellie's an artist, Lizzie, remember?" Veronica was sounding a little bombed. "Look at her. Does *she* look like a Smith girl?"

This isn't happening, Ellie thought. This can't be happening.

"No. She doesn't look like a Smith girl." Antonio took Ellie by the shoulders and studied her the way he had earlier in the evening. "She looks like . . ." His green eyes were looking deep into her.

Ellie spoke without thinking, "A cross between a whore and a cocktail waitress?"

"No, no, no, no." Antonio placed his index finger gently on her lips. "A cross between a poet and a movie star." He leaned into her and kissed her on the top of the head.

She was swirling in the tempest.

"Actually, *I* picked out her outfit." Peter finally spoke. He sounded proud and defensive.

"And we love it! Don't we?" Lizzie turned to Veronica. She actually sounded effusive.

"Yes! We love it!" Veronica was joining the backpedaling parade. "It's very . . ." she was searching ". . . gutsy! Ellie has great style."

Ellie tried to smile. She thought she was smiling. Are my muscles responding? she wondered.

"I always say to Veronica 'No one but Ellie Fuller or Mia Farrow could pull off that haircut.' You have to have perfect bone structure for that haircut."

Ellie looked around her. Everyone seemed distorted like through a fish-eye lens. A group of predatory WASPs, that's what they are, Ellie thought. All of them armed with their wineglasses. Just give a well-mannered WASP a couple of drinks and all the shiny paint comes right off. Everybody with a drink in hand; martinis, scotches, gin and tonics. *That's* what they teach at those Seven Sisters schools? Drinking! *That's* why I ended up a bulimic instead of an alcoholic? I didn't go to the right schools.

"Excuse me." Missy interrupted Lizzie and Veronica's chatter, which had digressed into a debate about Mia Farrow, Woody Allen, and Soon-Yi. "I have to powder my nose." She slipped her arm through Ellie's so they were hooked at the elbows. "Keep me company, El?" She didn't wait for an answer, she just whisked her away from the ruthless pack and off to safety.

"Lipstick?" Missy asked, holding up the shiny Bobbi Brown bullet like a lifesaver. Ellie took it without speaking and applied it carefully. She studied her face in the mirror. The harsh lighting of the basement bathroom was unforgiving.

"I'm getting to look *so* much like my mother it's startling." She leaned into the mirror to scrutinize the wrinkles above her mouth.

"She must be stunning," Missy said with a wink.

"Would you be my agent?" Ellie smiled and gave the lipstick back to her pal.

"Sorry about those two. I simply *adore* them both but I always forget how dangerous they can be after a couple of Chardonnays."

"What? You go out drinking with Cagney and Lacey?"

"Of course not, silly. Harper went to Park Avenue Playgroup, remember? And I also see those two at several charity functions every year."

"Charity functions, of course," Ellie said, feeling like the outsider in the leather mini.

"Listen, Tony and I are leaving early . . ."

"How can you do that?" Ellie felt panicked, betrayed. "Weren't you on the committee or something?"

Missy raised one eyebrow and smiled mischievously. "When we first arrived I told Veronica we had baby-sitter problems so we couldn't stay long."

"You are brilliant! See? I didn't think ahead. But I've been toying with staging a seizure since we arrived." Ellie fluffed her hair; it looked exactly the same.

"Well—" Missy leaned in conspiratorially "—just tell them the sitter called and said that Angus is fussy, she thinks he's running a fever."

"You are my idol."

"Tony and I will leave first and wait for you two on the corner."

Ellie looked at Missy, confused.

"Well, you're not going to let a perfectly good sitter go to waste, are you? Come to our place. Did you eat? Gloria can fix us something yummy." Missy had once again hooked elbows with Ellie and was leading her to freedom.

Chapter Nine

The doorman at Missy and Antonio's building was dressed to the nines: top hat, gold epaulets, the works. "Mr. and Mrs. Azcurra, beautiful evening." He nodded slightly, his gloved hands clasped behind his back.

"Gorgeous, Marco." Antonio nodded and smiled as they walked into the lobby. It was an elaborate display of marble and was big enough for a soccer game. This place looks vaguely familiar, Ellie thought. I must have catered some dreadful Christmas party in this building.

The ornate elevator had panels of burgundy and gold brocade that complemented the gold railings. I've definitely been in here before, Ellie realized. Who could forget this elevator? Missy put a key next to the word PENTHOUSE. Ellie and Peter stole a look at each other. He grabbed her hand and squeezed it. The elevator opens right onto the apartment, Ellie was starting to remember. And there's a Picasso sketch in the foyer. The elevator stopped; the doors opened.

"Gloria!" Antonio called. "We have guests!"

"Who's hungry?" Missy asked as they stepped into the foyer. Sure enough, a Picasso hung above a half-moon table that held matching softball-sized, skinny-necked topiaries. Between the topiaries sat an engraved oval tray that read:

The Piping Rock Club
Runner-up
1965
Member-Guest

A pair of green L. L. Bean boots sat on the pickled wood floor next to a Chinese-looking umbrella stand which held several silver and ivory-headed canes but not one umbrella.

The topiaries are new, Ellie thought, but the rest is just as I remember. "How long have you two lived here?" she asked.

"Seven years. It was an engagement present from Tony's father."

"That's a hell of a present," Peter said.

"Poppy likes to do things on a grand scale," Antonio said grandly. "It comes from generations of raising cattle: big steers, big land, big gifts."

Peter put his arm around Ellie and pulled her close. She nudged him in the ribs. She felt like they were two children in a strange and exciting land.

"When we moved in, we threw a huge party. Poppy called it an engagement party. We called it a housewarming." Missy hung her coat in the hall closet.

Oh, my God! I catered that party, Ellie realized. *That's* why Missy looked familiar to me that first day of the playgroup. Missy reached around Ellie and helped her with her coat. The butterfly pin flashed in the light. And that pin. Is that how I know the pin?

"I just love that pin, Missy. It's very unusual."

"It was my grandmother's, another engagement present."

Engagement present, aha! Ellie wished she could telepath to Peter her revelation. Details of the party she had catered were coming back in bits and pieces.

"There's a Matisse over the fireplace," she whispered to him as they followed their hosts into a tremendous living room. One wall was floor-to-ceiling windows. Central Park and the West Side stretched out in front of them. A large fireplace with a carved alabaster mantel was on the left wall. And, yep, above it hung a Matisse. Peter looked at Ellie, his mouth gaping. She gave him an *act normal* look as they settled onto a butter-yellow leather sofa. Antonio stood behind them at a wet bar.

"Who wants what?" he asked, silver ice tongs in hand.

"Seltzer," Ellie and Peter said simultaneously. Peter squeezed Ellie's knee and she had to suppress a giggle. She smacked him on the thigh and scowled. Antonio clinked ice into two heavy rock glasses and poured them each a Perrier.

"Gloria, are you here?" Missy headed out of the living room. "Excuse me a moment. It seems we have a missing cook."

"Gloria has been with my family since before I was born. Her empanadas are exquisite." Antonio handed them their drinks with cocktail napkins. "She came to us from Argentina after Missy and I married."

Sort of like a wedding present, Ellie thought disdainfully as she sipped her Perrier. Antonio sat across from them in an easy chair upholstered in bright Guatemalan fabric.

"Peter, Missy tells me you are a computer genius. That you're revolutionizing the medical insurance industry."

"Genius may be a bit of an overstatement, but . . ."

"Excuse me." Missy popped her head in. "Sweetie, could I have your help for a minute?"

"Duty calls." Antonio nodded to them and joined his wife. They spoke to each other in Spanish as they exited.

"I catered that party," Ellie said out of the corner of her mouth, like a spy passing information to a contact.

"What party?"

"Their engagement party." Ellie was whispering as fast as she could. "I was here, in this very room, seven years ago, in a polyester-blend tuxedo shirt with a strap-on bow tie."

"You're kidding!"

"I'm dead serious. I carved the roast beef. I passed puff pastries. I knew I'd seen Missy's pin before. That tipped me off. That and the Picasso in the foyer." She glanced quickly over her shoulder.

"That's how you knew about the Matisse."

She nodded, then giggled. "I feel like we're Susan St. James and Rock Hudson on *McMillan and Wife*."

"This is too much!"

"I know. Can you believe it? I *thought* Missy looked familiar since the first day I met her. Now I'm just waiting for *her* to recognize *me*."

"Oh, that'll be fun."

Ellie's attitude and carriage suddenly changed. " 'El, darling. Didn't we meet before over puff pastries? Do be a dear and freshen my drink.' "

"Check out the napkins." Peter held up his ecru cocktail napkin, displaying the brick-colored monogram.

"I know. She *is* my mother."

They heard muffled voices coming from the kitchen. Peter looked over his shoulder, got up, and walked to the windows. Ellie followed. They stood side by side looking over the park.

"Oh, my God. Look at this!" They gazed out and took it all in, silent for a moment. "Do you suppose it's possible to get depressed when you wake up every morning to this? We live in a hovel." Peter gave her a *watch it* look. She patted his ass and kissed his ear. "You know I love our apartment but . . ."

"Hey!" He frowned at her. "We have pocket doors in the dining room and—what's that molding we have?"

"Picture frame molding. I know—"

"And a river view! Do *they* have a river view?" Peter asked, waving his arm towards the endless park vistas.

"We can see a *sliver* of the river from our bedroom."

"And we have southern exposure and an eat-in kitchen and . . ."

"Peter, you know I love our apartment, but you have to admit it's humbled by this place."

"I'll admit nothing." He kissed her, reaching in her blouse and cupping her breast.

"I have to pee."

"No! Don't leave me here alone."

"Well, I could stay and pee all over their antique Oriental rug. That would make a nice impression. Besides, what are *you* worried about? You're not the one who catered their engagement party."

"What do I talk about? I don't know anything about cattle ranching."

"Ask him. I'm sure he'd love to tell you. My mother always says 'Ask a man about himself, he'll think you're fascinating.'" She kissed him, slipping her tongue in his mouth. He pulled her close. They kissed long and deep, grinding their bodies together. Ellie's hunger from earlier in the evening was re-ignited. She peeled herself away from him and tiptoed out of the room.

She knew exactly where the guest bathroom was. Once inside, she recognized the gold sink with the matching fish faucet and handles. The little shell-shaped guest soaps were unused and the ecru guest towels were monogrammed, of course. Ellie peed, then wiped with the ecru toilet paper from the gold fish holder. This bathroom is like something out of my grandmother's house, she thought. She pulled up her panty hose, smoothed out her leather skirt, and chose a pale green scallop soap.

"Isn't this wild?" She spoke to her reflection as she washed her hands. The anxiety and fear of the party had been replaced by a sort of giddy anticipation. "Empanadas with Antonio and Missy. Who would've guessed? Maybe they'll put on the Gipsy Kings and we'll all dance the tango." She found a well-used tube of Malt Shimmer in a tiny gold box next to the tissues and freshened her lipstick. The intimacy that Peter had talked about, of sharing Missy's lipstick came home to her. Missy *is* my friend, Ellie thought. She rescued me from those evil ones at the party; she's sweet and gracious to Peter; she would even give me her last lipstick if I needed it. That's friendship. She fluffed her hair and headed back to the action.

When she reached the foyer she could hear Peter explaining his latest computer program to someone. A familiar smell hit her. Pot! Oh, my God, it's pot! She rounded the corner to see Missy taking a hit of a big, fat joint. The earth is spinning off its axis, Ellie thought. Missy Hanover, preppy extraordinaire, is not only married to a sexy Latin type, she smokes pot. Now, I'm really lost.

"Ellie, you're back." Missy seemed startled, like a teen that had just been busted by her mother. She started to laugh. "This isn't what you think," she said between spasms of laughter. "Tony, tell Ellie this isn't what she thinks." She passed the joint to Antonio as she tried, in vain, to stop her laughing.

Ellie realized she was standing, hands on hips, staring at Missy in disbelief. She dropped her hands to her sides and shifted her weight.

"Oh, darling. Ellie does not care." Antonio took a hit. "She is an artist.

I'm sure Ellie has smoked her share of marijuana." Antonio said "marijuana" as if he were a science teacher about to list all the dangers related to this awful weed. Missy looked at Ellie sheepishly and patted the space on the sofa next to her. Ellie smiled and snuggled down between her and Peter, pot smoke swirling around her. Antonio offered the joint to Ellie.

"Still nursing," she said, waving it away.

"You were right, Missy, she is a gem. You must be a wonderful mother, still giving the precious milk to your darling boy. In Argentina, when I was born, no one used formula. If a mother had no milk, there was always a wet nurse in the neighborhood to offer her breast. My mother nursed seven children."

"Seven? I'm going to talk to the Mayor about a ticker tape parade in her honor," Ellie said. Antonio bellowed out a huge laugh as he passed the joint to Peter.

"What the hell," he said, examining the reefer.

This'll be interesting, Ellie thought, watching Peter suck the smoke deep into his lungs. She and Peter had never been stoned together. She hadn't smoked pot since before rehab. The munchies are not a good thing for a recovering bulimic. But, Antonio was right; Ellie *had* smoked her share of pot and more. After all, she grew up in Southern California in the sixties and seventies.

"Antonio's best friend from college is a botanist," Missy explained.

"He is a brilliant scientist, a professor at Cornell. This is from his private stock, grown on his farm. Every once in a while he leaves me a little package with the doorman. I found these when I got home last night." Antonio passed Ellie a silver Tiffany box. It was full of perfectly rolled joints.

"Wow. You guys get great gifts."

Antonio picked up a remote from the large antique chest doubling as a coffee table and clicked it toward a bank of stereo equipment. Paul McCartney's "Maybe I'm Amazed" came on at the perfect background level.

No maybe about it, Ellie thought.

"Whoa, I haven't listened to this album since high school," Peter said. Ellie examined her husband. He already had that sleepy-eyed look. Yep, he's high, she thought. This is going to be fun. *I'm* the responsible one. *They're* all on drugs. *I'm* in control. She watched Peter lean his head onto the back of the sofa, mouthing the words as the music washed over him. Missy kicked off her sling-back heels and took another hit. Then she stretched her long legs and rested them on the coffee table as she blew the smoke up toward the ceiling. She reached her arm behind Ellie and rested it on the back of the sofa. Antonio clicked the remote at the stereo and the music swelled. The three of them smoked and listened as Ellie watched like a scientist doing a field study.

Then . . .

"Maybe I'm amazed at the way I really need you."

Antonio started singing a duet with Paul McCartney, loud and strong. He closed his eyes and used the remote like a conductor's baton. He opened his eyes and stared at his wife. She met his gaze. They were locked in a private reverie. Missy sang with him.

"Oh! Ohh! Ohh . . ."

This just keeps getting weirder and weirder, Ellie thought as she watched the duo "oh" together, oblivious of anyone or anything. They're like Sonny and Cher, or Captain and Tennille. She felt a giggle rising in her throat and elbowed Peter, hoping for an ally. But when he turned to her, to Ellie's complete and utter shock, he began to sing, too, furrowing his brow and playing the rock star to the hilt. The stoned trio banged their hands on their legs, playing the air piano.

Ellie felt like she had been catapulted back to the early seventies, back to a time when every new album that came out seemed to be the perfect soundtrack for the chaos of her life. If ballet saved her sanity by getting her out of her crazy house, music saved her life by giving her comfort when she was forced to be *in* her house. She played it constantly and loudly: the Beatles, Blind Faith, the Stones, Joni Mitchell, and she always sang along.

What am I waiting for, she asked herself. She opened her mouth and sang.

"Baby won't you help me to understand?"

The two couples had been fast-forwarded to a level of intimacy usually reserved for friends from childhood. They all "oohed" together in seemingly perfect harmony. The song ended and everyone was pink cheeked and grinning like stoned idiots. I'm having a contact high, Ellie realized.

Just being in their stoned presence had taken her up, up. She had grabbed onto their pot-soaked coattails and was flying with them.

"Gloria!" Missy jumped up and greeted the tray-toting woman, taking on the busted teen persona once again. "Thank you!"

Gloria looked like something out of a Zorro movie, the Hollywood version of what a beautiful Spanish servant girl would look like. But she was clearly no longer a girl. Though her dark skin had that ageless quality, she carried the signs of a life of hard work in her body and her movements.

Missy kissed her cheek, took the tray from her, and placed it on the coffee table. It looked like a photo out of *Gourmet* magazine, with cloth napkins in autumnal tones that perfectly complemented the color of the empanadas and the burgundy stoneware. A beautiful salad shone in a glass bowl with richly grained wooden utensils. Their whole life is perfect, Ellie realized. Every aspect of it could be photographed for different periodicals at any given moment, even the joints in the Tiffany box. Do they have piles of unopened mail anywhere? Do their houseplants ever die and then sit in a pot for months before they are finally thrown out? Do they ever burp or fart or cry?

Gloria went to the stereo and turned the volume way down. We're in trouble, Ellie thought. She's gonna call my mom?

"Missy, Tony, why didn't you tell me that you were having a party this evening? I would've made churrasco." She spoke in a motherly tone with just a hint of reprimand.

"Gloria hates surprises," Missy explained to the group.

"Our life here is very predictable. My Gloria doesn't like her routine disturbed," Antonio said as he clicked the volume back up to an audible level. He smiled at her devilishly and began to serve the food.

Gloria exited in that invisible way that servants do and the party continued. The empanadas were unbelievable. Or was it the pot? Everyone ate silently, single-mindedly. The CD player was filled with Beatles CDs and set on shuffle. To Ellic's delight, the four of them were serenaded by the Fab Four throughout the meal. As Ellie stabbed the last of her mesclun lettuce, "If I Fell" was playing. John's plaintive voice gave her goose bumps.

"To which schools are you applying for Ahnika? All Souls, Brick Church, and Episcopal? The usual?" Antonio asked, blotting his mouth with his napkin.

"Uh, actually . . ." Shit, Ellie thought, I don't want to have the private schools talk with them.

"Where *did* we apply, El?" Peter asked. He had left the whole grueling process up to her. The competitiveness of private preschools in Manhattan was legendary. Even the act of getting applications was a grind. Ellie, along with every other yuppie mother in Manhattan, had had to decide which five or six schools to concentrate on in August, more than a year before their little darlings would attend. Then, the Tuesday after Labor Day at 8 A.M., the calling for applications had begun. Most schools would only send out a limited number. The most exclusive ones were so coveted by throngs of insane parents willing to pay as much as $16,000 for glorified day care that they had to conduct a lottery.

"All the good West Side schools," Ellie finally said, trying to sound confident as she put her empty plate back on the tray.

"West Side schools? But what about All Souls?" Antonio sounded worried as he reached for the silver box and took out a fresh joint.

"All Souls has a lottery system now, honey. They're way too late for that."

"But I play squash with Whit Simmons." Antonio put the joint in his mouth and lit it. "He's on the board. They have the best three's program in Manhattan." He took a big drag, holding the smoke in for a long time. The CD player click, clicked and "Why Don't We Do It in the Road?" blasted into the room.

And weirder and weirder, Ellie thought, trying not to giggle.

Missy sat on the arm of Antonio's chair and patted his shoulder. "You think it's the best because that's where we sent Harper and that's where we're sending Mason." He passed her the joint. "They live on the West Side, sweetie." She took a hit and held the smoke in as she spoke. "It's a whole different world."

Ellie grabbed Peter's empty plate and put it on the tray.

"Excuse me," she said as she picked up the rattan tray, now stacked with empty plates. I'm getting the fuck out of here, she thought. But she said, "I'm going to pick Gloria's brain about that empanada recipe of hers."

"Ellie, don't be silly. Put that down and relax," Missy implored. Ellie gave Peter a *back me up* look and headed toward the kitchen.

"Don't try to talk her out of it, Missy. When Ellie's in search of a recipe she's unstoppable." Which was a pile of crap, of course. Ellie was not a cook. She could make three things: damn good guacamole, fluffy whole-wheat pancakes, and a decent omelet.

Ellie, laden down with the tray, backed through the swinging kitchen door and found Gloria sitting on a stool in the big, homey kitchen watching *Ally McBeal* on a small TV. This is just like I remember it from the party, Ellie thought as she surveyed the glass-faced cabinets and the white-tiled counter tops.

"Oh, I would've cleared that," Gloria said, taking the tray from her.

"No problem. I've waited my share of tables." Ellie always felt compelled to let people who served her know that she was really one of them, a worker, not one of those *other* people.

"Great empanadas. Is it your grandmother's recipe or something?" Ellie asked as they began scraping plates and filling the dishwasher. She was willing to play the domestic role that Peter had cast her in, anything to avoid being grilled about private schools.

"Can you keep a secret?" Gloria asked.

"Of course."

"I get them from a little place on Forty-sixth Street." The two of them laughed. "I used to spend hours making them from scratch until I found this place. I never told Miss Missy or Señor Tony."

"My lips are sealed." The large stainless steel wall clock told Ellie it was 8:15. "Shit! Pardon my French. I've gotta go." Just then the door swung open and Missy entered. Her hazel eyes were red-rimmed. Her gait was slow and fluid.

"Why do you have to go? You have a baby-sitter."

"I told her we'd be back by eight."

Missy stood behind Ellie, reeking of pot, and whispered in her ear. "Call her, tell her you'll be a little late." She put her hands on Ellie's shoulders. Ellie stiffened, her crotch contracting. She looked for Gloria in vain;

the maid had done her disappearing act again. "Ellie Fuller, I don't think I've ever seen you relax." Missy began to press her fingertips into Ellie's trapezius muscles. It sent chills down her spine.

"A relaxed mother? Isn't that an oxymoron?" Ellie asked as Missy's fingers continued to knead her overworked muscles. Is this weird or is it me? Ellie wondered.

"That Peter of yours is a gem, so handsome and sweet and funny. He and Tony are in there reliving the World Series."

"Antonio's a Yankees fan? Thank God." Ellie was beginning to relax in spite of herself.

"He cried when they won the World Series. Isn't that sweet?"

"That's why God invented sports; so men could have their feelings," Ellie said dreamily, as her shoulders began to drop. "I've only seen Peter cry once, when Wells pitched that perfect game." Missy's fingers were walking down Ellie's spine, sending off little shivers at each vertebra. The door opened and Antonio stuck his head in.

"How are my beautiful girls doing? Ah, one of Missy's famous massages." His eyebrows raised in appreciation.

Missy wrapped her arms around Ellie's neck and gave her a playful squeeze. "They are leaving us," Missy pouted. "We mustn't let them go."

"Really, Missy, they've never gone to sleep without me. And I haven't nursed Angus in . . ." Like a reflex, she cupped her breasts, checking for fullness, just as Peter squeezed his head in next to Antonio's. He took in the scene; his face tightened when he saw his wife fondling herself.

Ellie looked down and was surprised to see where her hands were. "Oh!" She released her tits like they were hot coals. "Peter! Uh, excuse us but we have to go." She broke free of Missy. "Kimmie—uh, that's our baby-sitter—she was expecting us fifteen minutes ago and . . ." She scrambled past the boys and back into the living room. "Twist and Shout" was rockin' the place as she headed straight for the hall closet and her coat.

And even weirder still, Ellie thought as she put on her coat. Was Missy flirting with me? Is that possible? Is Peter's fantasy coming true? No, no. Missy Hanover a lesbian? I don't think so. She and Antonio are obviously wild for each other.

"Gabriela's? No, we've never been there. Sounds great!" Missy's voice came from the living room. Ellie, wearing her coat and with her purse on her shoulder, waited in the foyer feeling awkward as hell.

82

"I adore Mexican!" Antonio said as the threesome entered the foyer. "Ellie, you're not going to believe what Missy and I have decided to do. It's unprecedented."

"What?" Ellie asked.

"We are actually going to come to the West Side."

"No! Well, you better bring your passport or you might end up stuck there, and those radical West Siders might make you do something crazy like . . . grow your hair or . . ."

"Vote Democrat," Peter offered.

"Or get a tattoo," Missy said, joining the game.

"Yeah, we know a great guy," Peter said. Ellie's heart skipped a beat.

"You do?" Missy was helping Peter with his jacket. Oh, no, Peter, don't, Ellie prayed. Don't say it.

"Yeah, El went to a great guy last year. But he's in the Village. What was his name, El?" All eyes turned to Ellie. It felt as if all the air had been sucked out of the room. She was suddenly sweating inside her light jacket.

"Fritz," she said, as a drop of sweat rolled down her side from her armpit and soaked into her silk blouse at her waist. "Fritz something."

Ellie had met him less than a year ago. He had spent almost an hour bent over her bare ass, but she hadn't bothered to get his last name. Peter had mentioned tattoos and how sexy he thought they were countless times. Ellie had always pooh-poohed the idea. But last Valentine's day, pregnant as a whale with Angus and without a word to Peter, she found Tattoo World in the yellow pages, took the subway to Christopher Street, and met Fritz. He was a young energetic German with white-blond hair and countless tattoos.

Together, they designed Peter's Valentine's Day present: a blood red heart, about the size of a quarter, draped with a blue ribbon and fastened with roses on either side. "Peter" was tattooed on the ribbon in fancy script where it crossed the heart. On Valentine's Day, after Ahnika was put to bed, Ellie stripped, taped the top of a small box to her ass, covering the still-tender tattoo, and presented herself to Peter. He walked slowly around her naked body, found the box top, and then delicately removed it. With tears in his eyes, he gently kissed the heart. His cock swelled immediately and his arousal made Ellie moist. Despite the awkwardness of her huge belly and the tenderness of her tattoo, they had made love blissfully.

"Wouldn't you know she'd have a tattoo, honey?" Missy was arm in arm with Antonio and the two of them were admiring Ellie like she was some exotic species on the verge of extinction.

"It's right here," Ellie said, pointing to a spot just to the right of her pubic hair and looking deadpan at her audience. "It says SLOW CIRCULAR MOTIONS, EVEN PRESSURE. What do you think?" *I can't believe I just said that*, she thought.

"You're kidding!" Missy said, eyes like saucers.

"Gotcha!" Ellie winked at her friend.

"Oh, you!" Missy pursed her lips and shook her head. "She does that to me all the time." Everyone laughed, thank God.

"She is full of surprises, this one," Antonio said, ruffling her hair like a big brother.

"Oh, you have *no* idea, Antonio," Ellie said with all the bravado she could muster as she pushed the button for the elevator.

"As a matter of fact—" Peter started.

"If you suggest I *show* them my tattoo—" Ellie said over her shoulder, cutting him off "—I'm going to deny you access to it for an entire year."

Antonio laughed a grand Latin laugh, grabbed her from behind, and gave her a big kiss on the neck. "You are delicious," he whispered in her ear. She felt a tingling warmth deep in her belly that spread down to her crotch. All her fear and embarrassment had vanished and been replaced with an uncontrollable urge to turn to him and kiss him deep and long, to reach in his pants and feel his growing cock in her hand. To feel his long Argentine fingers in her wet pussy. But the exit gods were smiling on her and the elevator doors opened, thank you very much. She eased herself out of Antonio's arms, walked unsteadily into the elevator, and pushed *L*.

"Are you coming?" she asked Peter with a coy playfulness that she did not feel.

He was arm and arm with Missy and she was giggling something in his ear. *Now she's coming on to* him? Ellie marveled. She felt a pang of jealousy. But she wasn't sure which one she felt more proprietary about, Peter or Missy.

Peter gave Missy a peck on the cheek and started for the elevator. When he made it to Ellie's side, he put his arm around her and held her like a vise. Missy and Antonio looked like a taller, tanner reflection, facing them with two sleepy grins on their faces.

"I really had a great time. Thank you both so much." Ellie's own words sounded fake and hollow in her ears.

"It was great meeting you two. Thanks for the dinner, the drugs," Peter said.

"Let's do it again, soon," Missy said, waving as the elevator doors began to close.

"Gabriela's," Antonio called as the doors shut.

Ellie, wedged between her two sleeping children in their king-sized bed, was half asleep herself, with an endless loop of "Norwegian Wood" tormenting her and visions of Picassos and *Ally McBeal* dancing in her head. She struggled herself back to consciousness, trundled into the bathroom, and put in her diaphragm. Out in the living room, Peter was dozing on the sofa bed. She snuggled in next to his warm body and kissed his chest. He turned to her and hugged her for a long time. She felt dreamy and liquid as he floated down between her legs to her moistness and began to eat her. She sank into the pleasure, closing her eyes and drifting. Everyone came to her fantasy that night: Manny the tennis pro, Jeff Bridges, Antonio, George Clooney, and Missy. They were all there, all focused on Ellie and her enjoyment. But, somehow, despite Peter's persistent and consistent attention, she couldn't come. Oh, well, she thought, no big deal. She gently pulled Peter on top of her and inside her. They made love without a word. It was seamless and smooth.

Afterward, Peter was snoring before Ellie could catch her breath. She got a paper towel and cleaned herself off, had a drink of water, took her vitamins, and crawled back under the covers next to him. He rolled on his side and snuggled her close to him. His snoring stopped, thank God. The sweet peacefulness of their lovemaking had vanished and Ellie was suddenly wide awake. I really should work on the fucking pitch, try to come up with *something*. My meeting's in less than a week. But it's so warm and cozy here. She didn't budge.

Like sports highlights, flashes of the evening were coming back to her. The WASP vultures from the party, the grandeur of Missy and Antonio's life, Antonio's tall, strong body against hers, his breath in her ear. She eased herself away from Peter and reached down between her legs. She began to finger her clit, her hips raised in response. She could hear Antonio's voice; it was deep and rich. She could feel his lips on hers, his tongue in her mouth. Her fingertip circled faster and faster around her most sensitive part. Her back arched, Antonio's finger was suddenly there, she could feel his weight on her. Her legs locked straight as boards, toes stretching long. His finger faster, perfect, perfect! She came for what seemed like forever, silently, trying not to wake her sleeping husband.

Chapter Ten

I'm fucked," Ellie told her reflection in the mirrored walls of the elevator. "I'll never work in show biz again," she said, then pushed *28*. She tried to brush the wrinkles out of her pants as the elevator zoomed upward. "What could I have been thinking?" she asked her rumpled reflection. "I could be home right now watching *Teletubbies*." The elevator stopped and she took a deep breath. "Well, here goes."

The doors opened and three shiny gold letters, about two feet high, greeted her on the opposite wall: HBO.

She walked slowly toward the taupe and off-white reception area, feeling like Dorothy on her long walk down that ominous corridor on her way to finally meet the wizard. I'm screwed, she told herself, totally screwed!

. . .

Last night the digital clock on the VCR had read 12:53 when Peter, in boxer shorts, had wandered into the living room bleary-eyed.

"How's it going?" he had asked from the hallway.

Ellie pointed the remote at the VCR and hit *pause*. "Great!" She sat cross legged on the sofa with a pile of notes on her right, a pile of video tapes on her left and the remote in her hand. "I have a meeting with one of the most powerful women in women's comedy in less than ten hours to pitch my fabulous series idea and I have *nothing* to *pitch*!" She gestured at the pile of video tapes. "I've been looking at all my old stand-up tapes hoping to find some old bit to hang a series on."

"Can't you just call and reschedule?" He shoved aside the videos and sat down next to his harried wife.

"No, no, no. You don't get it. You don't reschedule with Lisa Bienstock."

"Bienstock?" Peter said. "Is she married to Jack-and-the?"

"Very funny. I either go to this appointment or I forget having a career in comedy. This woman is a shark. She's infamous for blacklisting comics. I have to come up with *something*." She pressed *pause* again and Ellie's miniskirted video image sprang to life. She stood on a small stage, mike in hand and spoke with ease and confidence to the comedy club audience.

"My husband and I are 'trying.'"

"I always liked this bit," Peter said.

"Thanks." Ellie took his hand and the two of them watched a younger, brunette Ellie work the room.

"It's very weird. After literally *decades* of trying to thwart that sperm we're actually encouraging it!" She looked at the audience with disbelief. "Pregnant on purpose; what a concept." The audience laughed.

Peter grabbed the remote from Ellie and pushed *pause*. "There's your title: *Pregnant on Purpose!*"

She stared at him for a moment. "Okay, okay. That's a good title, but what's it about?"

"Well . . . motherhood, pregnancy, sleep deprivation, all that stuff."

"*I* like it but they won't."

"Why not? There are millions of mothers out there."

"Believe me, I'd *love* to write something about that. But it'll never fly. Not at HBO."

"Why not?"

"*Sex and the City, The Sopranos?* That's HBO, y'know; sexy, hot, edgy. Motherhood is *none* of those things.

"But *you're* sexy and hot and edgy."

She kissed him. "You think I'm sexy and hot because you're married to me. And I'm edgy 'cause I'm sleep-deprived.

"Here's what I need." She got up off the sofa and faced him. "I need to be able to walk in and say 'I've got this great idea; it's *Will & Grace* meets *Survivor*."

Peter scowled at her. "But what kind of a weird show would that be?"

"It would be a totally stupid show." She had sat down on the sofa and put her head in Peter's lap. "But they *just* might make it, because it's a cross between two *already* successful shows. That's all they can wrap their little brains around." Ellie had taken the remote back and pressed *play* and the two of them had watched Ellie's video image spring to life once more.

I'm here to see Lisa Bienstock," Ellie said to the painfully hip, twenty-something HBO receptionist, who had choppy jet black hair and wore a macramé choker.

"Ms. Bienstock doesn't see anyone without an appointment," she said, the silver ball in her pierced tongue shining in the fluorescent lights. She didn't look up from *The Artist's Way*.

"Oh really? I was hoping I could just force my way into her office, tie her up, and then pitch my idea to her in the hopes that she would see how brilliant I am before security came and carted me off."

Miss Silver Tongue looked up, seeming a little worried.

"I *have* an appointment." You stupid little bitch, Ellie said silently. She heard the faint ding of the elevator behind her.

"Oh." Miss Silver Tongue put down her book, clicked her mouse a few times, and studied her monitor. "Your name, please."

"Ellie Fuller."

Just then Ellie felt a tug on her trench coat. She turned to see Lisa Bienstock swooping past her, cell phone mouthpiece dangling from her

ear. "Uh-huh, yeah. I know. I know. I spoke to him yesterday. He's a pig."
Lisa was talking into the mouthpiece and, like every other person on the
planet with one of these attachments, she looked like she was talking to
herself. In this case, she looked like a very trendy and very rushed schizophrenic as she dragged Ellie by the elbow of her trench coat into her
office.

Ellie looked back at Miss Silver Tongue and gave her a vicious grin.

Lisa close the door then gestured for Ellie to sit as she continued to
talk on the phone. "No. No! I don't care what he said. He can eat me!"

She's lovely, Ellie thought as she hoisted a large stack of scripts and
papers out of the only extra chair in the cluttered office. The office was
small but with a great view of the Hudson. Lisa plopped down in her
swivel chair and mouthed "Sorry" at Ellie, then rolled her eyes.

Well, *she's* had a makeover, Ellie thought. She was such a mousy little
thing when she worked at Comedy Central. Lisa's once-brown hair was
now highlighted with at least two different shades of blond. The stripy
hair was slicked away from her face and held back in a studied but casual
way by a big tortoiseshell clippie. Carefully chosen pieces of her hair
stuck out at angles from the jumble of hair in the back. She had small
ruby-studded hoops in her ears (real or fake, Ellie wondered) and, for
some reason, had not taken off her leather swing coat.

"He's a motherfucker and a has-been," Lisa said into her cell phone.
"What's he done since that pilot for Disney that tanked? . . . Okay, okay.
Call me after you talk to him. Bye."

"So!" Lisa said, as she pulled the earpiece out of her ear. "What've ya
got?" And she rolled her chair up to her paper-strewn desk.

"Well—" Ellie stopped. Lisa was rummaging through her faux-
vintage, straw and leather handbag.

"Go ahead," Lisa said. "I just have to jot something down before I forget." She pulled out her Palm Pilot and began to scribble on it as she
worked her tongue over her teeth.

Who does she think she is? When Robbie and I were writing for
Women Aloud she was bringing us coffee, for Christ's sake!

Last night, after they had finished watching Ellie's entire set on video,
Ellie had asked Peter, "Why am I even doing this?" Her head was still in

his lap, his hand on her hip. "I mean, I don't even *care* about all this stuff anymore, the whole fame thing. The one good thing about the split with Robbie is now I don't have to *pretend* to care about it."

"Look, if you want to do this Jack-and-the-bean-stock thing, do it! If you don't, don't. We have enough money without some development deal you might or might not get from HBO. Do it if *you* want to."

"You're right," Ellie said, closing her eyes.

"See, *this* could be one of the topics on your show."

"What show?"

"*Pregnant on Purpose*. This whole dilemma of working or not working. I'm sure hundreds of other mothers are struggling with this same issue. It could be like a panel discussion show that—"

Ellie had jumped up and started to pace. "Yes! That's it! *That's it!*" She had stopped and faced Peter a huge, triumphant smile on her face. "HBO, here I come!"

Lisa was still writing in her Palm Pilot when Ellie began, "It's a panel discussion show for parents—"

Lisa looked up from her Palm Pilot. "A panel discussion show for parents?" She had a look on her face like she'd just smelled cat shit.

"Yes!" Ellie spat back with tons of enthusiasm that she didn't feel. She stood. "Get this: It's *The View* meets *Politically Incorrect*." Lisa went back to her Palm Pilot.

"Look! Motherhood is very hot right now. *Everyone* is doing it! People are so desperate to be in on this whole motherhood thing that even movie stars are doing it whether they have a partner or not. Circulation for all those parenting magazines has *tripled* in the last three years." (Ellie was making that up.) "The guest list is unlimited. From Sting to Madonna; from Jodie Foster to Alec Baldwin. Aren't some of those babes on *Sex and the City* mothers? Heck, we could have the whole cast on the show! And there are endless topics to deal with from conception all the way through adolescence. And . . ." Ellie raised her index finger to the ceiling and paused for dramatic effect ". . . since it's cable we can tell the *whole* story. Unedited."

"How do you mean?" Lisa actually looked at Ellie.

"Well, we don't have to sugarcoat it. For instance, motherhood is a dirty job. Nobody tells you that. Nobody told *me*. None of the books *I* read when I was pregnant said, 'Look, after the baby is born you are going to have stuff oozing out of every orifice. Your breasts are going to be leaking constantly and weird stuff will be coming out of your vagina—for weeks!' "

Lisa's brow was furrowed as she nodded slightly. She's finally listening, Ellie thought, but I think she's about to vomit.

"The baby is going to be peeing, pooping, and spitting up all over you. No one warns you what a disgusting experience it's going to be."

"So the show is about how motherhood is disgusting?"

She hates me *and* she hates the idea.

"Well, yes and no. Motherhood, especially with a newborn, is fraught with big, conflicting feelings. I have never had a harder job in my life and I have never had a *better* one. But the minute anyone knows you're pregnant you're suddenly fair game. It's as if you have a sign on your chest that says 'I'm dying to hear *your* opinion about every phase of *my* pregnancy.'

"And once the kids are born—forget about it! *Everyone* wants to tell you how to raise them—family, friends, strangers on the street. For instance: Just the other day I had a woman glare at me in West Side Market because my double stroller was blocking her way. She said 'This store really isn't big enough for that stroller.' I said 'You're right. I've got an idea; why don't you give me your number, and the next time I need to go grocery shopping I'll call you and you can watch my kids. What d'ya say?' "

"You said that?" Lisa's eyes were like saucers, but Ellie couldn't tell whether she was impressed or horrified.

Ellie nodded. "I want to have a show about how to deal with unsolicited advice.

"My kids were born twenty months apart. Since the day Ahnika was born I've been on this relentless mommy train, and throughout this *entire* experience I've been thinking, 'This is harder or funnier or messier than I thought it would be.' And I've been thinking, 'Why isn't anybody talking about this?' I mean, *Pregnant on Purpose* could give mothers some real help *and* a few laughs. Because, let's face it, if you don't have a sense of humor through this whole thing, I can't see how it's possible to survive it."

There was a long pause, then Lisa went searching in her tiny handbag again. This time, she pulled out what looked like a book of matches. Don't tell me she's going to smoke. She opened the cardboard container and pulled out a small orange stick.

"Stim-U-Dent?" she asked, offering the small stick to Ellie.

"No thanks," Ellie said, struggling to keep the disdain out of her voice.

"There's only one problem, as I see it," Lisa said, picking her teeth. "It's not sexy."

"That's not true. I have girlfriends who were extremely horny when they were pregnant. And then there are some husbands who find a pregnant woman incredibly sexy. My husband couldn't keep his hands off me.

"And after the baby is born, one of the things I've learned is you *must* have sex. Not for the first six weeks, of course. First of all, thanks to giving birth, your vagina's been stretched beyond recognition, so you're not really looking for any action there. Second of all, if you nurse your baby—as I will firmly suggest on the show—Hell! I'd like to nurse right *on* the show! So, if you're nursing, your breasts are no longer your own. They now belong to this tiny little creature that needs them to survive. They are being sucked on, pulled on, and bitten until they're raw. Thirdly, it's exhausting and relentless. I can't remember the last time I got to go to the bathroom by myself with the door closed."

"I thought you said you must have sex?" Lisa asked, sounding irritated.

"You *must* do it to get some of your old self back. Because you are in danger of being totally swallowed up by motherhood.

"So there I am, Ahnika's six weeks old and I've been given the go-ahead from my gyno. Do I *want* to have sex? No. But I do it. Why? Because I don't have the desire or the time to take step classes or go out and do stand-up. But I have enough energy, just barely, to take a shower, put in my diaphragm, and let my husband make love to me. Now, this accomplishes several things. First of all it reminds me that I am sexy and that I am something beyond just a milk cow for my insatiable infant. Secondly, it gets my heart rate up, it's aerobic. And, thirdly, to have an orgasm is never a bad thing." Ellie paused, hoping Lisa would jump in and say something—anything. She took the Stim-U-Dent out of her mouth, tossed it in the trash, paused briefly, and then stood up.

"Is that it?"

I loathe this woman, Ellie thought as she searched her brain for more.

"Well, I want to do a whole show on—"

"Yeah, yeah. I get there are a lot of topics and a lot of possible guests."

She walked around her desk and once more took Ellie by the elbow. "But that's it? *Politically Incorrect* meets *The View* for parents? That's the whole show?"

"Uh, yeah, basically," Ellie said as she grabbed her purse. She wanted to sock Lisa in the jaw or crawl under her desk. The performer in her had been stopped midstream; she was experiencing *monologus interruptus* and she couldn't stand it.

"Lisa, have you ever heard a construction worker whistle at a woman who's pushing a stroller?" Ellie asked as she was escorted out of Lisa's office.

"What?"

"Construction workers don't whistle at women pushing strollers; it just doesn't happen. When you become a mother you disappear in a lot of ways. I could push my kids in the double stroller buck naked right past a construction site with a sign on my back that says FUCK ME and no one would notice."

There was a beat. Lisa puckered up her lips and stared at the ceiling as if she were trying to remember where she'd put her car keys. That was my closer, Ellie thought as they walked past Miss Silver Tongue. If she doesn't bite I'm a goner.

"Y'know, Ellen . . ."

She doesn't even know my fucking name!

". . . HBO doesn't really *do* any panel shows—"

"I know but—" Ellie interrupted.

Lisa put up one French-manicured hand to quiet Ellie. "But I don't really give a shit what HBO does because—I *love* it!" Then she whipped open her swing coat and thrust her slightly rounded belly at Ellie.

"Oh, my God!" Ellie screamed.

"I'm sixteen weeks!" Lisa was beaming.

"No!"

"Yes!" She closed her coat and took Ellie by the arm again. "I just *love* the show! It's fun, it's edgy, it's even sexy. I *love* the nursing on camera. I want you to host it, of course. I want a synopsis for six shows. Each show should have a topic—like—"

"Bodily fluids, sleep deprivation, how to handle your in-laws?" Ellie piped in.

"Yeah, stuff like that! So I need topics and possible guests for six shows. You need a major theme and then two different segments for each show. This is all sketchy, of course." They continued toward the elevators. "I'll need a three-minute monologue—funny and topical—to open each show." The two women now stood at the bank of elevators. "And separate from the monologue I need plenty of jokes or little stories that can be ready for use throughout the show." Lisa pushed the call button.

Ellie felt as if she were standing outside her body, watching herself nod mutely as Lisa rattled off instructions.

Lisa was still talking when the elevator dinged and opened. Ellie stepped inside. "I need all this on my desk by the end of February. That way we can pitch it to the bigwigs for next fall. Can you do that?"

"Yes!" Ellie stepped out of the elevator, took Lisa's foundationed face in her hands, and kissed her on the lips. "Thank you!" Back in the elevator she pushed *L*. "Thank you!" She called again as the doors closed on the blissfully pregnant Lisa Bienstock.

Chapter Eleven

Ellie pushed the double stroller down Broadway at the speed of light, dodging the evening foot traffic like the pro that she was. The early November evening had a little bite to it so she paused to pull the powder blue blanket up over the children's chests, then went back into overdrive. She checked the time on the Apple Bank for Savings over her shoulder as she passed Gray's Papaya. The sky was perfectly clear and that wonderful cobalt blue it gets just before the day gives way to night. She had four minutes to make the six blocks to Barnes & Noble and up to the third floor for the question and answer session and signing of her mother's latest book.

She had given herself ample time to be prompt this evening. She knew any lateness would be deconstructed and analyzed to death by her mother. But, at 5:30, when she was pulling on the only pair of "slacks" she owned (courtesy of a trip to Saks with her mother, of course), the phone had rung and Peter had told her he wasn't going to make it. He was stuck in Newark waiting for some CEO, or some bullshit. Bottom line, there was nobody to watch the kids, and Ellie had less than forty-five minutes to get them fed and looking "presentable" for their Grammy's big night. Through the grace of the toddler gods, everyone had cooperated.

Now, as they raced down Broadway, the kids were bathed and looking pretty darn cute as they snuggled in their stroller. Angus, in a blue jumper with green army men crawling over it, matching green corduroy padders on his tiny feet, and a navy blue hooded sweatshirt, was kicking his feet and sucking his pacifier like nobody's business. Ahnika looked smashing! She actually *wanted* to wear a dress, "To see Grammy at Bombs and Nobo," so she could wear the (previously unacceptable) precious flowered tights that her Grammy had sent her from the Hanna Andersson catalog for her second birthday.

Ellie was sweating by the time she pushed the stroller past Eddie Bauer. Barnes & Noble was in sight. She glanced at her watch: 6:28.

"Not bad," she mumbled to herself. "Hopefully they won't start on time."

"Mommy, Mommy, look! It's Grammy!"

Ellie scanned the crowds on Broadway, searching for her mother. Nothing. She looked down to see Ahnika pointing at the Barnes & Noble window. There she was, Sara M. Fuller, in all her literary splendor, staring out with quiet confidence from her very own Barnes & Noble poster. Her auburn pageboy, now quite gray at the temples, was pulled back with the same tortoiseshell headband she'd worn for as long as Ellie could remember. She held her folded reading glasses in her left hand, which supported her chin. Her patrician bone structure (and a little airbrushing, no doubt) gave her an ageless quality.

Wow, good for you, Mom, Ellie thought, feeling mature. You really did something; your own goddamned poster at Barnes & Noble. Better late than never. Because you were never much of a mother, that's for sure. Oops, there goes the maturity.

She paused at the entrance. God, if you could help me be happy for her, I would really appreciate it. Guide my thoughts and my actions. Okay? Better yet, guide my mouth, could you? I never know what's going to pop out of it when I'm around her.

The revolving doors were moving steadily with a stream of customers. The door that Ellie and her wide load could fit through was at the top of a small hill. She struggled to push the stroller up the slope and reached, in vain, for the door. It bore a sign which read, *Wheelchair Access on Columbus*.

"Wheelchair access?" Ellie grumbled to herself like a street person. "What about *mommy* access. Don't women and children count in this culture?" She stretched over the top of the double stroller for the door handle. It was just out of reach. She let go of the stroller, just for a moment, to grab the door handle.

"Mommy!" Ahnika called as she and Angus rolled backward, toward the teeming chaos of taxis and buses on Broadway. Ellie dashed to save her children and reached the stroller as it careened into a mountain of a woman known as the Dog Lady. She was a neighborhood mascot of sorts. She had six tiny Yorkshire terriers that she walked all at the same time all over the West sixties and seventies. She looked like a huge canine maypole.

"I'm *so* sorry," Ellie groveled. "Are you all right?" The dogs were yapping and the Dog Lady was rubbing her ankle.

"There ought to be a law," was all she said, glaring at Ellie. Then she picked up the yappiest of the group and continued on her way.

"It's the Dog Lady, Mommy! Did you see her? Did you see all her doggies?" Ahnika was unfazed, thank God.

Back at the slope, Ellie decided that dragging the stroller was the way to go. After getting the door open, she propped it open with her body as she pulled the heavy load up the small incline that led to the barely wide enough opening. A security guard (a woman, if you can believe it) stood less than four feet away and didn't make a move.

"Thanks a lot for your help. I *really* appreciate it," Ellie said, in an overly cheery tone as she headed for the elevator. The stroller bumped a display of Thanksgiving books and several tumbled to the floor. Ahnika jumped up and ran to push the button on the elevator and Angus dropped his pacifier. He started to whimper as Ellie scrambled to retrieve it from under a table. It was back in his mouth before he started to howl.

"You've got your hands full," said a grandfatherly type as he squeezed past Ellie, still on her hands and knees gathering books off the floor.

No shit, asshole, she thought, but, "Yeah. Bull in a china shop. That's me," is what she said.

I've gotta mention this on the show, Ellie thought—what a spectacle you become, how often you and your children are the object of pity and disdain in public places.

There was a nice-sized crowd of yuppies and college students waiting to hear the words of wisdom of Sara M. Fuller when Ellie and the kids rolled quietly up to the back of the group. In front of her were several rows of folding chairs, all full, and in front of them was a table displaying a smaller version of the poster from the window and stacks of *After the Dance*, Sara's follow-up book to *The Family Dance*. Next to the table stood an empty podium with a mike on a small riser.

God, stick with me, could you? The mixture of pride and envy was making Ellie sick to her stomach. She took a deep breath. Let go, she thought as she released the air, and let God, she prayed as she breathed in again. She tried to imagine that she was breathing in God's unconditional love. She could feel it . . . a little.

"Waaahhh!" Angus had dropped his pacifier, *again*. Ellie had it back in his mouth in a second. She crouched next to him and gently rubbed his fuzzy little head.

"Ssshhh!" Ahnika put her finger to her mouth and chastised her brother.

"Test one, two, three. Test one, two, three." A gangly teenager was on the podium checking the sound system.

"Why does he keep dropping it?" Ahnika asked with all the attitude of a bored thirteen-year-old.

"I don't know, sweet pea. Maybe he's . . ." Ellie checked her watch, cupped her breasts, panic spread through her ". . . hungry."

"Welcome to all of you." A heavy-set woman in her sixties with lots of amber jewelry and thick-rimmed reading glasses had stepped up to the podium. Ellie was studying Angus. How long would he settle for the pacifier? she wondered. Maybe I should just feed him now and hopefully he'll be done before my mom is. Or maybe I can keep him happy with the pacifier and teething biscuits till I get out of here.

"It is with pride and great pleasure that I introduce tonight's speaker. It would not be an overstatement to say that Sara M. Fuller's first book, *The Family Dance*, changed the course of countless families in this country. I know it changed mine."

Ellie was unbuckling Angus from the stroller—she had opted for nursing and hoping—when she heard a voice in her ear.

"She definitely changed mine."

"Missy! You came!" she said, hugging her pal.

"Didn't I say I'd come?"

"You said 'maybe.'"

"I'm up front. I saved you a seat."

"I can't." she said, gesturing to the kids and the stroller.

"I thought that Peter . . ."

"Business meeting."

Missy gave her a knowing look.

"You *are* coming to the party, aren't you?"

"Not another party?" Ellie asked, in a panic.

"Camille's birthday party, it's this Saturday."

"Oh, yeah. Of course, we're coming." Where the fuck did I put that invitation, Ellie wondered? And what the heck do I get the little French girl who has everything?

"So, please help me welcome the delightful and insightful Sara M. Fuller." The crowd erupted into loud applause, Chubby stepped down, and Ellie's mother, dressed in a knee-length Burberry plaid skirt, nude hose, sensible pumps, and a button-down cotton shirt, with her reading glasses hanging from her neck, stepped up to the podium. Ellie found herself clapping like mad and fighting back tears.

"Thank you. Thank you all very much." The applause died down. "Thanks, Margery." Sara nodded to Chubby, who was beaming on the sidelines. "Margery Voxworthy, my agent and very good friend." She took a moment to look at the crowd. "Well, thank you all for coming out tonight and for buying my first book. I hope you like this new one."

"Mommy, when are we gonna see Grammy?" Ahnika asked in that piercing tone of a two-and-a-half-year-old. Half the heads in the crowd turned to see the source of the interruption.

"Is that my Ahnika?" the author said into the mike as she searched the sea of people for her granddaughter. Ellie lifted Ahnika above the crowd.

"Grammy!" The crowd laughed.

"Hi, Pumpkin. I'll see you in a little bit. When I'm done talking, okay?"

"Okay, Grammy. Bye-bye."

The crowd was loving it. Here was the family dynamics expert showing off some of her very own healthy and happy family dynamics, live and in person. Missy took Ahnika from Ellie and pulled a brand-new activity

100

book with a set of markers out of her purse. The two of them found a vacant corner on the floor and went to work. She is perfect, Ellie mused, watching her friend bond with her daughter.

Sara M. Fuller had the crowd in the palm of her hand as she fielded questions about the family roles she'd defined in her first book and tossed in helpful tidbits from book number two to hopefully make some sales. It was clear that most of her fans viewed her almost as a guru. She spoke openly about her own life, which only further endeared her to them.

"When my ex-husband went to jail, my alcoholism went into overdrive."

Good, Mom, you've managed to reveal every fucking family secret we have in one sentence, Ellie thought as she stood nursing Angus. When she was a drunk it was really a walk in the park next to this. At least she had the brains to draw the curtains. It's this new reformed and reinvented version of my mother that just makes me want to get in a bell tower with an automatic rifle. If I know her, she'll figure out how to get my bulimia into the next sentence, then Missy will never speak to me again.

Ellie listened to her mother answering questions from the crowd and she found herself silently composing a few questions of her very own for the eminent Sara M. Fuller.

How do you reconcile your role as an expert on families with the reality that you were a horrible drunk when you were supposed to be raising your own daughter? Ellie was dying to get an answer to *that* question. And: *Have you done any research on the relationship between AA and neglect?* Ellie had spent the last twenty years witnessing what she called the hypocrisy of AA.

Once Sara had gotten sober and started talking in "AA-speak," as Ellie called it, she had proceeded to blame all of her bad behavior on the disease of alcoholism.

Perfect, Ellie had thought. Now she can say "Oh, I'm so sorry I've been such a bad mother, but you see it wasn't really *my* fault. It's this darned alcoholism." And now, here was her mother, on her little stand with her little mike, being applauded for that kind of logic. To all these people Sara Fuller looked like a walking confessional. As far as Ellie was concerned, her mother had never copped to anything.

Ellie wanted to run up to the podium, knock her aside, grab the mike, and tell everyone—through all her years of AA and self-discovery, the words "I'm sorry" have never crossed this woman's lips.

Right after Sara Fuller had gotten sober, Ellie's bulimia had kicked into overdrive. Sara's connection to AA could've—should've—helped Ellie get abstinent. But Sara's connection to AA had had just the opposite effect. Ellie was damned if she was going to go to one of those fucking Twelve Step programs filled with a bunch of hypocrites like her mother.

"Mommy, I have to go poo-poo and pee-pee." Ahnika's voice filled the room, pulling Ellie away from the bitterness of her childhood and back to the reality of motherhood. Ahnika had abandoned her art project and was dancing around holding her crotch.

"Honey, I can take you," Missy whispered, getting up and trying to take Ahnika's hand.

She pulled away. "No, I want Mommy!!"

A pretty woman with a Louise Brooks haircut in a trendy suit had stopped in the middle of her question about how to change the dynamics between adult siblings and was now glaring at Ellie and *her* family dynamics.

"Okay, okay, Ahnika. Mommy'll take you," Ellie said, crouching next to her scowling daughter while she continued to nurse Angus. Ahnika spotted the blissful Angus fastened to her mother's breast and gave him a nice, hard smack on the forehead.

"Waaahhh!"

You little fuck, Ellie thought. She felt a twitch in her arm and had to consciously stop herself from hitting Ahnika back, square in the face. She leaned into her.

"You must use your words, sweetie," she whispered. The entire crowd at Barnes & Noble watched and waited.

"Waaahhh!" Now they were both crying. Ellie snapped. She picked up Ahnika by the waist and tucked her under her arm.

Sara was trying to answer the unfinished question saying something about the impact of birth order and trying desperately, it seemed, to get the focus *off* her evil granddaughter and onto some *other* hateful siblings. Ellie carried her two crying children, one under each arm like footballs, through a corridor of judgmental eyes. If someone says "You've got your hands full," Ellie thought, I'm gonna belt 'em.

Mommy, look. My poop looks like a sheep!" Ahnika was perched on the toilet, legs dangling, looking between her legs and studying what she saw.

"That's great, sweet pea, it *does* look like a sheep." This fascination she has with her poop has got to be on the show, Ellie thought, as she sat on the floor of the tiny bathroom stall with Angus back on her breast. We'll call the segment, "Fun with feces."

The door to the bathroom creaked and Ellie saw a pair of suede loafers enter the bathroom. She felt like an inflatable toy with a slow leak. All the air was seeping out of her. I don't wanna go back out there, she thought. I don't want to have to face that crowd and my mother and Missy—motherhood sucks!

"Ellie? Is that you?" Missy was attached to those tasteful loafers, of course.

"Yep. I'm just in here playing 'name that animal.'" She knows my mom's a drunk and my dad's a jailbird and she's still talking to me, Ellie mused. That's a shocker. "You go back. I'm fine."

"Well, I was feeling a little hungry and I thought Ahnika might want to keep me company at the café."

"I wanna stay with Mommy," Ahnika sulked.

"Okay. I was just going to get this yummy treat they have that's a cookie shaped like a spoon and dipped in chocolate. But I suppose you don't like chocolate, do you?" Missy asked.

"I love chocolate. Mommy, can I go with Missy and get a chocolate spoon? Please?"

"Yes, you can go." Ahnika tried to jump off the toilet.

"Wait a minute, Miss Cutie Cakes." Ellie caught her midair with her free hand and plopped her back on the toilet, wiped her, then pulled up her undies and the precious tights and scrambled out of the stall all while her son continued to drink his supper from her breast.

"You are amazing," Missy said, as she lifted Ahnika up so she could reach the sink.

"You think?"

"I do."

The show was over and the fans were lined up, waiting for a signed copy of *After the Dance*, by the time Ellie returned. She sat on the floor next to the stroller and watched Angus suckling, willing him to sleep. She felt sad and defeated, totally stymied by this whole mother/daughter thing.

She was doubting every parenting choice she had ever made. I had Angus too early, she thought, I've totally fucked up Ahnika. She hates him, and that's totally fucking up Angus. He's getting hit out of the blue by his sister who he adores. What the fuck is that going to do to him? He's going to grow up and fall for angry, unpredictable women who treat him like shit.

Ellie watched her mother greet her fans. She was gracious and animated with each one. She has definitely survived her life, Ellie thought. Yep, Ellie concluded, I have to give her credit. A Gen-Xer with stringy hair, a pierced eyebrow, and baggy cargo pants was now at the front of the line and had made her mother laugh out loud. Ellie smiled. At sixty-six, Sara Fuller still had glimmers of the shining Smith girl that she was.

Ellie was suddenly transported back to a summer morning in the early sixties. She was sitting courtside in the dappled shade of a eucalyptus tree. The cool of the morning had not yet given way to the desert heat of the Southern California summer. Ellie, wearing red and white seersucker shorts and a puff-sleeved white T-shirt, was sitting cross-legged on a strip of lawn. She was coloring in her Barbie coloring book while Sara and Paul played their weekly game of mixed doubles. The fast-paced action of the game kept pulling her away from Barbie and her evening dress. She watched her parents in awe.

Their tennis whites matched their sparkling smiles as their athletic bodies darted effortlessly around the court. They played tennis together the way Fred and Ginger danced: easy, fluid, and fun. Paul's sandy blond hair seemed to glow in the early sun as he returned the ball at the net. Sara's auburn hair shined and bounced like a Breck ad as she ran for the ball and smashed an overhead shot to win the game. She thrust her racket into the air, Paul ran to her and lifted her up onto his shoulder, then he marched around the court, shouting, "That's my girl! That's my Smith girl!" Sara smiled down at him, loving the way he loved her. There was something magical about the two of them on that court. Before the indictment and the divorce. Before her father had been carted off to jail and her mother had descended into a bottomless martini glass. Back then Ellie was still a little girl and Sara and Paul were still her magical parents.

Ellie's tears spilled onto Angus's sleeping face. He didn't flinch. She gently wiped them with the sleeve of her shirt. The moments of perfection from Ellie's childhood always made what came afterwards seem more tragic. She looked up to see Sara giving the Gen-Xer a heartfelt hug. She seems to have moved on from all that, Ellie marveled. Why can't I?

"*Grammy!*" Ahnika was bouncing across the floor on a sugar high, with Missy in hot pursuit. She ran straight for her grandma, dethroning the Gen-Xer.

"I had a chocolate spoon, Grammy!"

Sara caught Ahnika under the arms, swung her around, and then sat her down on the edge of the now almost-empty table. Ahnika began to dance around the table as she told Grammy about her adventure with Missy. The Gen-Xer smiled in spite of herself. Ellie took her well-worn pad out of her purse, flipped past pages of Ahnika's drawings and "to do" lists and wrote:

Segment/bit on sugar bribes on the show? They work and are a godsend in certain situation (when you're being publicly humiliated by your child's behavior). However, there is a price to pay: a toddler who boings around the room with the energy of a new super ball, and/or a child who later crashes and burns in a puddle of tears. Fuck!

Missy pulled out the activity book again and lured Ahnika away from Sara. Ahnika took the book happily, crawled under the table, and settled in.

Ellie watched as Sara gave the Louise Brooks clone's book a quick signing and thanked her for coming. Then Missy stepped in and introduced herself, and the two Smith girls were off, chatting like the old club members that they were.

Ellie moved Angus, now fast asleep, to his spot in the stroller and tucked the blanket around him. I suppose I have to go over there and congratulate her, she realized. God, are you with me?

"Mom, you were great! I'm so proud of you." She gave her mother a big hug and a kiss on the cheek. "I'm sorry about the melee."

"Well, Missy and I were just talking about how you have *got* to give up this crazy idea that you can do it all and get yourself some help."

"Mom, you know I was in therapy for years."

"She always makes a joke," Sara said to Missy. "I'm serious. You look exhausted."

"Thanks, Mom. You look great, too." Uh-oh, less than a minute into the visit and sarcasm is springing from my lips.

"Sweetie—" Sara took Ellie gently by the arms "—that's not what I meant. It's just I worry about you.

"I know a great gal. Filipino." Missy was joining the campaign. "They have a wonderful work ethic."

"But do they have rhythm?" Ellie asked, feeling trapped and betrayed.

"I always had help when you were growing up and there was just one of you."

"Mom, don't remind me. I spent about a year in therapy on those two." She turned to Missy and went into her stand-up persona. "Mrs. Paxton had this too-tight nurse's uniform and teased up bright red hair. She made Joan Crawford look warm and fuzzy. And Mrs. Milton was as big as a house and spent all her time eating, napping, or yelling at me. Welcome to my childhood."

Ellie smiled meanly. The conversation felt to her like a huge boulder heading downhill, picking up momentum and heading for a village of innocent women and children. God, stop me, she prayed. Send a hurricane, some locusts, anything—just don't let me get in any deeper.

"I made some bad choices then. My judgment was impaired. I was an active alcoholic at the time."

I hate that term, Ellie thought. What a bunch of crap. *Active alcoholic?* Sounds like she was at some fucking camp for drinkers—canoeing, making baskets and playing badminton in between perfecting her martini recipe.

"Well, you can find someone that you can trust. Someone good that the kids will enjoy." Sara was still trying. But Ellie was locked in the struggle and she couldn't get out.

"Well, I have this crazy idea—I want to raise my own children. I know it's nutty but that's what I want." Had she just alienated Missy, who had a live-in staff, with that last one? She didn't care.

"I'm not suggesting that you don't raise your own children. All I'm saying is get yourself a sitter now and then so you can go somewhere or do something and just relax."

"Look, I know bringing them wasn't ideal, but . . ." She wasn't about to admit that she had planned to come without them. She thought it would make Peter look bad. "Would you rather I hadn't come at all, that I'd just missed the whole thing?"

"You did miss the whole thing." Sara was right on that one, but it just made Ellie go for the jugular.

"Well I guess I was mistaken. I thought you might want to see your grandchildren." A look of horror crossed Sara's face. Ellie didn't flinch. "Silly me."

Missy had disappeared. Ahnika was gone, Angus too. The table, the walls, the books, everything had vanished. All that remained was Ellie and Sara in their endless battle.

"Of course I want to see them. That's a horrible thing to say."

"Then why are you staying at the Carlyle? Why do you *always* stay at a hotel? You never stay with us." God? Hello, God. I'm waiting. Send in the locusts. Now's your moment.

"You have never invited me to stay with you, Ellie," Sara said slowly and evenly.

Ellie's heart had stopped beating, or so it felt, and her lungs seemed to have collapsed. She had no sarcastic comeback for that one. It had never occurred to her to ask her mother to stay with them. Her mother *always* stayed in a hotel and Ellie assumed that's how she liked it.

"Mom, I never even thought . . ." was all she could muster. Her mother's gaze had not faltered. She suddenly looked tiny and old to Ellie. "Mom, I'm so . . ."

"Daddy!" Ahnika screamed from beneath the table.

Ellie looked to see Peter floating up, up, up, like a miracle. Thank you, God, she thought. Her bodily functions started working again and every muscle in her body relaxed as she saw her handsome, business-suited husband hop off the escalator and stride toward her. Ahnika scrambled out from under the table and sprinted to him.

"Hello, daughter!" he said, effortlessly picking her up and slinging her over his shoulder like a conquering Hun. She giggled and kicked her feet in mock protest. "Is it over? Did I miss it? I drove like a madman." Ever the diplomat, he went right for his mother-in-law and gave her a big kiss. "You look wonderful. How'd it go?"

"She was great!" Ellie said as she put a protective arm around her mother's shoulders. "There was a bit of a scene caused by some poor misguided woman who actually brought her children."

Sara looked at Ellie defensively. Ellie smiled at her and gave her a wink.

"That's unconscionable," Peter said, feigning disgust.

"Can you believe it? It seems her workaholic husband's business meeting went late so he couldn't watch the children. Surprise, surprise."

"What a cad!" Peter said.

"Without a doubt," Ellie said, punching his arm. "But Mom handled it like a pro. She even got a few laughs. You see, it turned out that this poor harried woman was determined *not* to miss Sara M. Fuller's first-ever book signing in New York City. And, even though she missed most of it, she's really glad she got to see her mother in action." Ellie was now facing her mom. "And, as she was watching Sara M. Fuller, author, mother, lecturer, many thoughts raced through her brain. But most of all, I thought of what a miracle you are." She hugged her mother and whispered, "You really did something, Mom. You really did." Sara hugged her back. And the endless battle had ended. For now.

Chapter Twelve

Ellie wandered the aisles of West Side Kids scrutinizing all the toys. Barbie, Batman, Hot Wheels, toy cash registers, plastic fruit, army men, bath toys, Candyland, Clue, Sorry. Each new section seemed to hold promise, then was almost immediately rejected by Ellie as too something: too babyish, too old, too stupid, or too obvious. She looked at her watch. I'm fucked, she thought. Totally fucked.

"Ellie, is that you?"

She turned to see Arlene standing behind her.

"I didn't recognize you without your kids." Arlene pretended to search for Ahnika and Angus behind a stack of Lego kits.

"Very funny."

"You didn't do something wacky like—get a sitter, did you?"

"No. I did something insane, I left them with my mother."

"I'm calling Child Welfare Services right now. Is this a first?"

"Yes. I'm trying to strengthen our relationship and deepen my trust in her, or some such bullshit. She took them to the Museum of Natural History."

"Are you panicking?"

"Yes, but not because I'm worried about my children's welfare in the hands of a woman who was working on a crossword puzzle when God handed out the maternal instincts. No. I'm freaking out because Ahnika's classmate's birthday party is in less than an hour and I don't have a clue what to buy this perfect little East Side French girl who I'm sure already has everything. Look at these toys," Ellie said, gesturing wildly. "They all look really cheap or they're politically incorrect."

"Politically incorrect?"

"Oh, I don't know. This one is too gender specific," she said, pointing to a cute miniature porcelain tea set. "This one's too violent," she said, picking up a water pistol. "Do they look really cheap, or is it me? I almost bought her this way overpriced Madeline doll that I saw on the East Side, with about eighty matching outfits, but I thought, she probably already has it. I mean, she *is* Madeline, for God's sake!"

"Okay, okay. Calm down." Arlene was massaging Ellie's shoulders like a boxing coach between rounds. "Your first East Side birthday party. I've been there, it's a toughie, but I know you can do it." Ellie took a deep breath and relaxed a bit. "How much time do we have?" Arlene asked.

"Thirteen minutes."

Arlene took Ellie by the hand and pulled her out the door.

"Where are we going?"

"Books. You get 'em books. It's always a safe bet," Arlene told her, dragging her west on Eighty-second Street. "Makes you look like an intellectual and like you're concerned for their child's brain development and all that crap."

"But I was already in Barnes & Noble today. I spent over an hour reading and rejecting *every* Caldecott winner since 1943."

"Trust me," Arlene said, as they pushed through the revolving doors. "I was in here this morning and read this very book to the girls. They had four copies."

They headed up the long escalator, taking two steps at a time. "Excuse us. Sorry. Excuse us." Arlene was the running back to Ellie's linebacker, or whatever it is. Shoppers scattered as they passed.

They were now facing a wall of books. Arlene scanned the shelves, then handed Ellie a small midnight blue box with three tiny hardbound books inside. "Here's your answer."

Ellie took the shiny indigo box and studied it. On the front was a picture of a smiling bunny wearing a gold crown and a lavender gown. She held a sleeping baby bunny in her arms. They were both floating in space.

"*Voyage to the Bunny Planet,*" Ellie read aloud. "Well, I like the title," she said as she slid the three little books out of their home. *First Tomato, Moss Pillows,* and *Island Light* were their titles. The inside panels had brief summaries of each story, just like adult hard covers, only they rhymed. Ellie read to herself,

> *Felix thinks that no one cares.*
> *He hears no footsteps climb the stairs.*

"Done," Ellie said, closing the book and heading back downstairs to the cashier.

Out on the sidewalk Ellie looked at her minute gift, then back at Barnes & Noble.

"What? You don't like it." Arlene sounded hurt.

"No, no, I love it. I want a set for *my* kids. It's just that . . . I know this sounds really stupid, but it's such a—*little* gift."

"Brother." Arlene rolled her eyes. "You wanna go back to the East Side and drop a bundle on Madeline? Go ahead. But, I'm telling you—" Arlene pointed her finger at Ellie's nose "—little Miss Frenchy probably *does* have that stupid doll. And I can guarantee you she does *not* have *Voyage to the Bunny Planet.*"

Ellie was trying to trust Arlene but she couldn't get this picture out of her head: She's arriving at Camille's birthday party dressed in her usual T-shirt, jeans, and boots, carrying her humble yet thoughtful present. She's pushing her kids, who look like something out of *Oliver Twist,* in the double stroller. All of Ahnika's classmates are arriving, looking like they just stepped out of a Sears catalog from the 1950s. All the mothers are wearing crisp, coordinated party-going outfits and are carrying huge, elaborately wrapped gifts.

"I'm not going." She started to bolt.

"You're going." Arlene grabbed Ellie by the arm and turned her to face her. "Listen to me. They are all just as insecure and fucked up as everybody else. They just have bigger apartments and more expensive clothes. Not even clothes that we would want. Right?"

"Right!"

"You'll be fine."

"I will?"

"You will. *Taxi!*" Arlene had spotted an empty cab. It jumped two lanes of traffic in a nanosecond and screeched to a stop in front of the two women.

"Go, go." Arlene opened the cab door for her friend. Ellie hopped in the cab, clutching her tiny present. "And have some fun." Ellie nodded without an ounce of conviction. Arlene slammed the door. Ellie waved good-bye as the cab sped away from the curb.

"Lady, where're we headed?" the cabdriver asked.

"Oh, sorry. East Side, Eighty-second and York." She looked once again at her miniscule present, closed her eyes, and took a deep breath. Okay, God, I'm headed east again and, as usual, I need your help. I'm measuring my worth by the size of this stupid present. Help! And these women . . . these East Side women that I've bunched together in a huge group, like some multi-headed, well-accessorized spider. These women who have really been perfectly nice to me, God, could you help me to not dislike them *just because* they have huge diamonds and apartments and country homes and live-in help. But, God, am I allowed to dislike them because they're Republicans? She ran her hand across the surface of the gift; it felt smooth and solid in her hands. Maybe little Camille will really *like* her present, Ellie hoped.

The cab was now crawling north on York. Road construction had created a seemingly endless traffic jam. It had been almost three hours since she'd sent her babies off in the charge of her mother (who hadn't done any mothering *ever* as far as Ellie could remember) and she was starting to feel a little anxious. She scanned the traffic ahead to see if there was any movement. Nothing. Just lots of horn honking. She was missing her babies, needing them. It was a physical need, like a junkie. As much as she *did* need a break from mothering, after being apart from them for more than an hour or two Ellie began to feel a pull in her chest, like an invisible tether that had come to the end of its elasticity and was slowly snapping back to its normal length. She searched for a street sign. They were half a block from Eighty-first Street.

Shit! I forgot to show Mom how to fold the double stroller. Oh, God, it's impossible to figure out without help. She's probably pushing the damn thing through the park, giving herself a stroke.

Ellie opened the door in the middle of traffic. "This is fine," she told the driver, tossing a five and a single over the seat.

"Hey!" he started to protest.

"Sorry." She slammed the door and was running up York in search of her children. Visions of accidents and hospital emergency rooms sprang into her brain out of nowhere. The foot traffic on York dodged her; she dodged them. I don't see them; she was starting to panic. I don't see them! What could I have been thinking leaving them? What am I, an idiot? If something's happened to them I'll have to kill myself. I won't be able to live. She was Carl Lewis whizzing past people, dogs, buildings, trash cans.

And there they were.

"You made it!" Ellie fell onto her babies, snuggled under their blanket in the double stroller against the chilly November day. "Hi, cuties! I missed you." She covered them with kisses. "Did you guys have fun?"

"Mommy! I hate kisses!" Ahnika squirmed in her seat. Angus, holding a mangled soft pretzel with bits of gooey dough dotting his cheeks, just giggled. Ellie sat back and took them both in. She looked up to see her mother, looking a bit frazzled, but gazing at her grandchildren with the same wonder.

"We went to the museum and saw the movie with the dancers," Ahnika began.

"Didja? That's great." Ellie resisted the urge to kiss her a million times.

"And the whale and the penguins and—and—and . . ." She was so excited she couldn't finish her sentence.

"Go ahead, sweetie, I'm listening," Ellie told her as she pushed the stroller toward the entrance of a luxury building.

"You looking for the birthday party?" the doorman asked. Ellie nodded. "Around the corner on your right."

"Thanks." Ellie, Sara, and the kids found the entrance to Yorktown Gym. The door was flanked with helium balloons.

"I saw everything, Mommy! But Angus fell asleep."

"He did?"

"Yeah. He's still too little, Mom."

"You think?"

They entered a large gymnasium complete with gymnastics equipment, big tunnels for crawling through, and a trampoline. The place was decorated to the hilt with crepe paper, balloons, and oversized vases of sunflowers in each corner. How the heck did they find sunflowers in November? Ellie wondered. And what did it cost 'em? All of Ahnika's stocking-footed classmates were playing, jumping, and bouncing on the equipment. They were all flanked by mommies or nannies. Marie Claire, in a smart black pants suit and the ever-present Hermès scarf was chatting with Libby, who was dressed head to toe in emerald green. They were watching Devin and Camille, in leggings and a T-shirt (if you can believe that) roll down a large royal blue wedge.

"Hi there, cutie." A smiling woman in her early twenties, wearing gym clothes with a whistle around her neck, was greeting Ahnika. She sat at one of two folding tables near the entrance. A pile of nametags sat on the table in front of her. The other table was piled high with—you guessed it—large and elaborately wrapped gifts. Ellie surreptitiously put her puny gift on the table, silently cursing Arlene.

"My name's Christa. What's yours?" the woman asked Ahnika.

"Mm," was all she could muster.

"I guess she's feeling a little shy today," Ellie told Christa as she began to search through the nametags.

"Don't be ridiculous. She's not shy," Sara interjected, sounding embarrassed. "Her name's Ahnika," she told Christa, taking over for Ellie.

So we're going to have a scene here as well, Ellie thought. I was *really* hoping we'd avoid that. Ellie had found Ahnika's nametag and was sticking it to her turtleneck as Ahnika shrugged off her jacket.

"Don't label her that way, Ellie. You should know better than that," Sara whispered a reprimand to her daughter.

Okay, come in, God. This is Ellie sending up a flare. Why is she trying to humiliate me at Camille's birthday party?

"Mason! Mommy, Mommy, Mason's here!" Ahnika had spotted her pal crawling through a huge red foam doughnut across the gym.

"Go, baby, go," Ellie said, and Ahnika was off.

Ellie turned to her mother and spoke slowly and clearly. "First of all, Mother, I *didn't* label her. I've read all the fucking books. Even yours. I said she was '*feeling* a little shy today.' And second of all, whether I did or did not label her, it's really none of your fucking business, is it? And thirdly, thanks in large fucking part to your mothering skills—or lack thereof—I was a fucking bulimic for more than a decade and have been in therapy most of my adult life. So pretty much *any* parenting suggestion you make I'm going to do the opposite." Ellie unstrapped Angus, who had begun to fuss, and picked him up. The stroller toppled over backward, making a loud thud. Ellie bounced the fussy Angus on her hip, picked the stroller up, and put the diaper bag on his seat. Then, like a factory worker mindlessly performing an elaborate task, she lifted her blouse, unsnapped her nursing bra, and out popped her swollen breast.

"Oh, Ellie, no!"

"Oh, Mother, please!" she said as she put Angus on to suck. "You talk about the importance of breast-feeding in your book, for God's sake!" Ellie hated her mother more than ever at this moment.

"Of course, but . . ."

"But don't do it when I'm around in front of all these nice people from nice families. Is that it, Mother?"

"Well, no. It's just—in my generation nobody breast-fed. I'm just not used to it. I guess I'm just uptight, as you would say."

"It's not just your generation, Mom, believe me." Ellie had softened. Sara had admitted that Ellie was right, in her way. Something that Ellie couldn't ever remember her mother doing before.

"You made it." Missy was suddenly, magically, at her side. She had arrived, once again, like the cavalry, but a little late, this time.

"We did," Ellie said, with a big fat smile. The two women exchanged a real hug. Air-kissing had been abandoned since the "Maybe I'm Amazed" night. I've been shitty to my mother again, she wanted to whisper in her friend's ear.

"I'm glad you're here," is what came out instead.

"Sara, I didn't know you were coming. What a nice surprise." Missy air-kissed Ellie's mother.

Ellie watched her mother as she greeted Missy.

"Thank you dear," Sara said to Missy.

Look at her, Ellie marveled, watching the two Smithies chat. Mom must be reeling from all those "fucks" I just flung at her but, as usual, she's maintaining the proper decorum.

Tweet! Christa was now center stage, blowing her whistle.

"Okay, everybody, it's time for the obstacle course. Are you guys ready?"

All the children screamed "YEAH!" right on cue.

"Camille? Where's the birthday girl? Camille, where are you?" Christa put her hand to her forehead like an explorer and ceremoniously searched the room for the girl of the day. Camille ran to Christa and grabbed her by the hands.

"They do a wonderful job here. I had Harper's fourth birthday party here," Missy said.

"It's great," Ellie said. The three women stood on the sidelines and watched Christa and an assistant usher twelve little darlings through tunnels, over foam mountains, and across low balance beams.

"What are you planning for Ahnika's birthday?" Sara asked.

"I haven't given it a thought," Ellie admitted.

"Don't worry," Missy said, putting a confident arm around her. "I'm an old pro at this. We'll plan it together. When's her birthday?"

"June seventeenth."

Missy furrowed her brow. "Summer birthdays are tough. Come the end of school, everyone leaves for the summer."

"Right, right," Ellie said. But she thought—everyone except me and several million other plebes that don't have summer homes.

"But not to worry. We'll just do it few weeks early. We'll start planning next week." Ellie gave Missy a *you're kidding* look.

"Really. You have to start way in advance. Everybody gets booked. Marie-Claire started planning this in June." She gestured to the room and the group of blissful children. "I'm the one who told her about this space."

For Ahnika's first and second birthday parties, it had just been friends and family at the apartment with pizza and cake. Now what am I expected to do, Ellie wondered? She looked around the room and suddenly realized that she was going to be entertaining all these people before the school year was out. And it was going to cost a bundle.

"I know a great magician that did Harper's second birthday. Or there's a space on the West Side similar to this one with gym equipment and a staff. They do everything for you."

"Oh, that sounds like such fun!" Sara piped in.

She is so—so—perky and sweet around Missy, Ellie observed. I'd like to smack her. Magicians and gym equipment for three-year-olds? I had lemonade and Pin the Tail on the Donkey till I was seven and I was happy, Ellie thought. She silently cursed Peter for getting her into this competitive, warped, moneyed world.

"Sara, I thought you were leaving today. I didn't expect to see you here."

"I have to scoot soon, grab a cab back to the hotel, get my bags, and then head to Kennedy."

"I was a little worried about you, Mom. I forgot to tell you how to fold the double stroller and it takes diagrams and a degree in engineering if you've never done it before."

Sara gave her a *no kidding* look.

"What did you do? You didn't push it all the way here, did you?"

"No. Some nice mother at the museum saw me struggling with the damned thing and came to my rescue."

"They are the worst. I just thank God I never had to do use one. Mason and Harper are far enough apart."

"Sorry," Ellie said, putting her arm around her mom.

"No biggie, as you would say." Her mom eked out a smile. "We had a ball at the museum."

"I'm so glad. They didn't miss me?"

"Not a minute."

"See? They're fine without you. You *can* take some time away from them." Missy elbowed her friend. The conspiracy had been revived.

"Angus got a little fussy, so I just picked him up, put his head on my shoulder, and sang very quietly in his little ear."

"Really?" The image of her mother holding Angus and singing him to sleep gave Ellie an ache in her chest. Did *my mother* hold me and sing me to sleep? Ellie couldn't imagine such a thing. "What did you sing to him?"

"The same song I used to sing to you, silly. 'In My Room.' I *am* a mother you know."

"I don't think I know that one," Missy said.

Ellie sent up a quick prayer. God, please don't let her sing. Sara had lived her whole life under the delusion that she had a lovely singing voice. But it was too late. Sara Fuller sang:

> *"In my room there hangs a picture*
> *Jew-els can not buy from me."*

Sara's voice sounded fine, almost soothing in fact. Ellie didn't recognize the tune or the lyrics but somewhere in her body she knew the song. She was swallowed up by an overwhelming nostalgia, a longing for events long forgotten, as her eyes filled with tears.

> *"'Tis a picture of my Ellie*
> *She is the sweetest girl in the world."*

I'm *not* crying at Camille's birthday party, Ellie told herself. She clenched her jaw holding back the tears. Why does this happen to me every time I'm around this woman?

> *"And I love my little Ellie*
> *She is as sweet as sweet can be."*

"That is lovely. What's that from?" Missy asked.

"Ellie's dad made it up out of the blue. We were in the hospital, Ellie was only a few hours old, and he was holding her, studying her, she was so tiny and perfect. And it just came out of his mouth like he'd known it all his life." Sara looked at Ellie, her eyes sparkling with love for her daughter. Ellie wanted to hug her mother, to climb into her arms, to be carried away by her and sung to sleep. She didn't speak, she couldn't.

"Do you remember the song?" Missy asked Ellie.

"No, I—Well, yes, I think I . . ."

"Mommy, Mommy! Look, look at me." Ahnika was bouncing for all she was worth on the trampoline with all her classmates waiting and watching.

118

"I wish you could stay for the show," Missy said to Sara.

"There's a show? You mean there's more than this?" Sara asked.

"You're going to love it," Missy said to Ellie, who was in a daze.

"Sweetie—" Sara leaned into Ellie and gave her a peck on the cheek "—I've got to scoot. You can give me all the details later. If I don't leave in two minutes I'm going to miss my plane." She turned to Missy.

"Great to see you again, Missy. You keep an eye on my dolly, would you?" She gave Missy a hug.

"Why don't you take her shopping?" Sara stage-whispered in Missy's ear. "You have such style. Maybe it will rub off on her."

"She has *your* style, Mother." Ellie laughed, incredulous at her mother's nerve and lack of tact. "And I don't think it's going to rub off on me. Yours never did." She gave her mother a one-armed hug with Angus still nursing away. Sara gave his head a kiss and squeezed his chubby thigh.

"Bye, Mister Cutie, I love you," she whispered to the suckling boy. "I've got to say good-bye to my best granddaughter," Sara said, kicking off her pumps and heading toward the trampoline.

"I'm out of commission next week, you know," Missy said as they watched Ahnika jump off the edge of the trampoline and into her Grammy's arms.

"Why? What's happening?"

"I'm having surgery on my shoulder, an old riding injury."

"Wow, you never mentioned this to me. Is it serious?"

"Not really. I took a bad fall in a polo match in '91 and this shoulder has sort of bothered me ever since." She rubbed her right shoulder. "And I've just ignored it. But lately, carrying Mason—and he's so big—it's started to . . ."

"Would you *please* let him use the stroller?"

"No, I have been. I brought the stroller today. Anyway, I finally scheduled the surgery."

"Well, let me know how I can help. I can pick up Mason if you want or . . ."

"El, you have your hands full with Angus and Ahnika. I have Gloria and Candy who can help with that stuff. But I will be in this huge brace for six weeks—my shoulder has to be completely immobilized—so I'll probably need you for some things."

"*Bye, Grammy!*" Ahnika's piercing voice rang through the gym. She was back on the trampoline waving like mad as Sara walked backward across the gym blowing her kisses.

"She's a pistol, that girl of yours," Sara said as she wiggled back into her pumps.

"She is," Ellie and Missy said in unison. The three mothers laughed as they watched Ahnika give Mason a headlock of a hug.

"She's got more than her share of personality," Ellie said, watching the two buddies tumble over, giggling.

"Gee, I can't imagine where she got that," Sara said. Ellie gave her a look and shook her head. Then, Sara Fuller, esteemed author, grabbed her daughter and tickled her.

"Mother! Stop!" Ellie was laughing, trying to get away. I can't keep up with this woman, she thought. "I'm going to leave the kids with you more often. I like how it affects you."

"Promises, promises. Now I must run." She and Missy air-kissed. "Walk me out, El?"

"Sure. Keep an eye on Ahnika," she told Missy as she and her mother, with Angus going along for the ride, walked to the lobby. They stood just inside the front door.

"Listen. How was your meeting with HBO?"

"What?"

"I never heard about your meeting with Lisa Bienstock."

"It went pretty darn well, actually! Thanks to Peter I pitched an idea about parenting called *Pregnant on Purpose*. She *loved* the idea."

"It sounds great! Did you do that bit about labor before and after an epidural, the whole thing with the remote control and watching *Jeopardy*?"

"No, I'd totally forgotten about that bit." Ellie was reeling. Who *is* this woman, she wondered, studying her mother; she's remembering Lisa Bienstock's name and quoting old stand-up routines of mine. I never think she listens to a word I say.

"So, are they going to do the show?"

"I don't know yet. I have a February deadline. If she likes what I give her, then I think they give it to the L.A. people."

"Well, if they're smart, they'll see how funny and talented you are and snatch up this wonderful show of yours!"

"Mom, thanks." She thinks I'm funny and talented? That's news to me, Ellie thought.

They walked out of the building through the double glass doors and toward the street. A uniformed doorman stood under the awning.

"How do you know it's wonderful? You haven't heard a word of it." And I haven't really written a word of it, Ellie thought.

"Because *you're* wonderful—and funny and bright and strong." I can't believe this, Ellie thought, she sees me! She really sees me! She wanted to grab the doorman and say "Did you hear that? Did you? My mom sees me! She finally, actually . . ."

"You're *my* daughter, aren't you?"

Ellie collapsed on the sidewalk and buried her head in her hands, sobbing. Well, that's what she *felt* like doing. It's still about her, she thought, as she struggled to stay vertical. Even when she's talking about *my* show, it's *still* about her.

"Can I hail you a cab?" the doorman asked.

"Yes, thank you." He walked to the curb and effortlessly summoned a cab.

"Love you," Sara said, as she hugged her daughter, holding her hips back so as not to squish the now-sleeping Angus. "Sweetie, can't you—" she gestured to Ellie's exposed breast "—put that away?"

"You think I should? I was thinking of flashing the doorman."

"Ellie!"

"Just as a way of thanking him for getting the cab and all."

Sara shook her head and sighed.

"Okay," Ellie said as she gently pulled Angus off her breast, snapped up her nursing bra, and pulled down her turtleneck. "Happy?"

"Yes!" Sara said, scowling.

"Safe trip, Mom," Ellie said, as she held the door for her mother, resisting the urge to slam it on her size five and a half Ferragamo. Sara got into the cab, rolled down the window, and blew Ellie a kiss.

"And let Missy get you some help," she yelled as the cab pulled into traffic.

"Psychiatric help?"

"Very funny. Give Peter my love." And her mother's happy, hopeful face disappeared in the sea of East Side traffic.

Goddamn her, Ellie thought. The mood swings I go through when I'm around that woman. One minute she's the same old WASP witch that I know and love and then, just to get me off guard, she starts acting all sweet and thoughtful. I don't know who she is anymore. She shifted Angus onto her shoulder, marveling at his dark pink lips puckered in a perfect *O*.

"Will you stand on a curb and curse *me* one day?" she asked her sleeping boy. "I hope not."

God, why is it never easy with her, she asked silently, watching the foot traffic on York. A young Hispanic woman was rushing uptown with a toddler in tow. His little legs couldn't keep up so he stopped dead, whined something in Spanish, and reached up for his impatient mommy. She stopped and looked down at him, hands on her hips. But when she saw his face, she melted, picked him up, and put him on her shoulders. He giggled from his perch; she smiled and began cooing to him in Spanish as they continued their trek.

How many times has he gotten a ride thanks to those eyes of his? Ellie wondered. The woman saw Ellie watching her, spotted Angus, then shrugged her shoulders and smiled as if to say "What can you do?" Ellie smiled back at the twosome as they passed.

From the moment she became pregnant with Ahnika, Ellie had felt an immediate bond with mothers the world over, mothers throughout the ages even. She would smile like an idiot as she passed pregnant women or mothers carrying babies in Snugglis or pushing them in strollers. Usually they'd smile back, as if to say "Hey there, buddy. How's it going?" She and the young Hispanic woman had instantly understood each other, because they both had changed endless diapers, been thrown up on, and given in when they shouldn't have, just to hold onto a shred of sanity.

I love being a member of the Mommy Club, she thought. Maybe I could have something about that on the show.

As Ellie turned and headed back to the party, the picture of her mother's beaming face in the cab window popped into her head. But aren't *we* members of same club, too, she wondered? What d'ya think, God? Will she and I *ever* understand each other? Okay, maybe understanding *is* too much to ask for. How 'bout acceptance? Will she ever just *accept* me? Oh! I'm supposed to work on accepting *her?* Well, I don't know about that one.

Chapter Thirteen

They had llamas?" Peter asked Ellie as he opened up the sofa bed. "Llamas at a three-year-old's birthday party?"

"*A* llama, only one. But two goats, a lamb, a bunny, and a potbellied pig." She grabbed a chenille throw pillow and plopped down on the now-open sofa bed.

"Sounds like they brought in the entire children's zoo from Central Park."

"They did! Listen to this—Missy said that Marie-Claire's family is on the board there or something and has donated a shitload of money to the zoo. There's a big plaque somewhere with their name on it. So now, whenever they want to entertain little Camille, they just make a phone call and—*poof!*—an entire menagerie is delivered wherever they ask."

"You're kidding." Peter was looking a bit dazed.

"Well, I'm exaggerating a little. But I think they must have a lot of clout. I mean, you should've seen this. I come back into the party, after having yet another psyche-shattering conversation with my mother and . . ."

"I thought your mother left." Peter had settled into the easy chair.

"She did, thank God. I was sending her off to the airport. Anyway, I come back in and they've laid down a big sheet of AstroTurf in the gym and lined up all the children along one side. Like magic, circus music starts playing and this llama enters through a side door followed by two goats and a lamb and this little round pig trotting in last. The kids went nuts."

"Jesus Christ. This is unbelievable." He grabbed a throw pillow from the floor and hugged it to his chest.

"It is. As I was watching the llama take a shit right in front of me, I was calculating what it must've cost them. Between renting the space and the staff, the animals, about a hundred sunflowers, not to mention the party favor bags, it was probably over—"

"Party favor bags?"

"Basically it's how you get the kids to leave the party."

"What do you mean?"

"They were out of control. Arlene always says 'Giving sugar to a three-year-old is like pouring kerosene on a raging fire.' And she's right. They'd had cake *and* piñata candy *and* . . ."

"There was a piñata?"

"I'm telling you! I've never . . . By the end half of them are having meltdowns because it's naptime. They're all trying to climb on the gymnastics equipment, which has supposedly been put away. At one point, as Mason and Ahnika headed back to the trampoline, screaming at the top of their lungs, Missy and I just looked at each other and shrugged our shoulders. Then Marie-Claire claps her hands and says 'Whoever has their shoes on and is in their stroller gets a party favor.' So, all the kids, like little angels, scramble to get ready so they can collect their booty."

"So you're telling me that the parents who are throwing this elaborate party also have to shell out money for a gift for every kid there?"

"Uh-huh. When I was little, it was maybe Silly Putty and some Good & Plenty. Something like that. But not on the East Side in Manhattan."

"What was it? Season tickets to the Knicks?"

"How did you guess? The boys got season tickets and the girls got a week at Canyon Ranch."

"Really, tell me. I'm on the edge of my seat."

"Me, too," she said, jumping off the sofa bed and sprinting into the foyer. "After Marie-Claire gave Ahnika hers she wouldn't let me even look at it." Ellie grabbed a miniature straw tote off the handle of the double stroller, ran back into the living room, and jumped on the sofa bed. "How cute is this?" she asked holding up the bag. "All the girls got these and the boys got miniature vintage Lassie lunch boxes."

"Anything in it?"

"Let's see," she said, slowly unsnapping the tote and peering in, half expecting to see a Tiffany box. She pulled out a small gift, wrapped in a hankie and tied with pink grosgrain ribbon. "Oh, my God. Look at this!" She tossed the gift to Peter as if it were a bomb about to go off. "It's so perfect I can't stand it." She was up, pacing.

"It has AHNIKA embroidered on it," Peter said, examining the gift.

"You're kidding." She stopped, snatched the gift from him, gave it a once-over, and threw it on the sofa bed. "Forget it. I give up. I can't compete with this," she said gesturing to the box.

"What are we planning for Ahnika's party?"

"I don't know. I don't know!" She was yelling at him. "But suddenly I feel like I have to get David Copperfield on the phone and find out if he does parties for three-year-olds."

"Honey, you're shouting."

"Sorry," she whispered as she sat on the arm of his chair. "And then I wonder where to have it? If we have it here, surely we need to get the place painted and get some window treatments up. This whole Park Avenue Playgroup thing is warping my mind. I mean phrases like 'window treatments' are popping out of my mouth."

"No, no, no. We can't . . ."

"I know. You're right," Ellie said, cutting him off. She shook her head and took a deep breath. "I mean, these women are nuts. I don't mind being a mother. In fact I love it. But I think there's something a little nutty and obsessive about spending months planning your three-year-old's birthday party. Look at this!" She picked the gift up and studied it. "Do you know the man hours involved in wrapping twelve perfect little packages like this? Of course, Marie-Claire has a live-in nanny *and* a personal assistant, so it's a piece of cake for her."

"Do you want those things?" the ever-calm Peter asked. "Because we can afford those things, y'know."

"No, no. I have other things to do. I have a TV show to write, for instance." She headed for her desk and turned on her computer.

"What are you doing?"

"Well, I've got that February deadline and at this point I haven't written a word. I'm spending all my free time worrying about a birthday party that's months away." She booted up her computer. Peter retrieved the maligned gift from the rumpled sheets and began untying the bow.

"Aren't you even curious about what this is?"

"No. I'm frightened by it, to tell you the truth."

"Voyage to the Bunny Planet."

"What!" Ellie whipped around in her office chair to face Peter. He was holding a shiny, deep blue box just like the one Ellie had purchased at Barnes & Noble earlier in the day.

"Oh, no, no! It can't be. I don't believe it." Ellie was at Peter's side, staring in horror at Ahnika's party favor. "I'm so humiliated. This is my worst nightmare come true."

"What?" Peter stood up and shook the box at her. "Ellie, would you please tell me what the fuck is such a big deal about this stupid thing."

She took the box from him. "This stupid thing, this sweet, elaborately-wrapped party favor gift is the exact same thing that *I* gave to Camille for her *birthday* present!"

"You're kidding." He seemed to be suppressing a smile.

"I'm not." She shook her head and looked at her smirking husband, then started to chuckle. "Talk about your faux pas."

"Well, looks like you and Frenchy have the same tastes, right?" He tackled her and the two of them landed on the sofa bed laughing.

"How did I get such a fabulous husband?" she asked, kissing him. "You don't think I'm a loser, do you?"

"I think you are the sexiest mom on the planet." He kissed her and wrapped his legs around her.

"So, we agree that if we have a party in the city—and I mean *if*—it should be simple. We can just have it here. Something appropriate for a three-year-old, like cake, presents, Pin the Tail on the Donkey? Don't you think?"

126

"No, we can't have it here. First of all, we don't have enough room. Second of all, the kids will trash the new rug."

"So what are you saying? We rent out the Felt Forum and see if Barney's available?"

"What's What's-Her-Name doing for What's-His-Name's party?"

"Honey, you have to be a little more specific than that."

"You know who I mean, Missy. What's she planning for Mason Jar?"

"I really don't know what she's planning but you can be sure it won't include Pin the Tail on the Donkey. She knows all the ins and outs 'cause she's already been through it with Harper, Mason's big sister. You know Missy, she's ready to take me under her wing and plan Ahnika's whole party *for* me."

"Good. You two plan it together. I'm glad she can show you the ropes."

"Peter, you're kidding, right? You don't want to try and do some expensive and extravagant party, do you?"

"Well, why not?" he said, sitting up. "I'm not going to let these East Side lawyers and investment bankers make me look bad."

"What are you talking about?"

"I'm talking about the fact that *I* make as much money as these East Side fucks and we can throw just as fancy a party as they can."

"I've got it!" she said, trying to sound playful. "We'll lie. Since Ahnika's birthday is in June, we'll just say that we're going to celebrate it in Spain, at our summer home like always."

"You think this is a joke?" He stopped and turned to her. "This isn't a joke. It's a competitive world out there, and I'm going to make sure that our kids can win in every situation."

"Do you think this overblown and expensive birthday party that I just went to is going to make little Camille more competitive?"

"I don't really care about little Camille."

"Peter!"

"Look, that sounded wrong. All I'm saying is, let Frenchy and her bow-tied husband worry about Camille. My job is to worry about *my* kids. And I'm not going to throw some loser party for my daughter and let everybody think that we're a bunch of loser bohemians."

Ellie stopped breathing; the room around her faded to nothing but a blur. That's what he really thinks of me, she thought, horrified. He thinks

I'm this loser bohemian that he rescued from my pathetic little showbiz career and I'd be nothing without him. Slowly and carefully, she got up off the sofa bed and headed out of the living room.

"Where are you going?"

"Your loser bohemian wife is going to bed."

"No, Ellie, honey, you misunderstood me." She kept walking. "Wait! We have to figure out this party thing."

"Peter! Ahnika's birthday is *six months away*! We planned our *wedding* in seven weeks. What is the matter with you?" She stood in the doorway shaking.

"Now there's something wrong with me that I want my daughter to have a nice birthday?"

"No, you want to use her birthday to show all these shallow East Side assholes that you are just as shallow as *they* are."

"Is that what you think of Missy, your new buddy, that she's shallow?"

"No, Peter—God, you're missing the point. Forget it." She turned to go.

"*I'm* missing the point? You are so busy rebelling against what your mother wants you to do that you don't have any idea what *you* want to do. You don't want Ahnika to have a nice, fancy party because it would make your mother happy. And you couldn't stand that, could you?"

"Peter, I—"

"No. Don't answer, El. Just think about it. For once, don't give me an answer. For once, could you just think about it?"

Ellie's selfrighteousness and conviction drained out her in an instant. How many of her actions through the years had just been reactions to what her mother had wanted her to do? Wait a minute, she thought, I dealt with that in therapy about a million times. I'm pretty sure I stopped doing that awhile ago. I mean, I married Peter, didn't I? And he was her dream man for me. A nice WASP guy with an M.B.A. from Wharton. No, she decided, this is *not* about that.

"Maybe you're right," she said, hating him. "Maybe this is all some big rebellion against my mother. I'll have to think about that. In the meantime, why don't you call up my mother and Missy, and the three of you can plan whatever you want for Ahnika's party. Maybe a dinner dance on the *QE2*. Or perhaps Cirque du Soleil is available that week. I'm going to bed."

"El, don't . . ." he tried to respond. She slammed the hallway door behind her.

Ellie's mind raced with the clever and sarcastic things she could say to Peter as she tried in vain the sleep. All the while, she hoped he would come into the bedroom and apologize for his lapse of sanity. *He'll stroke my hair,* she fantasized, *and suggest that we withdraw Ahnika from the playgroup. Then, we'll move upstate to escape the empty materialism of the city. We'll live in a commune where the children can run naked on the ramshackle farm and play with handmade toys. Okay, maybe a commune is a bit much. I know I'd be miserable living out of the city where I couldn't get good Indian food or a decent bagel.* She waited.

The door didn't move. *Surely he would come in and they would make up. Is he sleeping? How can he sleep when we're fighting?* They had never gone to bed mad at each other. She thought she heard footsteps in the hall. *No. He's probably out there snoring up a storm, that bastard!* She closed her eyes and started to recite the twelve steps of Overeaters Anonymous in her head, her version of counting sheep.

We admitted we were powerless over food—that our lives had become unmanageable. No door. *Came to believe that a Power greater than ourselves could restore us to sanity.* Yep, I'm sure he's asleep. Damn him. *Made a decision to turn our will and our lives over to the care of God as we understood God.* Still no door. *Made a searching and fearless moral inventory of ourselves.*

"Fuck this!" she said, throwing off the covers. She climbed over Angus and Ahnika, tucked them in, then stomped into the living room.

"I hate that playgroup," she announced as she turned on the lights.

"What?" He rolled over and squinted up at her.

"I hate that fucking playgroup. I wish we'd never heard of the stupid place."

"Why? I thought—"

"If it weren't for *them* we'd be having sex right now instead of sleeping in separate rooms."

"Honey, I hate fighting with you, too." He reached up for her.

"And how can your sleep when we're fighting?" She climbed into his arms. "You're coldhearted."

He kissed her sleepily, reached between her legs, and gave her pubic hair a sweet stroke.

"Mmm," escaped her lips without warning. *Damn him,* she thought.

"I'm dying for some of this," he said, cupping her crotch with his hand. Her hips reached for him without her approval. He kissed her again, squeezing her tight. His pectoral muscles, hard and round, pressed against her. She was torn between wanting him and wanting to rehash their conversation. Surely he couldn't have been serious, she told herself. She bit his chest and held him close.

"Oh, God," he moaned. "I love making love to you. Do you want me to eat you?" he asked, kissing her again.

"No. I want you inside me now." She wanted him inside her quick to make sure that he was still *her* Peter. She needed to know that she still had him, owned him. He climbed on top of her; she guided him in. He felt so good, so familiar, so cozy. She wrapped her legs around him and pulled him in. I love this man so much, God. Don't you dare let him turn out to be an asshole. I couldn't survive it.

They fucked slow and deep as images of the day flashed through her mind: her mother waving from the cab window, Angus nursing and content, Missy's tall perfectness, llamas, goats, and potbellied pigs parading around the gym, a blissful, floating Ahnika waving from above the trampoline. As Peter came inside her, she dug her fingernails into his biceps. Not fueled by passion but by fear and desperation.

Chapter Fourteen

Ellie stood next to the topiaries and the Picasso in Missy's foyer. "Bye, my little cuties." She felt a little panic rise up in her throat as she watched the elevator doors start to close on Ahnika and Angus. At the last moment, she jumped in the elevator and whispered in Candy's ear. "Don't hesitate to call or bring them back."

"Don't worry, I know my babies," Candy said in her soothing Caribbean accent. "I've been with Miss Missy since Harper and Mason were born and I've raised nine of my own." She gave Ellie a gentle nudge out of the elevator. "Just ask Miss Missy. She'll tell you."

"Have fun, guys," Ellie called. Angus waved and kicked his legs from his backpack. Ahnika and Mason sat and made faces at each other in the double stroller, too busy to even say good-bye.

"Well, they're off to the park for a big adventure," Ellie said, trying to sound casual as they disappeared behind the elevator doors.

"They'll be fine." Missy, wearing an elaborate halter brace that kept her right arm immobilized, patted her friend with her left hand.

"You think?" She turned to her friend who was wincing. "Oh, Missy, is it really painful?"

"It's hurting right now but I took a pain killer before you came so . . ." She looked at her watch. "I should be fine any minute." It had only been three days since her shoulder surgery and she was moving slowly.

"Good. Well, I'm here to help. What's up?"

"You see I really didn't think this through when I scheduled the surgery. Tony's been out of town this week and Gloria went to visit her sister in Argentina." The two women were walking through Missy's rambling apartment to the master bedroom.

Whoa, Ellie thought, when they crossed the threshold. Like the living room, floor to ceiling windows covered the opposite wall and Central Park, all gray and wintry, spread out below them.

"I love this view," Ellie said.

"Thank you. We love it too."

"Great bed." She pushed the gauze aside and peeked in.

"Thanks. It's Italian."

Dominating the room was a king-sized bed with an elaborately carved dark wood frame. It had the tallest canopy Ellie had ever seen and was draped in white gauze. A raw silk bedspread in a muted gold covered the expanse of the bed and was expertly piled with pillows in bright Mediterranean fabrics.

"We found it on our honeymoon at a flea market in Florence."

Really, Ellie thought, we found *ours* at 1-800-M-A-T-T-R-E-S. It's a charming little thing.

"The two of us fell in *love* with it. It really wasn't *so* expensive but it cost a *fortune* to ship it here."

Flea markets in Florence? Jesus, Ellie thought, what am I doing here? Suddenly an image of Missy and Antonio's naked bodies tumbling onto the bed, pillows scattering in their wake, ran through Ellie's head like a flash cut from a music video. Yep, this is where Miss WASP USA and Mr. Swarthy Argentina "do it," she thought. Why do these images and ideas occur to me whenever I'm here? She remembered the steamy night of the pot and the empanadas. Is it them, or me? she wondered as she closed the canopy and turned back to Missy.

"Wow!" she said, as she stared at her image in a massive mirror. "What an incredible mirror!"

"It came with the bed," Missy said as she ran her hand across the graceful carvings on the frame. It was as tall as the bed, at least five feet wide and made of the same rich, dark wood.

"Well, I love the whole room." Ellie was suddenly picturing her own bedroom furnishings—a mixture of her grandmother's hand-me-downs and Pottery Barn—which up until this moment she had actually been quite happy with. She found herself reconsidering Peter's suggestion of *not* having Ahnika's birthday party at home.

"So, listen," Ellie said. "What exactly is it that you need me to do? You've been a little mysterious about it."

"Well, it's just I—I'm sorry to have to ask but . . ."

"Missy, really. I'm happy to do anything. Don't be ridiculous." Is she blushing? Ellie wondered.

"Well, what I really need you to do is . . . you see with this big brace I can't really do much for myself so I haven't . . ." Yep, she definitely *is* blushing.

"Honey, just ask me. 'Yes' is already the answer."

Missy took a deep breath. "I need you to give me a sponge bath." She rattled the whole phrase off as if it were one word.

"Not a problem," Ellie rattled back. Oh, my God, she thought, is she nuts?

"I haven't had one since the hospital and I didn't feel comfortable asking Candy and . . ."

"I said it's not a problem," Ellie assured her. A sponge bath? A sponge bath! She's got a live-in staff but needs *me* to give her a sponge bath. Is this weird? This is weird.

"Are you sure? Because if it is a problem I can . . ."

"You can what? Ask Marco, the doorman, if he's available?"

"Ellie!" Missy giggled like a fifteen-year-old.

"I was kidding."

"You are terrible."

"Don't tell me you haven't noticed those shoulders of his? But enough about Marco. We have a job to do." Ellie took her friend by her good elbow and pointed to a door in the corner of the bedroom.

"Bathroom?"

Missy nodded, and the two women headed toward the door for (drum roll, please) a sponge bath.

Yet another huge room with a breathtaking view, Ellie thought. My apartment is shrinking before my very eyes.

Ellie had taken off her boots and socks and rolled up her jeans and was sitting on the edge of the antique footed tub with a soapy washcloth in her hand. Missy, with Ellie's help, had stripped down and was perched on a small upholstered bench next to the tub. She was wearing nothing but some Hanro briefs and her brace.

She kept the undies on, Ellie observed. That leads me to believe I won't be in charge of pussy washing. Good news. And, thanks to the brace, only one of her perfect breasts is exposed. Okay, okay, one breast. I can handle one breast. Bah-dum-bump! she joked to herself.

Well, for all her stuttering and blushing she doesn't seem the least bit uncomfortable now, Ellie thought, studying her poised friend. I don't know why *I'm* making such a big deal of this, she told herself. Robbie and I used to take baths *together*, for Christ's sake. In a tub very much like this one, she realized.

Ellie and Robbie had been in Hollywood (okay, Culver City) punching up a bad Shelley Long script. The pay was lousy and the hours insane, but it was an important step (so they had thought) towards their certain superstardom as a comedy writing team.

Every day was twelve to fourteen hours of writing jokes to try and save a bad, improbable script. They would fall through the door of their thirties-style bungalow around eleven every night, too tired to eat. All they wanted was to soak in a hot bath. The first few nights, one friend would watch a *thirtysomething* rerun while the other one got to soak in the huge footed tub. On the third night, as Ellie relaxed in the steaming tub, the bathroom door burst open.

"I can't wait, I'm comin' in," Robbie said, pulling off her T-shirt and stepping out of her undies.

"Okay." Ellie skooched over. It didn't seem strange or sexy to share a tub with her friend, merely practical.

"Check this out."

Ellie looked up to see Robbie standing stark naked in the bathroom doorway, pointing to the living room.

"You are amazing!" Ellie said. Robbie had turned on *thirtysomething* and moved the TV so it could be viewed from the bath. And from that night, till they were replaced by the director's brother and his wife, the two women had soaked together in the cozy tub, in their little Deco bungalow, watching Hope and Michael agonize over the problem of the day.

Ellie wrung the extra water from the washcloth and gazed beyond the blanket of leafless trees of Central Park to the West Side. Well, *that* feels like it was a million years ago, she thought. Days of hashing out rewrites, working on setups and punch lines with Robbie have been replaced by—by—sponge baths with rich WASPy girls? Nothing makes sense anymore, Ellie thought, squeezing a glop of Anik Goutal shower gel onto the washcloth. The smell of gardenias filled the room.

"Well, let's start with the feet, shall we?" Ellie said, thinking, that feels both safe and biblical.

"Sounds great."

"That's what they taught us in sponge bath school—'start with the feet and work your way up.'"

"You went to sponge bath school?"

"I got my master's in sponge baths. I never told you that?"

"You're teasing me again."

Ellie chuckled as she picked up one of Missy's beautiful slender feet. "Can't fool you, Missy Hanover." Her toes were painted a tasteful shell pink.

"Is that warm enough?" she asked as she washed the bottom of her foot.

"Heavenly." Missy smiled warmly and giggled. "I'm starting to float a little," she whispered as if she were a Catholic girl confessing a naughty thought.

"What?"

"The Percodan, it's working," she said dreamily.

Jesus, Peter's not gonna believe this. I'm giving an almost naked perfect specimen of a woman a sponge bath and she's high as a kite, Ellie thought as she cleaned the foot thoroughly. No calluses, she marveled as she rinsed the foot. This woman *is* perfect. Well, that's done. Should I do the other foot or move my way up to . . . ? She glanced up to the top of Missy's leg, and there was her vulva making a little white cotton bulge in the crotch of her panties. Ellie grabbed the other flawless foot and washed it. She was trying to think of *something* to talk about but her brain wasn't working. She looked up at Missy to find her smiling with her eyes closed. Oh, yeah, the drugs have definitely kicked in. Good, now at least I don't have to try and make conversation. As Ellie washed foot number two her eyes scanned the long, graceful slope of Missy's hairless, tanned legs. They *are* lovely, she thought. She wanted to touch them, to rub them, to feel their smoothness. I could just wrap my arms around her golden thighs and rest my head in her lap and . . .

Whoa, Ellie! Get back, girl. Focus! Focus on the task at hand. Am I acting casual? Or can she tell I'm freaking out? I know! I'll just pretend I'm washing Ahnika or Angus. Yeah, that's the ticket. Ellie went to work—ankle, calf, shin, not a problem. She started on the knee and . . .

"*Ahh!*" Missy screamed and kicked her leg, sending the washcloth into Ellie's chest. "Oh, I'm so sorry." Missy giggled, opening her eyes. "I'm very ticklish on my knees. I should've told you." Her speech and movements, thanks to the drugs, were slightly slower, smoother.

Phase One, Ellie thought as a wave of recognition shot through her bones. She's acting like Mom after two martinis. I used to actually *like* Phase One. It was the only time in the day when Mom seemed relaxed and happy. Of course, it never lasted and Phases Two (sarcastic and bitchy) through Five (sobbing and passing out) were always sure to follow.

"Oh, no. You're soaked!" Missy said dramatically as she grabbed a monogrammed hand towel and began to blot Ellie's chest.

"No big deal," Ellie told her, then tossed the washcloth into the tub. "I'm a little damp."

"At least take your sweater off. You must be roasting."

"No, no. I'm fine," she tried to protest, but Missy was already up and pulling her sweater off. For a one-armed, stoned woman, she's fast, Ellie marveled. And before she knew what was what, Ellie was standing in Missy's fancy bathroom wearing nothing but her jeans and her nursing bra. She cupped her milk-swelled breasts with her hands. They were huge

136

(she hadn't fed Angus since early that morning) and her left breast was leaking so much it had soaked through the breast pad, leaving a little damp circle on her bra. This is lovely, Ellie thought.

"Ellie," Missy said, sounding concerned and surprised. She was staring, it seemed to Ellie, at her crotch. "Come here."

"What?" Ellie said, inching toward her cautiously.

"What—is—*this?*" Missy spoke very slowly as she stepped oh-so-close to her friend and gently hooked her baby finger through Ellie's belly button ring.

"Oh, that." What the hell is she doing? Missy, almost on top of her now, smelled at once musky and flowery sweet. The fragrance sent a surge of lust through Ellie's torso. "Are you trying to seduce me, Mrs. Robinson?" Ellie heard Dustin Hoffman's nasal voice in her ear and saw Anne Bancroft's tanned and toned body in her mind.

"I did that when I found out I was pregnant with Angus," Ellie managed to continue.

Missy gave the ring a little tug. A slight pain shot into Ellie's stomach and down to her groin. She felt paralyzed as Missy towered over her. Her friend seemed suddenly menacing, with her big metal brace like some sort of futuristic Amazon, ready for battle. She wasn't moving, just leaning into Ellie, smiling. Is she going to kiss me? Their eyes locked. Missy's face seemed to inch toward hers. She was dying to feel Missy's lips on hers, her tongue in her mouth, to touch that perfect pink breast. Missy unhooked her finger and then crouched down so her nose was inches from Ellie's belt buckle, her hot breath warming Ellie's belly. Oh, my God! She's—she's—she's going down on me! Ellie raced back in her mind through the morning. Oh, no! I didn't have time to shower. This is not good. This is *really* not good. I was not planning on having sex this morning. Missy tilted her head up and gazed at her friend from her crouched position, then lost her balance and started to topple over onto her immobilized shoulder. Ellie moved quickly and caught her friend's head with both hands, like a basketball, as Missy hooked the fingers of her good hand into the top of Ellie's jeans for support.

"Whoops," Missy said, grinning goofily at her friend.

"You okay?" Ellie asked, still holding her head. Missy nodded, her fingers pulling down Ellie's jeans for balance and revealing the lacy top of her underwear. The two women were locked in this odd embrace for the longest time. This is one of the sexiest moments of my life, Ellie thought. She resisted the urge to press Missy's face into her throbbing crotch. I want this woman. God help me. I want Missy Hanover, the woman without a vagina. What the hell am I doing? She was both aroused and frightened, adrenaline gushing through her veins. Realizing that she and Missy could be lovers—would be lovers—sent everything in her life flying off in different directions. This is it. It's going to happen. Peter's *Penthouse* fantasies are all about to come true.

"Well," Missy said as she pulled herself up by Ellie's waistband.

"Well," was all Ellie could manage. Both women stood inches apart, Missy's face still in Ellie's hands, Missy's fingers still inside Ellie's jeans.

"We'd better get back to work." Missy, eyes still locked with Ellie's, slowly slid her fingers out of her jeans, then abruptly returned to her place on the bench.

"Right." Ellie fished the washcloth out of the tub. This one's crazy, Ellie thought, feeling weak kneed. She could feel dampness in her pants. Missy smiled innocently at her friend, put her foot back up on the edge of the tub, leaned back, and closed her eyes. Ellie went to work. Her task seemed suddenly tame next to what she *thought* had almost happened.

When she got to the second knee she stopped. "So how am I supposed to wash this tickle spot?"

"Do it fast and hard," Missy said dreamily, eyes still shut.

That's a setup if I ever heard one, Ellie thought. She scrubbed the knee "fast and hard"—no hysterics. Hmm, now the thighs. Just how far up do I go? The white cotton mound of Missy's pussy was just waiting there at the top of those thighs. Is it wet like mine? Ellie wondered. She steadied herself with her right hand and did some vigorous, nonsensual washing of Missy's thigh—top, side, back—then took a deep breath and inched up her inner thigh with the warm, soapy washcloth. Think Ahnika, think Angus, she chanted silently. She was just inches from the top when . . .

Oh, my God, even *she* has that slightly poochy stuff right at the top of her thigh. She began to wash the little pocket of fat, her washcloth brushing against Missy's mound. How many times have I looked in the mirror and cursed that little pooch? Now, here it is, right under my washcloth and it's so—so—yummy. She wasn't sure how she was going to keep her fingers from finding their way into Missy's underwear and beyond. She willed her hand away from Missy's crotch, turned to the tub, rinsed the washcloth, and then rinsed Missy's thigh.

"Mmm. You are fantastic."

"Glad to do it," Ellie said, suddenly sounding like an Avon lady from the Midwest who'd just demonstrated the latest lip and cheek colors to a valued customer. She took the clean leg off the tub and knelt next to thigh number two. Missy hand was suddenly on Ellie's neck. Ellie's breath went out of her. Missy began to play with the hair at the nape of Ellie's neck. Ellie dissolved inside.

Think Ahnika, think Angus. She began to wash the last and final thigh as Missy continued to caress Ellie's neck. She tried *not* to picture Missy's mouth, her breast, the white cotton mound of her panties. She kept seeing herself standing up and climbing onto her friend, kissing her, taking her. Is that what *she* wants? Is she waiting for it? Is it what *I* want? Is it what *Peter* wants? The thigh was almost clean. All but the inner thigh. The final frontier, Ellie thought. She began at the knee and worked her way up. Every inch was sexier than the one before. Missy's fingers on her neck were delicious. Ellie's pussy ached, her breath was heavy, her nipples erect. I can't stand this, she thought. I've got to have her. Peter would understand. He wants it too. She dropped the washcloth and . . .

"Hello, girls!"

Ellie looked up. Standing in the bathroom doorway was Antonio, smiling and handsome, wearing an olive green suit that showed off his incredible eyes.

"Hi, sweetie," Missy said lazily, her eyes at half-mast. Antonio bent over his wife and kissed her deep and long. Missy took her hand from Ellie's neck and put it around her husband's. Ellie was unable to move her hands from Missy's wet thigh. I want her, Ellie thought watching the beautiful couple kiss. No, I want to *be* her. No, that's not it, I want *him!*

"You're home early," Missy said, licking her lips.

"The meeting was over before I expected. I flew all night." He stepped back, seeming to be taking it all in. Jesus, with Missy's breast and that brace and me on my knees between her legs with my tits bursting out of my bra, he must think he's stumbled upon a Helmut Newton photo shoot.

"I see the sponge bath is working out nicely," he said, casual as could be.

"It was Antonio's idea to ask you to help me out. Isn't he clever?"

"A genius." Ellie smiled up at him. He leaned down to her.

"Nice to see you, Ellie," he whispered in that wonderful accent of his, eyeing her overripe breasts. Then he kissed her right on the mouth, his lips slightly parted. Oh, God! Ellie thought, trying not to crumble. I've landed smack in the middle of some French film—I'm Isabelle Huppert, Missy's Fanny What's-Her-Name, and Antonio is Gérard Depardieu. What's going to happen next? What? The promise of sex was hanging thick in the air.

"Don't let me interrupt," he told them and left.

Well, I just don't know what the heck's going on. Weren't we about to have a three-way, or am I making things up? Ellie picked up the washcloth and went back to her duties, washing the final frontier like a robot. As she turned to rinse, she caught a glimpse of Antonio through the crack in the door. He was unbuttoning his shirt. I can't believe this! She glanced at Missy—whose eyes were closed—then went back to spying on Antonio. He threw his shirt on the bed, then unzipped his pants. Oh God, oh God! She tried to keep one eye on the floating Missy and one eye on the stripping Antonio. He stepped out of his pants. His white briefs accented his dark skin and the beautiful bulge of his cock. Jesus, she thought, I'm surrounded by naked people. Bulges and tits and mounds and—and—he's unbelievable! She forced herself to look away, only to be confronted with her next project—Missy's flat, milky white stomach. She washed quickly and efficiently, vividly aware that Missy's flawless breast was only inches away and next on the agenda. Is Antonio watching us? she wondered. I think he's watching us. She glanced furtively through the crack and saw him on the bed, lying on his back, his hands behind his head. Are his eyes open or shut? I can't tell.

Time for the breast, Ellie, it's time for the breast, she instructed herself. She blinked hard and set her jaw. Here goes. She started at the bottom, easing the washcloth under the slight fold between Missy's ribcage and breast, then gently moved on to the side, the top, the cleavage. Finally, Ellie's washcloth-covered hand was cupping Missy's breast, massaging it clean. Okay, Ellie, that's enough, she admonished herself. I'm pretty sure it's nice and clean now. Move on! She was trying to, but the fullness and softness were exquisite.

"Mmm." Missy moaned softly, a tiny little growl from deep in her throat. Ellie's pussy contracted, moistened. Did Antonio hear that? she wondered, peeking at him. Their eyes met . . . or did they? The crack was so small and he was so far away. Ellie's hand was still covering her friend's breast. He's watching me, Ellie thought. He is! Isn't he? Move on, Ellie. Move on! She finally acquiesced to her own demands and slid her hand off the wonderful roundness and up quickly to Missy's good shoulder, then her armpit, arm, hand, all the while keeping her eyes on Antonio. Every inch was erotic. Every twitch or slight movement by Missy was foreplay for her and her distant lover on the bed. She felt light-headed, high, strangely separate and yet entrenched in the events at the same time.

"Just a minute!" Antonio called to some unseen person and rose from his spot. Where's he going? she wondered as she cleaned Missy's back. She heard muted voices. Oh, my God! Ahnika and Angus must be back! Her already heavy breasts began to tingle at the thought of her baby boy. Angus must be starving.

"The little ones have returned from the park." Antonio, wearing a white terry-cloth robe stuck his head into the bathroom and delivered the news.

Ellie, instantly snatched from her roll of erotic foot-maiden, dressed in a heartbeat, then racewalked down the long hallway to see her babies, that tether once again pulling her along. A smile overtook her whole body when she saw them rosy cheeked and passed out, all three of them—Mason and Ahnika in the double stroller and Angus slumped over in the backpack. Thank you, God, she thought, marveling at this gift she had been given.

"The cold air put them all right to sleep," Candy whispered as she eased the bulky backpack off her shoulders and placed it on the foyer floor. "I hate to tell you this but they didn't miss you for a moment."

"That's the good news and the bad news, right?" Ellie whispered back. Candy unbuckled the sleeping Mason while Ellie pulled Angus slowly out of the backpack.

"See! They *can* survive without you," Missy said quietly as she and her brace—now covered by an ivory terry-cloth robe—entered the foyer.

"Candy, my sweet!" Antonio, in his robe, called from the hallway. "Have you worked your magic again?"

"*Shhh!*" all three women said in unison.

Candy, with the sacked-out Mason now in her arms, smiled and shook her head. "Mr. Azcurra, getting tired children to sleep is not magic, it's just necessary. Now, please excuse me while I put this boy in his bed," and Candy headed down the hallway.

"Thanks again, Candy," Ellie stage whispered to her retreating back.

"Anytime."

"She's a miracle worker," Antonio told Ellie when he joined the group.

"And so is Ellie," Missy said. "I'm clean, relaxed . . ."

"You smell delicious," Antonio said, nuzzling his face into Missy's neck.

"My shoulder isn't hurting."

"Well, I don't think Anik Goutal and I took the pain away," said Ellie, strapping the still sleeping Angus in next to his sister. "I'm pretty sure serious drugs were involved there, don't you think?"

"You did a *great* job. Thank you." Missy kissed her firmly on the cheek. "How many people do you know that would give a friend a sponge bath?" she asked. Ellie blushed and shrugged her shoulders.

"She is our little jewel." Antonio put his arm around her and gave her a fatherly squeeze. "Didn't I know that only Ellie would do the job right?"

"Gosh, golly. I just don't know what to say. I only hope you put *my* name on that list for the Nobel Prize. I'm pretty sure I'm a shoe-in."

As the group laughed, Ellie wiggled out of Antonio's grasp and headed for the hall closet.

"Well, I'm outta here," she said, putting on her red pea coat. "I have this foolish dream that I can actually get some grocery shopping done before these two wake up."

Chapter Fifteen

Ellie had the vague feeling that she had narrowly escaped some horrible disaster when she pushed her babies out of the elevator. A chilly fall wind smacked her face as she exited Missy's building. The center median of Park Avenue was already all dressed up for Christmas with lights and garlands.

She pushed the stroller east at breakneck speed. Not really going *to* anywhere but going away *from* her morning of soft-core porn. Like a lemming on a suicide mission, she headed to Lexington and turned downtown. By the time Ellie crossed the threshold of an East Side health food store that she hadn't been to in years, she had already consumed a bag of barbecued potato chips, a Reese's Peanut Butter Cup, a bag of Peanut M&M's, and half a bag of mint Milanos. She wiped cookie crumbs from her lips as she snaked the stroller down a narrow aisle stacked high with bags of blue corn tortilla chips, organic refried beans, and boxes of whole wheat muffin mixes. She stopped when she saw the familiar green and yellow box. Her heart rate and breathing quickened at the sight of it. She started to reach for the box; Angus fussed in his spot. She froze, about to be caught. He settled down again; she grabbed the Herblax and headed to the cashier before she could think. The line was short, thank God.

She stared at the box. It had been twelve years since she had held a box of Herblax in her hand. Twelve years since she had abused her body with laxatives. She could almost feel the sweet, clean, empty feeling that this box could bring. The feeling of power, of renewal, of control. One time, she thought, her palms sweating. One time isn't going to matter.

She was about to toss twelve years of abstinence out the window, but no decision had been made, really. It was like countless stories she'd heard at OA meetings, women who'd lost their abstinence and didn't know how the hell it happened. Everyone always compared it to alcoholics who found themselves sitting on a bar stool, glass in hand, without having made a conscious decision to drink. But there had always been a common thread—no meetings, or not enough meetings. Ellie had always listened to these stories rather smugly. But she hadn't been to a meeting since— since—well, she couldn't remember.

A string bean of a man with a long, thick ponytail was interrogating the cashier about Saint-John's-wort. C'mon, buddy, Ellie thought. What's the problem? You writing your thesis on it, or what? Her foot began to tap on the linoleum at ten beats per second. She was about to lunge for Mr. Ponytail, take him by the neck, and toss him onto Lexington. She looked over her shoulder in search of another employee. He droned on.

"Excuse me." She plopped her box on the counter. "Could I just buy this, quickly, before my children wake up?" She smiled at Mr. Ponytail and hoped she had achieved the perfect mix of urgency and ass-kiss.

"Ellie! How are you?" the cashier asked.

"Danny!" It was one of the guys from Health Nuts, her West Side health food store. She was caught. "What are you doing over here?"

"Excuse me," Danny told Mr. Ponytail as he picked up the precious box. "Let me just do this for my friend, may I?" His Indian accent was inherently gracious.

"Certainly." Mr. Ponytail bowed deeply (a move perfected at countless Renaissance Fairs, no doubt) and stepped aside.

"My brother-in-law owns this store. I'm helping him out while he's away."

"Oh," she said, her eyes glued to the Herblax box in his hand. It sailed through the air as he gestured.

"The babies are sleeping. That's a first."

"Yes." She smiled weakly and gave him a twenty. Let's go, let's go, *let's go*! she screamed inside her head. Just gimme the shit and let me outta here!

"Thanks." Her hand was shaking as Danny handed her the change. She squeezed passed Mr. Ponytail and out onto the sidewalk. She took the Herblax out of the bag and stared at her drug of choice.

Ring!

"Shit!" She searched in her Coach bag for her cell phone. She read the number on the readout: *Call from private.*

Ring! "Shit! Who the hell . . . ?" She reluctantly pressed *send.* "Hello."

"Ellie, hi, it's Lisa Bienstock."

"Oh, hi."

"Listen, I just had to call you. I just had the funniest conversation with this woman and I think it would be great for the show."

"Great," Ellie said, rolling her eyes.

"I'm standing in line at Fairway reading *What to Expect When You're Expecting* and this woman in line behind me says, 'Where are you delivering?' And I say 'New York Hospital.' So she looks at me horrified and says, 'Well, it's not too late to change.' Then she pulls a business card out of her purse and presses it into my hand and goes, 'You *must* call my midwife. She's fabulous! I had no drugs, no episiotomy, and I didn't rip.' And I'm like, 'Really?' Then she tells me how her midwife massaged her inner thighs and vagina with cocoa butter for more than two hours. Can you believe that?"

"Yes, as a matter of fact," Ellie said, wishing Lisa would disappear.

"But wouldn't it be a good story for the show?"

"Definitely. Listen, Lisa, I've gotta go. Angus is fussy," she lied, "and if I don't stick my breast in his mouth soon I'm going to cause a scene. And I'm on the *East* Side."

"Okay. How's the writing going?"

"It's going great!" she lied again. "Lisa, you're breaking up. I can't hear you. I—" Ellie pressed *end* then *power* on her phone, clicked it closed, and shoved it back in her purse. "I never should've given her my cell number," she mumbled.

She felt as if she was floating as she ripped the plastic wrap off the box of laxatives, suspended on another plane, away from motherhood and wifedom, the fruits of her abstinence. She had been transported back to another place, to another person, really, a person who had been trapped in the vacuum of bulimia for more than a decade. A person whose entire life had been swallowed up by her all consuming obsessions with food, her weight, and her body. When she wasn't eating she was thinking about eating, planning her next binge. When she *was* eating she was thinking about throwing up. When she was throwing up she was making promises to herself—tomorrow I won't binge. I'll stop throwing up on the first. Five more pounds and I'll quit barfing. A person so filled with shame and secrets that she had no present and no future. A person who, during the darkest time in her life, had been throwing up more than ten times a day. And, somehow, through sheer will and perfectionism, she had fooled them all. Been the envy of her classmates, even. Somehow she had continued a full load at Juilliard, which included taking three or four dance classes daily. And when she *was* dancing, surrounded by mirrors, her perfectionism about her body drove her to fantasies of suicide. Dance classes, once her salvation from a drunken, self-pitying mother, had become a form of torture. But none of these memories came back to her now, just the need for the release, the emptiness, the control.

She headed down Lexington in search of a deli where she could get hot water to make her tea. "Don't they have any goddamn delis on the East Side?" she grumbled to herself as she marched. Each step took her closer to salvation, so she thought. Each moment the children continued to sleep was a blessing, so she told herself.

"Eli's!" she almost shouted when she remembered the trendy East Side bakery was only two blocks west. Her mouth was dry with anticipation, her breasts heavy as a couple of boulders, but hot water and deliverance were right around the corner. She pushed the sleeping babies west with the single-mindedness of the junkie that she was. The buzz of East Siders was a blur around her. Just this once, just this once, she kept repeating like a mantra. Suddenly the stroller stopped dead.

"Shit!" She had steered right into the bottom step of a large stairway jutting out from an old church. She checked out the babies. Still sleeping, thank God.

"Oh, my God, they're gorgeous!" A perfectly fit woman in her late forties, with jet black curls and cool blue eyes, was cooing over Ahnika and Angus. "Look at him! And her with the leaves! So precious."

"Thanks," Ellie said quickly, hoping to avoid a long tribute to her sleeping children. The woman stopped and stared at Ellie. She knows what I'm up to, Ellie thought, feeling quite paranoid.

"Do we know each other?" the woman asked. "You look *so* familiar."

Ellie studied the woman. She *did* look vaguely familiar. Listen, lady, she thought, I don't know how the heck I know you and I really don't care because I don't have time to chat.

"Yeah, you do too, but . . ." Ellie shrugged her shoulders and resumed her place at the helm. "I'm really late for a doctor's appointment. So . . ."

"Oh, well." The woman said sweetly. She seemed to want to say more.

"Carrie!" A short, chubby woman called to the fit woman from the stairs. Carrie, huh, Ellie mused? That really *is* familiar. How the hell do I know her?

"Aren't you chairing this meeting?"

"I am, I am," Carrie called back.

Oh, my God, "chairing this meeting"? I know her from OA. Yep, she's thinner than she used to be, but—Oh, fuck! Ellie, considering her immediate plans, had no desire to share her realization.

"Well, it seems I'm late, too," she said to Ellie, then turned and hurried up the steps. "You have beautiful children," she called back and was gone.

"Okay, God, I get it. I get it," Ellie said quietly to the heavens as she started toward Madison. She stopped, closed her eyes, and took a deep breath. So you planted an OA meeting *right in my path* to save me from myself. Is that it? She reached in her pocket and felt for the Herblax. There it was, just waiting for her. I know, God, I'm supposed to turn around and fly up the stairs to that meeting, right? She took the box out and looked at it, looked over her shoulder at the church steps, then headed toward Madison. Her lips were tight across her teeth, her gait heavy and slow. At the corner, she opened the box and ripped into the plastic bag inside. She could see Eli's Bread across the avenue. A blond woman, laden with baguettes and holding a coffee cup, was leaving. Over her shoulder, she could also see the stone steps of the church. A few latecomers were still arriving, rushing through the door at the top. She took the opened plastic bag out of the box and held it high in the air. Her heart was pounding; there was no saliva left in her mouth. Slowly, she turned the bag over and shook it. She watched as the loose tea floated down into a city trash can. Then she pulled the half-empty bag of cookies out of her purse and dumped them in the trash can as well.

Well, that's it, she thought. There's no turning back now. She knew from years of experience that just throwing out the box would not have been enough. Oh, no. That left open the possibility of her changing her mind, of walking back to the trash can and fishing out the box. She had thrown out plenty of food, disgusted with herself halfway through a binge, only to retrieve it after she had purged. Later, a more seasoned bulimic, she had taken to pouring laundry detergent on her food (to avoid any changes of heart) when the taste of hand lotion had proven too easy to stomach. She watched as the wind blew some of the laxative out into the noontime traffic on Madison.

"You happy?" she asked God, looking up at the gray fall sky.

Step Two—Came to believe that a Power greater than ourselves could restore us to sanity." The chubby friend of Carrie's read aloud from a three-ringed bind. She passed it to a grave-looking, white-haired woman next to her.

Ellie had followed a latecomer into the church and found the meeting in the basement. She had managed to park the stroller in the back corner without causing too much commotion.

It's nice to be in a meeting, she conceded as she listened to the rest of the steps. I don't recognize anyone from the old days except What's-Her-Name.

"Step Twelve—Having had a spiritual awakening as the result of these Steps, we tried to carry this message to compulsive overeaters and to practice these principles in all our affairs." The steps were finished and the notebook made its way back to Carrie, the woman from the steps.

"Are there any newcomers here today that would like to say hello?" She searched the room for a raised hand. A frail arm slowly ascended right in front of Ellie. Oh, my God. Ellie put her hand to her mouth to stifle a gasp.

"Hi." Carrie spoke with incredible gentleness. "Would you tell us your first name, please?

The girl mumbled something as everyone strained to hear her.

"I'm sorry, could you speak up so we can give you a proper welcome?"

"My name is Frances!" the girl said, almost shouting, her sticklike arms now folded across her sunken chest.

"Hi, Frances, welcome!" Ellie said along with the group, trying to telepath love and acceptance to her. Frances seemed to recoil at the sound of the friendly voices.

Oh, God, oh, God, please help her to stay, Ellie prayed. She felt sure Frances was about to spring from her seat and bolt from the room.

"Well, we're glad you're here. There are . . ."

"Well, *I'm* not glad I'm here," she said, cutting Carrie off. "I'm only here because my fucking therapist said if I *don't* come she's going to hospitalize me—again."

"Mm-hmm," Carrie said softly, nodding. The whole room went tense, quiet.

"I don't know why I'm here, anyway. I'm not an overeater, as you can see." She laughed, flinging her arms open to reveal her cadaverous body. Carrie waited, seeing if she had anything else she needed to say. Nothing.

"Well, there are lots of people in this room whose food plan is about eating *enough* food, not less food. If you stay and listen you will find plenty of people here who have been through what you're going through."

Frances rolled her eyes and shook her head. "Yeah, right," she mumbled.

Ellie wanted to put her arms around Frances and move to the other side of the room at the same time. She *was* Frances, or at least had been. When she had first gone to OA—fresh out of rehab, skinny and jittery, angry at the world—she had hated meetings, hated every friendly, mawkish person that told her everything was going to be alright.

"There are beginner's packets for newcomers that are free at the literature table, along with meeting lists. I'm glad you're here." Carrie smiled and nodded at Frances, then glanced down at her notebook. "Is there anybody at *this meeting* for the first time who would like to say hello?"

Ellie's heart skipped a beat; she almost raised her hand, then didn't.

"Okay, then," Carrie continued, "at this meeting we have a speaker who speaks on a topic for fifteen to twenty minutes."

I don't suppose the topic will be "extramarital lesbian affairs," Ellie joked to herself.

"I'm very excited about our speaker today. Will you please help me welcome Grace." Carrie clapped as she turned to the woman seated next to her, and the room followed suit. Grace was an olive-skinned, solid woman in her late twenties.

"Hi, I'm Grace and I'm an overeater," she told the group in a Brooklyn accent when the applause stopped.

"Hi, Grace," came the group response.

"And I am *so* happy to be speaking today. I'm just back from vacation in Florida. No, no, no, no, I shouldn't say 'vacation.' That was the idea, that was the plan but . . . it was more like a test. Some sort of bizarre test by God to see if I'm *really* working my program. You see, I made the *unbelievable* error in judgment to stay with—" she gave the crowd a grave, deadpan stare, paused, and then whispered "—my mother."

There were groans of recognition, laughs all around, and one big guffaw popped out of the white-haired woman. Grace smiled and shook her head. I like this woman, Ellie thought.

"But I'm here to say I survived without killing myself . . . or her." The group laughed. Ellie stole a glance at Frances. Was the laughter helpful or annoying to the angry newcomer? Ellie could remember how happy *she* had been to hear laughter and jokes when she first came to OA. It was the thing that made her stay.

"But, more amazing than that," Grace continued, "I didn't steal into the dark kitchen late at night and scarf large quantities of carbohydrates. No, I followed my food plan to the letter." She shook her head as if to say "I can't believe it myself." "And I have done that *every* day, one day at a time, by the grace of God, for the last two and a half years."

Ellie took a deep breath and was filled with the wonder of her early days in OA, when every day of abstinence had felt like a miracle. God, that seems like a million years ago, she thought. But it was really just a second ago, she realized, quickly checking to see if her own miracles were okay. They were still conked out in the stroller. She was so overwhelmed with gratitude and relief that she wanted to stand on her chair and shout "Hallelujah!" She wanted to hold up Ahnika and Angus and say "Look at this! Look at these beauties! They are mine! I am happy! I live a normal, happy life!"

She started to cry; slowly, quietly, a steady stream of tears flowed down her cheeks and onto her collarbone. She was so happy, so scared, so confused. How had she almost thrown everything away? What the fuck is wrong with me? she wondered. She felt unhinged, totally unmoored, as if nothing in her life were solid and real, as if all her years of abstinence and a "normal life" were only some elaborate denial that she had concocted for herself. She was dying to feel Peter's warm body next to hers, to see his sweet smile and hear his annoying jokes. It felt like years since she had seen him. There was an eruption of laughter.

"So, my mother gives me one of her deadly looks," Grace told the room full of rapt overeaters, "and instead of reaching for the basket of carbohydrates I just thought, 'Easy does it.'"

Easy does it, Ellie repeated in her head. And she closed her eyes and let the simple, sweet wisdom of Grace's experience wrap around her like a warm blanket.

Chapter Sixteen

I'm a mommy sandwich, Ellie thought, as she lay smooshed between her sleeping babies and listened intently for the sound of Peter's key in the lock. He had been away all day for a meeting in D.C., so they hadn't spoken since her brush with lesbianism and bulimia. After several hours of being back in the sanity and security of their cozy, rent-controlled, two-bedroom apartment, Ellie was counting the minutes till their reunion. She wanted to feel his arms around her, the weight of his hard body on top of her. In fact, she had already put in her diaphragm in anticipation of his return. Like a Catholic girl waiting for confession, she couldn't wait to tell him about the events of the day. She started, once again, to rehearse the long and heartfelt monologue in her head.

Listen, I've decided to get a sitter for a few hours a day so I can get to some meetings and get some writing done. You know that there's nothing more important to me than you and the kids. But today I came very close to throwing it all away. I need to tell you about it because I want to make absolutely sure that it doesn't happen. We have a saying in OA—you're as sick as your secrets. And I don't want to have *any* secrets from you so . . .

"Hi." Ellie heard a husky whisper in the darkness. She opened her eyes to see Peter's business-suited silhouette in the doorway, briefcase in hand.

"Hi, handsome," she whispered. "They're asleep. I'll be out in two minutes."

"Okay."

"I love you."

"Love you, too," Peter said, then disappeared down the hallway. Ellie started to panic. Shit, what do I tell him? What the fuck do I say? Her morning of tanned, slender legs, flowery scented suds, and Argentine men in briefs flew up in her face like a tacky montage from a daytime soap. I didn't *really* do anything, did I? I mean, Missy and I didn't *do* anything, right? Antonio and I didn't even *touch* each other. Do I tell Peter? Should I tell him? Somehow, she had totally skipped over the lesbian affair/ ménage à trois part of her day when she had been working on her monologue. For some reason, the wild events of the morning, the ones that had no doubt caused her to binge and almost purge, had seemed irrelevant when she had been composing her confessional. But now! Now that her sweet, trusting husband was back and waiting patiently for her, not telling him seemed wrong. She had never kept anything from him before. Never even considered it. She closed her eyes and took a deep breath. Let Go, she thought as she exhaled. And Let God, she thought as she breathed in again. Then she waited. Waited for something, for a sign from God as to what to do, how to handle this whole sponge bath . . . situation. She waited . . . and waited.

"You coming?" Peter's husky whisper came again. She saw his now boxer-shorted silhouette in the doorway and her chest contracted.

"Yes." She eased herself out from between Angus and Ahnika, her heart racing. She and Peter stood at opposite sides of the bed, watching their children sleep in the dim light from the hallway.

"I missed them today." He bent down and gave them each a gentle kiss on the cheek.

"You are the best father in the world," she said, tucking them in.

"You think?"

"I do." And they walked into the living room together.

Peter hopped on the sofa bed and patted the spot next to him. "Come here. I've been thinking of your pussy all day."

"Oh, you say that to all the girls." Ellie straddled him and rubbed his chest as she kissed him, suddenly anxious for sex. He placed his hands on her ass and pushed his pelvis up towards her, his already hard cock pressed against her vulva. She reached between her legs and wrapped her fingers around his—

"Tell me about your day with Missy," he whispered in her ear. "What did the two of you do together?"

She squeezed his dick harder that she'd planned to.

"Hey!" He grabbed her wrist gently.

"Sorry." She loosened her grip.

"What exactly was it that she needed your help with?" He turned her over onto her stomach and began to pull down her panties. "Hmm?"

Oh, my God, these are the same panties that I wore to Missy's, she realized. Do they smell like sex?

"Did she need help—" he was easing the panties off her feet "—getting undressed, perhaps?"

"Yes. But she kept her panties on." A picture of the perfectly stoned Missy in her Hanro briefs filled her head. Is he psychic, she wondered? He began caressing her cheeks, slowly, gently. She floated to the ceiling, feeling all fuzzy and blurry. All rational and linear thought dissolved in her and came dripping out between her legs. She ached for him. I wish he could keep nibbling me and be inside me at the same time, she mused. Her hand was between her legs and she massaged her clit with slow, circular motions.

"Did you touch her breasts?" He continued with what he thought was just fantasy talk in between nibbles. She had a feeling suddenly that Missy was in the room with them, sitting on her little bench in her briefs with her brace and her breast, watching them, smiling her drugged-up smile.

"I did. It was round and pink and beautiful." All the forbidden excitement of the morning returned, mixing with Peter's soft lips and rough beard, Antonio's white cotton bulge, his green eyes, watching her, watching them. Ellie was so aroused she wasn't sure where she was. Peter turned her over and opened her legs. He had to push her hand away to get to what he wanted. He studied her for a moment, then plunged into

154

her. His tongue and lips sent waves of pleasure through her body. She was lifted up, up, out and away. Far beyond that room or their life. She came almost instantly—again and again, sailing through space, floating, flying, where all that existed was her pussy and Missy's tongue. Oh, right, it was Peter's tongue wasn't it? She pulled his head into her and slammed her thighs together, trapping him, holding him there till it was too much and she had to push him off. When he climbed on her she was spent. But the feel of his slippery cock inside her was like a spark of energy. She lifted her hips to meet his and wrapped her arms around his neck.

"Did she eat you like that? Did she?" he asked as he fucked her slow and sweet.

"Yes, yes, she did." They were on the big wooden bed suddenly and Antonio was standing over the two of them.

"Was it good? Did you love it?"

"It was perfect, delicious. He was watching us."

"Mmm, I like that. Him watching you." He put his hands underneath her ass, tilting her just so, fucking her deeper, faster, his face buried in her neck, his breath thick and warm. Every thrust sent her back to the edge again. She was lost again. Was she home? Was she on the massive bed? Was it Peter inside her? Antonio? Was Missy watching them?

"I'm gonna come," Peter whispered in her ear, bringing her back to their life and their home.

"Good. I want it. I want your cum inside me." She wanted, needed to be his, with him, in their life, their bed, their love.

"Oh! Oh! Oh!" He called out with each thrust. Closer, closer. "Ohh-hhh!" He came, squeezing her, so deep in her it felt as if they would fuse together and become one, attached at their crotches. She loved it, loved him.

They fell away from each other, panting and sweating. He put his hand on her hip and gave it a pat. She put her hand on his. God, don't let me blow this, please don't let me fuck this up, she prayed.

"That was incredible. Did it feel good?" she asked, even though she knew the answer.

"Are you kidding. It was perfect!" He rolled over and kissed her shoulder. "I'm dying of thirst. You want some seltzer?" he asked as he sat up and headed for the kitchen.

"Yeah," she told him, grabbing some Kleenex from the coffee table and wiping off her messy pussy. "Then get back here and give me some postcoital snuggling, you insensitive pig!" she called after him.

"Honey, guys don't like the word 'coital.' It makes them think of spoiled milk," he said as he walked toward the kitchen.

"Very funny." She laughed in spite of herself.

"Postcoital snuggling? What kind of feminist propaganda bullshit is that?" he called from the kitchen.

"I'm married to Archie Bunker," she mumbled to herself, smiling. "How did that happen?"

"So, are you going to tell me what Missy needed from you or not?" he asked as he sat on the bed, seltzer in hand. She took the glass from him.

Here's my moment, she thought. To tell or not? She sat up and took a long, long drink. I'm gonna tell him, she decided.

"Are you stalling?" he asked, taking the seltzer midswig. I can't tell him, she decided. She smiled at him, trying to act natural. "What exactly was it that only *you* could do for her?" he asked as he settled back into their cozy spot.

"She needed me to . . ." Ellie pulled the covers up to her chin and stared at the ceiling as her brain scrambled to come up with a good lie. It came up empty. "Give her a sponge bath." She looked for his reaction.

He turned to her. "You're kidding." His eyes narrowed, scrutinizing her.

"I'm not."

"You're not?"

She looked him straight in the eyes and shook her head slowly.

"You gave Missy the preppie heiress a sponge bath?"

"Yep!"

"I can't believe it." He propped himself up on one elbow. "This is unbelievable! What happened?"

"Nothing happened. I gave her a sponge bath." So far, I'm not lying, she thought.

"That's it? There you are, the two of you naked and nothing happened?"

"Peter, we weren't naked. That's only in porno movies and in *your* fantasy. *I* wasn't naked and she kept her panties on." Still not lying.

"But wasn't it erotic? Didn't you love it? So you saw her tits?"

"Tit. I only saw one. The other one was covered by this huge brace she has to wear for weeks. She really is immobilized."

"I can't believe that she even *asked* you to give her a sponge bath. Women are so weird. A guy would never ask another guy something like that."

"That's 'cause men are so uptight. What's the big deal? I wash Angus and Ahnika every night, don't I?" Still not lying.

"But, come on. She's a beautiful woman. You've got to admit it's a little different from washing the kids. It wasn't the least bit erotic?"

"Look, I'm a heterosexual woman. I was doing a friend a favor. I washed her, I rinsed her. That was it." And that *was* it, Ellie told herself. As she reframed the story for Peter it somehow got reorganized in her own mind. It *wasn't* a big deal. Nothing happened. She gave him a kiss on the neck and closed her eyes.

"Well, it's very sexy for me." He kissed the top of her head and chuckled. "So, if Missy ever wants another sponge bath or a full body massage or anything like that, just know that you have my blessing." They lay still and contented, their breathing in sync, their bodies intertwined. Ellie started to drift off.

The monologue! What about the monologue? A voice out of nowhere was asking her, shaking the sleep from her head.

"Peter?" she asked tentatively.

"Hmm?"

"You sleeping?"

"Mmm."

I guess that's a yes, Ellie thought, staring up at his profile. Well, I can do the monologue tomorrow. There's really not much to say anyway, right?

Chapter Seventeen

Ellie skipped out of Liana's with her new sexy (yet classic) Nicole Miller cocktail dress. At $258, they had thrown in the hanger for free and provided a plastic garment bag to protect it from the almost frozen December rain. Liana herself, a very smart-looking Asian woman who owned the Columbus Avenue boutique, waved at Ellie as she headed uptown. Ellie had passed the store countless times over the last few years, always admiring its display of timeless dresses in the window. But before today she had never even crossed the threshold. Until now she had never had the occasion to wear the type of dressy dresses that Liana's sold. But tonight . . . tonight she and Peter, in his custom-made navy blue suit, would be celebrating New Year's Eve at Antonio and Missy's annual party.

. . .

*A*fter the sponge bath incident, things with Ellie and Missy had remained virtually unchanged. For their first few post–sponge bath encounters, Ellie had searched high and low for some sign that something *had* in fact happened between the two friends in the steamy bathroom on that gray fall day. But there was not a clue to be found. They had still spent all their playgroup time together, at the coffee shop or at Missy's apartment.

At Missy's they would chat and eat snacks (whipped up by Gloria) as they watched Angus progress from supercrawler to supercruiser, pulling himself up on various antiques and then squealing with delight at his triumphs. All the time the HBO deadline loomed somewhere in the back of Ellie's mind.

During this time, Missy had begun her campaign to help Ellie orchestrate the perfect birthday party for Ahnika. She was guiding Ellie through the seemingly endless maze of caterers, magicians, and animal acts. Ellie went along for the ride, looking at flyers, taking notes, and nodding at Missy's suggestions. Never saying yes, but never saying no either.

Peter's parents, after years of prodding, had finally relented and spent some of their nest egg on a dream vacation to Australia. So, while her in-laws were bringing in the Yuletide with the Aborigines and kangaroos, Ellie had been able to prepare for her first-ever Christmas in *her* home with *her* family. She decorated the apartment with evergreen boughs, pinecones, and candles and ordered personalized stockings for the entire family from Lillian Vernon. Ahnika, being finally old enough to catch the consumerism frenzy, compiled a mile-long list that was sent off to the North Pole, of course.

It was past midnight on Christmas Eve, and Ellie and Peter were wrapping the last of the presents, when they heard a wailing cry from the bedroom. Ellie sprinted to the bedroom ready to nurse Angus, only to discover a sobbing Ahnika lying in a pool of her own vomit. Like only a mother can, Ellie scooped up her barf-covered child and comforted her without skipping a beat. Then she changed her out of her soiled *Star Wars* pj's, oblivious to the smell and feel of the vomit. Angus, true to form, slept through the melee. Ellie stayed by Ahnika's side while she threw up a record seven times in two and a half hours.

Peter went to Duane Reade in search of Pedialyte, and Ahnika, on nice fresh sheets, finally settled down into an exhausted sleep with Ellie by her side.

I gotta have this barf phenomenon on the show, she thought as she listened to Ahnika's breathing. How, once you become a mother you're impervious to how gross it is. Barf, pee, poop, snot—none of it gets to you. Maybe a whole segment on bodily fluids, she was thinking when she felt something wet on her arm. She turned to see Angus spewing vomit all over her and the nice clean sheets.

That night they went through three sets of sheets and countless towels, and were on the phone with the pediatrician three times.

Around noon on Christmas day, when the four of them were lolling in the living room opening presents in slow motion, the phone rang. It was Missy calling from Argentina to wish everyone a Merry Christmas.

When Ellie told her about their night of nausea she said, "You poor darlings. I'm sending over your Christmas present now."

"Great. Bye," Ellie said, too tired to even be curious, and went back to dozing on the sofa.

An hour later, the doorbell rang. Standing in the doorway was a tall, thin black woman. Ellie's Christmas present from Missy, it turned out, was two weeks of free baby-sitting. The woman in their hallway was Candy's cousin Bibi, newly arrived from Trinidad. Bibi had needed a job and Ellie, as far as the greater world was concerned, needed a sitter. It was a perfect match.

"Uh, Bibi, I don't know what to say. I really don't—"

"I have strict instructions from Miss Missy," Bibi said as she eased herself into the apartment. "I can't take no for an answer. I'm prepaid for the two weeks and I'll be in big trouble if you don't let me do my job," she told Ellie as she walked into the living room.

"Bibi, please! It's Christmas. Go home and enjoy the holiday with your family." Ellie was following Bibi around the living room as she grabbed a wastebasket and started shoving wrapping paper into it.

"My family is back in Trinidad," she said as she began straightening the scattered gifts and boxes. "I prayed all year for a job and a chance to work in America. And the Lord has sent me to you."

Ellie had no comeback for that one. So Bibi stayed and while Ellie and

Peter napped she bathed Angus and Ahnika. Then she disappeared into the kitchen.

Later, while the four of them were watching *Frosty the Snowman*, Bibi appeared in doorway.

"Dinner's ready," she had announced quietly. And the entire family (plus one) had sat down to a wonderful Christmas dinner of curried chicken with roti bread.

𝒜 week had passed since Bibi's surprise arrival into the family. And, thanks to the knowledge that her children were in good hands, Ellie, with her fabulous new cocktail dress over her shoulder, found herself strolling (not rushing) up Columbus in the freezing rain. She stopped to check out the latest groovy footwear in the window at Sacco. A pair of black strappy sandals was calling her name.

I could buy those, she realized. I have the money *and* the time. Unbelievable! Thank you, God. Thanks for sending us Bibi. Life is good, she told herself as she headed into the shoe store in search of a saleslady.

"Mommy, Mommy!" A sock-footed Ahnika, wearing her new cowgirl outfit, came sliding around the corner as Ellie took her key out of the lock. "Come see what we did to Bibi!"

"Okay, sweetie. Just let Mommy put down her packages." She dropped her new purchases in the middle of the hallway as Ahnika dragged her into the playroom.

"Mama!" Angus called from Bibi's lap when she entered the room.

"Hi, handsome! Oh, my God!"

Bibi sat on the floor of the playroom immobilized. Her head was wrapped in an Ace bandage, leaving only part of one eye with any possibility of seeing. She wore plastic handcuffs on her wrists, Scotch tape covered her mouth, and her legs were piled with throw pillows.

"She's our prisoner," Ahnika told her with pride. Bibi was smiling, thank God.

"You okay, Bibi?" Ellie asked. Bibi nodded and her mouth struggled against the tape. "Sweetie, I think the prisoner has something to tell me. Can you remove the tape?"

"Sure, Mom," Ahnika said, sounding like a ten-year-old. She climbed over Angus and ripped off the tape.

"Ahnika!"

"What?" she asked, totally clueless.

"Don't worry, I'm fine," Bibi said, rubbing her lips.

"Well, Bibi, you won't be needing to get your upper lip waxed after all," Ellie said. Bibi laughed softly.

"We were just having some fun playing bad guys," Bibi said with a smile.

Ellie surveyed the trashed playroom—dress-up clothes, blocks, and Play-Doh everywhere. "Bibi, you are worth your weight in gold," she told her.

"Look!" Ahnika said, holding up a jump rope. "We'll tie her legs!"

Angus squealed with delight and scrambled off Bibi's lap and crawled toward his sister. Ellie slowly backed out of the room. She waited and listened just outside the playroom for some reaction to her departure. None. They don't need me, she realized. She felt a mixture of relief and deep sadness as she headed to the hallway to retrieve her party outfit.

The freezing rain had turned to fluffy snow by the time Ellie and Peter headed east in their holiday duds.

"I love the snow," Ellie said, sounding like a kid as she looked out the cab window. "If it's gonna be cold, it might as well be pretty."

Cars, cabs, and buses were slipping and sliding all over the slick road. Their cab driver drove down Central Park West cautiously.

"Look, Peter. Look at Tavern on the Green." She squeezed his leg, feeling like a tourist as she gazed at the leafless trees surrounding the famous restaurant that sat on the edge of the park. As was the tradition, every branch had been meticulously wrapped with about a million Christmas tree lights, creating a magical, storybook effect.

"It looks like a postcard, doesn't it, with the perfect amount of fluffy snow falling?"

"Yeah, it's great," he mumbled, his head leaning back against the seat, his eyes closed.

"Are you okay?" she asked, skooching closer to him.

"I'm just exhausted. Working on New Year's Eve sucks."

"This'll cheer you up." She plopped her leg over his and hiked up her skirt to show off her lace topped stockings and garter belt.

He smiled weakly and gave her thigh a pat.

"Boy, if that's the best you can do I'm gonna have to find some young Argentinean stud tonight at Missy's to replace you."

"I'm sorry, El. You know I always want you. I only had a protein bar for lunch. I'll feel better after dinner."

Zocalo, their favorite East Side restaurant, was empty when they arrived. Streamers of bright pink, yellow, and mango-colored ribbon hung down from the ceiling brushing their shoulders as they followed the host to a table in the back. He was dressed like a biker in black jeans and a tight black T-shirt, and had a Fu Manchu mustache but walked like Marilyn Monroe.

Peter sat down with a thud.

"Your waiter will be right with you." He smiled broadly, then he handed them each a menu. "Enjoy your dinner." And he was gone.

"Jesus. You're not looking so good. Are you sick?" Ellie asked.

Peter took a deep breath. "I'm not feeling so good," he told her, brows furrowed.

"Oh, my God! You've got the kids' flu." She recoiled inside. "I really thought we had dodged that bullet. Do you think you have it?"

"No!" he said, almost defiantly. "I'm not feeling nauseous, just exhausted,"

"Oh, honey. Do you want to go home?" she asked. "We can just go home if you want."

"No. I *have* to eat. All day I've been dreaming about their Aztec soup.

The waiter arrived. He was short and dark with slightly Mayan features and also clad in a tight black T-shirt and black jeans.

"Hi," Ellie said, taking over. "We'd like to order our appetizers right away." She didn't even give him time to nod. "He'll have the Aztec soup, and I'll have the special quesadilla. And we'll split a large bottle of Pellegrino."

"Right away," he said and was gone.

The two of them sat silently for a while. Ellie looked out the front windows and saw the snow falling, still in perfect little Hollywood puffs. She could feel her perfect evening slipping away.

Tonight would've been the first night we've ever done anything like this, she realized. Ever. She looked at her exhausted husband, looking so handsome in spite of his condition, and remembered the morning, less than four years ago, when he had shown up at the front door of her East Village walk-up.

She had been in a deep sleep when she heard banging on her front door.

"Okay! Okay!" she yelled as she grabbed her crimson thrift store Chinese robe and headed for the door. "Robbie, if that's you, I'm gonna kill you."

She and Robbie had worked past midnight, trying to make a deadline the night before, and it would be just her style to show up at an ungodly hour the next day with coffee and croissants.

"Are you playing coy?" Ellie shouted through the door, then unlocked the three deadbolts that kept her feeling safe in the still iffy East Village. "If you didn't bring coffee, you're in big trou—" She swung open the door with a dramatic flair. She stopped short.

"Hi," Ellie said, flooded with shock, embarrassment, and elation all at the same time.

Standing in the yellow light of her dingy hallway was not her best friend Robbie, but her ex-boyfriend Peter Moore, a cup of coffee in each hand.

"Well, I brought coffee, but I still might be in trouble." He offered her one of the blue and white Greek to-go cups.

"Thanks." She smiled as she took the coffee, stunned out of her mind. She hadn't seen or spoken to Peter since before she went into rehab.

"Nice place," he said, straining to look past her into her small funky apartment.

"Would you like to come in?" Her heart raced; her crotch moistened. She was vividly aware that she was almost naked and that Peter Moore had been one of the best lovers she'd ever had.

164

"I'm just gonna say this and go, if you don't mind," he said, lowering himself onto the edge of her coffee table.

"Sure," she said, still stunned.

"Okay. Here goes." He took a deep breath and looked out the window as he spoke.

"After you disappeared, and no one at Juilliard would tell me how to find you, I gave up. I figured, if you were trying so hard to get away from me, what was the point? I dropped out of Juilliard because once you were gone it was clear to me that I wasn't really an actor. I mean, I wasn't an artist. I didn't have the passion that all you guys had.

"Not knowing what else to do, I applied to graduate school like every other boring person on the planet with a college degree and without a plan. I got into Wharton and I went. Then I moved back to the city and started my own company.

"Anyway, I was sitting in my apartment two weeks ago, channel surfing and eating cold sesame noodles, and suddenly there you were." He stopped now and looked at her for the first time since his speech began.

"After so many years of wondering what, how, why—there you were, right in my living room." He looked down at the hardwood floor and slowly took a sip of coffee.

"Well, I couldn't stop thinking about you. I thought about that time you dragged me to see Martha Graham and you wept at that crazy dance. I hardly knew you and I didn't really like the dance, or I missed the point. Anyway, I remember how I felt sitting in that dark theater watching you weep because of a dance. I remember thinking 'This person is special, Peter, don't let her go.' But mostly I thought about how much you used to make me laugh. And I realized that in all the years since you left, no one has ever made me laugh the way you did." He got up, walked to the window, took a sip, and stared into his coffee cup as he spoke.

"So, two days ago, I called the cable channel, told a couple of white lies, and got your phone number and address. I thought of calling but I thought you might hang up on me. I had to *see* you and ask you why you left. Find out what I did to make you go."

"Peter, that's not—"

"Wait. I'm not done. Let me do my little closing speech. I've been rehearsing for three days." He smiled and looked embarrassed.

"For the last four years, I have been very focused on changing my life. And I've done it. I have my own company doing something I really like that I'm good at. I live in a great apartment. I have friends that I care about. But I have been looking for—Oh, God, this is the hard part." He turned away from her and looked out the window. "I know this is going to sound like a bad personals ad but, here goes.

"The thing is, when I saw you on TV two weeks ago I just went 'That's it! There she is! It's Ellie I've been waiting for, or looking for.' When I sat next to you in that theater back at Juilliard, I knew." He turned toward her and looked her in the eye.

"Look, I know you don't really know me and I probably seem like some sort of a stalker right about now. But I have really—missed you. Eight years later I still miss you." His eyes filled with tears. "I know that sounds crazy.

"Listen, I've dated plenty of women, but when I saw you I . . ." He stopped and closed his eyes. "I couldn't *not* come. I couldn't *not* find you and say these things to you."

Ellie sat on the couch, her eyes locked with his. She willed herself to stay put. Every molecule in her body wanted to jump up and run to him, to wrap her arms around him and kiss him a million times. To say "And I've been waiting for you, too. I didn't know it till this moment but I have!" He was so handsome and vulnerable and full of balls all at the same time that she couldn't stand it. She couldn't imagine loving anyone more than she loved him at that moment.

"So, what d'ya say? Want to be my girlfriend?" he asked, looking down at the floor again.

"Sure," she told him, without skipping a beat.

They spent that morning catching up. Ellie had changed into some jeans and a T-shirt, then made French toast while she told him the gory details of her bulimia rehab and the connection she had made with Robbie. It felt easy and fun between them, like two old friends getting together. As she soaked the bread in the egg batter and listened to him give the *Reader's Digest* version of the last four years, she remembered how much she had liked him when they were dating. But back then there hadn't been room in her life for anything. Dance and her eating disorder had been more than a full-time job.

They were doing the dishes together when there was a knock at the door. It was Robbie with coffee and scones, and she was shocked to find her Ellie unavailable to her. Peter smiled and chatted with her in spite of her coolness. But Robbie never softened. Never.

Less than a month later, ignoring all of her best friend's warnings, Ellie had packed up her East Village apartment and moved in with Peter.

From that moment to this, their lives had been on fast forward. First there was the pregnancy (oops!), then planning the wedding, then there was the wedding, then Ahnika's birth, then life with a newborn, life with a toddler, then (oh, my God!) pregnant again. In this scenario there had been no room for romantic nights out in lace-topped stockings and cocktail dresses.

S'cuse me." The waiter was standing at the table, appetizers in hand.

"Oh, hi," Ellie said, suddenly pulled back from her reminiscing.

Peter's head was resting in his hands.

"Honey, your soup's here."

When he looked up his complexion was green. There goes New Year's. The waiter placed the food in front of them both and left.

"How are you feeling?"

"Like I'm gonna throw up."

"Oh, shit. I'm so sorry. Let's go." She scanned the room for the waiter to get the bill.

"No, no. You stay, eat your dinner, and go to the party. I'll be fine."

"Are you sure?" She felt like a rat for even considering the idea. But she *was* starving and terrified at the thought of catching the stomach flu, something that hadn't even crossed her mind when her babies had been barfing everywhere.

"What is the point of you coming home? Bibi is staying over if the kids wake up. I'll be fine. I just have to ride it out."

"I really hate to send you home alone on New Year's, but you know how much I hate the stomach flu. I swear I'd rather go through labor—*without* an epidural—than get the stomach flu."

"I know, I know. I don't blame you." He was moving in slow motion, getting up and putting on his coat. "But it is a little ironic that an ex-bulimic would be so fearful of the stomach flu, don't you think?"

"Not really, because bulimia is all about control—control over your body, your food, your weight. When I used to make myself throw up, *I* was in control. When you have the stomach flu, you are totally out of control of your body. Am I right?"

He nodded slowly and sighed deeply as if he were willing himself not to barf all over the table.

"Oh, honey. I'm gonna eat my dinner and then come right home. I'm not going to the party without you. I wouldn't have any fun."

"Oh, go, go! Then when you come home, you can entertain me with stories of the rich and shallow."

"No. I'm gonna eat and come home. I'll have them wrap your soup to go. By this time tomorrow you'll be all better."

He shook his head wearily. "Whatever you want, sweetie. But you look so great. Just think about going, okay?"

"Okay."

He blew her a kiss and then shuffled out the door.

Ellie ate her quesadilla as the restaurant filled up with festive people in New Year's garb. She ordered the special—grilled chipotle-rubbed tuna served with a pineapple-mango salsa and jicama relish. And then tried to act casual.

Eating alone in a fancy restaurant was not an easy thing to do. But eating alone in a fancy restaurant on New Year's Eve dressed to the nines felt surreal. Is everyone watching me? she wondered. They are. They probably think I've been stood up, she realized. The waiter cleared her dinner plate.

"Thanks." Oh, my God, Ellie realized suddenly, *he* probably thinks Peter and I had some big fight and *that's* why he left.

"On the house," the waiter said as he placed the dulce de leche crepes in front of her.

"Oh! Thank you. That's so sweet!"

He smiled down at her, and Ellie thought she detected a hint of pity in his expression.

"My husband went home sick," she explained, then thought it sounded like a pathetic lie. He looked at her confused.

"Me husband is *muy mal*," she tried again.

"Yes, he ees," the waiter said with malice in his tone.

Shit, did I just say he is very bad or very sick?

"You are buteeful woman." He leaned toward her. "To be left alone on such a night ees not right." His dark eyes looked deep into her.

Oh, my God, he's wants me! she realized. This is too much!

"No, it's just he's sick. Sick. Blah!" Ellie acted out throwing up. "Not *bad* but sick. *Comprende?* Blah! Throw up, barf?" She waited. He looked at her and shook his head. His dark eyes were penetrating her, broadcasting sex across their language barrier. She was speechless.

"I hope you have wonderful New Jeers," he told her, dripping with subtext.

"Oh, you too." She forced herself to look down, breaking the spell. She reached for her purse and started rummaging for her wallet. She was sweating, her skin all tingly and hot. She found her credit card and stood up. They were now face to face, inches apart. He was exactly her size, compact and fit.

"I'll take the check please." She tried to sound all business as she handed him her credit card.

"Right away," he said, but didn't move. There was a slight smile in his eyes, which made him incredibly sexy, but not at all scary.

Is he gonna fuck me right here?

"Excuse me." She squeezed past him and their chests touched briefly. Whoa, she thought as her knees started to buckle. "I have to use the ladies' room." She didn't look back. As she rounded the corner for the bathroom, one of the heels on her sexy new sandals slipped and she almost went down. She caught herself and made it to the sanctuary of the *Baños* without injury.

"You *are* lookin' pretty hot for a forty-year-old mother of two," she told her reflection. The hair was working. The dress showed off her full breasts. And the foundation and under-eye had managed to conceal her dark circles, the result of three years of sleep deprivation. She peed and took out her Malt Shimmer to freshen up her lipstick.

"Ellie, you're just going home, remember? Do *not* put on lipstick just to say good-bye to Enrique Iglesias out there. Uh, uh, uh. That would not be wise." She scrutinized her naked lips, considered her lipstick briefly, then put it back in her purse.

She managed to sign the check without making eye contact with Enrique. As she walked the long stretch past the crowded bar toward the stairs, freedom, and home, she could feel his eyes glued to her ass.

Well, that was pretty fun, she thought as she mounted the steps. Kind of nice to have some young, sexy foreigner want to jump my bones. She stopped at the top of the stairs and put on her coat, resisting the urge to turn and see if he was watching her. Peter'll like this story, she mused. She pushed the door open and walked out onto the snowy sidewalk, feeling triumphant. She scanned the streets for an empty cab . . . none. Just then a taxi pulled up right in front of her, and a group of Gen-Xers, looking all shiny and sparkly, piled out and headed into Zocalo. Ellie grabbed the door handle, about to climb in—but stopped. She bent down and peeked into the basement restaurant. Yep. There he was, watching her. She waved at him. He waved back.

"Happy New Year, handsome," she whispered to the snowy night, then climbed into her cab and headed west.

"Seventy-sixth and Amsterdam," she told the driver as she peered out at the scenery.

The serious East Side, all dressed up for Christmas and covered in sparkling snow, looked stunning and cozy at the same time. The cab moved slowly through the slushy streets, and Ellie watched all the party-goers scramble out of cabs and limos and into fancy buildings flanked with doormen dressed in regal uniforms. They look like they just stepped out of a *New Yorker* cartoon, Ellie thought, feeling once again like a tourist. As the cab traveled toward Fifth Avenue, the Metropolitan Museum of Art glowed huge and stately in the distance.

She pictured the scene she was rushing home to: two sleeping kids and a barfing husband. The cab idled at a red light at Madison.

"Driver!" Ellie called through the opening in the Plexiglas partition. "Make a right here. There's been a change of plans."

Chapter Eighteen

Ellie could see Marco opening the door of another cab when they pulled up to Missy's building. A pasty-looking man with wispy hair in a dinner jacket got out and turned to help his fur-clad date negotiate the snow. Ellie shuddered. *What am I doing here? What am I gonna do at a party where people murder innocent animals without giving it a thought?* She considered staying in the cab and just going home, but felt too silly to change her mind yet *again* in front of the cab driver. *I just hope I don't end up in the elevator with them,* she thought as she shut the cab door behind her.

"Good evening, Ms. Fuller. Happy New Year," Marco said, holding the elevator for her. She entered the elevator and smiled curtly at the animal killers, then stared at the floor. As they got off the elevator into Missy's foyer, the smell of pine hit Ellie and made her smile. A tuxedoed unemployed actor greeted them. Ellie studied him. We've never catered together, thank God. He took everyone's coats in exchange for a plastic coat check number and disappeared.

Missy and Antonio's apartment had been transformed; candles and fresh pine and holly garlands strategically placed throughout looked Christmasy but still tasteful. Someone was playing Mel Tormé's "The Christmas Song" on a piano somewhere. Ellie tried to put on a holiday smile, but her heart was thumping as she scanned the festive group for a familiar face.

The fact that she had carved roast beef at a party very much like this one, in this very apartment, came back to her in spades. I should've gone home, she told herself as she watched the animal murderer and her wispy husband head into the party with ease and confidence. Look at those two, she thought. He's got that timeless preppie thing going with the dinner jacket and she's got that nonsexual generic old money thing happening. That emerald green suit of hers is something my mom would've worn in 1965.

Ellie checked out her own outfit in the foyer mirror. Oh, my God, she thought, I look like a punk Betty Boop. She pulled in her nonexistent stomach, pushed out her full breasts, and strode into the grand, glowing living room with an armor of attitude. A tuxedo-clad man sat at the piano finishing "The Christmas Song." Clusters of gorgeous, polished people chatted and drank as stealth waiters floated through the crowd, anticipating everyone's food and beverage needs. The thumping of her heart seemed to be getting louder as she ventured into the thick of the group. She grabbed a glass of champagne off a passing tray and took a slug. One glass is okay, she told herself, thinking of her nursing boy. The stuff warmed her throat and seemed to slow her heart a tad. She took another slug and scanned the room for—for— For who, Ellie? she asked herself rather harshly. Just who do you expect to see here? If Peter had come you would've known exactly *three* people here. Without him it's two—Missy and Antonio. Yep, that's it. You know the host and hostess, and you are alone in a sea of shiny plastic people with no sex organs.

"Celia, you look marvelous!" The animal murderer, her auburn helmet of hair barely moving, was rushing to embrace a petite blonde in a red-checked taffeta party dress. She wore her hair in an up-do and looked like a paper doll from the fifties. The two women air-kissed and their large, pricey earrings clanged together.

Well, El, you've done it again. Everyone here except you knows the secret handshake.

"We had a marvelous Christmas in Vail this year. You know the Knickerbockers, Cooper and Slim? They've built a place right down the road from us and blah, blah, blah . . ." Mr. Wispy was talking to Celia's bookish husband.

Ellie emptied her champagne glass, took a deep breath, and then marched toward the food table. I can do it, she told herself. I can. I've done it before. I'm a grown woman. I survived bulimia, for God's sake. I can do this! She arrived at the food table, shoved a strawberry in her mouth, and looked around for a likely victim.

Time to mingle!

"I love Gershwin," a voice from behind her said. The piano player had moved on to "Someone to Watch Over Me." Ellie turned to see a tall, gray-haired man, dinner jacketed of course, a damp cocktail napkin wrapped around his glass of champagne.

"Me, too," she said smiling. That was brilliant. "My father was a huge Gershwin fan." Oh, good. Bring up Dad. That's a smart move.

"Mine was too."

"He had this Ella Fitzgerald record *The Gershwin Songbook* or something like that. I knew all the words."

"I just bought that CD," he said enthusiastically.

"Really? God, I should get it. That and *Ella Digs Cole*. That's a great one. Do you know that album?" Wow, this guy seems nice and genuine.

"Love it," he said and thrust his hand at her. "Buzz Albright."

"Hi, Buzz. Nice to meet you." Ellie suppressed a grin. With his big, square jaw and swelled chest he actually looks a little like Buzz Lightyear, Ellie thought. She took his hand and shook it firmly. "I'm Ellie Fuller. Nice to meet an Ella fan." They smiled at each other and watched the piano player for a moment.

"Are you related to the Fullers of Hancock Point—Dee Dee and Ogden?"

"No, no." Actually, she went on in her head, I'm related to Sara and Paul Fuller: The Fullers of the Betty Ford Clinic and San Quentin. "I don't think I have any relatives there. My family's from Michigan." Why are all these WASPs obsessed with this crap? Can't a person just have a conversation about music and then move on to movies, something like that? She smiled at Buzz, wishing she were home with her barfing husband.

"Michigan, where in Michigan? My father-in-law was blah, blah, blah . . ." The white noise in Ellie's head was drowning out whatever he was saying. I gotta get outta here, she thought, as she nodded and smiled sweetly. I'm going to find Missy, tell her about Peter, and split.

". . . He sold the whole thing in the sixties blah, blah, blah . . ." His sweet friendly persona had been replaced by a big puffy important one and Ellie hated him. She was beginning to panic when she saw Antonio's head of dark wavy hair across the room.

"Excuse me, Buzz. I haven't had a chance to say Happy New Year to our host." She gave Buzz another nice, firm handshake. "It was nice talking with you," she said and bee-lined it toward her swarthy host.

Now, where the hell did he go? She wandered into the dining room and saw Gloria heading into the kitchen.

"Gloria!" she called as the kitchen door swung shut behind her.

The kitchen was bright and bustling when Ellie slipped in. Two prep chefs, in their kitchen whites, were filling hors d'oeuvres trays as the waiters filled champagne glasses. Gloria was taking a tray of piping hot mini-empanadas from the oven.

"From your family's secret recipe?" Ellie asked.

"Miss Ellie!" Gloria said as she put down the tray. The two women hugged. "I'll kill you if you tell a soul," Gloria whispered in her ear. Ellie zipped her lips to reassure her friend.

"Happy New Year, Gloria. You have to stop calling me 'Miss Ellie.' It makes me sound like a sitcom character. It's Ellie, okay? Just Ellie."

"Okay, Ellie, Happy New Year. Where is Señor Peter?"

"Home with the stomach flu."

"Oh, no!" Gloria put her hand to her face.

"Yes. Can you believe it? He got sick *during* our New Year's dinner. I can't stay. I have to get home to him."

"Oh, Miss Missy and Señor Antonio will be so disappointed. You can't stay for just a little?"

"No, I really can't. I just dropped in to wish everyone a Happy New Year. Do you know where I can find Missy or Antonio?"

"Ellie? Ellie, is that you?"

Ellie turned to see a small round man in his thirties standing in the doorway. He was wearing a chef's hat and struggling with a huge destroyed cheese platter. The Brie had been stabbed into submission and nothing was left of the chèvre but some powdery mush. Ellie stared at the familiar face.

"Jose! I don't believe it!" Jose put the platter down and leaped to Ellie's side.

"Look at you!" he said, taking her hands and giving her the once-over. "I love the hair." He squeezed her tight.

"Look at *you*! Are you still working for Perfect Party People?"

"Hey, I'm head chef now," he told her, tapping his hat.

"That's great!"

"You must be doing pretty good yourself. I heard you got married."

"Two kids."

"No!"

"Yes. I'm a wife and a mother. Can you believe it?"

"Good for you. How's it feel to be on the other side of the party?"

"You have no idea," Ellie said. "If I have to talk to one more Buzz or Buffy or Bitsy I think I might have to put a gun to my head."

Jose laughed. "New hair, new life, but you're still funny."

"Oh, Gloria, this is my friend Jose. We used to work together, in another life. Jose, Gloria."

"Oh, we're old friends," Gloria said. "Jose is in charge of all our parties."

He put his arm around Gloria. "Who's in charge?"

Gloria smiled and shook her head.

"Gloria, now you know that *you* run everything and everyone in this house. Including me."

The kitchen door swung open and a pretty young waiter came in carrying an empty silver tray.

"I need more Thai shrimp. They're devouring them. It's like *Lord of the Flies* out there." Jose took a large sheet of steaming shrimp from the oven and placed it on the counter as a tall chiseled waiter pushed through the door with yet another empty tray.

"More empanadas," he told the group.

Jose was artfully arranging the hot shrimp on the first tray with his bare hands, his fingers immune to the heat after years of abuse. "Gloria, are those empanadas ready? Send them out."

As Gloria started filling tray number two with her mini-empanadas, Ellie took the tired-looking garnish off the tray and replaced it with some fresh dill and radicchio from a pile on a nearby chopping board.

"Miss Ellie, you don't have to . . ."

"Gloria, I'm happy. I like being a worker in the kitchen; I always have. If you make me go back out there I'm going home." She stopped and waited for a response. Gloria and Jose exchanged a look, then shrugged their shoulders. "Thank you," Ellie told them as she took the empty saucer off the now-full shrimp tray and pointed to a metal bowl full of a dark brown sauce.

"For the shrimp?"

Jose nodded, too busy to talk. Ellie cleaned off the saucer, filled it, and put it back on the tray. Ellie, Jose, and Gloria worked quickly and silently, redressing and filling the trays. In less than a minute, the two waiters were sent back into the fray, their silver trays armed and ready.

"We're a heck of a team," Jose said as he began to rebuild the pathetic cheese tray.

"This is fun. I haven't done this in years," Ellie said.

"We used to work a lot of parties together in the old days," Jose said. "In fact, didn't you work Missy and Antonio—"

Ellie gave Jose a quick knee in the butt. He stopped and looked at her.

"Ix-nay on issy-May's arty-pay in front of oria-Glay," she said under her breath, hoping to God he knew Pig Latin. She looked at Gloria, who was at the fridge taking out more empanadas, out of the corner of her eye; she seemed unaware of their little deception.

Ellie joined Jose at the cheese platter and began to freshen up the garnish—off with the half-eaten strawberries and the trampled-on dill. She held up a grape stem that had been picked clean by guests.

"Grapes?" she asked.

"Fridge."

"I got it," Gloria said, handing her a large glass bowl brimming with fresh, plump bunches of grapes.

I am good at this, Ellie thought as she arranged the grapes on the platter. All thoughts of finding Missy or Antonio had vanished from her mind. Worries over her children and her sick husband were no longer swimming restlessly in her brain. No, she was focused on her latest project—the cheese platter—and she was content.

"Ellie, what the heck are you doing?"

Ellie looked up to see Missy standing in the kitchen doorway, looking gorgeous. One hand was holding the swinging door open; the other hand placed firmly on the hip of a deep red, raw silk blouse.

As always, she's looking classy and elegant, Ellie thought, and I'm dressed like a tart. I give up.

All movement stopped. The three cohorts glanced at each other surreptitiously. Ellie smiled weakly and popped a stray grape in her mouth.

"I came in here looking for you and they looked a little swamped. So I thought I'd . . ."

"Sweetie—" Missy let the door fly "—I didn't invite you to my party so you could help in the kitchen."

Black pants and flats, why didn't I wear black pants and flats? Ellie chided herself as Missy headed toward her. Look at her, with the ponytail at the nape of her neck. It's understated, classic. Ellie touched her hair self-consciously. Of course, short of a wig, there's nothing I could've done with *this*. Just then Missy put her arms around her slutty friend and gave her a kiss on the cheek.

"I'm so glad you're here. You look smashing in that dress," she whispered in Ellie's ear.

"Thanks," Ellie whispered back. "You look stunning. I love the red lipstick."

"I was inspired by you."

"Really?"

"Yes. I thought of you when I bought it. I thought, Ellie would wear this color and I'd love it. So . . ." Missy winked at her friend and then turned to Jose.

"This cheese platter is gorgeous, Jose. You are an artist," she said, shifting into her hostess persona. "I guess you've met my best friend."

Ellie gave Jose the hairy eyeball in the hope that he wouldn't blow her cover.

"We've met," was all he said.

"Has she already recruited you for *her* next party?"

Jose was about to say God knows what when Ellie jumped in. "As a matter of fact, he's going to hire me and Gloria for *his* next party."

Gloria and Jose laughed and Missy joined in.

"I told Miss Ellie not to help but . . ."

"You don't have to tell me, Gloria. She just wouldn't listen, is that right?"

"That's right," Gloria and Jose said in unison.

"Well, I'm going to steal her away from you two," Missy called over her shoulder as the two women pushed through the door and back into the sparkling party.

"Antonio has been asking and asking about you and Peter. Where *is* that handsome husband of yours?" Missy was still holding Ellie's shoulders firmly and guiding her to some unknown destination.

"Peter's sick."

Missy stopped and faced her. "What?"

"Remember that flu the kids had?"

"Oh, the poor thing. Well, I'm glad *you* came." She hooked her arm through Ellie's and continued on.

"Listen, Missy, I can't stay. I just dropped by to wish you and Antonio a Happy New Year, and then I really have to get back to Peter and the children." She got it all out quickly before Missy could object.

"Of course, dear. Just give Tony a quick New Year's kiss and then I'll have Marco hail you a cab." They were heading down the hallway, but not toward the bedrooms. Ellie realized that even though she'd been in this apartment a dozen times, there were still parts of it she'd never seen. Where the heck is she taking me? To some secret passageway?

When they arrived at a heavy wooden door, stained a deep brown, Missy stopped, took Ellie's hand, and gave her a mischievous grin. She grasped the brass doorknob, slipped a key in the lock, and turned it slowly.

A key? Jesus, what's up, Ellie wondered? The steamy morning of inner thighs and one perfect breast came back to her in an instant. She felt adrenaline rush into her chest. Now what the hell am I getting into? When the door opened, the smell of pot hit her smack in the face. Here we go again, she thought. And Peter's gonna miss it.

The women slipped through the doorway, Missy closed the door silently behind them, and locked it. The smoke-filled room was dimly lit, and "Riders on the Storm" by The Doors was playing from some unseen stereo.

Where am I, and what decade is it? Ellie thought. The dank smell of marijuana and Jim Morrison's woeful voice in a room where she could barely see had transported her. She was tempted to look down and see if hip-hugger bell-bottoms and a ribbed poor boy had magically replaced her cocktail dress.

"We would ride all day—from sunrise to sunset—driving the cattle." Ellie followed the sound of Antonio's deep accented voice to find her host holding court at one end of the smoky room. When Ellie saw his handsome face glowing in the firelight, her heart quickened. On a cluster of dark leather furniture surrounding a white marble fireplace, a group of six guests (very special guests, Ellie was thinking) were huddled together, hanging on his every word.

"At night, totally exhausted, we would make camp." He held a big fat joint in his right hand; it drew orange lines in the air as he gestured. "Then—" he paused for dramatic purposes "—one of the gauchos would make Carbona Cariolla—a traditional Argentinean stew with peaches and apricots, so delicious!—over an open fire."

Missy nudged Ellie and rolled her eyes, as if to say, He's at it again. Ellie smiled.

"Then the gauchos would tell stories about cattle ranching in the old days. I was only a boy, fourteen or fifteen. It was magical. When the last story had been told and the fire was just an orange glow on the pampas, I would crawl into my bedroll, full and happy, and fall asleep under the stars." He stopped and took a long deep hit on the joint. His stoned audience was transfixed, waiting for more.

"And then you met a girl, am I right?" Every head in the group turned in unison to Missy. "An American girl?"

"Darling!" Antonio opened his arms, calling his wife to him. "Yes. I met a long-legged beautiful American witch."

The potheads laughed.

"A witch?" Missy said, settling into his lap. Antonio held the joint to her lips and she took a ravenous hit.

Will I ever *get* this woman, Ellie wondered? Is she Missy Hanover the preppie heiress without a vagina, or Missy Hanover—witch, seductress, pothead?

"Of course she was a witch. How else could you explain that this, this—girl of thirteen could make the meanest stallion in my father's stable as sweet as a little rabbit?"

What a ham, Ellie thought, enjoying every moment.

The cluster of preppie potheads continued to be held firmly in his sway.

"And of course *I* met an evil Argentinean sorcerer," Missy told her guests.

"Who was a sorcerer?" Antonio asked in mock indignation.

"Well—" Missy had taken on Antonio's grand style of speaking. "How else could you explain how this—boy of fifteen could turn a nice bright American girl into a babbling, lovesick dope." She kissed him on the nose.

"That's so cu-u-u-u-te!" A blond-haired dandy with bloodshot eyes and a bow tie cooed.

"Riders on the Storm" ended as Missy whispered something to Antonio. "Nonsense! She can't leave."

Uh-oh, Ellie thought, how am I gonna get out of this one? But in her heart she was very flattered and not completely sure she really *wanted* to get out of this one. The bass strains of "L.A. Woman" filled the library as Missy climbed off of Antonio's lap and the two stood up.

"Excuse us," Missy told the group as she took the joint from Antonio and handed it to the blond boy.

"Ellie, darling." Antonio was suddenly by her side. He smelled smoky and earthy as he enveloped her with his strong arms. "You mustn't leave us," he whispered in her ear. She shivered.

"Antonio, Peter's sick." Ellie was struggling to stay focused, serious. She wriggled against his grip to face him. "How can I leave my sick husband alone on New Year's?"

"Ellie, my sweet, thoughtful girl." He paused and looked up to the ceiling, searching for—what? Inspiration? He had the slow, measured movements of someone as high as a kite that was struggling to maintain. It made Ellie giggle inside. "Peter is a man . . ."

"Yeah, I had kind of figured that out," Ellie teased.

He laughed big and loud. "I love this girl," he told the room as he hugged her again. "What I am trying to tell you is this: when a man is sick he does not *like* a fuss. He does not want a fuss. He wants—he *needs* to be alone. I know the woman always wants the pillows fluffed and the flowers—lots of attention. Men do not. When I was a boy . . ."

Antonio began to wax philosophically about men and their needs, and Ellie tried to listen. She did. But her mind began to wander.

Those eyes of his—uh, uh, uh—I bet women throw themselves at him all the time.

"The men in my country blah, blah, blah . . ."

Should I let him talk me into staying? Do I want to stay? It's not like I don't *want* to stay. God knows I've been looking forward to this thing since Missy mentioned it. Peter doesn't care if I come home, does he? Maybe I should call him.

"When Harper was born, Missy needed me to blah, blah, blah . . ."

Its not like I don't *like* Missy and Antonio. I do. I mean, he's a bit much with all his macho bravado, but he *is* sweet. And of course I like Missy.

"I think when God made man blah, blah, blah . . ."

She nodded and smiled at Antonio, not hearing a word that he was saying. He didn't seem to notice. Boy, if I could take a coupla hits on that joint I'd stay in a second, Ellie thought. Just the thought of getting high gave her a little rush. Uh-uh, El, don't you dare. You can't get stoned and keep your abstinence.

Jesus Christ! What I'd give to be normal. Just to be able to smoke a joint now and then. Is that too much to ask for, God?

"New Year's Eve 2000, the true beginning of the new millennium, will never come again and Missy and I . . ." Antonio put his arm around his wife and pulled her in close, ". . . would love for you to stay and share it with us."

"Stay!" someone called. Ellie turned to see it was Mr. Wispy from the elevator. Who knew, she thought. The blond, bloodshot one hoped off a leather ottoman and headed toward Ellie, waving the joint at her.

"Come on. Stay. Have a couple of hits, a little champagne, it's New Year's." He put his arm around Ellie and held the joint under her nose.

"I feel like I'm in one of those movies that they showed in science class in junior high about the dangers of drugs and peer pressure," Ellie told the group.

Blondie Boy laughed and waggled the drug at her like an evil dealer. The smell of pot was overwhelming; she stared at the glowing roach.

"Now, I know from that movie that if I take a puff on this marijuana cigarette . . ." She took the roach from him and held it high in the air. ". . . that I will be immediately hooked. And in a very short time I will move on to heroin, become a junkie, and lose everything in my life that matters to me."

Everyone laughed.

Ellie looked at the roach again, dreaming about what it had to offer.

Ellie had been thirteen when her cousin Jack had first turned her on to pot and its magic. That first summer, she was pretty sure that she and Jack had gotten stoned *every day*. They would meet at six-thirty, when Ellie got back from ballet and Jack got home from his job selling bell-bottoms at Jeans West, and repeat a daily ritual. They would climb into the rafters of Ellie's garage, roll six joints, and smoke them *all*. Down they would climb, giggling and sputtering, then sneak past Sara (also anesthetized) on the sofa and steal into the safety of Ellie's bedroom. They'd always head straight for the stereo; choosing the perfect album was part of the ritual. Which album would complement the mood of the high that they had achieved that day? Whether it was The Who, Joni Mitchell, or Crosby, Stills, and Nash, it always seemed to be a perfect fit.

That summer of pot and music changed the course of Ellie's life. Pot changed it. Pot took the harsh glare off of her life and replaced it with a soft easy light that soothed her at every turn. It introduced her to the comfort of food and stopped her from caring. Caring whether Sara was sloshed or not, caring whether she came to Ellie's dance recitals or not, caring that her only father was away in jail. She had Jack, she had dance, she had music, and she had pot. She was invincible.

But that was a long time ago, Ellie thought as she studied the glowing roach in her hand, a different world with different rules.

"No thanks. I really have to go. My husband's . . ." She tried to hand the drug back to Blondie Boy. He waved it away.

"Aw, c'mon, have some fun," Celia, the one in the red-and-white-checked dress called from the sofa.

Ellie looked around. All eyes were focused on her. She felt a chill. The dark room, the pre-war apartment, the shadowy faces—another scene from *Rosemary's Baby* sprung to mind.

"Don't be a spoilsport," a bone-thin woman in a strapless velvet dress with a Locust Valley accent called from the sidelines.

Now I'm gonna seem square next to some preppie bitch who looks like a Q-Tip wrapped in velvet? She surveyed the group of hopeful faces, the WASPy elite potheads.

What would Emily Post suggest in this situation? Do I refuse the drugs and run the risk of seeming ungracious? Or do I take a couple of hits, just to be sociable, and put my abstinence and the health of my child in jeopardy? Her survey of the room ended on Antonio's smiling face. He winked at her.

She winked back, put the roach to her lips, and inhaled long and hard. Her lungs burned; her eyes began to water. She struggled to keep from coughing out all the precious smoke so it could release its magic into her bloodstream, then she exhaled.

"I guess I'm staying."

Chapter Nineteen

Ellie drifted back into the party. Two hits of Antonio's superpot did the trick; she was now in the soft, easy light. She was past caring, above and beyond it. No more caring about accessories or summer homes or the secret handshake. No. She floated back into the WASP-infested waters without fear. She was invincible once again.

Once the drugs had kicked in, the idea of calling Peter was immediately forgotten. She was engrossed in the task at hand—partying. The old paranoia that can come with being high was nowhere to be seen. She moved effortlessly in and out of rooms and conversations and nibbled on countless hors d'oeuvres passed by faceless waiters. Then she wandered back into the living room, where she saw Miss Q-Tip (Allison Beaumont), clearly suffering from a bad case of the munchies, hunched over the food table. When Ellie arrived at her side, Allison was piling a spoonful of caviar on top of a slab of chèvre that had been spread onto a slice of strawberry that rested on a piece of flat bread.

"That's a heck of a combo," Ellie whispered to her fellow library veteran.

"You *have* to taste it." Allison had the concoction poised at Ellie's mouth before she could refuse. "Trust me."

Ellie took a reluctant bite. "Oh, my God!" She chewed and moaned her way through the bite. "This is unbelievable!" She licked her lips and ran her tongue across her teeth, savoring every last bit.

"Isn't it fantastic the way the flavors and textures almost dance in your mouth? I don't know what made me do it but I just . . ." Allison paused and seemed to go somewhere else for a moment. ". . . walked up to the table and put those ingredients together like I was driven to do it." She took a bite, chewing slowly, reverently.

She is on another planet, Ellie realized. I only had *two* hits and I'm flying. Everybody else in that room smoked an *entire* joint.

"Ellie! There you are!" Ellie and Allison turned to see Missy floating toward them. She had a glass of champagne in each hand and was flanked by the chiseled waiter.

"It's almost midnight." She handed Allison a glass of champagne.

"No!" Ellie looked at her watch, stunned. It was quarter to. A pang of fear and guilt shot through her. The kids, Peter, what have I done? What am I doing here? The reality that she had *done* something else, *been* someone else besides a mother and wife for—well, for hours—just floored her.

"Midnight already?" Allison asked as she crammed the last of her treat into her mouth.

"Yes, already. And everyone *must* have champagne to bring in the New Year. Allison, can I steal Ellie from you?"

"Of course." Allison waved the two women away, still chewing.

"Bulimic," Missy whispered to Ellie as the two women, with Mr. Chiseled in tow, zigzagged through the party, giving champagne to all.

"Really!" Ellie felt a pit open in her stomach.

"Yes. For years, poor thing. Been to all the fancy eating disorder clinics."
"And?"

Missy just shook her head as she took two more glasses of champagne from Mr. Chiseled and handed them to an elegant-looking older couple standing next to the fireplace.

Ellie glanced over her shoulder at Allison. She was still glued to the food table, building a new masterpiece with God knows what. Yep, she's got the look, Ellie realized. Beneath Allison's paper doll perfection, Ellie could see the sallow complexion, the deep purple circles under the eyes, the vacant stare. I should've spotted it. She had a moment of wanting to save her. Of wanting to go back and give her an OA meeting list. For years, Ellie had carried an extra one in her purse. Not anymore.

"Ten minutes and counting," Missy kept repeating as she handed out supplies. By the time they'd gotten the precious elixir to all the stragglers, it was four minutes to midnight.

Four minutes, Ellie thought, studying her watch. She felt a chill run through her. I don't want to spend New Year's without Peter, she realized as she looked around the room feeling lost.

Missy had stopped to chat with the some Junior League poster girl.

Ellie watched her perfect friend do her hostess thing with her usual style and grace. Missy touched Miss Junior League on the arm and laughed at something she said. Miss Junior League beamed with delight.

She makes everyone feel special, Ellie thought. That what's so special about *her*. She makes everyone think that she's your best friend.

Bong!

A kettledrum of recognition vibrated deep in Ellie's chest. Oh, my God! It's all just part of her shtick. I'm not her best friend. I'm not special to her. What the hell am I doing here?

The soft easy light of the pot had turned harsh and ugly on one little thought. Was it paranoia or a revelation? Ellie couldn't be sure. A thin veil of sweat now covered her body.

"Farewell 2000," someone called.

"It's almost midnight?" a startled voice asked.

Shit, midnight! Ellie looked at her watch—three minutes and counting. And midnight means kissing. Oh, God! She had a vivid flashback of a pre-Peter New Year's party without a date. She had ended up French kissing some unshaven, self-absorbed screenwriter whom she happened to be standing next to when midnight had struck.

I have to get out of here, she thought as she scanned the scene for a possible escape route. Missy was chatting on with Miss Junior League. Ellie turned and racewalked away from her and the party—past the little guest bathroom, down the hall, past the family photos that lined the wall, past Mason's room and Harper's, all the way to the end of the hall.

Once she was inside the master bedroom, the quiet darkness was comforting. Ellie breathed a sigh of relief, walked to the mammoth windows, and gazed out at Central Park. It was a study in white, gray, and silver, with clusters of people braving the cold here and there; some of them carried sparklers that glowed brilliantly against the monochromatic park.

"Unbelievable," she whispered to the empty room. Her breath made a little circle of steam on the glass.

"Two minutes, everyone! Two minutes to go!" a faint voice announced. The din of the party rose slightly.

Ellie looked beyond the park and stared lovingly at the West Side. There's the Dakota; that's Seventy-second Street. She counted north four blocks to Seventy-sixth Street. In her mind she walked the two crosstown blocks to the apartment building where her family was.

"Happy New Year, Peter," she whispered into the glass. "Sleep tight, my sweet babies." She kissed the window, leaving her lip marks in the circle of frost.

"Ellie?"

She turned to see Missy's silhouette in the doorway.

"Hi." Missy closed the door behind her and seemed to disappear.

"It's almost midnight," she whispered to the dark room as her tall dusky form crossed the unlit room. "I didn't know where you'd gone." She held Ellie's arm gently when she reached her.

Just like with Miss Junior League, Ellie thought cynically. "I just needed a break," she said, turning back to study the park.

"But it's almost midnight," Missy said again, stepping closer.

"One minute and counting!" the same faint voice called. The din rose again.

"Midnight's a little tricky when you're without a date on New Year's."

"Why?"

"It's the kissing thing, the kissing at midnight. New Year's is the one holiday where you *must* have a date. I know women who've put off breaking up with their boyfriends for *months* just to avoid experiencing this.

"Dicky Reinhardt's stag."

"The blond frat boy?"

Missy nodded. "I'm sure he'd jump at the chance to kiss you at midnight."

"No, no, no, you're missing the point. I'm not worried that no one would want to kiss *me*. There's no one out there that *I* want to kiss."

"Got it."

"Good."

"Let's just stay here then. I'll be your date."

"*Ten, nine, eight.*"

Missy put her arm around Ellie, and the two women stood side by side looking out at the last few moments of 2000.

"*Seven, six, five.*"

"I'm glad you're here," Missy said, giving Ellie's shoulders a squeeze, eyes steady on the park.

"*Three, two . . .*"

"Me, too," Ellie said, putting her arm around her friend.

"*ONE!*" There were shouts and horns from the party, from the street, from the park.

"Happy New Year," Missy whispered in Ellie's ear, then kissed her on the cheek. Her moist lips seemed to rest there forever.

Oh, my God, not again, Ellie thought. But her cunt said yes.

"Happy New Year," Ellie said, focusing on the West Side, not moving an inch.

Do I have to kiss her back? she wondered. Do I want to? This is another Emily Post moment. What *is* the protocol when you suspect that your hostess is coming on to you? Do you kiss her back, just to be polite, and end up tousled in the bedcovers? Or do you stand still as a statue and hope she goes away?

"Don't you want to be my date?" Missy asked, holding Ellie's shoulder tightly.

"Uh, of course—sure. Hey, why not." Ellie puffed out an embarrassed laugh, then looked Missy in the eyes for the first time. She is so beautiful, Ellie thought. And so poised, as always.

Missy was just waiting . . . calmly . . . innocently, so it seemed.

Just kiss her on the cheek, El. What's the big deal? Missy smiled. Ellie giggled, put her hand on Missy's shoulder, pushed onto her tiptoes, and aimed for her cheek. Missy turned her head and intercepted. Ellie's lips landed squarely on Missy's. Oh, Jesus! Ellie swooned. She dug her nails into Missy's shoulder to keep from collapsing. She was waiting, ready for Missy's lips to part, dying to feel her tongue in her mouth. The pot seemed to kick in again and she felt transported to another plane. Her cunt was instantly aching for her friend, for her New Year's date. Then Missy pulled away.

"Oh, I almost forgot," Missy said as if they had been chatting on the phone about the latest George Clooney movie. "I have a surprise for you." She stepped away from the window. "Close your eyes."

"What?" Ellie was lost, reeling.

"Close your eyes."

Ellie followed orders. She heard some clothes rustling and—Was that a zipper?

"Okay, open," Missy instructed.

Ellie opened her eyes, and there stood Missy, holding her blouse up with one hand and her cute little capri pants down with the other. She was smiling proudly as she showed off her stomach to Ellie and all of Central Park.

"What?"

"Look!" Missy pointed to her navel. Ellie leaned in so she could see in the dim light. "What do you think?"

"Oh, my God. I don't believe it." Missy Hanover had a brand-new navel ring in her freshly pierced belly button. A dead ringer (no pun intended) for the one Ellie wore.

"Isn't it great? I just love it."

"Missy! You wild woman."

"You were my inspiration," Missy said, grabbing Ellie and hugging her tightly. Ellie hugged her back, thinking of Missy's naked belly pressing against her.

"Missy?" Antonio's voice came faintly from the hallway. Ellie started to pull away from her friend.

"Shhh. Wait," Missy said ever so softly in Ellie's ear as her arms tightened around her. "Quiet." The two women stopped and waited.

"Missy? It's midnight." His voice sounded closer.

"Come," Missy whispered, taking Ellie by the hand and guiding her to the ground next to the bed. Ellie felt as if she was in some forties movie. They were Ingrid Bergman and Joan Fontaine, sisters perhaps, running for their lives, hiding from the Nazis.

"Missy?" They could now hear Antonio's footsteps tapping on the wooden floor. "Where in the world could she have gone?" He was right outside the door. The two women lay side by side on the Oriental rug next to the bed. They were staring into one another's shadowy faces, wide eyed, waiting. They heard the doorknob turn. Missy put her index finger to her lips and made the "shhh" sign. She smiled as if they were playing a joke on Antonio. Ellie smiled back, heart pounding, totally into the game. The door opened and a yellow light spread through the room.

"Missy? Are you in here?" He stepped into the room.

The women's eyes were locked together.

"I can't even kiss my own wife on New Year's Eve," Antonio muttered to himself.

Ellie felt a giggle start to rise up inside her. She grinned and hunched her shoulders. Missy put her hand over Ellie's mouth and gave her a *don't you dare* look. But Ellie could feel the giggle growing in her belly, her chest. Go, Antonio, go! She screamed in her head. Go away! She clenched her jaw to try and get a grip. Missy's hand was still guarding her mouth.

As if he had heard Ellie's silent pleas, Antonio turned, stepped out of the room, and closed the door behind him. The two fugitives didn't even breathe till they heard the sound of his footsteps fading down the hallway. Then Ellie allowed herself a tiny giggle.

"Can't a man kiss his wife on New Year's Eve?" Missy whispered an imitation of her frustrated husband.

Ellie laughed. "He *is* dear, though, searching for you."

"*You* are dear," Missy said, holding Ellie's face in her hands and studying her. She kissed Ellie gently on the lips. "I want *you* to be my New Year's date." She kissed her again, longer, parting her lips this time. "Always." And again. And Ellie was ready. She was already gone, captured by the spell of Missy's touch and adoration. She met Missy's wonderful lips, wanting them, wanting her. This time Missy's mouth was open, and her tongue slipped into Ellie's mouth easily, sweetly even. Ellie's tongue met hers and they danced around each other. Their bodies inched closer, like magnets.

This is—this is—Ellie's brain struggled to finish the thought. But she was deep inside Missy now, in her heart, her mouth. She had gotten on the roller coaster and there was nothing to do but hold on tight and wait for the end of the ride. She felt aroused in every part of her body, not just her vagina. Aroused, but safe too, comforted. Never had Ellie experienced anything so erotic and so sweet at the same time. She felt the firm touch of Missy's hand on her thigh.

"I've been dreaming of touching you for so long," Missy said between kisses.

You have? Ellie wondered.

Missy's hand traveled slowly, deliciously, up Ellie's thigh. When it reached the lace top of Ellie's stocking, Missy stopped kissing and looked at her.

"I should've known," she said, smiling, then slipped a finger under the lace and traced a circle around to the back of Ellie's thigh. Ellie reached up for Missy and pulled her mouth back onto hers. Missy's hand abandoned Ellie's lace and traveled up over her hip and across to her stomach.

Ellie rolled onto her back. Missy explored Ellie's stomach for what seemed like an eternity. Ellie's pussy was pulsing now, jumping and flinching with every caress. But there was no rush, no frantic need for her to move on to the next thing, the next phase of the lovemaking.

"And I've dreamed of these," Missy said as she passed her fingertips over the mound of Ellie's breast. Her nipples tingled as the milk let down, anticipating Angus's mouth. Ellie lifted her hips and hiked her dress up to her chest. Missy climbed onto her knees and was poised next to her friend, leaning over her. Ellie unsnapped her nursing bra—pop! pop!—and like a party trick unleashed her full, white, veiny bosom in an instant.

"They're beautiful," Missy whispered and she began stroking them in that sweet erotic way—softly, reverently. Ellie closed her eyes and rode the roller coaster, up and down, turning, twisting. Then Missy's lips were on hers again and they kissed longer, deeper, and not so sweetly. Missy's breath was coming faster and harder, her kisses more urgent. And Ellie was with her breath for breath. Missy grabbed one of Ellie's idle hands and—

Oh, my God, she thought, when Missy placed Ellie's hand smack on her naked tit. There it is, that breast, that perfect breast. They were kissing and fondling, fondling and kissing. The symmetry of it, Ellie thought, it's exquisite—my breasts, her breasts, our breasts.

She was speeding on the roller coaster now, zooming down, down, down. . . .

When Ellie regained consciousness—if consciousness can be defined as the ability to have a conscious thought—she was thinking, how does she do that? Oh, my God, how does she do that?

They were still on the floor of the bedroom, but Ellie was stripped down to her stockings and garter belt and Missy was between her legs. She was caressing Ellie's labia with her lips and just skimming her clit every now and then with her tongue. One hand was stroking Ellie's inner thighs, worshipping them, really. Ellie was on the last leg of the ride, climbing up a long, slow, easy hill. Missy was getting her to the top with every lick and flick and stroke and caress. Ellie rode up, up, up the hill. Flick and lick and touch and—

"Oh, God!"

And up, up, up, and stroke and skim and flick and . . .

"Oh, God!"

Flickflickflick—she was at the top, yes, the very top, so high up, so high—and flickflickflick—her whole body quivered and paused and wavered—flickflickflick—for the longest moment—and—then—she— *sailed!*

"OOOHHH!!!"

Not down, but out—out and away on the strong, swift wind of her orgasm. Her pussy opening and opening, wider and fuller and juicier. And Missy was there, inside her, it seemed, licking her perfectly.

So sweet, Ellie thought as she sailed off, her pussy leading the way— out and up to another place, a deeper wider, wilder place than she had ever been.

Then the wind passed, and Ellie floated back down to earth, back down to the floor, back down to Missy and Antonio's bedroom, back to New Year's Eve. Missy emerged from Ellie's crotch and kissed her on the cheek, then put her head on her shoulder. And the two lovers breathed together in the big, quiet bedroom.

Ellie stared out at the cloudy night sky. At the bottom of the window, she could see the tips of the buildings from the West Side. Tears spilled onto her cheeks, and she struggled not to let her body heave while she cried silently at what she had just lost.

They dressed in silence, then Missy stole out for a moment and returned with Ellie's coat.

When they ventured from the bedroom, the whole party had moved into the living room for a sing-along. As Missy escorted Ellie to the elevator, they could hear "Night and Day" being mangled by the drunken crowd. Missy took Ellie's head in her hands and planted one more long wonderful kiss on her lips. Then Ellie slipped into the elevator and pressed L. She waved silently as the doors closed. Missy blew a final kiss.

Marco scored a cab like magic. Once inside, Ellie was craving a cigarette. I don't know why I ever quit, she thought as they passed the Metropolitan Museum heading down Fifth. The cab turned west on Seventy-ninth Street and a flash of Ellie's dark, quiet apartment sprung into her head.

I hope Peter's asleep, she thought. The idea that, thanks to the stomach flu, he could still be awake at 1 A.M. shot fear right through her. She stared out the window blindly at the snow-covered park.

Jesus, all I did tonight was eat, she thought. How many of those crab cake things did I eat, and those shrimp, and empanadas? I must've eaten a million calories. And all that cheese . . .

By the time the cab exited the park and headed north on Central Park West, Ellie was deep into her calculations:

Eight, maybe nine of those little crab cakes, about 75 calories each. That's—Jesus, that alone is almost 700 calories. Okay, and the shrimp, about ten of those. They're, what, 80 calories each? That's another 800 calories right there.

When the cab pulled up in front of Ellie's building, she had reached a grand total of 3,680 calories. She paid the driver and entered the building knowing what she had to do.

The apartment was quiet and dark, thank God, when she eased the front door open. She shut it without a sound and slipped off her strappy sandals. The sofa bed was open in the living room, and Ellie could see a faceless form under the quilt. She padded silently and quickly to the kids' bathroom.

Once inside with the door closed, she lunged for the toilet and jammed three fingers down her throat. All the crap from the evening came rushing up and spilled out of her, splashing into the toilet. She flushed and watched the 3,680-plus calories disappear down the drain.

Like it never happened, she thought. Her temples pounded and she was sweating as she shoved her fingers down again, deeper this time, and managed to bring up a little more, perhaps some of her dinner. She was panting, eyes closed with her head deep in the bowl, spitting and gasping—

"Ellie!" Peter's voice filled the bathroom.

Oh, my fucking God! I'm caught! She looked up into his concerned eyes.

"Peter, I—" She was about to blurt out a confession and promises of "never again" when he cut her off.

"Honey, you're sick. I'm so sorry. I thought through some miracle you weren't going to get it." He leaned down and helped her to her feet. "It doesn't last long. I'm already through the worst of it."

"Oh," she managed to say as she rinsed out her mouth and washed her hands. He took her by the arm and led her into the living room.

"The kids are in our bed with Bibi. I'll get you some pj's then make you some ginger tea."

"Peter, that's crazy. You're sick, too."

"No, I'm fine. I haven't thrown up for over two hours. I think that part of it is over." And he was gone.

Ellie—feeling somewhat detached, thanks to the pot and the purging—undressed and stashed her soiled undies in the hamper in the kids' bathroom.

"Here." He handed her some flannel pajamas, then headed to the kitchen.

"Thanks."

By the time she got under the covers, she was shivering. Maybe I *am* sick, she told herself. Her stomach, empty as a drum, was gnawing at her. It felt cozy and familiar, like an old friend.

The events of the evening were safely at bay, pushed away by a light-headed detached feeling. The consequences of those events were nonexistent, for the moment. She closed her eyes, waiting to drift off. She heard the click of the kitchen light and Peter's footsteps in the hall. She opened one eye a slit to peek at him. He stood in the glow from the hallway light, holding a steaming mug.

"Honey?"

She closed her eye.

"Honey, I got your tea."

She heard him cross the room.

"Are you sleeping?"

She didn't move.

"Wow, that was quick," he said, and she heard the tap of the mug being set on the side table. He crawled into bed behind her. "Good night, sweetie," he whispered, barely audible. "Happy New Year. I love you," and she felt his lips on her neck.

Chapter Twenty

T hat's not how Mommy does it." Ahnika's whining voice pierced the veil of Ellie's foggy sleep.

"Well, Mommy's still sleeping because she's sick and this is how Daddy does it." Peter's tone was exasperation covered by a thin, taut layer of patience.

"Daddy! Ow! My finger!"

"Ahnika, if you could just—where's your thumb? Don't you have any mittens?"

Ellie slit one eye and she could see Peter's back as he bent over the double stroller in the hallway. They're going out, she thought. Thank God!

"I want my gloves! Mommy always lets me wear my gloves." The sound of tears was creeping into her voice.

"I didn't say you *couldn't* wear the gloves. You can wear the gloves."

Ellie stayed still as a stone, wishing them out the door. Her head was heavy from the pot and the champagne. Her throat ached from the assault of her fingers. Her stomach twisted, longing for food.

She had slept like a rock until Angus had woken up starving at about 6 A.M. Peter—already up, of course—had brought him to her. She had been nursing her boy when Ahnika had come toddling down the hall moments later, and the three of them had snuggled back to sleep in the big sofa bed.

"I don't know why your mother—grumble, grumble—for a child who's not even three."

Because she *wanted* fucking gloves asshole! Ellie shot back in her head. And she's the most headstrong child on the planet.

"Daddy, it's not right!" Tears creeping in again.

"Honey, please wear the mittens. We'll get you a treat on the way to the park."

"Aaahhh!"

"Jesus Christ! Bibi, can you help me out here?"

Ellie closed her eye and heard Peter walk into the kitchen. It took all of her strength to keep from jumping up, putting the fucking gloves on Ahnika, and getting all of them out the door!

"Here sweetie, let Bibi help." Bibi's lilting voice calmed Ahnika immediately. "Hey, where's that thumb? Where's that crazy thumb of yours? Did you eat it?"

Ahnika giggled.

They are taking *for—ev—er* to get ready, Ellie screamed inside her head.

After endless negotiations about mittens and scarves and hats she finally heard the front lock click, the swish of the door as it opened, then another click as it was locked.

I'm free, Ellie thought as she sat up and looked around the apartment. She got up and turned on the stereo, something she hadn't done in months. She put "Court and Spark" in the CD player and pressed *play*. Joni Mitchell's clear strong voice filled the apartment and sent Ellie into an immediate spasm of nonspecific nostalgia.

She cranked it up and sang along as she headed to the kitchen for some coffee.

"Help me, I think I'm falling in love again," Joni sang. A note on the refrigerator said:

El—

Gone sledding and to the museum. Will try to keep them out so you can get some rest. See you around 1:00. Feel better.

Love you! P

P.S. Happy New Year!
P.P.S. Sent Bibi home since it's New Year.

"Thank God, thank God, thank God," she mumbled to herself in amazement. "When was the last time I was in this apartment by myself?" she asked the microwave. "By myself, listening to music with nothing that I'm *supposed* to be doing." She sipped her coffee as she toddled back into the living room and Joni.

Faking the stomach flu has its pluses, she thought. Maybe "When to Fake the Stomach Flu" could be a bit on the show. She went to her desk and found her *Pregnant on Purpose* file as Joni continued to serenade her.

"Help me I think I'm fallin' in love with you . . ."

The image of Missy blowing her a kiss at the elevator flashed in Ellie's head, and the thought that Missy might be in love with her hit her like a sucker punch. She walked to the stereo and hit the power button. Joni's voice was gone and the big empty apartment reverberated with silence.

"What now?" she asked her quiet home. Her stomach growled. "Eat. I've got to eat." She headed back to the kitchen and made herself a protein drink. Images from her encounter on the floor with Missy came back to her in her mind and body.

"Shit," was all she said as she gulped down her drink. Are Missy and I still friends, or are we lovers now? "What the fuck have I done?" She rinsed out the blender and headed for the bedroom.

"Who the hell can I talk to about this?" She was talking to herself as she pulled on her workout pants. "I'm fucked," she said, struggling into her jog bra.

"Well, you had better go to a meeting today, miss." She waggled a finger at her reflection. "Where's the Twelve Step Program for happily married women who sleep with their best friend? I go looking for a best friend and end up with a fucking lesbian lover."

She grabbed her aerobic shoes and sat on the bed. "If I could just talk to Robbie about this. She'd have some good advice." She tied her shoes and stood to check out her outfit in the mirror. "Yeah, right. She'd say 'Drop Peter, I never liked him anyway.'" She stared at herself with disdain and shook her head. "You are an idiot."

Ring!

She picked up the cordless without thinking.

"Happy New Year," came Missy's voice, sounding very sexy.

"Oh, hi. Happy New Year to you, too," Ellie said, once again donning her Avon lady persona.

"I woke up this morning very disappointed."

Good, Ellie thought, she thinks it was a mistake, too. "Really?" she said hopefully.

"Yes. I woke up and rolled over and there was Antonio," Missy whispered. "I was *so* disappointed it wasn't you."

"Really?" Ellie's vagina responded against her will.

"You can't talk?" Missy asked.

"Not really." She started to pace.

"Call me later. I love you."

"Bye." Ellie held the dead phone next to her ear. "She loves me? She loves me! What the fuck have I done?"

Ellie rushed into Jorge's body-sculpting class five minutes late.

"Well, hallo, miss. How nice of you to come," Jorge bellowed over the loud music at Ellie in mock reprimand. She smiled and tried to act cool as she grabbed an armful of weights. Then she snaked her way through the crowded class to a vacant spot up front, walking like Groucho Marx in an attempt to cause as little disruption as possible.

"I guess she have such a wild New Jeer she cannot make class on time, huh?" Jorge asked the class, getting giggles from a few women.

Ellie shook her head and smiled, thinking: Oh, you have no idea.

"Happy New Year, you!" Ellie heard a stage whisper from behind her as she got into the runner's stretch.

"Arlene! Hi, honey!" she whispered back. "What are you doing here?"

"I'm here to have an assignation with Jorge, my secret lover."

"Is he good?"

"He's fantastic. Look at him." The two women gave the baby-faced stud the once-over and smiled at each other.

"What do you think I'm doing here? I'm trying to sweat off about fifteen glasses of champagne from last night and the eight pounds that was the first thing on my list of resolutions from *last* year."

"You have B.I.D." Ellie was so happy to be talking to her ballsy, irreverent friend that she wanted to cry.

"Keep it down!" the woman next to Arlene snapped.

"Sorry," Ellie and Arlene said in unison and gave each other an *uh-oh* look.

Jorge dragged the room full of moaning and sweating women through a grueling class. And Ellie was ecstatic to be there. She was, as always, transported out of her life and into her body and the task at hand. In fear of Miss Snappy, she resisted the urge to chat with Arlene.

"EIGHT MORE!" It was the home stretch for abs and Jorge had dimmed the lights. "SEVEN, SEEX, FIVE, FOUR, TREE, TWO, AND . . . eight more."

Groans and complaints all around.

"I lied. No time to cry, ladies. SEVEN, SEEX, FIVE . . . It ees a new jeer and we all have work to do. TREE, TWO, and ONE! Das eet. We are finish." Jorge switched tapes and dimmed the lights. Ellie closed her eyes and k.d. lang's gorgeous voice filled the room. "Jus' lie on your back and take a deep breath."

Ellie followed Jorge's instructions. She loved the cooldown, loved getting permission to relax, even if only for five minutes.

"Das eet. Breathe in . . . an' out."

"You are rude and inconsiderate!"

Ellie opened her eyes to see Miss Snappy leaning over her.

"Excuse me?"

"If you can't be on time, you should stay in the back," Miss Snappy told her, then stomped out of class.

Ellie shot a look to Arlene, who had heard the exchange. Arlene shrugged. Ellie jumped up and followed Miss Snappy out the door, hopping over reclining bodies as she went.

"Excuse me! Excuse me!" Ellie was jogging to catch up with her before she reached the elevators. Miss Snappy spun around and faced Ellie with a bored-to-tears expression.

"What?"

"Listen, honey, I am very sorry if I disturbed you. And I believe my friend and I already apologized. But there weren't—"

"Don't call me 'honey.'"

Okay, I'll call you "asshole," Ellie thought. She took a breath, determined not to lose her temper.

"Well, you just called me rude and inconsiderate. I think 'honey' is rather nice, considering. The point is, there weren't any spaces in the back. Besides, if you don't want anyone in front of you, you should get in the very front row yourself," Ellie said, then turned to go back to class.

"Everyone else in the class manages to get here on time!" Snappy called after her.

Ellie kept walking.

"I see you come to class all the time and you are *always* late." She had the taunting tone of a sadistic grade school teacher. "Maybe it's something you should take a look at!"

"I happen to have two small children and it's very hard to get out of the house," she told her evenly, then continued on her way.

"Oh, gimme a break. I have a ten-month-old son and *I'm* here on time."

Ellie turned and fired, "A ten-month-old?" She stomped toward Snappy. "A ten-month-old? You don't know shit! Talk to me when he's two, and he has an opinion. Get back to me when you have to negotiate every little thing that he eats, does, or wears before you can get out the door. We'll talk about how prompt and perfect you are when he has to wear his favorite new gloves, but it's a ten-minute ritual just to get the fucking things on! Talk to me when he's inconsolable because you pushed the elevator button instead of him and—"

"Ellie."

She felt a hand on her shoulder.

"Ellie." It was Arlene. "Honey, forget her. Let it go," she said softly.

Ellie realized that she was inches from Snappy, with her index finger jabbing at the air around her face. Snappy looked terrified. Ellie dropped her hand and looked at Arlene.

"She's insane!" Snappy said.

"Look, I'm sorry I—"

"I'm dying for a nice long whirlpool, aren't you?" Arlene took Ellie by the elbow and guided her away from her nemesis.

I thought you were gonna hit her," Arlene said as she lowered herself into the churning water.

"I really lost it, didn't I?" Ellie said, blasting the backs of her thighs with her favorite jet.

"She had it coming to her. I mean, you can't chat with a friend? It's a body sculpting class. Not a fucking monastery."

Okay, good, Ellie thought, Arlene doesn't think I'm out of my mind. She skooched down so the jet pummeled her butt. She closed her eyes and wished the world away.

"So, how was your New Year's?" Arlene asked.

"You go first."

"Well, Scott and I had our traditional New Year's fight. So it was a lot of fun, as you can imagine."

"I'm so sorry."

"I hate New Year's." Arlene was leaning back, eyes closed, as a water jet ravaged her shoulders. "I wish I could just sleep through it. But of course you can't. Of course it's this holiday where there is *so* much pressure to have fun. And if you don't have fun, if you don't have an unbelievably fantastic time, then you're some kind of loser."

"That is so true. I don't get the big deal. I really don't. What was the fight about?" Ellie asked, dying to hear some one else's juicy story.

"Well, six years ago when he had the affair . . ."

"He had an affair?"

"I never told you that story?"

"No."

"I must have."

"I'm pretty sure I would've remembered if you had."

"Well, Scott had an affair with a dancer."

"Scott had an affair with a dancer and you didn't kill him? You are a saint."

"How can you say that when you're an ex-dancer?"

"Well, I understand what the words 'had an affair with a dancer' mean to a nondancer."

202

"You do?"

"Yes. It means he slept with, not only another woman, but another species. Someone you can never even hope to compete with. Someone that you can never look like or act like. Someone who can twist and turn her body into all sorts of fun and erotic positions that you can only dream of. Someone who is sexy and aloof and powerful all at the same time. Someone who can be described by the word 'willowy.'"

"That's exactly it! She was willowy. Willowy! I will *never* be willowy." Arlene sat up and pointed at her huge breasts. "That's exactly how I felt. How could you know that when *you're* willowy?"

"I know that because I spent years *trying* to be willowy. It turned me into a bulimic."

"So you can understand that even though it's been six years I still get upset."

"Yes, of course. But why on New Year's?"

"Six years ago on New Year's Eve, out to dinner at our favorite restaurant, he took that opportunity to tell me he had been having an affair. He told me that he had already ended the affair. He was sorry, etc. etc. And he felt like shit and he thought if he didn't tell me that he was being a heel."

"Well, he's got a point."

"No, he doesn't! He doesn't have a point! He told me because *he* felt bad and he thought *he* would feel better by telling me. I didn't know anything. I was walking around with this illusion that we had a happy marriage. I wish he'd never told me. Because, even though I've forgiven him and I've moved on, even though he's a great husband and father and all that, I can never forget that he did that thing. That he deceived me in that way and let someone else into that intimate space that used to belong to only us."

"So—you—think . . ." Ellie began, choosing her words slowly as if Arlene's answer could determine the future of her own life ". . . if someone *does* have an affair and they regret it and they want to stay with their spouse, that they should just keep their mouth shut?"

"Absolutely!"

The door swung open and a tall, beautiful, light-skinned, naked black woman entered the whirlpool area.

"Karen. Hi, how are you?" Arlene called.

"I'm great, great. How are you?" Karen walked to the edge of the whirlpool.

"Karen Oberman, this is my friend Ellie Fuller. Ellie, Karen."

"Hi, Karen. Nice to meet you." Ellie waded across the bubbling water, hand outstretched.

"Nice meeting you, too," Karen replied, and the two naked women shook hands.

"Karen's kids go to Calhoun," Arlene told Ellie. "Ellie's looking at Calhoun for her daughter."

"We *love* Calhoun." Karen's face lit up.

"We love it, too. I wept at the open house. Really. It's our first choice so far," Ellie gushed.

"Are you applying to a lot of schools?"

"Only four. I've seen three so far. One more tour to go."

"Isn't it grueling?" Karen asked.

"Grueling," Ellie replied.

"Well, Calhoun is wonderful, very progressive," Karen said, shivering.

Ellie noticed her erect nipples. They were a deep cocoa brown. Her breasts are lovely, she thought.

"We wanted a school that was very nurturing."

"That's what we loved about it," Ellie said, trying hard to look at Karen from the neck up. One time with a woman and suddenly I'm a lesbian? Is that how it works?

"Listen, I've got to do the steam room. I'm fighting a sinus infection. But I'd be happy to tell you all about it. Call me. Arlene can give you my number."

"Okay. That would be great," Ellie said in her most un-seductive tone.

"Nice meeting you." Karen and her erect brown nipples headed toward the steam room. "Bye."

"Bye," Arlene and Ellie called. Karen opened the door and disappeared into a cloud of steam.

"She seems nice. How do you know her?" Ellie asked.

"She's in my book group. She is nice, very smart. Used to be a bigwig at IBM and now she's a stay-at-home mom."

"Good for her."

"Don't give her the mother-of-the-year award so quickly. She has a live-in nanny *and* she just left her Wall Street husband for her daughter's gymnastics instructor."

"You're kidding me?"

"No. He's this twenty-something hunk that teaches at Circus Sports."

"I took a mommy-and-me class there with Ahnika."

"This guy's name is Christian and—"

"Christian? He was Ahnika's teacher. Dark hair, perpetually tan?"

"That's the guy. And Karen just told the entire book group last week that she and Christian are madly in love."

"Wow," was all Ellie could manage. Arlene's husband fucked a dancer, Miss Corporate IBM is fucking her daughter's *gymnastics* teacher, and I'm having a lesbian affair. Is nothing what it seems?

"Anyway, every year I promise myself I'm not going to cause a scene on New Year's. And every year, sometime during the evening, I burst into tears and start screaming at poor Scott."

"Oh, really? Tsk. What does *he* do?"

"He takes it. What *can* he do but take it? He's the one who was fucking little Miss Willowy while I was fighting the crowds at Fairway, shopping for his favorite olive bread."

"So you two had a horrible night?" Ellie feared she was staring into her own future. She and Peter would never be happy again, but they would stay together for the children, torturing each other for the rest of their lives.

"Not totally horrible. We had really great make up sex during the cab ride home."

"You did?"

"Well, we didn't exactly fuck *in* the cab. But it got pretty darn steamy."

"That's so sweet," Ellie said, dewy eyed.

"I don't know how sweet it was but . . . Actually, it gets a little less horrible every year."

"Thank God!" So maybe Peter and I can survive this.

"But enough about me and my dramas."

"Please! Didn't I vomit up—no pun intended—all my skeletons to you just a few months ago? I'm just relieved that you're not perfect."

"You didn't think I was perfect, did you?"

"I guess, sort of. I thought you and Scott were. I mean, look at Karen," Ellie whispered.

"Yeah," Arlene said looking at the steam room door. "Who would look at her and suspect she had tossed her marriage aside for great sex?"

A flash of Missy between her legs popped into Ellie's head. Her pussy tingled; she was bathed in guilt.

"Your turn. How was your New Year's?"

Drum roll, please. "Different."

"That's intriguing. What happened?"

How do I handle this? Do I tell her the whole thing? Do I skip the juicy parts?

"It's never warm enough in this whirlpool. This water is tepid. Am I right?" She was stalling, doing a rewrite in her head.

"It's always tepid. I've written five complaints. So . . . ?"

Ellie told Arlene the story. A few stragglers came into the whirlpool now and then, but the tepid water drove everyone away.

"So you're in her fabulous bedroom, checking out the incredible view, hoping to be alone at midnight, and she finds you?" Arlene was on the edge of her seat.

"And Missy . . ."

The glass door to the whirlpool area swished open, and both women stopped to look at who was invading their privacy.

"Oh, my God! Oh, my God!" Arlene was almost screaming. She jumped out of the tub.

"Happy New Year, sweetie!" A dark-haired, zaftig woman in her forties, wrapped in several towels, bellowed as she ran to embrace the dripping Arlene.

"What are you doing here? I had no idea. Oh, my God!" They hugged and screamed and jumped. Ellie sank into the tepid water.

"Ellie, this is my best friend in the whole world, Lorraine Heyman."

Best friend?

"So *this* is Ellie. I have heard all about you," Lorraine said as she bent down to shake hands.

"Really?" I haven't heard a fucking thing about *you*, Ellie thought. This is unbelievable. She felt betrayed, like some woman who was on a date with her new boyfriend only to be introduced to his wife.

"Lorraine moved to London three years ago and—"

"We're back!" Lorraine broke in.

"What?"

206

"I wanted to surprise you. I've known since November."

"Oh, my God. This is the best New Year's present I could have."

Ellie felt like crying as she sat shivering in the whirlpool, and the best friends prattled on and on about some damn crap.

"Gosh, look at the time!" Ellie said finally, sounding like an actor doing a bad line reading. "I've gotta meet Peter and the kids." She waded to the stairs.

"That's it? I'm not gonna hear the end of the story?"

"What story?" Lorraine piped in.

"Well, nothing happened, really." Ellie marched up the stairs and grabbed her towel from the railing, then turned to the soaking women. She hated them both.

"Missy and I just had wild sex on the floor of her bedroom while her swarthy Argentinean husband searched for her in vain." Then Ellie wrapped her towel around her with a flare and headed toward the showers.

There was a beat—then—

"You are funny!" Arlene called after her. "Didn't I *tell* you she was funny?"

And Ellie could hear the empty-headed women laughing as the door closed behind her.

Chapter Twenty-One

The OA meeting was in what seemed to be an abandoned cafeteria. The fluorescent lights flickered and cast a depressing light that gave everyone a rather grave look. Who arranged these chairs? Ellie wondered as she looked for an empty seat in the unorganized room. The speaker, who looked startlingly like the angry anorexic woman from Ellie's last meeting, sat at the far end of the cafeteria, her back to some long forgotten steam tables. Ellie found a seat far off to one side and settled down. The speaker was staring down at her lap as she spoke.

I can't hear a fucking thing, Ellie thought. She looked around to see if anyone else was straining to hear and saw several people chatting. What the hell's going on here, she wondered? No one's listening. Jesus, and I need a meeting so badly. She saw a vacant spot near the front. Maybe if I move my chair closer I'll be able to hear. She got up and tried to lift her chair.

"Shit!" It wouldn't budge.

"Shhh!" Several people shushed her in unison. She gave them an apologetic smile. Is this thing nailed down? she wondered, and knelt to examine the legs. Oh, my God. They're nailed to the floor, she realized. She looked around. They're all nailed down. That's weird.

"So, thanks to OA, now I only throw up every two or three weeks." The speaker was suddenly shouting. The group cheered.

What? What *is* this? Ellie wondered as she looked at the beaming faces around her. You can't be the speaker in an OA meeting if you're still throwing up. What the fuck's going on? I have to get out of here. She grabbed her coat and purse. But when she headed to the exit she was stopped dead in her tracks. What the . . . ? She turned back to see that her purse strap was caught on the chair. This is unbelievable, she thought as she struggled to liberate herself and her purse.

"Thank God," she whispered to herself when she had gotten her strap free. She beelined it to the exit, wondering what else could possibly go wrong when—

"You are being very rude and inconsiderate!" A voice rang out from behind her. Ellie felt a mix of panic and outrage rise up in her as she turned.

"Oh, no. Not you. Not you again," Ellie said wearily at the glaring woman. Before her was Miss Snappy from body-sculpting class.

"If you'd only obey the rules," she said, shaking her head, hands on her hips. "Do you *ever* obey the rules? Do you *ever* think of anybody but yourself?"

"You self-righteous bitch!" Ellie said, then lunged at her, and the two women went over. When they hit the ground, Ellie was on top, her hands around Miss Snappy's neck, and she was squeezing with all her strength. It felt wonderful.

"Fuck you, bitch," Ellie said as she squeezed. Miss Snappy's eyes looked as if they were about to pop out of her head. "You don't know me. How dare you judge me?" She squeezed even harder.

"Ellie?" She heard a faint voice behind her. It sounded like Peter.

What's he doing here? she wondered. She kept squeezing; Miss Snappy's complexion went ashen.

"Fuck you, bitch! Fuck you!"

"Ellie." Peter's voice was louder, more insistent now. She tightened her grip. Miss Snappy's eyes closed; she was turning from ashen to blue.

"*Ellie!*" She felt a hand on her shoulder. She rolled over and opened her eyes.

"Peter?" His handsome face was over her.

"Oh, shit! Did I fall asleep?"

"I guess so."

I missed the OA meeting, she realized. Damn it!

After leaving Arlene and Lorraine in the whirlpool, Ellie had had two hours to kill before the one OA meeting that she could find on New Year's Day. She had come home to change her socks, soaked from trudging through the snow. She had lain down on the bed just for five minutes and, apparently, fallen asleep.

"What time is it?"

"One-thirty. Why? Did you have some big plans?"

"No, no. It's just—I was just curious."

"You were moaning in your sleep. You must've been dreaming."

"I guess so," she said, picturing Miss Snappy's blue face.

"How are you feeling?" He stroked her forehead.

Like shit. Like I wanna kill myself. Like I've ruined everything that's important to me just like I always knew I would, she thought. But—

"Okay, how are you feeling?" is what she said.

"Pretty good, really. I was able to eat a big breakfast and I feel like I'm operating at about 85 percent."

"How are the kids?"

"Angus is hungry and Ahnika is tired. We went sledding." He smiled a big proud daddy smile.

"Really? Did Angus do it?"

"Sure. I took him down that tiny slope near Seventy-seventh Street on my lap."

"You are something, taking them sledding after throwing up all night." She reached her arm around his neck and pulled him in for a kiss. He kissed her sweetly and she began to cry.

"What's wrong?" he asked when he saw her tears.

"I don't know."

Tell him! a voice screamed inside her head. Tell him now and there's still a chance.

"It's just, last night at the party you weren't there, and I didn't know anybody, and . . ."

Shut up! another voice called. Remember what Arlene said. Don't do it. He doesn't have to know. He never has to know. Besides, the whole thing was his idea in the first place.

"What? Did you miss me? I missed you, too."

"I really missed you. And when it was almost midnight, I stood in Missy's bedroom, staring out the window towards the West Side, wondering why I was at the stupid party, why I wasn't home with you and the babies. And then Missy came in and—"

"Aaahhh!" Angus's cry echoed through the apartment.

"I guess he's pretty hungry," Peter said. "Do you think you're up to feeding him or do you want me to give him another bottle?"

"You gave him a *bottle*? Formula?"

"El, he was starving, you were sick."

"So, why didn't you give him some baby food?" She threw the covers off. "That's it! No more formula. *I'll* feed him. *I'm* his fucking mother, for Christ's sake!"

"Honey, I was just trying to give you a break."

"Well, you know how important breast milk is. Suddenly I don't care about my kids?"

"Nobody said that. You've been sick, that's all. Nobody is suggesting that."

"Aaahhh! Aaahhh!" Angus's cries grew louder.

"Where is he?" Ellie asked, and she stormed out of the room and away from Peter.

Chapter Twenty-Two

Here we go again, Ellie thought as she climbed the stairs to a spectacular white marble townhouse on East Seventy-ninth Street. She glanced at her watch and walked quickly to the receptionist's office, the sound of her boots echoing in the cavernous entryway. Would Ahnika be happy in this palatial setting? she wondered as she gazed at the huge marble staircase at the far end.

She followed the receptionist's directions to a conference room. When she entered, she gave the group of Upper East Siders a smile, found her name tag on a side table, then headed for an empty seat at the large oval conference table. Every one of them, it seemed to Ellie, turned and gave her the once-over. She scrutinized their outfits—three business-suited dads and six mannequin moms. Thank God for Bibi, she thought as she looked down at her crisply ironed pants. I look a little more together today. But these people, they all look like confident adults *every* day. They must have entire closets—walk-in closets, probably—full of adult clothes. Why did I ever apply to this East Side school? she wondered.

"Good morning, everyone." Sasie Benedict, admissions director, breezed into the room, wearing a simple strand of pearls, a pale blue cashmere sweater set, and charcoal gray pants. "Have a few more sips of coffee, and then we must begin.

"We'll start at the top and work our way down," Sasie explained as the group crowded into the small, gated elevator. She pushed 6 and they began their slow ascent.

"As some of you already know, Wilhelm Reiker was a German sociologist who developed an education philosophy that was widely adopted throughout Germany and Europe in the twenties." The elevator struggled its way up as Sasie did her pitch.

Ellie's stomach rumbled as they poured out of the elevator. I'm starving, forgot to eat breakfast, again. Shit! Trying to get everything ready for Lisa is really screwing me up. I'll make sure to eat a good lunch, she promised herself. At least I haven't barfed since New Year's. Ten days and counting. No more of that, Ellie vowed as she shuffled towards an open classroom door. No more of that.

"These are the fours," Sasie said in a stage whisper as the group huddled around her in a corner of the bustling playroom. Four-year-olds of all shapes and colors were engaged in painting, dress up, blocks, etc. "As you can see all the toys are made of wood or other organic materials."

"Oh." "Hmm." Little noises of approval were heard all around.

Organic materials, Ellie thought. Who're they kidding? She pictured the warehouse of PlaySkool and Fisher-Price toys that lined the shelves of Angus and Ahnika's playroom. Our house is like a plastic shrine, Ellie thought. And none of *your* kids have plastic toys? she was dying to ask the others.

Sasie made a subtle *follow me* gesture and they left the happy scene behind them.

Ellie's stomach growled again. Man, I'm dyin' here, she thought as the collection of parents headed down a flight of stairs. Sasie's spiel droned on. This isn't good, Ellie thought as she tried to shake off the familiar light-headedness. This really isn't good.

The next stop was a huge kitchen and dining area where twelve or so kids and three teachers were busy mixing, measuring, and chopping.

"The children make all their own snacks and meals." Sasie continued her commentary in her well-perfected stage whisper. "We use only organic foods."

That's great, Ellie thought, really. She was *trying* to like the place, she was. I'd feed Ahnika organic stuff if she'd eat it. But all she'll eat these days is Rugrats macaroni and cheese, jam sandwiches, and pepperoni. Maybe they'd let me pack her a lunch, Ellie considered as they left the perfect little tykes to their soy milk and tofu cookies.

"How about microwaves?" a balding man in a gray suit asked as they entered the stairwell again.

"Oh, no. No." Sasie's eyes widened and she shook her head. "Of course not," she told him, as if he'd asked whether or not pornography was allowed. There were mumbles of approval all around.

Wait a minute, Ellie wanted to stop the group and ask them a few pointed questions. So you're telling me, that none of *you* have a microwave? Come on, she thought as she watched them heading down the stairs. And none of your little darlings are addicted to Rugrats macaroni and cheese?

There were more classrooms and the sales pitch continued.

"The children keep journals . . . blah, blah, blah . . . They are never pushed into reading before they are ready . . . blah, blah, blah . . . a sense of safety and belonging . . . blah, blah, blah . . . They start learning French in the first grade, Sanskrit in the second grade."

Sanskrit, Ellie thought, they're learning Sanskrit? But she bit her tongue.

"This is our last stop," Sasie said as she led the earnest parents into an old-fashioned gymnasium.

"Oh, I love it!" cooed a blond mom with a perfect pageboy.

"Yes," Sasie agreed. "We think it looks like the gym in *It's a Wonderful Life*, doesn't it?" And it did.

A wild group of five-year-olds was running and laughing and bouncing balls everywhere.

"The children get time in the gym every day and time in Central Park when the weather allows." Sasie paused and let the wistful parents watch the happy scene. It was beautiful and timeless. Fifteen jubilant kids were batting around three of those soccer ball-sized red rubber balls that every kid born after 1950 played with growing up.

What a great space, Ellie thought. She could picture Ahnika and a future Angus dashing around the big marvelous gym playing dodgeball.

"Let's go back to the conference room for some coffee, and I'll answer any questions you all might have." They left the boisterous children reluctantly.

As they entered the conference room, Ellie grabbed a currant scone before she found a seat with the rest of the group.

The bald one was the first to talk. "What about sports—basketball, baseball?" he asked.

"We have no competitive sports here, only games that foster cooperation."

"Ah." The bald one nodded in approval. More nods and smiles all around.

"So no dodgeball?" It was out of Ellie's mouth before she realized it. Every head turned.

"No," Sasie said with finality, a huge smile plastered on her face. "No dodgeball." And she scanned the room for more questions.

"You're telling me that you have that fantastic gym and the kids aren't allowed to play dodgeball?"

"No," Sasie said again, irritation seeping into her tone. "But they play plenty of other games. The children have plenty of fun as you all just witnessed."

"How 'bout kickball. Surely they get to play kickball."

"No," Sasie said curtly, locking her eyes with Ellie's. "There—are—no—competitive—sports—here—at—the—Wilhelm—Reiker—School!"

Ellie felt a challenge; she couldn't turn back. "Maybe I'm nuts, but as a kid I loved dodgeball. No?" She looked around at the others for support. No one would meet her gaze. "I mean, there were a lot of things wrong with the public school that I went to as a child, but dodgeball wasn't one of them."

There was a strained silence. People shifted in their seats.

"Do you have a *question* that I can answer about the school, Ms. Fuller?"

Let it go, El, let it go, she told herself. Sasie's gaze was steady, confident. Fuck you and your snooty superiority, another side of Ellie piped in.

215

"Yes, I guess I do." Ellie slowly surveyed the sea of horrified faces. "What exactly did Wilhelm Reiker have against dodgeball?"

"Oh, please!" someone blurted out.

"Honestly!" said another.

"Look, I think she's answered the question. Dodgeball is a competitive sport; they don't have competitive sports," the bald one said.

"He's right," Miss Perfect Pageboy piped in. "Obviously if dodgeball is *that* important to you this is *not* the school for your children."

What the hell have you done, Ellie? You've alienated everyone, you're trapped here, and you didn't even get to ask her about the fucking Sanskrit.

"Well, you're probably right," Ellie said with mock seriousness. "I guess I'll just have to search Manhattan high and low for a private school with a more dodgeball-heavy curriculum." She searched their faces for a smile, a giggle, something, anything. The evil group didn't give an inch.

"Well," Sasie said turning away from Ellie. "Anyone else?" And the questions and comments flowed from the WASPy crowd.

But Ellie was blissfully oblivious to it all as she climbed deep inside her scone. The next thing she heard was the sound of a chair scraping on the wooden floor. She looked up to see that Sasie Benedict, all perfect, pearly, and cashmered, had stood up.

"I'm sad to say that that's all the time we have today. I have another tour waiting. If any of you need to talk to me further, don't hesitate to call my office."

Ellie grabbed her coat and managed to escape from the cold white fortress without having to make eye contact with anyone. She walked down the stairs toward Seventy-ninth Street with one thought chanting in her brain: mixed nuts, mixed nuts, mixed nuts . . .

Chapter Twenty-Three

Ellie popped three more cashews in her mouth and shoved the half-eaten bag of nuts into her coat pocket as she walked to the concierge desk.

"I'm here to see Missy Hanover. She's here watering her mother's plants," she said, smiling at the concierge. The line sounded like bullshit in her head but she didn't care. What's he gonna do, Ellie wondered, tell on us? He doesn't know what we're doing up there. She giggled to herself in the elevator, giddy with the secrecy and the intrigue. I forgot what a good liar I am, she thought proudly. Well, growing up with my parents, it was a must.

As she floated up to Lally and Woody Hanover's apartment, Ellie remembered her first big elaborate lie. It had been at her first dance recital. At ballet classes, she had made a new friend—a girl named Janine who was tall and silly and laughed at her jokes.

Janine and all the other ballerinas lived on the other side of the hill and went to different schools. So Ellie had started there with a clean slate. She had loved that, loved being just Ellie the dancer, not Ellie the girl with the convict dad and the lush for a mom.

But backstage after that first recital, when only Jack, her cousin and best buddy, was there with hugs for her, the questions began.

"Hey, El, where's your mom and dad?" Janine asked as she and her parents approached.

"Uh—well—" She turned to Jack; he shrugged his shoulders, his eyes like saucers. "My father's dying of a rare bone disease," she blurted out suddenly. Jack nodded gravely. "He's being treated in London where there's been a breakthrough. My mother's there with him, of course." A perfect lie had sprung from her lips like magic.

"What a bummer," Janine whispered in Ellie's ear as she hugged her.

"Why don't you two come back to our house for dinner?" Janine's mother asked.

Ellie smiled a brave little smile and accepted the invitation thinking— well, *that* worked like a charm! From that moment on Ellie always had a good lie ready for the curious or concerned.

As the elevator ascended, Ellie's vagina contracted in anticipation of her afternoon with Missy. This would be their third afternoon together since New Year's, and Ellie was on another planet. Her lifestyle as a stay-at-home mom was tailor-made to deceive Peter. He was at work all day, and she had Park Avenue Playgroup and Bibi to watch the children. So she had hours of free time to spend with her lover. The fact that she was neglecting her children, ignoring the HBO deadline, and ruining her life and marriage by having an affair was obscured by how Missy seemed to adore her. Being loved by Missy made Ellie feel special beyond description. The perfect and elegant Missy Hanover had chosen *her* to be her lover.

Ellie rang the doorbell, her palms damp, her pussy wet. Missy opened the door to her parents' tasteful apartment, threw her arms around Ellie, and kissed her deep and long. Within seconds the two women were tumbling in Lally and Woody's bed, their naked bodies writhing beneath the crisp white monogrammed sheets.

Missy, wearing her father's flannel robe, walked into the bedroom with two mugs of steaming tea. "I went to Farmington with Sasie Benedict. She got kicked out." She raised an eyebrow and gave Ellie a mischievous grin.

"Sasie Benedict, admissions director at the Wilhelm Reiker School, got kicked out of boarding school?" Ellie asked, reaching for her tea.

"Yes! For stealing." She dropped the robe to the floor and climbed back into bed.

"Miss Cashmere Sweater Set is a thief? No!"

"Well they never proved anything but . . ." Missy shrugged her shoulders and sipped her tea ". . . it seems all her roommates ended up missing jewelry."

"She *was* wearing a nice string of pearls," Ellie said, and the two women laughed. "I just can't believe that about Sasie Benedict. She seems so perfect. So straight."

"Ellie, you are so naïve."

"Look who's talking, Miss Gullible."

"I am gullible. I'll admit it. And *you* are naïve—about certain things."

"I am not naïve," Ellie protested. "There are a lot of things you could call me. Naïve is not one of them."

"You think just because you lived in the East Village and hung out in comedy clubs that you're not naïve. Ellie, everybody's got a story to tell. Everybody has secrets."

"Do *you* have secrets?"

"Maybe. Don't *you* have any?"

Well, I'm a bulimic and I was hired help at your engagement party, Ellie thought but didn't say.

"Well I never stole jewelry from anybody and—Missy, cut it out." Jesus, Ellie realized, I really don't know anything about this woman, do I? She grabbed the bag of nuts from the bedside table and shoved a handful in her mouth.

"All I'm saying is, just because someone went to a certain school or has the right address or wears family jewels doesn't make them invulnerable to flaws and temptations."

Ellie stopped. This was a revelation, although it shouldn't have been. After all, she had grown up with a mother whose family jewels and good education couldn't save her from *her* flaws and temptations.

Ellie downed some more nuts, sipped her tea, and pulled the monogrammed sheets up to her chin. "It's freezing in here."

"My mom turns the thermostat down to fifty degrees or something insane like that when she leaves for the winter. She's a typical heiress—cheap."

"So she's gone all winter?"

"Yep. She and Daddy leave after Thanksgiving and come back just before Easter."

"Where do they go?"

"Loblolly."

"Loblolly? Is that an island or something? I've never heard of it."

"It's the name of our house in the Caribbean, on Antigua. It was named after a tree that grows in the patio."

"Wow. How great!"

"It is. It's a wonderful house. My parents went to Antigua on their honeymoon, and they fell in love with the place, so Daddy bought a house there."

"Do you ever go?"

"I used to go a lot. When we were growing up, my brothers and I went all the time." Missy put her tea on the bedside table and snuggled down under the covers. "Every year, we'd go for two weeks over Christmas, a week in March, and sometimes we'd go in August for Carnival."

"You don't go anymore?"

"I haven't been since I was pregnant with Mason."

"Jesus! Why not?"

"Tony's not crazy about it. Says it's too remote," Missy said, yawning. "Can't stand to be so out of touch with the business. And we always go to Argentina over Christmas to see his family since he sees my family all the time." Missy was talking slowly, more quietly. "I keep meaning to. Every year I say I'm going to take the kids and go without him." She turned suddenly. "Hey! Let's go!"

"What?"

"Let's go! You, me, and the kids. Let's go at Spring Break."

This caught Ellie totally off guard. "I love that they call it Spring

Break. I mean, just what exactly are they getting a break from? Finger painting and napping? It's not like they've been cramming for finals."

"Ellie." Missy was sitting up now. "I'm serious. We can send Tony and Peter to Argentina. They can camp out on the pampas and eat raw meat or whatever men do, while we lounge in the cabana, drinking iced tea and watching the kids play in the perfect turquoise water."

"Wow, I—" Ellie shoved the last of the nuts in her mouth.

"We could do it. Listen. The kids get two weeks off from school, right? Mother and Daddy will be there, but they have their own wing, so we'd only have to see them at meals."

A home in the Caribbean with wings, Ellie thought. This is the life my father dreamed of.

"And if you and I wanted to play tennis or something like that, without the kids, my parents would be delirious to watch them."

"Missy, it sounds wonderful, really. Sounds like the best vacation I could imagine, but I already have plans."

"Well, you just have to cancel them." There was an edge in her voice.

"Missy, we've had these plans for forever. We're all going to see my mom in California."

"Oh, that sounds delightful."

Is that sarcasm? Ellie wondered.

"Two weeks in Los Angeles with Peter and the kids. By all means, go! How could the Caribbean compete with that?" She rolled away from Ellie and pulled the covers up to her ear.

"I'd change it if I could, you know I would. But I haven't been out there since I was pregnant with Angus, and Peter's never been." Ellie's words hung in the air. "Every time we've tried to plan a trip out there, his business has gotten in the way. So this one's been planned since last May."

There was a beat, then: "He'll cancel," Missy mumbled into her pillow.

"What?"

"I said 'He'll cancel.' You know he will." Missy was still facing away from her, talking in loud, clipped sentences. "Peter doesn't *want* to go to California and spend time with your mother. Really, Ellie, here's your naïveté again."

Missy's tone was so patronizing, Ellie was ready to smack her. "Missy, what are you talking about?"

When Missy turned back toward Ellie, her face was hard. "Look, Ellie,

Peter loves you and all that, but men want what they want and they do what they have to do so they get it. It's biological, probably. Peter tells you he wants to go to California with you to visit your mother, but he's never gone? *That* tells me he doesn't *want* to go. So, I'm just saying, like every other male on the planet, he will work this situation and get what he wants. You'll end up taking the kids to L.A. by yourself—which is five hours on an airplane with Angus and Ahnika and no help. And because it will be all about *his* precious business so he can make money for you all to have a nice lifestyle—blah, blah, blah—you won't even have the satisfaction of getting angry about it."

"For someone who's only met my husband once for a few hours, you seem to think you know him pretty well."

"Oh, for goodness sake, Ellie, you are impossible!" Missy threw off the covers and stomped into the bathroom. Ellie could hear cabinets slamming and the shower being turned on. What is with her, she wondered? I'm supposed to abandon my life suddenly? Brother! I don't know what I'm doing here, anyway. I have to get these shows to Lisa in less than six weeks and—

"I know Peter because I know men, and they are *all* the same." Missy was standing naked in the doorway, her long slender body making an exquisite silhouette.

"That's an incredibly sexist thing to say," Ellie said, trying to keep her mind on the subject and off Missy's breasts.

"Just because it's sexist doesn't mean it's not true." And she turned and was gone. Ellie was out of the bed and in the bathroom in a second. Missy was already in the shower. Ellie flung the shower door open. Missy stopped and looked at her sadly, her soapy sponge in her hand.

"What are we doing here, Missy?" It was out of her mouth without a thought. She wasn't sure what she meant by it, or what kind of response she was hoping for. Missy just stared at her. Ellie stood motionless with the shower door in her hand.

"I'm taking a shower and you're standing there shivering," Missy said, starting to smile.

This woman, this woman, she thought. I don't understand her at all.

"Get in here," Missy said, grabbing her wrist and pulling Ellie into the nice hot shower.

Missy wrapped her arms around Ellie and began washing her back.

"Remember our sponge bath?" Missy whispered, kissing her ear as the sponge traveled down to her ass.

"That is something I will never forget," Ellie said. They washed each other, their bodies slipping and sliding together. Then Missy's finger found its way into Ellie's swollen cunt. She pushed it in deep, deeper. Ellie was gone in an instant; she came in waves and waves.

Clean and pink from the hot shower, the two women snuggled under the covers of Lally and Woody's bed. A thought that had been plaguing Ellie since New Year's came again: shouldn't I eat her pussy, too? Missy was drifting off next to her. If I think about it too much it'll never happen, she thought as she slipped her head under the covers and headed south.

"Uh, uh, uh," Missy said, taking Ellie by the shoulder and gently pulling her back up.

"What?" she asked when she emerged from the covers. "Don't you want me to?"

"No, I don't." Missy kissed her on the cheek. "I just like doing it to you. I love making you happy. Seeing you satisfied is enough for me." Missy put her arm around Ellie's neck and settled into her. "It's all I want, really," she said sleepily.

But isn't she horny? Ellie wondered. Isn't her pussy aching like mine?

"I don't need any payback. That's such a male thing, don't you think?"

"I don't know if it's male. I just thought I was being polite," Ellie said, feeling a little embarrassed and very relieved. Even though she was terribly attracted to Missy, she didn't find the idea of going down on her erotic. As much as she had tried to over the last few weeks, she just couldn't picture it.

"Oh, it's a completely male thing. Men are always focused on the goal, the payoff. Everything they do is just so they can get their dick in your pussy."

"Missy!" Ellie said in mock surprise.

"What?"

"I didn't think nice girls who went to Smith used such language," Ellie teased.

"There's your naïveté showing." Missy smiled slyly. "But I'm serious. Hugging, kissing—any kind of foreplay is just that—foreplay. They don't enjoy the act for the act itself because they are so cock oriented."

Whoa, Ellie thought, she sounds like Susan Faludi. Missy the angry feminist? That's a first.

"Their cocks are in charge, always telling them 'get pussy, get pussy, get pussy.' "

Not Peter, Ellie thought. He sits at his desk at work and dreams of going down on me. But she wasn't about to say that. No. Though the rules of their relationship had not been clearly defined, Ellie was pretty sure that she was not allowed to brag about her husband's appreciation of her pussy to her lesbian lover.

"Here's what sex is like with Tony . . ." Missy continued ". . . sex with any male I've ever been with, really: I do something to him, then he does something to me, then we fuck."

So just how many lovers have you had? Ellie wondered, reaching for the empty bag of nuts. And how many of them were women? She licked her finger and worked it into the corner of the bag, pushing out of her mind the possibility that she was not the only one, the special one. Her stomach grumbled as she sucked off the salt and bits of nuts.

"And that's how sex is with you and Peter, am I right?" Missy yawned and put her hand on Ellie's stomach.

Yeah, that's pretty much it, Ellie thought, but she said, "Well, we've been together for a while. Maybe we've gotten into a bit of a rut." She was feeling defensive. Even though she was out of control over Missy, she was not about to trash Peter. He was a wonderful lover and she didn't love him any less than she had before New Year's. *He* hadn't done anything wrong. *She* was the bad guy.

"You know what I hate the most? I hate when you're giving them a blow job and they ask you a question. It's like being at the dentist when he makes conversation." Missy giggled dreamily. "I mean how are you supposed to respond with a mouth full of cotton or a big dick in your mouth?"

Ellie was speechless. Missy Hanover talking about dicks and blow jobs? Once again she's thrown me a curve, Ellie thought.

She looked up to see Lally Hanover staring at her. A huge portrait of Missy's mother hung in an ornate frame on the opposite wall. A shiver went down her back. Jeez, it's like she's watching us, she thought.

Do you know what your daughter's doing in your bed while you're away? Ellie asked the picture silently, then looked at down at Missy. Her eyes were shut.

How can I be in love with her? Ellie's chest contracted, her eyes filled with tears. Jesus Christ, I'm insane. She surveyed the bedroom. The easy chair across the room was piled high with pillows of all shapes and sizes. A tiny needlepoint pillow read: *God, give me Patience and do it right now.* Oh, my God! I think my mother has that exact pillow, she realized. I can't escape her. This is the East Coast version of my mother's bedroom. She had a sudden urge to call Peter and tell him her discovery. He would appreciate it. I wonder what he's doing, she thought. Does he suspect anything? Does he notice that I haven't called all day? She looked at the phone on the bedside table. Her heart ached. Later, she thought, I'll call him later.

A memory of a lazy Saturday flashed through her head. It had happened last summer when the four of them had spent all morning just snuggled in bed together—Angus nursing and sleeping, Ahnika giggling and playing, Ellie and Peter beaming and basking in this incredible life that they had created.

"Fuck!" she said out loud, putting her head in her hands. Have I ruined my life? Is it too late to go back? Her stomach growled. Missy was snoring softly. Ellie slipped out of bed, formulating a plan as she went.

"First I have to eat something," she said to herself as she put on Woody's robe and headed for the kitchen. "Then I'll get dressed and get the hell out of here." She padded down the long hallway, passing pictures of Missy and her brothers boating, skiing, on a Caribbean beach, dressed in Halloween costumes.

"I'll call and find an East Side OA meeting," she said, crossing the large formal dining room. "I'll go, get my hand up, and hopefully get called on." She entered the big empty kitchen feeling happy, renewed. "Then I'll go straight to Peter's office and tell him everything." She was speaking loudly, with conviction. "He'll forgive me, I know he will. I won't answer Missy's calls. I'll pull Ahnika out of Park Avenue Playgroup if I have to." She could fix it, make it right. She opened the refrigerator. "Shit!" Nothing, except for a lone shriveled lemon on the bottom shelf. The shelves on the door were lined with jars of cocktail onions, capers, pickles, and pimiento stuffed olives. She began to shiver.

"Just like home," she whispered. "Are they alcoholics?" She felt sick at the thought. "El, come on, they're away, makes perfect sense."

As Ellie, wrapped in Woody Hanover's plaid flannel robe, stared into the refrigerator of her childhood, she could hear her mother's voice in her head:

"Count your blessings. Think of all those poor starving children in China," Sara would slur as she gulped down her third martini of the evening. Ellie would just stare at the TV dinner in front of her, trying like hell to muster some appetite. This was during the really dark years, when Sara Fuller had only managed to make her daughter dinner two or three nights a month. The rest of the time she was too bombed to even consider any motherly duties.

Years later, Ellie had found a punch line to that depressing scene from her childhood: "I wonder what the mothers in China say to *their* kids," Ellie would ponder in front of a raucous audience at Caroline's or Stand-up New York. "'I know you hungly—'" she'd say in an exaggerated Chinese accent "'—but count your blessings. Think of all those poor children in Amelica with alcoholic palents.'" It always got a big laugh.

Ellie began searching through Lally and Woody's bare cupboards. Mugs, slam—glasses, slam—spices, slam.

"Aha!" She had discovered a cupboard with food, sort of. Two bags of marshmallows, a jar of Ovaltine, three cans of sardines, two cans of vichyssoise, more olives, and a box of Godiva chocolates with the ribbon still on.

"Come on! Vichyssoise and sardines?" She opened the last cupboard. "Perfect." The sick feeling was back. Gallon bottles of vodka, gin, and scotch sat waiting for Woody and Lally's return. Of course there was also plenty of tonic water, soda water, and vermouth.

"My people," she mumbled to herself.

"Fuck it. I'll eat out. But I need *something* to tide me over." She knew she was lying to herself as she reached for the gold box. She opened it quickly, fearing discovery, grabbed a dark chocolate almond cluster and popped it in her mouth. As she chewed, her breathing became thick. She could feel the rush as the sugar swam into her veins.

She ate all the dark chocolate ones first, thinking "just one more" after each one. By the fifth chocolate she had passed the point of no return; she was no longer tasting them, really, just hurrying to finish. To get them *all* in, all gone, away. She stuffed the last one, a milk chocolate strawberry cream, in her mouth. She hated milk chocolate *and* strawberry cream. She was in a stupor as she sat at the kitchen table and swallowed.

"Hello-o! Missy darling, hello-o!"

"Oh, my God!" Ellie heard the front door close, footsteps in the entryway, a closet door slamming, then more footsteps. She was trying to think through the thick fog of the sugar. It felt as if she was moving in slow motion as she stood and rewrapped Woody's robe around her, tied it in a bow, and wiped chocolate from her mouth with the back of her hand. Footsteps approaching. She put the ravaged box and the ribbon in the cupboard and closed it quietly. More footsteps. I'm caught, she thought, I'm caught.

"Missy, honey? Are you here? Sanford said you were here." And Lally Hanover walked into the kitchen.

Fuck, Ellie thought. She recognized her from the painting and the engagement party, all those years ago. She was elegant and graceful, like her daughter.

"Hello," Lally said sweetly. "I'm Lally Hanover, Missy's mother." She put out her hand as if she were meeting Ellie at a fund-raiser, not finding some strange woman in her kitchen wearing nothing but her husband's robe.

"Hi. I'm Ellie Fuller." She took Lally's hand and gave her a nice firm handshake. "I'm a friend of Missy's. Nice to meet you."

"Ellie, I've heard *so* much about you. You're the comedienne, aren't you?"

"Yes, I guess I am."

Lally smiled and nodded, waiting for more, it seemed.

"I was um . . . Missy is uh . . . We were just ha . . ." She was trying to come up with a story, any story, but her sugar-addled brain couldn't cope.

"Mother, you sneak!" Missy, fully dressed and looking as crisp as could be, glided over to her mother and gave her an air-kiss and a hug. "What are you doing here?" She sounded delighted at the surprise.

"I'm here for my mammogram. I got in last night. You know I come back every year for it."

"Mother, I told you to have Dr. Sheffield reschedule that till after you and Daddy are back." Missy took out a rocks glass from a cabinet and filled it with ice.

"Well, honey, I don't mind. By this time, I need a break from your father, quite frankly." The two women laughed.

Ellie was outside her body watching the whole scene, wondering when the director would yell, "Cut!" so she could go back to her trailer and relax. This can't be real, she was thinking as she watched Missy pour Lally a generous vodka on the rocks. Surely I'm in a movie and this scene will end soon. Good casting, she mused, as she admired Lally's timeless pantsuit and bone structure. Missy handed Lally the rocks glass.

"Thank you, dear." She took a long, slow drink.

Ellie glanced at the kitchen clock. Vodka on the rocks at 12:20, she thought. Okay, she's a darn good drinker.

"Mother, you and Ellie have introduced yourselves, I'm sure."

"Yes, we have," Lally said, looking at Ellie warmly. "But, I think we've met before. You look awfully familiar."

"No, no," Ellie said, a little too quickly. "I would remember that, certainly."

"You know, I thought that too when Ellie and I first met. Isn't that funny?" Missy piped in.

"Well, I get that a lot. I have that kind of face."

"Maybe at a fund-raiser. Are you on any committees? The Met or the Cooper-Hewitt?" Lally continued.

"No." Ellie was starting to sweat all over. "Maybe at the New Year's party." I'd like to stop this chitchat and get the fuck out of here, she was thinking.

"No, no. We were in Antigua on New Year's. Besides, it wasn't recent. I remember your face but the hair was different. Hmm."

"Mother has an uncanny memory for people."

"But it was at a party, I'm certain of that."

Ellie had a flash of a memory from the engagement party. Lally, bombed out of her mind, had dressed her down in front of a crowded buffet line for not carving the roast beef thinly enough.

"Well, I'm sure we had a nice time together wherever it was," Ellie said, smiling graciously. Lally was sipping her drink and studying Ellie, trying to place her. God, get me out of here, Ellie pleaded.

"She'll figure it out, believe me," Missy said, trying to ease the awkwardness. "I hope she didn't scare you when you walked in, Mother. The boiler in Ellie's building is out and—"

"Oh, these darned old buildings," Lally said.

"She called me desperate for a shower."

"Of course, darling." Lally finished her vodka.

"I told her she could meet me here and take a shower *if* she promised to help me with your damn plants."

Lally laughed. "Missy has a brown thumb," she explained as she poured herself another drink. "I'm sure you know that."

"Oh, yes," Ellie said, laughing along with them.

"Well, scoot, scoot," Missy said to Ellie, shooing her out of the kitchen. "You don't want to be late picking up the kids."

"Oh, yes. If you'll excuse me." Ellie stole a *can you believe this?* look at Missy as she left.

Shit, shit, shit! I'm busted. I'm busted all over the place. Ellie rushed into Lally and Woody's bedroom. The place was neat as a pin; Missy had made the bed and folded Ellie's clothes in a little pile. She grabbed her clothes and headed into the bathroom, then took off Woody's robe and hung it on a hook. She was feeling fuzzy and heavy from the sugar. She looked down at her naked stomach. It seemed to be bursting with chocolates. She glanced at the toilet, put her hands on her belly, grabbed a handful of nonexistent flab, and squeezed it hard, her nails digging into her flesh. She studied the toilet again. A full-length mirror was taunting her over her shoulder.

Come on take a look, it seemed to be saying to her. See what you've done to yourself. She turned and examined her naked body.

"Oh, no!" Ellie saw a chubby girl in the mirror. "I look like I've gained ten pounds since I left the house this morning." She walked to the mirror and pressed her nose to her reflection.

"You are a pig!" she said with complete conviction and contempt, then turned and knelt at the toilet. The chocolates came up easily. She hoped that the two women were out of earshot. But, after years of practice, she had perfected the art of barfing almost silently.

Ellie stood motionless in her third shower of the day. The hot, firm stream of water pounding on her shoulders, she cupped her breast in her hands. They were full and leaking. But she was empty now—hollow and clean. Empty.

Chapter Twenty-Four

Ellie sat at her desk typing away. Thank God for insomnia, she thought. I might actually get these shows written in time. The kids and Peter were fast asleep; the house was dead quiet.

"I thought you were going to wake me."

Ellie jumped. "Oh, God. You scared me." She turned to see Peter squinting at her from the hallway in his plaid boxer shorts.

"Why didn't you wake me?" He sounded annoyed.

"I tried," she lied. "I gave you a shake and whispered in your ear. You didn't budge." She smiled sheepishly. Fuck, fuck, fuck, she thought.

"I guess I'm exhausted." He crossed the living room and put his hand on her shoulder. "You're writing? That's great!"

"Yeah. Thank God. I haven't gotten much done lately."

"You're kidding?"

"No! Yes! I mean, I'm getting stuff done, it's just—"

"Are you going to make the deadline?"

"Oh, sure. Sure, I am. It's just—Lisa Fucking Bienstock calls my cell about ten times a day with all her ideas and it's driving me nuts. And . . ." She was scrambling in her head, panicking. "There's grocery shopping to be done and—and Missy and I are trying to plan Ahnika's party. Jesus, I feel like you're checking up on me." She turned away from him and stared at the monitor.

"I'm not checking up on you. It's just the reason we decided to keep Bibi was so you could get some writing done, no?"

"Yes! Yes!" She stood up and marched down the hallway. "What a stupid question," she mumbled and disappeared into the kitchen.

"El, I'm not sure what we're fighting about," Peter called as he followed her into the kitchen.

"I'm not the one who wanted to have some stupid elaborate birthday party for our three-year-old daughter." She slammed open the dishwasher and began unloading it. "Missy has got me meeting jugglers and musicians." She clanked mugs onto a shelf. "I've seen three different possible locations and met I don't know how many caterers." She was lying through her teeth as she stacked bowls in the cupboard. She and Missy hadn't done a thing on Ahnika's party since New Year's.

"El, I'm sorry. We can make it simpler and smaller if you want. I really didn't realize how much work it would be."

She stopped banging the cupboards for a moment and looked at Peter. God, he's all sexy and vulnerable in his boxers. And with his hair falling in his eyes—he's adorable.

"No, no. It's me. It's not you. It's just—it's just—" She stopped.

It's just what? a stern voice spoke in her head. It's just you're spending all your free time with Missy between your legs. It's just that binging and purging can take up a lot of time. Right, Ellie?

"What honey? It's just what?" Peter asked.

She started to cry.

"Ellie." He opened his arms and beckoned her in.

She snuggled into his warm embrace and kissed his chest. He always smells so good, she thought as her tears spilled onto him.

"I love you, sweetie." He kissed her on the top of the head.

"I love you, too." And she wrapped her arms around him. What have I done? What the fuck have I done? She wished she could turn back the clock to New Year's Eve. Back to the moment in the restaurant when he went home sick and she went to the party without him.

"I'm just freaking out about the deadline," she told him through her tears, "and it's my own fault I haven't done anything. I've never written without a partner. I don't know what I'm doing. I just waltzed into Lisa Bienstock's office and pulled a Paul Fuller."

"Pulled a Paul Fuller?"

"Well, I *am* my father's daughter. It's in my blood, literally. So I went into Lisa's office and I conned her, just like my father would've done. I smiled and told funny stories. I charmed her into thinking that I could write a TV show!"

"And what makes you think you can't?" He tucked her under his arm and walked her slowly back into the living room. "You wrote for *Women Aloud.*"

"With Robbie."

He sat them both on the sofa. "You wrote 'Daddy's in the Slammer.' You wrote that all by yourself."

"But I had Robbie to bounce it off of."

He pulled away from her. "What is this obsession you have with Robbie?"

"I'm not *obsessed* with her. Jesus! It's just— I don't know. After I left Juilliard and ended up in rehab, she's the only one who stuck by me. Y'know? Then we became best friends instantly. Maybe because I was an only child. I'd never really had a girlfriend before. Jack, my gay cousin, was the only thing that I had growing up that was like a best friend. But I'm not *obsessed* with her; it's just when I'm struggling with this fucking show I really—*need* her."

"What about Missy?" Peter took Ellie's hand. "She's a mother. Why don't you bounce stuff off of her?"

"Yeah, I guess I could." If he only knew what he was saying, Ellie thought. They sat together silently for a moment. "I've missed you," she said finally.

"Me, too. I've been working so hard on Union City that I haven't seen you in days, it seems."

"How's that going?"

"It's an administrative nightmare. That's why I'm working all these crazy hours."

"I'm sorry it's so much work. But look, the trip to my mom's is right around the corner. We'll have ten days just to hang out. I know spending time with my mother might not sound like fun but Southern California is gorgeous in March. She's gonna crank up the heat in her pool so we can swim every day, if we want. Angus and Ahnika should love that. And I'm sure she'll watch the kids so we can go out. I'll show you the sights of my childhood, such as they were. Where I first got stoned, where I lost my virginity, where I was when my father told me he was going to the big house." She smiled up at him. She was suddenly very excited about showing him around her past. He was silent. "Are you at all excited about going?"

He didn't respond.

"Peter! What's wrong?"

"I'm not sure I can go."

She hopped off the sofa and glared at him. "You're kidding."

"I just said I'm not sure. I just wanted to put that possibility out there so you won't be floored if it happens."

Missy's prophetic words sounded in her head: *He'll cancel.*

"I knew this would happen." She began to pace. "I knew this would happen."

"Honey, I'm sorry, really. I had no way of knowing that Union City would be so difficult to install. Really."

"Why don't you just admit that you don't *want* to go instead of always getting me excited about it and then not going?"

"But I *do* want to go."

"Ha!"

"Look, I run my own business and that takes a lot of time."

Ellie sank down into the easy chair, defeated. Oh my God, Missy was right, she realized. She stared at her sulking husband. What if he's not the man that I think he is? What if he's just like every other schmuck out there?

"Look," Peter said finally. "I *might* be able to go if I can get it done on time. Or maybe I can go, but not for the whole time. Y'know, meet you guys out there."

"If you don't go, we're not going."

"No. You should go. Have fun. See your mom."

"Peter, think about what you just said—'Have fun, see your mom.' Do you see that those two things are mutually exclusive? First of all, five hours on the plane with the two kids and without you?" She gave him a *c'mon now* look. "Sounds like a nightmare. Second of all, visiting my mother without you there for a buffer? I'd end up on the front page on the *L.A. Times*. REKNOWNED AUTHOR KILLED IN HER SLEEP. DAUGHTER HELD FOR QUESTIONING. Besides, I have another invitation."

Peter blinked at her. "Well, are you going to tell me what it is?"

"Missy's parents have a house in the Caribbean, and she's invited me and the kids."

"Well—wow. That sounds like a lot of fun. That's very generous of her."

"Okay," Ellie said flatly. "So I'll cancel the L.A. tickets and book the Antigua tickets. Is that what I should do?"

"Listen, I'm not canceling. I'm just saying that because Union City . . ."

"I know, I know, I know. You *might* not be able to go. So I'm just supposed to be in limbo and let some assholes at Union City decide my fate, is that it?"

"Those assholes at Union City are going to make a shitload of money for us."

"Fine. I don't care. Whatever you think." But, in her head, she thought, I'm calling the airlines tomorrow.

"Honey, everything I do is for you and the kids. Don't you know that?" He sat on the arm of her chair and put his arm around her.

Yeah, right, she thought as she smiled up at him.

"We're spending June at the shore; that's going to be a bundle. Ahnika's tuition, Manhattan is expensive."

"I know, I know," she said, softening a little. "You know I appreciate how hard you work."

"I know you do." He reached down and caressed her breast.

Shit! Ellie thought. Can't we just snuggle? Can't we ever just snuggle? She closed her eyes and tried to relax into him. She *had* missed him, hadn't she? His hand on her breast felt strong and rough. She put her hand on his and tried to soften his caress. He didn't get it. Now both his hands were on her, hard and strong. She willed her vagina to respond. Nothing.

234

"Peter."

"Yes?" he breathed in her ear.

"I'm exhausted."

"That's okay. You don't have to do anything. Just let me take care of you." He picked her up and carried her to the sofa and began kissing her.

But I don't *want* to have sex, she screamed inside her head, so you fucking me wouldn't really be taking care of me, would it? It would be taking care of *you*.

"Peter?"

"What?" There was an edge to his voice.

Can I turn him down? she wondered. It *has* been almost a week since we did it.

"I just . . ."

"You don't want to?"

"I'm just not feeling very sexy right now and I have the deadline and—"

"Fine." And he was up, standing in the middle of the room staring at her.

"Peter. That's not fair."

"Oh, *I'm* not fair? *I'm* not fair? That's perfect!"

"Peter." He was starting to scare her.

"I really don't know what the fuck's up with you these days," he said, narrowing his eyes, examining her. "You spend all this time on the East Side—a place you supposedly hate. I'm paying a fortune on childcare so you can write your fucking TV show, yet you don't seem to be writing. We've barely seen each other for the past week and you don't even care. In fact, it doesn't even seem like you *like* me."

"Peter!"

"It's true. When I touch you, it's like you can't stand my hands on you."

"No, no, that's not true." But it was. God, help me out here, wouldja? Is it too late to fix this thing? She was angry about California, but couldn't stand to have him angry at her. It was like falling into a black hole to have him reject her.

Tell him, a voice told her.

What? That's the answer? she asked God silently. This isn't about Missy. This is about me not wanting to have sex—for once. I'm not allowed that?

You've got to tell him, the voice urged.

"It's just with the news about California and all this pressure from Lisa and us not seeing each other—" She reached for him. He looked at her hand but didn't budge.

"Peter, c'mere." She leaned off the sofa, grabbed his hand, and pulled him to her. "Can we just snuggle a bit? Don't you ever just want to snuggle?"

"We snuggle plenty." He sat next to her grudgingly.

She heard Missy's voice in her head: "Everything they do is just so they can get their dick in your pussy." She placed his limp arm around her. She waited. He squeezed her ever so slightly. Thank you, God.

"I love you," she whispered, not knowing what else to say.

"Do you?"

"Jesus, Peter!" She sprung onto her knees and faced him. "One time. One time in our *entire* relationship that I don't want to have sex and that means I don't love you? That's not fair."

"Ellie, I've got news for you, this isn't the first time you've turned me down."

"Okay, ten, maybe fifteen times in four years I've said no to you. I'm not allowed to not be in the mood? Doesn't that ever happen to you?"

"No. It doesn't."

Missy seemed to whisper in her ear: *Their cocks are in charge, always telling them "get pussy, get pussy, get pussy."*

"Well, you ask your friends. Ask your friends how often *their* wives fuck them—then you'll thank your lucky stars." She walked to her desk and stared at the jumble of words on her monitor, her mind and body racing.

"So, what is it, Ellie?" He was behind her now, his breath on her neck. She didn't budge. "Are you too exhausted, or is it that you have to write? Which is it?"

"Peter? I really don't even recognize you."

He spun her chair around so she was facing him. "Well, we're even then, because I don't recognize you either." They were face to face. Ellie's body was almost vibrating from a strange mixture of rage and fear. She stared at his stony face, weighing her options.

"Okay, let's do it." She got up and headed towards the bathroom.

"What? Where are you going?"

"To put in my diaphragm." She stopped at the hallway and explained. "If it's so important to you, then we'll fuck." She flashed him a big grin laced with hate and was gone.

"Fuck him, fuck him," Ellie mumbled as she stomped down the hallway. "What an asshole. I hate him," she told the empty bathroom as she squirted contraceptive gel into her diaphragm. "I just hate him." She shoved it up inside her and stormed back into the living room. He had opened the sofa-bed in record time and was calmly waiting for her. She climbed over him to her spot, laid face down, and waited. He started caressing her ass.

I do something to him, then he does something to me, then we fuck. Missy's voice was in her head again.

His fingers searched for her vagina; she winced and held her breath.

I hate him. I just hate him. She was motionless as his fingers explored her crack. He turned her over and stroked her pubic hair. She stared at the ceiling, feeling nothing but rage. He opened her legs and dived for her pussy. His tongue was urgent and insistent.

I'm never gonna come, she thought. There's no way.

"Peter," she said quietly as she took his head between her hands.

"What?" He looked up from her pussy. Her pubic hair made it look like he had a dark bushy mustache. She hated him more.

"I want to suck you."

"You don't want me to eat you?" He sounded disappointed. She was hoping he would be.

"No. I just want to suck your big cock," she lied, playing the role of porn queen that she knew he loved, then scooted down into place and wrapped her fingers around his stiff dick. She gripped it hard, imagining that she was squeezing the life out of it.

"I like doing it to you. I love making you happy. Seeing you satisfied is enough for me," she said, parroting Missy's line from the morning. She went to work, doing her best to "make him happy." She was determined to get it over with as soon as possible. He moaned and groaned, she sucked.

"Do you like that? Is it sexy for you?" he asked.

She thought about the dentist and hated him more than ever.

"Mmm," she said finally.

She stopped and rolled onto her stomach; she couldn't bear to look at him.

"I'm dying to feel you inside me," she lied again.

He entered her and fucked her. She gripped the sheets as he banged into her, feeling nothing. He nuzzled his face into her neck and kissed her sweetly.

"I love you so much, El," he whispered.

Her tears spilled onto the pillow as he came inside her. He relaxed onto her and kissed her neck.

"Thank you, sweetie. That felt so great." He rolled off of her. "Did it feel good for you?"

"It felt great," she said flatly, then turned away from him and dried her wet cheeks on the sheets.

"Let me get you a paper towel." He was up and heading toward the kitchen before she could respond.

So much for snuggling, she thought.

Ring!

She sprung up and lunged for the phone but Peter was right next to it.

"For crying out loud!" he said as he put his hand on the receiver. "Who would be calling? It's after midnight. Hello? Oh, hi, Missy."

Shit, Ellie thought.

"No, no, no. We were up actually . . . Oh no. Is he okay? . . . Sure, sure. She's right here. One second." He walked the phone to Ellie.

"It's Missy. Mason's sick. She needs Dr. Granger's number."

"Missy? What's wrong with Mason?"

"Oops," Missy said, giggling. "I thought Peter was working late these days."

"He doesn't work till midnight. What's wrong with Mason?"

"Oh, he's fine, silly. I was making up a story for Peter. But you better say something that makes you sound concerned."

"Oh, my goodness, a hundred and four? Did you give him any Motrin?"

"Good girl. Is he still there?" Missy asked.

Peter was hovering next to Ellie. She looked up at him. "Everything's fine, honey. Can you get me that paper towel?" She smiled innocently at him.

"Sure." And once again he headed for the kitchen.

"Paper towel?" Missy asked. "You weren't fucking him, were you? You didn't give him any pussy, did you?"

"Missy, are you drunk?"

"That's *my* pussy now, you know."

Despite her irritation, Ellie's vagina sprung to attention. "Missy! Why are you calling me at midnight?" She spoke quickly and quietly, keeping an eye out for Peter's return.

"I *had* to talk to you about my mother's unexpected arrival today. Wasn't that unbelievable! When I heard her footsteps in the hall, I just froze."

"Where are you? Where's Antonio?"

"I'm in the library and Tony's fast asleep in our bed. I wanted to hear your voice."

Peter's silhouette appeared at the end of the hallway.

"Take his temp again in fifteen minutes." Ellie spoke with authority, playing the part to the hilt. "If his fever hasn't gone down by then, call Granger and talk to a nurse."

Peter handed her a paper towel and sat on the bed next to her.

"Thank you," she said, smiling.

"Oh, just tell him to go to bed, for goodness sake." Missy was sounding impatient.

Ellie wiped her husband's sperm off her crotch as she spoke to her lover on the phone. "Yeah. His number's 555-0002 . . . No they're great. They won't mind." She was ad-libbing effortlessly, even though her heart rate must have been about two hundred beats per minute. "Of course, you can call me back." She rolled her eyes at Peter and gave him a *what're you gonna do?* look.

"Ellie, darling, get rid of him!"

"Hang on." She put the phone on her lap. "Honey, go ahead and go to bed. I gotta try and get some writing done."

"You sure?"

"Yeah. Missy's worried about Mason. She might call back in a bit, so turn off the phone in our room." They kissed good night, and she smiled and waved at him as he left. She waited till she heard their bedroom door close, then said, "Missy, are you trying to get me divorced?"

"Maybe." Missy laughed loudly. "You get rid of him, I'll get rid of Tony, and you and the kids can move in here. There's plenty of room."

"Listen, I wanted to ask you something. Remember what you said about inviting me and the kids to Antigua?"

"Oh, I was just hoping. I shouldn't have been so bossy about it. It's just so beautiful and peaceful there. I'm sorry I got mad at you. If you have to go to California with Peter, then . . ."

"That's what I wanted to tell you. Peter and I just had—" Ellie stopped short. "What was that?"

"What was what?" Missy asked.

"I thought I heard talking in the background. Is someone there?"

"What kind of a question is that? I'm calling you at midnight, planning our divorces, and you think that Tony is here?"

Ellie was quiet, listening hard. She was suddenly frightened. She thought she heard Missy cover the mouthpiece and then muffled talking.

"Missy, who's there? I just heard you talking to someone. I know I did."

"I had the TV on. I just shut it off. Honestly, Ellie, you are sounding absolutely paranoid. Let's have pillow talk. You be Doris Day and I'll be Rock Hudson."

"You must be drunk. I've never heard you like this."

"I had wine with dinner, then I couldn't sleep because I had to hear your voice."

"Really?"

"Really. Now, what were you saying? You and Peter—go on."

"Oh, nothing. I just hope Peter didn't suspect anything, that's all." She still hadn't shaken off the feeling that Missy was not alone.

"Are you mad about my mother's arrival today? Don't be mad."

"I'm not mad. It's just it's so late and I have so much work to do on the show, Peter and I just fought . . ."

"Fought? I thought you just fucked." Missy giggled.

"Missy!"

"I'm sorry. I just wanted to tell you that I don't think that my mother suspected a thing and that she really liked you."

"She liked me? That's funny. I don't think I formed one coherent sentence the entire time I was standing there sweating all over her husband's robe."

"No, she liked you, she really did. But it's driving her crazy that she can't figure out how she knows you."

"You're kidding." Fuck, Ellie thought. My cover's blown.

"No. She's called me three times since then, determined to solve the mystery."

"Wow." Should I go ahead and tell her? Ellie wondered. If I don't tell her and Lally figures it out . . .

"Missy, listen, I want to tell you something."

"What, sweetie? You can tell me anything."

"Well, this is something I've wanted to mention for a long time, and I've been trying to figure out how or if I should say anything. But after today . . ."

"Wait!" Missy whispered urgently into the phone. "I think I hear Tony. Yes, I think he's up. Gotta go. Love you. Bye."

"Bye," Ellie said into the already silent phone. She stood motionless in the dark hallway, trying to digest the events of the night.

"What the hell was that?" she asked herself as she hung up the phone. She wandered across the living room towards the glow of her computer like a moth to a flame, fell into her chair, and stared blindly at her monitor. "Did Missy just ask me to move in with her? Was she serious?" Yes or no, she was petrified of either answer. "Would she really divorce Antonio?" She rubbed her eyes and tried to focus on her work.

Do they even *have* lesbians on the East Side? Would Missy's snobby friends accept us, invite us to fund-raisers? Or would we have to move to the Village and get a whole new wardrobe and circle of friends? Would we then go to lesbian dinner parties where everyone talks about Rita Mae Brown and Ellen DeGeneres and listens to k.d. lang and Melissa Etheridge CDs? Am I a lesbian? Is my marriage over?

She shut down her computer and headed for the kitchen, took out a box of Triscuits, some peanut butter, and some all-fruit jam. She stood in the harsh kitchen light and made a tiny peanut butter and jam sandwich with two Triscuits and popped it in her mouth. She made and ate another, then another—and another. She crammed each one in her mouth, tasting nothing until she was scraping the bottom of the peanut butter jar. Then she walked to the bathroom like a zombie, got down on her knees, and purged all of her sins out of her for the second time in one day.

Chapter Twenty-Five

"My name is Pinky! But don't call me stinky, cuz that's my grandma's name," a loud cheery voice boomed through Missy and Antonio's apartment as Ellie pushed her new double baby jogger into the foyer.

"Mommy, it's started. The show's started!" Ahnika whined.

"Sit down, sit down!" The voice came ringing from the living room. Ellie looked in to see the living room decorated to within an inch of its life with crepe paper, mylar balloons, and a huge HAPPY BIRTHDAY MASON banner stretched across the floor to ceiling windows. In front of the fireplace, an animated woman in pink satin short-alls was trying to wrangle a passel of preschoolers.

"I can't start until everyone's bottom is on the rug," she continued.

Ahnika jumped out of the double jogger, fell to the floor, and started crying hysterically.

"Ahnika, sweetie," Ellie tried in vain. This is good. Always make a big entrance, she thought, struggling to take Ahnika's coat off as she writhed. Angus sat in his perch in the double jogger, destroying a cinnamon raisin bagel and watching silently.

"We missed it! We missed it!" Ahnika screamed.

Ellie was too humiliated to even look up to see how many well-dressed, on-time mothers were witnessing her nightmare. She finally got the coat off the squirming, sobbing Ahnika only to reveal, yes, her Darth Vader costume.

She leaned into her daughter and whispered, "If you don't calm down we are going straight home."

"It's all because stupid Angus had to nurse," she screamed through tears.

"Sweetie, we don't say 'stupid' in our house." Ellie pulled off one glove. "And it *hasn't* started yet. She's just getting everyone settled." She pulled off the other glove.

"We're not *in* our house; we're in Mason's house."

Ring!

"Fuck!"

"What does 'fuck' mean, Mommy?" Ahnika stopped crying on a dime and asked calmly.

"It means darn it," Ellie explained as she scrambled for her phone in her purse. "Why didn't I shut this thing off?" She hit *send*.

"Hello?"

"Get off the phone, Mommy! We're missing it!" Ahnika's screams were back.

"Ellie, hi, it's me. I have great news."

"*We're missing it!*" Ahnika screamed.

"Lisa, just a second." Ellie held her hand over the phone then barked at Ahnika. "*We aren't missing it! Just STOP IT!*"

Ahnika froze for a moment. So did Ellie.

"What's up, Lisa?" Ellie felt hollow and shaky from too little food and too much exercise. She hadn't thrown up since the night of peanut butter and Triscuits, but she had started running every day, hence the double jogger.

"Well, great news; Larry and Michelle are flying in from L.A. next week and they want to see *Pregnant on Purpose*."

"Great!" Ellie didn't have a clue who Larry and Michelle were, but it was clear from Lisa's tone that she was *supposed* to know.

Ahnika was now whimpering softly. Ellie, the phone still to her ear, picked her up with her free hand and carried her into the living room.

"You're going to pitch it to them a week from Friday, like you did for me. Only now it'll be more polished, and you'll have all the monologues and the show ideas set."

"Uh-huh." Ellie was only half listening to Lisa as she put Ahnika down next to the gaggle of kids. The instant Ahnika saw Mason, she made a miraculous recovery and sat down next to him in the front row.

"Aaahhh!" Now Angus was screaming.

"Listen, Lisa, I have to go," Ellie said under her breath as she sprinted back to the foyer to rescue him.

"Okay, talk to you later."

"Bye . . ."

"Oh, Ellie, I wanted to ask you, I'm having horrible heartburn at night now that I'm so fucking pregnant. What—"

"Sleep sitting up," Ellie said, cutting her off. "It works like a charm. Lisa, I've *really* gotta go!"

"Friday!" Lisa chimed one last time as Ellie hit the power button, flicked her phone closed, and put it in the diaper bag.

"Sorry, sweetie." She gave Angus a squeeze. "Let's go see the show, okay?" and they headed back to Pinky.

"I'm here today because it's Mary's birthday and . . ." Pinky continued to talk in her loud, obnoxious voice.

"No. Mason, not Mary!" Camille called.

"Oh, right, it's *Jason's* birthday party."

"NO!" The children called in unison. "Mason!"

"Oh, right, right, right. It's Mason's birthday today." Pinky hit herself hard on the forehead. The children roared. "And he's eight years old today, and I'm sure . . ."

"No!"

"What?" Pinky looked scared now. "He's not eight?"

"No!" they yelled.

"Then he must be ten. Anyway, I'm sure . . ."

"He's three!" someone called.

"Are you sure?" Pinky looked suspicious.

"YES!" the group bellowed.

"Well, where is this three-year-old Mr. Mason?" Pinky turned her fists into binoculars and searched the crowd. Mason raised his hand; Pinky grabbed it and pulled him from his seat. Mason, wearing a navy cardigan, a white shirt with a Peter Pan collar, gray wool shorts, knee socks, and little navy blue oxfords, stood next to Pinky red faced.

He's got the Little Lord Fauntleroy outfit on again, Ellie realized. Just like at the Christmas party. This is another East Side thing that I don't get. Forget the pansy factor and the fact that shorts in March are completely impractical, how in the hell does Missy get him to wear that outfit? I can barely talk Ahnika into leaving her Darth Vader mask at home.

"Who likes bunnies?" Pinky asked, holding up a large blue-and-white-striped box.

"Me!"

"I do!"

"I like bunnies!"

All the children were yelling and waving their arms.

Ellie looked around and noticed that she was surrounded by more than a dozen kids and four nannies. All the other mothers and nannies were off eating, drinking, and chatting.

Where's Missy? she wondered, scanning the party. Oh, great, she thought when she spotted Missy at the bar, looking timeless in red cashmere sweater set, black slacks, and loafers. Uh-oh, Ellie thought, she's parler-ing avec Frenchy. What is it about Marie-Claire that I don't like? Ellie asked herself as she scrutinized her charcoal gray pants suit with the ever-present Hermès. Maybe it's because she's lived in New York for I don't know how long and she *still* doesn't speak the language.

"Now, when I bring out Larry you all have to be *very* quiet," Pinky whispered. "Cuz bunnies don't like loud noises. Can you do that?" There were nods and mumbles of agreement from the kids. "What? I couldn't hear you. I said 'Can you do that?'"

"Yes!" the children yelled, and Pinky fell over backwards as if blown over by their sheer volume. The crowd went nuts.

A bunny named Larry; that's damn good, Ellie thought as she and Angus headed for the bar.

"Isn't this Pinky person wonderful?" Libby Merrill had appeared out of nowhere. Ms. Monochromatic was a symphony in teal today—teal skirt, blouse, hose, and pumps.

"She's great," Ellie agreed. Now where the heck did Missy and Frenchy go? she wondered.

"Do you know where Missy found her?" Libby asked surreptitiously, as if they were trading government secrets.

"No, I really don't. I think it was a last minute thing."

"Missy has a knack for finding the best everything," Libby said, pouring herself a Diet Coke.

"We really hadn't talked about it much," Ellie told her as she plopped some ice in her club soda. They really hadn't talked about much of anything lately. Oh, Missy and Ellie had seen each other—twice a week, like clockwork. But after the fight with Peter, Ellie had decided to really crack down. She had told Missy that she couldn't waste her Park Avenue Playgroup time lolling in bed. She *must* make her deadline. And Missy hadn't argued. In fact, she had done her best to help; when Missy was finished licking Ellie to delirium, Missy would give her about five minutes to recuperate, then shove her out of bed and to her laptop. So, thanks in large part to Missy, Ellie just might have something to pitch to the all-powerful Larry and Michelle next Friday.

"Mason!" Pinky yelled in mock reprimand. "What have you done to my magic wand?"

Mason stood next to Pinky with a limp wand in his hand, giggling furiously.

"Go! Go!" Angus was yelling and pointing to Pinky.

"Okay, sweetie, just a minute." He was squirming to get down and get back to the fabulous Pinky. He had started walking less than a week earlier, so he was raring to go.

"Do you want me to take him?" Bibi arrived right on cue.

"Yes, Bibi, thanks." She handed her wriggling boy over. "I didn't know you were here already."

"I've been in the kitchen helping out. Did you just get here?"

Ellie nodded sheepishly. "I had to nurse Angus then Ahnika was adamant about wearing her Darth Vader helmet. It was a tad chaotic."

Angus scrambled out of Bibi's arms and beelined it for Pinky.

"Bye," Bibi called over her shoulder, and she was off in pursuit of the toddling Angus.

"She's great with him," Libby said, sipping her Coke.

"She's the best."

"Where in the world did you find her?" Libby asked, as they watched Bibi snag the giggling Angus and give him a big hug.

"Missy, of course."

"She is unbelievable."

"Hello, ladies." Faith Roberts had arrived at the bar in a casual but painfully preppy outfit—navy turtleneck, khakis, and the loafers with the tiny bows again, this time in navy with green trim. Frightening. "Who are we talking about?"

"Missy," Libby told her. "She found Pinky at the last minute, apparently. Isn't she amazing?"

"I suppose 'amazing' is a word that would describe her," Faith said and crammed a Brie-slathered cracker in her mouth. She was carrying a Thomas the Tank Engine paper plate piled high with hors d'oeuvres.

"What's that supposed to mean?" Ellie asked.

"Look," Faith said as she chewed, "I know you two are friends and she's never been anything but gracious to me, but I heard a story about her that made my skin crawl. That's all."

"Wha-a-a-t?" Libby asked, dying for the dirt.

"I really can't say. I was sworn to secrecy."

"But you just did, didn't you?" Ellie said, ready to pop her.

"All I'm saying is Missy Hanover may not be what she appears to be."

"What, Faith? Tell us!" Libby said, closing in, the ice in her Diet Coke clinking.

"Well—"

Ellie shook her head and started to walk away but Faith grabbed her by the elbow.

"Look, Ellie—" Faith's expression was grave "—If what I heard is true you had better—"

Ellie turned and fired, "You know what's really going on here, Faith; you are just completely intimidated by Missy and you can't stand the fact that she is nice and pretty and—well, flawless, really. So you stand at her party—stuffing your face with *her* food—and spread rumors about her."

Ellie's face was pulsing with rage. "That doesn't show very good breeding, now does it, Faith?"

"Just be careful with her, Ellie," Faith said. "Just watch your back."

"Aaahhh!" There was a scream from the group of spellbound kids.

"Devin, stop!" a three-year-old voice called.

"Excuse me," Faith said, popping a shrimp dumpling in her mouth. "Seems Devin needs my help." And she walked away on her loafers with the tiny bows.

"*Devin* needs her help?" Ellie said, "More likely, thanks to Devin, someone needs a blood transfusion. Excuse me, Libby. I have to find the bathroom." She headed off in search of her lover.

Watch your back. Faith's words rang in her head as she entered the dining room. What the heck could the story have been? It made her skin crawl? Jesus! Ellie's need to find Missy felt all the more urgent after the cryptic exchange with Faith. Okay, she's not here, Ellie concluded, scanning the room as she passed through it toward the kitchen.

"Miss Ellie!" Gloria called the moment Ellie came through the swinging door. "What are you doing in here?"

"I thought maybe I could put on an apron and pass some puff pastries."

"Don't you dare start helping, or Miss Missy will never forgive me."

After her run-in with Faith, hiding out in the kitchen sounded pretty darn good, but her first priority was finding Missy.

"Just kidding," Ellie said, giving Gloria a squeeze. She stole a fat strawberry off a fruit platter. "I'm in search of Missy. Have you seen her?" She tried to sound casual, then bit the strawberry in half.

"Not for a while. She's not out there watching the show?"

Ellie shook her head. "She seems to have disappeared."

Gloria shrugged her shoulders. "She'll be back. She always checks in with me."

"Well, back to the show." Ellie put the rest of the strawberry in her mouth and was off. This is weird, she thought as she headed down the hallway. Where could she have gone? Certainly she's not smoking pot in the library during Mason's birthday party. The idea of Missy and Marie-Claire sharing a joint in the dimly lit library sent a chill right through her. She began to racewalk toward the master bedroom. Maybe she's peeing? Maybe she's putting on lipstick? As she got closer to the bedroom door, she thought she heard Missy laughing on the other side. A stab of fear shot through her stomach. Suddenly there were arms around her and a hand over her eyes from behind.

"Guess who?" Antonio's deep, sexy voice whispered in her ear.

"Antonio." She tried to keep annoyance out of her voice. He released his hold and turned her to face him.

"Where are you sneaking off to?" He studied her with mock suspicion.

"Can't a girl use the powder room?" She was anxious to get to Missy. "The guest bath was occupado," she lied. He held her arms firmly and locked eyes with her, his specialty.

"And how is the famous writer?"

"My mother? Oh, she's fine."

"I'm talking about the soon-to-be-famous Ellie Fuller, star and creator of her own TV show," he boomed.

Why is he talking so loudly? Ellie wondered.

"From your mouth to God's ears," she said in her best Jewish grand-mother voice.

Antonio laughed one of his grand laughs and pulled her into him, hug-ging her for a long time. "You will be very famous, my little Ellie." His hot breath in her ear made her legs go wobbly. He began rubbing her back. "Believe me." He continued and showed no signs of letting her go.

"Thank you, Antonio. I hope you're right." She pulled back, struggling against his embrace. It's not you I want, silly, it's your wife, she thought, fighting an urge to plant one on his full Argentine lips.

She stretched onto her tiptoes and whispered in his ear. "Antonio."

"What, darling?" He gripped her shoulders tightly.

"Can I tell you something?"

"Anything."

"If you don't let me go, I'm going to pee all over your floor."

His grip relaxed immediately, and another laugh escaped his lips. "Go! Go and pee."

When Ellie turned to go, he smacked her on the butt. She just laughed. It felt like the most natural thing in the world.

"I must get back to my son's party." And Antonio turned and walked away, leaving Ellie to her search.

Her hand was on the doorknob to the master bedroom in a second. The sound of laughter came again. It stopped Ellie in her tracks. She felt suddenly scared of what she might find on the other side. She opened the door; the bedroom was dark, the curtains drawn. She thought she could see two figures standing on the far side of the big Italian bed.

"Missy?"

"Yes." Her voice was flat. Ellie felt cold suddenly. Her eyes adjusted to the darkness, and she could see it was Marie-Claire standing next to Missy. They were looking at her silently, waiting, it seemed, for an explanation.

"Oh, uh, sorry. Missy, I was looking for you."

There was a beat, then—"Well, here I am," Missy said coldly.

Marie-Claire said something quietly to Missy, in French, Missy responded, then the two women laughed.

What the fuck are they saying? Ellie wondered, feeling like an idiot. Are they talking about me?

"Excusez-moi, Marie-Claire, but I need to parler avec Missy, s'il vous plaît." Ellie shot daggers at Frenchy in the dim light, hoping she saw them. Marie-Claire just shrugged her shoulders and began to giggle. The two women began to babble in French again.

"Missy! I need to talk to you." She was trying hard not to scream.

Missy looked at her lover/best friend with disdain. "Honestly, Ellie, you are being impossible again."

What is going on here? Ellie wondered. What the hell is going on? She studied Missy's detached demeanor. She felt hot and prickly all over and her breathing was shallow. Marie-Claire whispered something to Missy. They laughed. Visions of playground meanies crowded Ellie's brain. She had an almost uncontrollable urge to march over to the two women and shove Marie-Claire over. No one moved or said a word for what felt like forever.

"I hope you two enjoy the bed," Ellie said finally, and she shut the door with a bang.

Chapter Twenty-Six

"Wine?" A smiling waiter, holding a tray of white wine, intercepted Ellie when she entered the foyer.

"Why not?" Her hand was shaking as she reached for the glass. "Thanks." She took a big gulp.

"*Reediculous!*" Pinky was saying with eyes crossed when Ellie entered the living room. Faith, Libby, Sophie, and the tall Indian nanny had made their way into the living room and were standing around the edges, eating and chatting. Ahnika sat beaming in the front row, and Angus was jumping on Bibi's lap, happy as could be.

They didn't even notice I was gone, Ellie thought sadly as she sipped her wine.

"Who wants some of my pinkalicious pink lemonade?" Pinky asked, holding up a small gold pitcher.

"Me! I do!" The crowd responded.

The minutes ticked by as Ellie numbly watched Pinky's show. Where's Missy? Why isn't she back at the party? she wondered. Ellie could see the dining room table crammed with endless platters of food. They seemed to be calling her like a siren.

Okay, El, it's been seventeen days. Don't blow it now. Don't blow it, she told herself. *We admitted we were powerless over food—that our lives had become unmanageable. Came to believe that a Power greater than ourselves could restore us to sanity. Made a decision to turn our will and our lives over to the care of God as we understood Him.* She recited the first three steps in her head. All I have to do is not binge today, she thought. Just don't binge between now and when you go to bed, that's all you have to do, El. As she sipped her wine, she could feel her heart rate slow and her nerves soften. Then there was a hand on her shoulder; she smelled the familiar powdery perfume.

"Missy. I'm—"

"Don't you ever embarrass me like that again," Missy told her, a stiff smile pulled across her lips.

The room disappeared; Ellie was in suspended animation.

"Do you understand?" Missy asked.

"No, I don't, quite frankly. I don't understand you at all," she said with all the cool detachment she could muster and headed for her lifeline.

Nobody here, thank God, she thought as she took an inventory of the spread. Missy had managed to make it all look elegant even with a Thomas the Tank Engine tablecloth. Ellie started with a big chunk of Brie, then checked over her shoulder. Pinky had the crowd in the palm of her hand; Missy was watching and laughing with the rest. Ellie shoved the hunk of cheese in her mouth. While she chewed, she poured herself another glass of wine, washed down the Brie with a couple of gulps, then moved on to a platter of empanadas. Her breathing was shallow. Her heart beat loud and strong as she downed them, tasting nothing. A handful of raspberries were next, followed by more wine, then back to the Brie. She kept one ear trained on Pinky's voice, making sure the show wasn't ending. She was pouring her third glass of wine when she saw Marie-Claire walk into the room.

Let's see how bad her English really is, she thought, smiling at the bitch.

"Why, hello, Marie-Claire, you annoying little twit," she said, feeling bulletproof, thanks to the wine.

Marie-Claire's eyes widened; she put her hand on her collarbone. "Excusez-moi?"

"Oh, I was just thinking what a stupid cow you are," Ellie told her, piling crackers and cheese onto a paper plate.

"Je ne comprends pas."

"Really? You don't comprend? Isn't that a shame?"

Marie-Claire started to babble in French.

"Excusez-moi, Marie-Claire—" Ellie cut her off "—but I was just wondering when the fuck you're ever going to learn to speak English? What? Not a good enough language for you? Too vulgar?"

Marie-Claire was responding in French, her voice was becoming louder and shriller. She began to gesture wildly. Ellie could see heads turning in the other room. Libby Sinclair caught Ellie's eye with a concerned look. Ellie shrugged her shoulders and gave Libby a *beats me* look.

"Pipe down, Frenchy. You're causing a scene." Ellie patted her on the shoulder, then took her plate full of drugs and left the irate Marie-Claire alone in the dining room.

Ellie stared blindly at the little shell-shaped soaps in the guest bath as she downed the last of four dumplings. Each bite dulled the pain a little. Each swallow stuffed down the rage a bit.

"Do I dare sneak out for another round?" she asked Thomas the Tank Engine, who stared up at her from her empty plate. She felt suddenly overwhelmed as she pictured the day of mothering still ahead of her— nursing Angus at two more times, getting the kids home, bathed, fed, into pj's, into bed, and to sleep. "How can I do it? How can I possibly do it?" All she wanted was to be alone with her food. To be able to eat and purge, then eat some more.

Someone jiggled the doorknob. She jumped.

"Just a minute," Ellie called, tossing Thomas in the trash. Then she turned around onto her knees, placed one hand near her mouth and one hand on the handle, ready to flush. With precision timing, she purged and flushed simultaneously. The sound of the toilet covered, she hoped, the sound of her retching.

"Ellie, is that you?" a voice called through the door.

"Yes. I'll be out in a minute!" She rinsed out her mouth. "Jesus, can't a person get any privacy?" she mumbled as she dried her mouth on a monogrammed towel. The little box with the lipstick in it was sitting in its usual place. She took out the Malt Shimmer.

"You look like shit," she whispered to her reflection. She was staring into her past again. Her face was pale and drawn from weeks of too much running and not enough food or sleep.

"This is it, no more barfing. That's it!" She put on the lipstick, pinched her cheeks, and opened the bathroom door.

Libby Sinclair was just outside the door. Ellie nearly fell over her.

"Are you okay?"

"I'm fine. Why?" Shit, she knows.

"Well, I saw you and Marie-Claire . . ." she paused, searching for the word ". . . chatting, and there seemed to be a problem. No?"

Okay, she didn't hear, Ellie realized.

"You know those Parisians, so emotional," Ellie explained. "I'm not sure *what* she was talking about, to tell you the truth. Her English is so limited."

"But what . . . ?"

"IT'S TIME FOR CAKE!" Gloria called from the dining room. There were screams and cries from the living room as thirteen crazed preschoolers stampeded toward a sugar high.

"Excuse me, Libby, I'm dying to get a look at this cake." Ellie joined the rest of the troops in the dining room. She searched the room for her lover—nothing. A child-size banquet table with tiny chairs and Thomas the Tank Engine tablecloth, napkins, party hats, etc., had been set up at the far end of the dining room.

"Okay, everybody find a seat," Gloria called. The children scrambled to obey. Mason sat at the head with Ahnika by his side. Bibi put Angus next to his sister. He grabbed a party hat and put it in his mouth. Gloria turned off the lights, and Missy emerged from the kitchen carrying the cake.

Everyone broke into a rousing chorus of "Happy Birthday." Ellie felt numb and detached as the off-key voices bounced off her. She studied her beautiful and confounding friend; the candlelight cast ghoulish shadows on Missy's perfect face.

"*. . . Happy birthday to you!*"

254

When the song ended, everyone applauded as Missy placed the train-shaped cake in front of Mason.

"Make a wish, make a wish," someone called.

Mason blew his little lungs out. It took three attempts and a little help from his mother for him to do the job. More applause.

"I want the face!" Mason shouted.

"And you shall have it," his mother told him. A waiter took the cake back into the kitchen. Moments later, he and a pal returned, loaded down with plates of birthday cake. They passed them quickly and efficiently to the unruly hordes. Ellie headed to the kitchen.

"How can I help?" she asked Gloria, who was carving up Thomas at breakneck speed.

"Miss Ellie, don't you dare . . ."

"Gloria, please," she said, arranging three cake plates in her right hand. "Never take away a person's job when they really need one," she told her as she grabbed a fourth plate with her left hand and was gone.

This is good, Ellie thought as she placed cake in front of perfect little Camille. This I can do; passing, smiling, this I'm good at. And she headed back to Gloria for a refill. In the kitchen with the waiters she loaded up again.

"Clearly you're a veteran," the headwaiter said as he watched Ellie's plate technique.

"Yep. I was passing pâté to snooty assholes when you were still in diapers."

Everyone laughed and they all headed out. Ellie walked to the kiddy table only to realize that all the children had been served.

Shit, she thought staring at her armload of cake. I didn't think this through. She considered the group of cakeless adults.

"Look at you!" Libby screeched. "Where'd you learn the plate trick?"

Oh, shut up, Libby, Ellie thought. "I don't really remember, to tell you the truth," she lied and handed Libby a plate. Missy was next in line.

"Oh—my—God!" Missy said.

"What?" Ellie was suddenly petrified.

"I've figured it out. I have *finally* figured it out!"

"What, Missy?" Libby asked. "What in the world are you talking about?" Libby looked around at the group with a *what a fun party game* look on her face.

Now it seemed the whole party was waiting for Missy's answer. Ellie was frozen.

"Well," Missy began as if she had a really good one, "ever since we first met . . ." she put her arm around Ellie ". . . ever since that first day at Park Avenue Playgroup, Ellie has looked familiar to me."

I'm dead, Ellie thought. I'm fuckin' toast.

"And when my mother met her, she also thought Ellie looked very familiar. In fact, she's been going nuts trying to figure out how she knows her."

"And you just figured it out?" Libby piped in.

"Yes!" Missy looked at her friend, still holding the plate full of cake. "I just figured out that she and I met, in a manner of speaking, in this very apartment seven years ago. She was at our engagement party, right in this very room, as a matter of fact. The hair was longer and not quite so blond, but I'm certain it was she—standing behind the buffet table at our engagement party, carving roast beef for all our guests!"

"No!" Libby said as she examined Ellie.

"Really?" Faith said.

All heads turned to Ellie. It was clearly her turn.

"Oh, my goodness. You're right!" Ellie wanted to take a plate full of gooey cake and mash it in Missy's face, but instead she smiled at her captive audience. "I always thought Missy looked familiar, and this apartment did, too." Ellie put her arm around Missy and gave her a deadly squeeze. "Thanks for solving the mystery, pal."

Her brain was aching, her empty stomach churning, but she was gonna get out of this one, somehow.

"But the funny thing is *why* I was carving roast beef at that party." Okay, El, now's your moment. "I—had—just been cast in a movie as a waiter. And I was doing research."

"Really?"

Libby bought it. Is Missy buying it? Ellie wondered. She couldn't look at her.

"Yes. And to prepare for the role, I worked for this catering company for a few parties."

"You were in a movie?" one of the nannies asked.

"Yes." She felt light and somehow detached from the surreal scene.

"What was it called?" the nanny asked.

"Road to Ruin." The title popped into her head like magic. "It was a big bomb, and my scenes were all cut out. It went straight to video, thank God. You can see me in the background in a couple of scenes."

You're babbling, El, that's enough, she admonished herself.

"Anyway, that's how I learned the plate trick." She held the plates up for the crowd, then handed one to Missy. Their eyes met briefly. Ellie tried hard to send a message of hurt and disbelief to her lover in that moment.

"I had to do it in one of the scenes that was cut." She smiled hopefully at her audience. "Now, if you'll excuse me, I'll be back in just a minute with your drink orders."

There was a smattering of laughter as Ellie exited. She marched through the foyer without a plan. I could just leave, she thought, eyeing the elevator as she passed. But the kids, I have to get the kids. Fuck! I'm trapped in a birthday party not of my own design. She whipped past the family photos that lined the hallway, toward the master bedroom, not knowing where else to go. She felt her way to the bed in the darkness, dove onto the Italian bed and buried her face in the endless pillows.

I'm not going back to that room full of snobby preppies, she vowed silently. I'm not! Her heart was racing, her whole body vibrated. She wanted to cry or scream but she couldn't connect. She felt empty and light-headed, floating on the Italian bed in the dusky room. She wasn't really in her body, one of the perks of bulimia.

"Okay, God, help me out, could you?" she whispered into the pillow. "I'm sorry, I really am. I've really fucked up, I know I have, but I need you. Help me to get back in my body. Please! I can't stand this. I know it's my own fault but I can't stand this feeling." She waited—floating, vibrating, hoping. She waited for some kind of click, some sort of switch to feel grounded again. Nothing. "Can you at least help me to make a plan to get out of here?"

She felt a hand on her back. Missy, she thought. She looked up. Her eyes met Antonio's, soft and green, in the dim light.

"Are you all right?" He sat on the bed next to her. She tried to respond, but her throat closed up. She put her face into the pillows again and barked out loud, uncontrollable sobs. "Ellie." He patted her back. "Ellie, darling. Don't. Don't be so sad." He stroked her hair. "It's all right." His voice sounded sweet and paternal. "It's all right."

Her sobs came harder. He lay down beside her, his face inches from hers.

"Okay, okay. I'm here. Okay. Everything's all right," he cooed to her and held her close to him. She felt safer and her sobs eased up a bit. "You mustn't take Missy too seriously. She doesn't think before she speaks half the time."

He's so sweet, Ellie thought. He's always been sweet to me and I'm sleeping with his wife. I'm a horrible person.

"Okay, that's okay." He held her and cooed to her for a long time and she began to feel real again, more grounded. She was back in her body. "You are so beautiful and dear, my Ellie. Don't be so sad."

Her crying had stopped; her breathing was returning to normal.

"Don't be so sad, my beautiful Ellie." She felt Antonio's breath on her neck. "Missy loves you, you know she does. She doesn't think sometimes, she just doesn't think."

Ellie looked up. He locked onto her with those eyes of his. He's so kind, she thought.

"Ellie, darling, everything's all right." He kissed her forehead, then pressed his cheek against hers.

She wrapped her arms around his neck and held on tight. She wanted him so badly, wanted to crawl into him and never leave, wanted to put her lips on his, to feel his body against hers, his tongue in her mouth, his hands on her breasts.

"Ellie, darling." His hips pressed in to her.

I want you now, her body screamed, *now!* He kissed her ear. She wrapped a leg around him and pulled her crotch toward his cock. Was it hard? She knew it must be; she ached for it. They didn't speak or kiss or even look at each other, as if avoiding those things meant they weren't really doing what they were doing. Their breathing came quickly now as their pelvises ground together. His stiff cock, straining against his pants, pressed into her. She loved it. Their clothes were an annoying inconvenience. She wanted them gone, wanted them to melt away and him to enter her now, *now!*

"Ellie?"

The two panting lovers froze. Ellie opened her eyes and saw Missy's silhouette in the doorway.

"Is that you?"

258

Ellie and Antonio rolled away from each other and onto their backs.

"I wanted to apologize." Missy walked slowly in the darkness to the bed, crawled onto it, then lay down on Ellie's left. "I didn't mean to upset you so."

"Oh," was all Ellie could muster. She was now a Missy/Antonio sandwich. Did she see us, Ellie wondered? She must've heard us. Is she angry?

"I wasn't thinking," Missy said. "Sometimes I just don't think before I speak."

My God, Ellie thought, that's just what Antonio said.

Missy put her hand on Ellie's cheek, cool and damp from tears.

"Were you crying?" Missy kissed her on the cheek. "I'm so sorry I made you cry," she whispered in her ear.

Jesus Christ, Ellie thought. Isn't she going to say something about catching us humping in her bed? Missy's breath on her ear, with Antonio so close and so hard, was so erotic that Ellie thought she might faint.

"I'm sorry." Missy put one hand on Ellie's stomach and kissed her cheek again. "Can you forgive me? Can you ever forgive me?" Missy's hand, pressing hard into her, traveled down Ellie's belly and cupped her dampness. She was transported, out of her body again, floating on the feel of Missy's firm hand on her pussy and the thought of Antonio so close. Did he know about the two of them? Did he care? Did Missy see what they had been doing? Did *she* care? Her mind was swirling.

"I'm sorry," Missy whispered again as she pressed her fingers deep into the folds of Ellie's pants.

The three of us together, Ellie thought. She turned away from Antonio, toward Missy and kissed her. It was perfect and delicious, like always, but better, better than before, better than ever because Antonio was there, close, behind her, watching them.

Like Peter's fantasy, Ellie thought. She was hoping Antonio would hold her, stroke her, enter her. These damn clothes!

Missy's hand was inside Ellie's pants now, struggling against the Lycra, searching for her wetness. And she was helpless in Missy's grip. Any thoughts of anger or mistrust were drowned in the luscious sea of fingers and lips and tongues. Missy was kissing her belly now. Kissing it sweetly as her fingers did their magic, and Ellie floated higher and higher. Missy was between Ellie's legs now, her pants around her ankles. She opened her eyes and she thought she saw Antonio still beside her, watching her, smiling at her. She closed her eyes again as she came and came and came. Trying not to scream, only gasping quietly as she grabbed Missy's head, wrapped her legs around it, and pushed it deep into her pussy. She panted on the Italian bed, slowly, slowly floating back down to earth again. She opened her eyes and looked to her right; Antonio was gone. When had he left, she wondered? Had he really ever been there? Did he watch us or not? Ellie wasn't sure of anything anymore.

five miles a day and she hadn't thrown up since the debacle at Mason's party. But she was whiteknuckling it this time, doing it without help, without meetings or phone calls or a sponsor—or God. Oh, she was still talking to God, of course. But she wasn't surrendering to him, no way, uh-uh. She was doing it all on sheer will.

Ellie hadn't seen Missy since Mason's party over two weeks ago; Missy had been busy with some sort of charity function, so their regular Tuesday and Thursday rendezvous had been put on hold. Instead of being disappointed by this, Ellie had actually felt relieved.

She had been spending all her "Missy time" doing what she should've been doing all along—writing. And when the day of the big meeting with the all-powerful Larry and Michelle came along, Ellie's pitch was just about perfect.

Ellie was feeling pretty darn confident as she stepped into a cab and gave the driver HBO's address. She was even happy with her outfit. She sat back to go over the pitch in her head and her purse began to ring. She clicked open her phone and checked the readout: *Call from Private.*

"Lisa? I'm going to see her in ten minutes. What could she *possibly* have to say to me?" She pressed *send.*

"Hello."

"Hi, Ellie. This is Josh, Lisa Bienstock's assistant. Listen, the meeting's been canceled."

"You're kidding me!"

"No. I'm sorry to call at the last minute. Larry and Michelle had some sort of a conflict."

"What? But I'm on my way there."

"I know, I'm sorry but . . ."

"Where's Lisa?"

"Well, you're not going to believe this; first I get a call from Michelle, then Lisa called from a cab." He paused. "She's in labor."

"Really?"

"She's on her way to the hospital even as we speak."

"Well, that is fabulous!" At that point Ellie had actually smiled. Fuck Larry and Michelle, she had thought, then she had said good-bye to Josh, turned off her phone, and told the cab driver to turn around.

Chapter Twenty-Seven

I'm really on top of things," Ellie said to herself as she surveyed the r
piles of clothes, shoes, and toiletries that she had laid out on the sofa. S
went over her crumpled packing list. "Sippy cups and baby spoons." S
marched off into the kitchen, gathered four sippy cups and three b;
spoons, and tucked them into the cold pack.

"This time tomorrow we'll all be poolside," she said to the quiet kitch
as she zipped up the cold pack. "Maybe Peter and I can actually have a cc
versation. This may be good. This visit with my mom may actually be oka

I'm going to give everything up slowly," she had told herself the morni
after she had shared a bed with Missy and Antonio. "That's how I did
the first time," she told herself. So she had cut her running back to on

. . .

The idea of the trip to L.A. had kept her going through all of this. The idea of getting out of New York, away from HBO—and her lover—well, it just seemed like a good idea.

She and Peter had drifted so far apart that she wasn't sure how to get back to him, back to how sweet and wonderful it had been. She hoped it was still possible.

"We'll work it all out in California," she told the dark hallway as she headed back for the living room. "I know we will. Where the heck is he?" She looked at her watch. "It's after midnight. Jeez." She began filling the suitcase, slowly and methodically. "Maybe I can be all packed by the time he arrives."

The suitcase was half filled when she heard his key in the lock. She dropped a handful of clothes and ran to him. "Hi, there," she said, stretching onto her tiptoes and kissing him on the mouth. "Long day, huh? I'm almost packed." She skipped back into the living room and did a grand gesture at her accomplishments.

Peter just stared, looking shell-shocked. She felt a twinge of fear burrowing in the base of her spine. She forged on.

"My mom called today," she told him, falling to her knees to resume her packing. "She is *so* excited we're coming, it's almost cute. She said the weather has been perfect, around seventy-five during the day. It got up to eighty last week. And she's got the pool cranked up to like ninety-two! I know this sounds crazy, but I think we may actually have fun."

"I can't go."

She wanted to jump up and take him by the neck but she continued packing, placing Angus's clothes into the suitcase like pieces of a puzzle as she focused on breathing and trying not scream.

"I'm sorry, El. I'm really sorry." He wearily put down his briefcase.

She didn't respond.

"El, c'mon, you know I'd go if I could."

"No big deal," she said flatly as she grabbed her new turquoise bikini from the piles of clothes on the sofa and threw it into the suitcase.

"New suit?"

"Yes. I bought it for our trip." She hated him, hated that he had ruined their chance to connect again.

"I'm sorry, El. You know I am." He collapsed into the easy chair, his face in his hands.

"I know." Goddamn him, she thought as she studied his crumpled frame, he's managed to make *me* feel bad. He's canceled again at the last fucking second and *I* feel bad for *him*.

"Don't worry, honey. It's not a big deal." She didn't mean a word of it. She stared at the half-filled suitcase and the folded clothes on the sofa. "Peter?"

He looked up at her, defeated.

"Would you do me a favor?"

"Sure."

"Would *you* call my mother and tell her that we're not coming."

"But you guys can still go. Maybe I can change my ticket and meet you."

"Forget it! I'm not going to spend five hours on a plane with a baby and a toddler just to be tortured by my mother for ten days. I'd rather have gum surgery. Every time I go out there—*every time*—I vow that I'll never do it again."

"Honey, I'm so sorry . . ."

She was out of the room before he could finish his sentence. That's it, it's over, she realized, our marriage is over. He won't do me this one little thing and visit my mother with me. That says it all.

She stood in the playroom, staring at the shelves crammed with books. She grabbed a random handful and put them in a stack on the floor.

"*He's* the one who wanted Ahnika to go to Park Avenue Playgroup, not me. And *that's* where all the trouble started," she mumbled as she grabbed some markers and a pad of construction paper. Her eyes welled with tears. She sank to the floor and stared blindly into space. "Fuck him," she whispered to the wall of toys and books, "just fuck him." She sat on the playroom floor, hugging her knees.

"I thought I could do it. I thought I could get the fuck out of this Missy thing and pull us back together. But he doesn't even care." She put her forehead on her knees and wept. "He doesn't even care."

"El, honey, I'm so sorry." She heard his voice from the doorway. She didn't look at him.

"It's just this is such a big account and it could—"

"Fuck the account! Fuck that stupid account!" She stood up and faced him, fists at her sides, ready for battle. "What about our marriage? Doesn't that mean anything to you?"

"Wait a minute? Did I miss something? What the hell is wrong with our marriage?"

"Peter, my God. Where have you been?"

"I've been right here, Ellie. I've been right here working my ass off so I can make a nice life for you and the kids."

"God, I hate that sacrificial bullshit! You work hard because you like it. You *love* being good at what you do and running your own company. Don't make it sound like some big sacrifice you do for me and the kids, 'cause I don't want it! I don't want that on my back!" She swooped up the art supplies and squeezed past him. He followed.

"I don't need more clothes or money or stuff. We have plenty of stuff." She threw the art supplies on the sofa.

"So what about this?" He took her new bikini out of the suitcase and dangled it in her face. "What's this if you don't need more stuff?"

She grabbed it from him and threw it back in the suitcase. "I got that for you, for our trip together. I thought you'd like seeing me in it."

"But you'd hate wearing it."

"I thought it might spark some interest. When was the last time we made love?"

"A week ago yesterday."

"And when have we *ever*, in our entire relationship, not fucked for a week?"

"Look, I'm sorry about all this. I'm sorry I ruined our vacation, but—"

"Oh, you haven't ruined *my* vacation. You've ruined *your* vacation."

"What do you mean?"

"*I'm* going to have a vacation. The kids and I are going to have a great vacation!"

"You are?"

"Yes." She walked to the phone, feeling vengeful and renewed. "We're going to Antigua with Missy." She dialed.

"Don't you think it's a little late to be calling?"

"This is an emergency; Missy's a good friend." The phone rang once. "She'd call *me* in an emergency."

"You're inviting yourself?"

"She already invited us." It rang again. "I said no because we were *supposedly* going to California as a family. Remember?" Ring number three.

"Hi. We can't come to the phone right now, please leave a message after the tone. Thanks."

"Missy, hi, it's me. I'm sorry to be calling so late. There's been a change of plans. We're coming to Antigua. Isn't that great?" Her voice cracked. She swallowed hard to force back tears. "I hope the invitation still stands. Call me. Any time." She waited on the line as the machine continued to record, hoping that Missy was there and would pick up. "Okay? Call me. Call me, okay? Bye." She hung up. She felt like she was dangling in midair between Peter and Missy—hanging over a huge crevasse. Peter held one hand and Missy held the other and—in both cases—her grip was slipping.

"Ellie, what the hell's going on?" His voice was like ice.

She could feel his eyes on her as she went back to her packing. "Well, I'm packing and you're watching."

"El, talk to me."

She looked up finally; his face was ashen, his eyes cold and angry. He knows, she realized in that instant. But how could he? Her heart leaped into her throat and she thought she might throw up. "And what is it you'd like me to say?"

"Ellie, what is going on? I heard the tone of your voice when you left that message. There's something not right here."

"Yeah, what's not right is you canceling our trip at the last minute and never fucking me," she said, throwing things into the suitcase, "and not giving a shit about our marriage and . . ."

He grabbed her wrist. His grip was steel. "Stop!" he shouted. The two of them froze. "Look at me." She didn't budge; he squeezed her wrist tighter. "Look at me!"

He knows, he knows! Oh, my God, he knows! She lifted her head slowly and met his gaze, trying like hell to keep the terror and guilt out of her eyes.

"Tell me what I heard in your voice isn't true. Please! Tell me I'm just imagining things between you two."

"You are imagining things." She peeled his fingers off her wrist. "Missy and I are friends. Friends! That's it." She looked in his eyes again and did her best Stanislavski. "You wanted me to find a friend at Park

Avenue Playgroup. Well, I did. Don't try to turn it into some Penthouse pictorial because of your overactive libido." She pushed out a laugh, praying it sounded light-hearted.

"Penthouse pictorial? What are you saying?"

"Well, that's what *you're* saying, isn't it? That's what you're picturing—some wild lesbian affair between the two of us."

"What?"

Ellie continued stuffing and organizing things in the suitcase.

"*What?*" He leaped over the suitcase and grabbed Ellie by the shoulders. Her grip on Peter and Missy had slipped and she was sailing down the deep ravine toward a rushing river.

"Peter, stop! You're hurting me."

"Tell me! Tell me what you were saying."

"I was just saying out loud what you were thinking. That Missy and I are lovers."

"That's not what I was thinking."

She splashed into the icy water; her whole body ached.

"It's not?" Her voice was a tiny whisper.

"No, no. That's what *you* were thinking."

I'm dead, she thought, as the wild water carried her down river to some unknown disaster.

"What I thought was that you and Missy had planned this whole Antigua thing all along, hoping and praying that I'd cancel. But you just told me the real deal, didn't you?" His voice was low and soft, his fingertips burrowing into her shoulders.

"Peter, you're talking crazy. I only thought—"

"It's too late, El, no backpedaling now. You just solved the mystery for me. You just told me why I've never really liked Missy. Why we've been seeing less and less of each other for months. Why lately I feel like I don't even recognize you anymore . . ."

"Peter, please! Missy and I are friends. You've . . ."

". . . AND WHY WE NEVER FUCK ANYMORE!" he roared in her face. His grip felt as if he were crushing her bones.

"Peter, you're hurting me." Tears spilled onto her cheeks. He released her and turned away.

"Get the fuck out of here before I kill you."

"But— Peter, no. I never wanted to—" She had never pictured this moment; she had no plan, no ammunition. Her brain scrambled for a defense. "But whose idea was it? Huh? Not mine. You're the one who talked on and on about how much you wanted me to be with another woman. It was Missy this and Missy that. That's all you ever talked about. It wasn't my idea, Peter."

"Well, it sure the fuck wasn't my idea. You think this is what I wanted? You deceiving me, shitting all over me? No, that was definitely not my idea." He was pacing and panting. He stopped and stared off silently, shaking his head. "All this time. All this time I've been the fucking chump?" He turned to her. "Fuck you!" He clenched his fists by his face like a boxer.

Ellie braced herself, ready for a punch.

Thwack! He kicked the suitcase.

"Fuck you!" Another kick.

"But, Peter, I thought it was what you wanted." She was sobbing now.

"You did, that's what you thought?" Kick! "I never got to watch Missy eating your pussy, did I?" Kick! "Or sucking your tits." Kick! "No, I was working like an asshole! Oblivious! The joke was on me!" Kick! He picked up the now-full suitcase, lifting it over his head . . .

"Peter, stop!"

. . . then turned it over and rained bathing suits, suntan lotion, and their future down on Ellie. She covered her head and fell to her knees.

"It wasn't me. Peter, it wasn't me." She heard the suitcase drop to the floor, heard Peter's footsteps in the hall, heard the deadbolt turn.

"Peter!" She shot up and raced for him. "Where are you going?"

"Away from you!" The door slammed behind him.

She opened it; he stood at the elevator.

"Peter!"

"You would take our life, this wonderful life that we had, and just throw it away on some lesbian affair?"

"I didn't, really! I . . ."

"If you think you're getting custody of the kids, think again."

"Peter! Peter, don't!"

The elevator doors opened.

"I'll spend every penny I have to keep you away from them." He stepped in.

She lunged for the buttons to stop him, but the doors closed, and the elevator clicked away. She fell to the floor next to the elevator. Her cold, bruised body was now careening down the rapids, bumping from rock to rock.

Chapter Twenty-Eight

He'll be back. You know he'll be back." Arlene lit a Marlboro Light, then handed it across the small round table to Ellie. She took a long deep drag as if she'd been smoking all her life. That is heaven, she thought as she watched the foot traffic that passed the outdoor café at Ocean Grill.

"Look. Peter loves you, right?"

Ellie nodded and mumbled an agreement, then searched the sidewalks in a vain hope that Peter would pass.

"I've left ten messages." She smoked and stared at her cell phone, which sat on the table next to a basket of untouched bread.

"He'll call." Arlene's voice sounded soothing.

"I've been sittin' up waitin' for my sugar to show." The woman at the next table seemed to be talking to them.

"What?" Arlene said as she turned to the woman.

A big-toothed woman with long sandy blond hair sat at the next table with a cigarette in her hand and a full ashtray in front of her.

"I've been listening to the sirens and the radio," the woman continued.

Oh, my God, Ellie thought. She looked at Arlene and widened her eyes as if to say, Do you know who that is? But Arlene was clueless.

"So, are you having man trouble, too?" Arlene asked.

"He said he'd be over three hours ago. I've been listening for his car on the hill."

Arlene gave Ellie a puzzled look.

"That's a lyric from 'Car on the Hill,'" Ellie explained to Arlene. "And you're Joni Mitchell, right?"

Joni winked at Ellie, then opened her mouth and sang like the heavenly genius that she is, *"I'm just livin' on nerves and feelings / With a weak and a lazy mind . . ."*

"That's it!" Ellie said grabbing Joni by the arm. "That's how I feel. How did you know?"

Ring!

Ellie's cell phone was ringing; she threw herself on herself on it.

"Peter?" She pressed the phone to her ear so hard it hurt. Joni was still singing—loud.

"Hi, it's me." Peter's sweet voice soothed every part of her.

"Where are you?"

"I'm on the street, on my cell phone. Where are you?"

"I'm at Ocean Grill with Joni Mitchell."

Arlene gave her a *hey, what about me* look.

"And Arlene."

"With Joni Mitchell? What are you talking about?"

"Never mind. It's just, I'm sorry and I love you and I want you see you."

"I know. I'm coming to you. I'm coming to you right now."

"You are?" She stood up and her napkin fell to the ground.

"Yes! I'm walking across Broadway."

Ellie crawled under the table to retrieve her napkin.

"I'll be there in less than five minutes."

"Great!" She was on her knees with one hand on the cell phone and the other on the elusive napkin. "I love you."

"I love you, too."

There was a screech of tires, a loud thud, then silence.

"Peter?" Ellie was still under the table on her knees and elbows. "Peter? Peter, are you okay? Answer me." She could hear voices and traffic in the background. "Are you there? Are you all right?"

"Call 911," Ellie heard on the phone.

"Oh, my God! Is he dead?" Another voice.

"PE-E-E-E-TER!" Ellie screamed into the phone.

"Jesus, the poor guy, he just stepped off the curb without looking."

"Get his cell phone. Call 911."

"Is he breathing?"

"PETER!" she called again. She heard a scraping sound, then the line went dead. She placed her forehead on the cool tile floor and screamed. "NO!"

"Laughin' it all awayyyy . . ."

Joni was still singing as Ellie keened under the table.

"Excuse me." A faint voice was calling through her sobs. "Excuse me."

Ellie tried to lift her head from the tiles but she couldn't.

"Miss, hello?"

Why doesn't Arlene help me? she wondered.

"Miss, excuse me."

Why doesn't someone help me?

Ellie felt a hand on her shoulder, shaking her. With every ounce of effort, she raised her head and opened her eyes. She saw a stern face with perfectly etched eyebrows staring down at her.

"Yes?"

She felt something being pulled from her ears, and Joni's voice finally stopped.

"Your daughter is wandering the aisles in first class."

"What?" Ellie looked around and realized she was on a plane, realized she must have been dreaming. "It was just a dream," she said aloud, and tears of relief sprang to her eyes.

"Miss, your daughter is wandering the aisles in first class!" A twenty-something flight attendant was the owner of the eyebrows.

Ellie looked to her right; Ahnika's tray table was littered with juice boxes, paper, and crayons, but her seat was empty. "My daughter? Where is she? Is she all right?"

"She's fine. She's up in first class bothering the passengers." Miss Sternbrow held Ellie's earphones in her hand with a *get it together, lady* look on her face.

"Jesus, I must've fallen asleep."

"Apparently," Miss Sternbrow said, her voice dripping with disdain.

Ellie rubbed her face, trying to gather herself; it was damp with tears. Scenes from the dream came back, and relief rushed through her. Peter's not dead, she realized, he's not dead. Thank you, God. She glanced to her left and noticed that Angus's car seat was empty.

"Angus!" Dread shot through her. "Where's my baby?" She looked at Miss Sternbrow in a panic. She pointed at Ellie's lap with a deadpan expression. Ellie looked down to see her baby boy quietly nursing, at the edge of sleep. "Oh." She smiled sheepishly at the still glowering stewardess.

"Is this the mother?" A slight, overly tanned steward with strawberry blond hair had joined Miss Sternbrow. She nodded.

"Listen, ma'am, you've got to get your kid out of first class. This is really not acceptable."

"Of course." Ellie began clearing the debris off of Ahnika's tray table. "I'm sorry. I just nodded off for a moment. Let me . . ." She closed the tray table, then unbuckled her seat belt.

Heaven forbid these two should help me out and just walk Ahnika back here, she thought. Flight attendants, Ellie mused as she strained to get out of the cramped airline seat. Talk about your misnomers. With Angus on her breast, she only had the use of one hand to pull herself and her baby boy out of the tiny space. She struggled for what seemed like forever as the two evil flight attendants stood watching and waiting.

"Thanks for your help," Ellie said with a big fat grin, then squeezed past them. As she made her way to first class, the horror of the fight with Peter came back to her.

. . .

After he had left, Ellie had lain on the hall floor listening to the sounds of the elevator, an engine of fear vibrating in her chest. Every time the elevator click-clicked up or down, she felt sure it was Peter, back to reconcile. She lay frozen on the floor for over an hour, feeling, for some reason, that leaving that spot would jinx his return. When she finally peeled herself off the floor and stumbled back into the apartment, she was numb and disconnected.

"Of course, he'll come back and we'll make up," she said, as she began to repack the suitcase. "He'll come back through the door any minute. I'm sure of it."

When the repacking was done she knew sleep would be impossible, so she opened the sofa bed and channel surfed, waiting to hear his key in the door.

Through Conan, Mary Tyler Moore reruns, and even Robbie in a Miracle Duster infomercial with Robbie's fem-bot smile taunting her, she waited. With every tick of the clock, her guilt and remorse began to shift to anger and resentment. By 3:30, she started calling airlines about flights to Antigua.

At 6 A.M. she began to stack the bags by the door, still expecting him to walk in at any minute. As she woke and dressed the children, she was sure she'd hear his footsteps in the hall. No such luck. As they waited for the elevator, she hoped his handsome face would be inside when the doors parted. Even as the three of them walked through the lobby to the livery cab waiting curbside, she had still prayed that Peter would appear at the last minute, take her in his arms, and tell her how they'd work it all out. He hadn't.

No cavalry this time.

With Angus still on her nipple, Ellie did her best to hurry up the aisle to rescue the first class passengers from Ahnika's precocious rampage. Over her shoulder she could see Miss Sternbrow and Mr. Too Tan still standing next to her empty seat talking (about her, no doubt).

"Some people," Ellie mumbled to the still suckling Angus. "They act as if bringing children on an airplane is some sort of social gaffe. Like I've brought livestock with me that's pooping and peeing everywhere." She shook her head as she did an awkward sort of side step up the aisle to keep from bumping Angus's head on the passing seats.

"My daddy couldn't come cuz he has to work on computers." Ahnika's high clear voice rang through the cabin.

Ellie smiled at the red-faced businessman who was enduring her patter. "Hi. I hope she wasn't bothering you."

He grunted a response. Ellie saw his eyes rest on her exposed breast. She pulled her T-shirt down as much as possible.

"Sweetie, let's go back to our seats, okay? I've got some Goldfish. You hungry?"

"I'm sick of Goldfish. I like it up here behind the curtains."

"Yes, honey, we all do, but only some people are allowed here." Ellie took her hand.

"Why, Mommy?"

"Because they've paid a lot more money, so they get these special seats and fancy meals and stuff." Ellie smiled at Old Redface again, trying to win him over.

"So we won't be bothered by wayward children," he harrumphed to himself, rustling his *Fortune* magazine.

"I beg your pardon?"

"None of my children went wandering the aisles when they were little. And if they had, they would've gotten the back of my hand, I can tell you that."

"Well, I suddenly feel very lucky to have had the father I did," Ellie said. "And if you ever met my father, you'd know what a huge insult that really is." She smiled, then turned and walked away with Ahnika in tow. She could still hear him mumbling as they passed through the first class curtains.

"Why was he mad, Mommy?"

"Because he just wants to read his magazine and think about money."

"Why?"

"Because he's a bitter, unhappy man who doesn't like children," Ellie said as every passenger, it seemed, craned their necks to see who the troublemaker was.

"Yes, it's true. I actually had the bad taste to bring my children on a plane with me," she announced to coach class. "Shocking, isn't it?" Ellie noticed a sixty-something woman with bleached yellow hair staring at Angus in disbelief. "And worse yet, I'm nursing! In public!" She pulled up her T-shirt and thrust her naked breast at her fellow passengers. "I know, I know—it's disgusting, it's indecent! I should be arrested, shouldn't I."

"Mommy?" Ahnika tugged on Ellie's hand.

"*What?*" she snapped as they arrived at their seats.

"Stop yelling, Mommy?" Her little face crumbled into despair as tears sprung from her eyes.

"I'm not yelling! I'm speaking emphatically!" Ellie plopped into her seat and—*whap!*—smacked Angus's head into his car seat.

"Waaahhh!"

"Oh, Angus, sweetie, I'm so sorry!" She began rubbing the back of his head.

"Excuse me!" Ellie heard over the din. She looked up to see Mr. Too Tan, toting the beverage cart and glaring at Ahnika, who stood whimpering in the aisle.

"Ahnika, sweetie, can you let the man by?" Ellie said, still frantically rubbing Angus's head in the hope that his cries would wane. Ahnika didn't budge. "Sweetheart, the man needs to get by!"

Ahnika stood stock-still in the center of the aisle, glaring at her mother through watery eyes.

"*Get in your seat!*" Ellie bellowed as she grabbed her whimpering daughter by the arm and yanked her out of the way.

"*Waaahhh!*" The wailing was now in stereo.

Fuck! Fuck! Fuck! Ellie thought as she waggled her nipple into Angus's gaping mouth. He latched on, his sobs stopping on a dime. Thank God for the secret weapon.

"Mommy, you hurt me!" Ahnika's accusation rang loud and clear through the cabin.

Welcome to single motherhood, Ellie thought as she put her free arm around her weeping daughter. This is what my life's going to look like twenty-four/seven if Peter divorces me, she realized, and was instantly flooded with dread and regret. I can't do this, God, I can't. She started to sweat as the cabin began to close in on her, the stale air felt scratchy in her lungs, and Ahnika's wails continued like icing on the torture cake. She closed her eyes and took a deep breath. "God, grant me the serenity . . ." She mumbled the prayer quietly to herself as she gave her daughter a gentle squeeze.

"I'm sorry, sweetheart," she managed to push out between labored breaths as she fought back her own tears. "I'm so sorry I lost my temper. I was wrong and I'm sorry."

Ahnika's cries softened as Ellie stroked her forehead and kissed her cheek, all the while praying silently for her own panic to subside.

"Would you like a treat? I brought some treats."

Ahnika nodded and sniffed as she licked a tear off her upper lip.

"A Blow Pop or a Pixie Stick?"

"Pixie Stick!" Her face brightened.

Ellie pulled an assortment of Pixie Sticks from the seat pocket. "Choose." Ahnika grabbed a grape one, tore the top off with her teeth, and poured a small hill of the purple powder into her tiny hand.

Ellie heaved a sigh of relief as she watched Ahnika eat the precious powder with her damp index finger. She's so perfect and sweet. How could I have hurt her? Ellie's brain and body felt rubbery and worn out. She closed her eyes for a moment.

Uh, uh, uh, a voice called in her head, look what happened last time you fell asleep. Her eyes shot open. You're right, you're right, she answered silently. If Peter's gonna divorce me, I'd better get used to this. Oh, my God! He could get custody. He didn't do anything wrong. I'm the adulterer! I'm the lesbian adulterer! He could really get sole custody and I'll never get to see them! She clapped her hand to her mouth and reached for the airsick bag, then swallowed hard to keep the bile down.

"What's wrong, Mommy?"

Everything, she thought, but "Nothing, sweetie." is what she said, giving her purple-tongued daughter a weak smile. Then she put the airsick bag back in its spot, buckled her seat belt, and felt the engine in her chest turn over again; an engine of panic, dread, and fear was varooming deep inside her.

Chapter Twenty-Nine

Ellie, with Angus on her back in a backpack, Ahnika squirming in her stroller, and a huge canvas suitcase by her side, stood in the stuffy car rental office, trying to keep her cool.

"I'm sorry, but there's nothing I can do if the reservation isn't in your name," the rental agent told Ellie with a curt smile.

"Okay," Ellie said, "then I won't take *that* reservation. Give me *another* car, any car." She smiled a *you fucking idiot* smile at the *Bay Watch* wannabe who held the key to her future.

"We're all booked. I don't have any other cars." Malibu Barbie seemed pleased with this revelation.

"But you *do* have an extra car," she continued with a facade of calm, "because Peter Moore is not coming for his car."

Malibu Barbie hit some keys and stared at her computer monitor. "According to my records, Mr. Moore hasn't canceled, ma'am."

As always, being called ma'am grated on Ellie's nerves like fingernails on a blackboard. "I know he hasn't canceled because we're him! We're here and we need the car!" She was starting to raise her voice.

"Ma'am, without the proper ID I can't give you that car."

"I see."

"If you'd brought your marriage license or . . ."

"Come on . . ." Ellie read her name tag ". . . Tricia, how many people travel with their marriage licenses?"

"Well, do you have any proof that Peter Moore is your husband?"

"Let me see," Ellie said, fumbling through her wallet. This is a test, she thought, some horrible, ironic test?

"Mommy, Mommy, I wanna see. Uppy, uppy!" Ahnika yelled tugging at Ellie's pants.

"Ahnika, please. Can you just give Mommy a break for a minute?" She riffled through her purse.

"Okay. How 'bout this?" She pulled out the airline tickets, triumphant. Angus bounced wildly in the backpack and pounded on her head. "Angus! Sweetie." She spread the three tickets on the counter with one hand and reached up to block Angus's attack with the other.

"Go, go, go!" he called as he bounced.

"Mommy, I can't see!" Ahnika whined. "Why does Angus get to be in the backpack? I wanna be in the backpack!" Ellie hoisted Ahnika up and set her on the counter.

"Look, here are my plane tickets. I'm Ellie Fuller and here are my kids. See, their last names are Moore, just like my husband's."

"My daddy couldn't come. He's working on computers," Ahnika added.

"Listen, Mrs. Fuller . . ."

"Ms. Fuller," Ellie corrected her. "I kept my maiden name, remember?"

"Whatever. The point is she can't sit up here, it's not safe."

Ellie could feel the line behind her fidgeting, but she wasn't giving up. "She won't fall, trust me." Ellie picked up the tickets and waved them in her face. "Look, I'm Ellie Fuller, my children are named Moore, the reservation is under—"

"Ma'am, I'm terribly sorry but—"

"Tricia," Ellie said, straining to keep it together, "if you call me ma'am one more time, I can't be held accountable for my actions."

"All right, Mizzz Fuller," she hissed back, "I'm terribly sorry but there's nothing I can do." Then Malibu Barbie looked past Ellie to the head of the line and called, "Next!"

"Listen." Ellie leaned in and spoke in a deadly whisper. "I'm on the verge of a divorce and I didn't sleep all night. If you don't rent me the car then I . . ." She stopped as tears began to roll down her cheeks. "Forget it! Just forget it!" She stuffed her tickets into her purse.

"Come on, you guys, let's go." With Angus still fussing in the backpack, Ellie put Ahnika back in the stroller and then did her best to push the stroller as she dragged the huge suitcase behind her.

"What's happening, Mommy? Why are you crying?"

"Nothing, sweetie, it's nothing." She was outside her body suddenly, detached and separate from the humiliating scene. *If I could just lie down,* she thought as they inched their way to the exit. She stared at the beige linoleum; it looked cool and inviting. *I just need to lie down.*

"Come on! Do her a solid!" Ellie heard a faint voice pierce the fog around her.

"Yeah, she's a mother, for Christ's sake!" another voice called from somewhere.

"Okay, okay!" a woman's voice answered. "Mizzz Fuller! Wait."

Ellie stopped and turned slowly toward the voice. The room came back into view. Malibu Barbie was actually smiling at her.

"What?" Ellie asked.

"Come back. Let me call my supervisor, see what she can do."

"Thank you, Tricia," Ellie said, and she meant it.

"The Hill"—the setting of Ellie's childhood—sat fat and proud in the distance, dotted with white stucco houses topped with red tiled roofs. They shined bright and clean in the California sun, like set pieces atop perfect green lawns.

Ellie put her arm out the window of her white Chevy Lumina and caught the passing breeze. *About seventy-five,* she thought, *just like Mom promised.*

The smell of new grass, salt air, and eucalyptus trees filled her nostrils. An overwhelming collage of feelings, thoughts, and images from her childhood danced and overlapped in her mind. She turned on the radio. The perfect harmonies of Crosby, Stills, and Nash rang out as the car swung away from the coast.

"Thank you, God," she said and joined in.

"It's getting to the point where I'm no fun anymore . . ."

The sun bounced off the iridescent leaves of the eucalyptus trees as she turned onto Portuguese Bend Road and pulled up to a little white gatehouse.

"Hey, Benny, how the heck are ya?" she called to the gatekeeper. Jesus, he must be 110 by now, she thought as she watched him struggle out of his chair.

"Why, it's Ellie Fuller! Little Miss Ellie Fuller come back from the big bad city," Benny called back, walking up to the car and peering into the backseat at the sleeping babies.

Benny had worked at this gate for as far back as Ellie could remember. When she was little she had thought that he actually lived in the tiny house. She turned down Crosby, Stills, and Nash reluctantly.

"Who do those children belong to? Don't you dare tell me they're yours."

"Yes, Benny, it's true. I actually grew up. I'm a mama now."

"Don't you tell me such things. I don't wanna hear it," he said, opening the electric gate and waving her through. She waved back, cranked the music again, and sped away.

When she turned onto the steep driveway of Number 5 Bridle Lane, the relentless engine in her chest shifted into overdrive. The house that had been her home for the first eighteen years of life came slowly into view. It was a dark gray, shingled ranch nestled among pepper, eucalyptus, and olive trees, the opposite of the red tile roofed, stucco houses typical of the area.

"It keeps getting smaller," Ellie said as she studied the place. "The trees get bigger and the house gets smaller." The mixture of melancholy and fear that gripped her every time she came home for a visit seized her whole body. She focused hard on steering and managing the accelerator and brake.

"Suite: Judy Blue-Eyes" was just ending as she pulled in behind her mother's pale yellow Mercedes. She turned off the car and listened to the silence.

"Okay, El, this is it. You have to get out of the car now." She didn't move. "Come on, now. You can do this." She opened the car door and walked up the brick walkway. "What are you afraid of, El? You've messed up your life quite nicely all on your own, thank you very much. What can she possibly do or say that could make it any worse?"

She stood at the big wooden front door, staring at the wrought iron handle. Pictures of the roomy kitchen with its oak cabinets, terra-cotta tiles, and walk-in pantry swam in her head suddenly. Since Sara had gotten sober, she had made an effort to keep the pantry stocked—nuts and crackers and Oreos were always on hand.

A shiver came over her as the crunchy, creamy taste of a freshly milk-dunked Oreo filled her mouth.

Is it too late to stay in a hotel? Ellie wondered as she studied the deep grain of the wooden door.

"One day at a time, El. If you didn't binge after last night, you can survive this." Her fists were clenched, her fingernails digging into her palms, as she took the last step toward the door. But before she could reach the handle, the door swung away from her.

"Welcome!" Sara M. Fuller was beaming, arms outstretched. "You're alone?" Her face fell.

"Hi, Mom, nice to see you, too. The kids are asleep in the car. Peter couldn't come," she said quickly and pushed past her mother and into the house, her sandals clicking on the stone floor. Jenny and Penny, Sara's two ancient and chubby dachshunds, came clicking and sliding around the corner.

"Hi, you two." Ellie crouched down and gave each one a good pat; their slim whiplike tails beat each other as they wagged them wildly.

"You're just going to leave the children in the car?" Sara stood in the doorway staring at the Lumina. "Do you think that's wise?"

That's gotta be a record, Ellie thought. Less than ten seconds into the visit and she's criticizing my parenting choices.

"Well, if I move them, they might wake up. Then they'll be cranky all night," Ellie said, putting her purse on the window seat, the same spot she'd been putting it since the day she had started carrying one. She turned to see her mother almost sprinting for the car.

"*I'll* move them," Sara called from the driveway. "If they wake up, I promise I'll watch them."

"Am I being sensitive?" Ellie asked Penny and Jenny as they sniffed her red toenails and licked her ankles. "Am I making this up, or is she really the most annoying woman on the planet?"

"I've made up the guest room for the two of them," Sara said as she breezed through the foyer, a crashed-out Angus in her arms.

"Mother—" Ellie was following her down the winding hallway, Penny and Jenny on her heels "—they sleep with me, you know that. I don't want them in another room."

"They're *still* sleeping with you? I felt certain they'd grown out of *that* by now." She crossed the threshold of the guestroom.

"Mother, Angus is barely a year."

"All I'm saying is . . ."

"We are the only mammals on the planet that don't sleep with their young. No, that's not true. Western civilization is the only group that doesn't sleep with their young. Globally, we—"

"I know, dear. Globally, we're in the minority. You've given me this speech." She placed Angus under the plaid blanket of the double bed and tucked him in. Ellie grabbed a wicker chair from the corner and placed its back against the side of the bed to serve as a railing as Sara headed out of the room. Ellie jogged behind to keep up, Penny and Jenny slip-sliding behind and bringing up the rear. "I just hoped that you and Peter had finally moved them out and given yourselves a little privacy, that's all. But I defer to you, of course. You're the mother." She was headed down the front walk again.

"Yes, yes, that's right. I am the mother and I would really like you to respect my wishes."

"Of course, dear. Whatever you say." Sara opened the other door and began unbuckling Ahnika.

"*Stop!*"

Sara jumped, then froze, hovering over her angelic sleeping grand-daughter. There was a long silence, then she took a deep breath, straightened her five-foot-two frame, and faced her fuming daughter.

"What is it, Ellie? What have I done to make you *so* angry at me?" Sara's pale blue eyes seemed to be pleading with her.

Ellie wanted to answer her, she did. And her mother was waiting. So, it seemed, were Penny and Jenny. Completely still for the first time since her arrival, the two graying dogs gazed up at the two women, waiting. Ellie searched her brain but a coherent thought was nowhere in sight; pictures of Oreos and dry roasted peanuts crowded in. She stole a look toward the back door. The big kitchen of her childhood was calling her—loud and clear.

And her mother was waiting.

No! A voice came sternly in her brain.

"Ellie, answer me. What have I done to make you so angry?"

"Nothing, Mother. Forget it." Ellie walked to the back of the car and opened the trunk; Penny and Jenny toddled along.

"Let go and let God," she whispered quietly as she heaved the huge suitcase out. The dogs sniffed it frantically. "Girls, there's nothing but clothes in here, believe me." She unzipped it right there on the driveway as her mother carried Ahnika, still sleeping, into the house. Penny and Jenny, convinced there were no treats for them, trotted back up the brick walk after their master.

"Let go and let God." She pulled out her running shoes, found a pair of socks. "Let go and let God." She dug down deep and felt the slippery nylon of a pair of running shorts and pulled them up. Clutching them to her chest, she looked to the heavens.

"Thank you, God. Now, just a jog bra and I'm home free." She fished around the suitcase for the last piece of the puzzle. The midafternoon sun warmed her back and she could feel the engine in her chest relenting slightly. "Yes!" She pulled out a black jog bra and zipped the suitcase up in one motion, then rolled it into the house through the kitchen door and changed quickly in the back bathroom.

"Going for a run, Mom," she called from the foyer.

"Aren't you hungry? I made us a big sa . . ." Sara Fuller's voice faded as Ellie zoomed out the front door and sprinted down the driveway, away from her mother and Oreos, away from her past and her sleeping children.

She jogged down the driveway, turned right off Bridle Lane and onto a horse trail, then climbed the dusty hill past pepper and eucalyptus trees.

At the top of the hill she reached a ridge. She had a perfect view of Georgette Canyon—the small canyon that ran through Palos Verdes and had been her backyard when she was little. Sprouts of new grass dusted the dark brown canyon walls and sloping horse corrals with a vivid green. The earthy and sweet smells of wild sage and fennel mixed in her nostrils, bringing back long ago adventures. She and her cousin Jack had spent hours hiking and horseback riding, fishing for pollywogs, catching poison ivy, and, of course, getting stoned, in this huge playground over the years.

As she ran across the ridge, Catalina Island, floating quietly and serenely in the deep blue Pacific, popped up beyond the far edge of the canyon.

"Oh, my God," she said, starting to pant a little, "it's so pretty here. I can't believe Peter—" The thought of him made her chest rev wildly. She took a deep breath, trying to calm the engine. "Fuck him. Just fuck him." Then like B following A, Missy popped into her brain.

Is she lolling on a white sand beach with pitchers of iced tea by her side? Is she still in New York? Did she get any of my calls? The trail took a turn and sloped down into the canyon, her beautiful vista sinking out of view. "Fuck them both," she said and picked up the pace.

Over an hour later, Ellie slipped into the kitchen through the back door, sweating and panting.

"Gra-ha-hammy!" The laughter in Ahnika's voice was ringing through the house. "Don't! Grammy! Stop tickling me!" Ahnika yelled.

Ellie smiled at the sound of her giggling girl. Mom was always a helluva tickler, I'll give her that, she thought as she sneaked through the kitchen to spy on them. Angus, in his turquoise swimmie diaper, was toddling around the round coffee table, grinning at Ahnika and Grammy as they tussled on the Tiffany blue sofa.

"Oh, I'm terribly sorry," Sara was saying as she mercilessly tickled Ahnika, whose tie-dyed suit was only half on. "If you would just sit still, I could get your suit on and we could go swimming."

"*Grammy!* You're tickling me!"

She's in heaven, Ellie realized. She tiptoed back into the kitchen, grabbed a paper towel, and wiped the sweat from her face.

Ellie had been on the far side of the hill when she realized she'd been gone for almost an hour. Visions of Ahnika and Angus freaking out had swum in her head as she sprinted home in record time, and all for naught.

She opened the fridge, searching in vain for seltzer or bottled water. No longer the refrigerator of her youth, it was filled with yogurt and salami and other luncheon meats. A tossed salad covered in Saran Wrap sat on the bottom shelf with a note: *Thought you might be hungry. XOXO Mom*

"Not really," Ellie said, reaching for the orange juice.

When she closed the refrigerator she was eye level with a small stone refrigerator magnet which read: *God give me Patience and do it right now!*

"Just like Lally's pillow!" Missy's mother's bedroom and all that she and Missy had done there tumbled into Ellie's brain in a moment. A dull ache began to grow in her head as her eyes landed on the picture beneath the stone magnet—Peter, holding a wispy-haired Ahnika, stood next to a puffy-faced Ellie, who held a newborn Angus. Ellie closed her eyes and held onto the refrigerator for support.

"What the fuck have I done?" she asked herself once more, then walked slowly across the kitchen and grabbed a Flintstones jelly jar glass out of the wooden cabinet.

"I really should eat something," she said, examining the vintage jar. Dino and Fred were barely there after decades in the dishwasher.

"She never throws *anything* out."

Ellie had thought that when her mother's book turned out to be a big seller, Sara would redo the whole house, after all the lean years with her father and all the dark years after that. But no, she had reupholstered a few things, bought herself a Mercedes, and put in the pool. Aside from that, everything had stayed exactly the same. So, whenever Ellie came to visit, she really was coming back to the home of her childhood.

She filled Dino and Fred with OJ, downed it, then filled it again.

"Who's ready for a swim?" Sara's melodic voice came from the living room.

"Me!" Ahnika responded as the three of them scrambled out the side door toward the pool.

Ellie was about to follow them then stopped. What are you doing? she asked herself. They are happily playing with their grandmother. A miracle, yes, but true. Let them be. If there's a problem, *then* you can get involved.

I could nap, Ellie thought, watching her giggling children, bobbing in the shallow end with their grandmother. The kids are totally safe in their little inner tubes. I could actually nap.

Her old room was spotless and also unchanged since the day she had left. She was time traveling once again as she studied the framed pictures of Gelsey Kirkland, Baryshnikov, and other dancers that hung above her bed. The plastic horses that had been her fascination in second and third grade still stood proudly on the top shelf of the built-in bookshelves that lined the wall opposite her bed. The autographed *Yellow Submarine* poster that her father had scored from some unnamed source still hung on the back of her door. After his second conviction, it had occurred to Ellie one night that the autographs were probably forged. But she had still never been able to bring herself to take the poster down. Postcards from long forgotten friends were stuck in the frame of the dresser mirror, and an old puka-shell necklace that she had made in tenth grade was draped over one corner. Then she spotted her suitcase set up next to the dresser on an ancient suitcase stand.

"How the heck did she . . . ?" Ellie shook her head at the thought of her tiny mother hoisting the heavy suitcase onto the rack. "She's amazing."

"Subtle, Mom," she said, eyeing her new turquoise bathing suit on her bed which her mother had obviously laid out for her.

"Ahh!" There was a scream of delight from the backyard.

Ellie examined her bikini, then eyed her bed. "Okay, Mom, you win." She stripped off her damp running clothes and put on her skimpy new suit, then stood at the back door, spying again.

Sara Fuller was twirling her grandchildren round and round by their inner tubes like a human carnival ride. She's been body snatched, Ellie thought, and she swung open the hallway door onto the pool area. "Hey! Any room for me?"

"Mommy!"

"Mama!"

"Get in here, young lady, and have some fun with your children," Sara commanded.

"Yes, sir!" Ellie said, giving her mother a salute and diving in the deep end. The water slipped and slid over her as she swam to the shallow end.

"Hey! Who likes California?" Ellie asked.

"Me!" Ahnika yelled.

"Me!" Angus imitated.

She pulled her two babies to her and gave them each a big kiss.

"Watch this, Mommy. I can swim!" Ahnika swung her arms wildly and kicked her feet like mad, making lots of splashes but not much progress.

"That's great, sweetie."

"Climb on," Grammy told Ahnika, backing into her and patting her shoulders. "I'll swim you to the deep end and back."

"To the deep end!" Ahnika yelled and the two of them headed off.

The engine in Ellie's chest had slowed to a quiet hum, and she felt almost content as she and Angus bounced in the warm water of the shallow end, blowing bubbles and laughing while Sara and Ahnika "did laps."

The sky had turned a deep indigo and the L.A. basin sparkled yellow and blue in the distance when the four of them finally scooted out of the now steaming pool and snuggled into the towels that Sara had laid out. Ellie wrapped Angus tightly into a tattered pink towel with "Ellie" stitched in a deeper pink script across the front. She hoisted the terry-cloth sausage over her shoulder, then patted his back, watching Ahnika, another tattered "Ellie" towel draped over her shoulders, climb into Sara's arms.

"I'm glad you never threw these out," Ellie told her mother as they headed into the house.

"Every year I put them in the box for the Tic Tocker Thrift Shop and every year I take them out at the last minute," she said, smiling at her daughter.

As the four of them walked into the warm house, shivering and making little cold moaning sounds, a fleeting thought slipped into Ellie's brain: I'm glad I came.

Chapter Thirty

$\mathcal{N}$ot bad, Ellie thought, squished between her two sleeping children in the bed of her childhood, not bad at all. I was sure things would get ugly at dinner. But we got through it without a hitch. She closed her eyes and waited for the exhaustion that she had felt all day to take her away—but no such luck. She felt the dull ache from this afternoon return behind her eyes.

Peter's gone, and who can blame him? How did this happen? Her brain was unrelenting—going over and over the events of the last few months. Her head was beginning to pound. Jesus Christ, I'm an idiot!

I *have* to find some Tylenol or I'll never sleep, Ellie thought, as she eased herself out of bed. She closed the bathroom door behind her and reached for the light switch. The bright light shot daggers of pain through her eyes; her stomach heaved. She shielded her eyes with one hand and felt her way to the medicine cabinet with the other, then rifled through the contents of the medicine cabinet through slitted eyes: Bayer aspirin, Neosporin, Band-Aids.

"Midol? Jesus! No wonder there's no Tylenol. Everything in here was purchased before 1976."

Ellie stared at the aspirin longingly. She didn't know *why* you weren't supposed to take aspirin when you were pregnant or nursing, what the danger was to the child; she just knew she wasn't allowed to. She reached for the bottle of aspirin and an image of Angus with fins instead of arms popped into her head. She closed the cabinet, then pressed her fingertips into her brow bone—hard, hoping the pressure would relieve the gripping pain in her head. It didn't.

"Fuck." Salvation, she knew was as close as the kitchen. Her mother always kept a bottle of Tylenol in the junk drawer. She squinted at her watch. "It's only 7:40? Shit! Okay, okay, okay, okay." She lifted her head and stared at her pale face in the medicine cabinet mirror. "You can do it. Just get the Tylenol and get out."

Hi, sweetie. Kids asleep?" Sara asked from her easy chair by the fireplace when Ellie crossed the living room.

"Yeah. They were exhausted," Ellie said as she opened the drawer where relief waited. Yes! She grabbed the bottle of Tylenol and opened the childproof cap.

"You okay, sweetheart? You look kind of tired."

"I have a bit of a headache, Mother, that's all." Just get 'em and get out. She spilled two capsules into her hand.

"Maybe it's a hunger headache. You didn't eat much dinner."

"I had plenty of dinner, Mother. I just need some Tylenol and some sleep."

"I bought some fresh strawberries at Annie Ishibashi's stand today." Sara had left her chair and was heading for the fridge. "Why don't we have a nice little dessert of strawberries and half-and-half, sprinkle a little sugar on?" She took a basket of strawberries out of the fridge and showed them to Ellie. "Just us girls, what d'ya say? You used to love that when you were little, remember?"

"Mother, my head hurts so badly that I'm nauseous and—" She

stopped when she noticed a bright green Post-it on the cabinet above the phone. "Mother?" She peeled it off and held it out to her mother.

"Oh! I forgot to tell you; Missy called while you were running."

"Missy?"

"Yes. She left a number."

"She called when I was running? When exactly were you going to tell me this? When I was getting on the plane to go back to New York?"

"Sweetheart, I wrote a note. You just saw the note. Is there a problem?"

"I don't know why I even came, I really don't." She slammed the Post-it onto the counter, grabbed a Flintstones glass, and filled it from the tap. "I always think it's going to be different and it never is."

"El, I don't think that's fair." Sara was still holding the gleaming basket of fruit. "I wrote the note, you got the note. I just don't think that's fair."

Ellie's head was throbbing; the kitchen light made it worse. She closed her eyes and downed the medicine.

"Life's not fair, Mother. Wasn't that your famous line to me when I was little? 'Well, life's not fair, sweetheart. Get used to it,' you'd say to me, then make yourself another martini. That was always your answer, remember?"

"No. I don't remember ever saying that to you."

"Oh, my God!" Ellie actually chuckled. "That's unbelievable. It was your pat answer for every problem I had for my entire adolescence, until I finally had enough sense to stop coming to you for advice or comfort. But it's not surprising that you don't remember, really. You were bombed nonstop for over four years—from the day Daddy was convicted till the day you walked into AA. Do you remember that much, Mother?" Ellie looked her mother straight in the eye.

"Yes, I do. And I know you're angry about that and I—"

"We're not talking about *my* anger right now mother, we're talking about the fact that *I* got a phone call and *you* didn't tell me."

"I said I was sorry."

"No, you didn't. You said 'Is there a problem?'"

"Well, you know what I meant."

"I didn't know that 'is there a problem' meant 'I'm sorry.'" She put the Flintstones glass in the dishwasher. "Can't you just say it, Mother? For once in your fucking life, can't you please just say it to me?"

"What? Say what?"

"Forget it!" And she turned to go.

"Ellie, stop! Please. Can't we stop this? Can't we be different together?"

"I don't know, can we, Mom? Can we?" Don't cry, El. Don't you dare cry. Anger and tears were fighting for airtime in her body. Her head pounded; she felt weak and shaky, but she was determined not to crack.

"I'm worried about you, sweetheart. You look tired and thin. Are you eating enough?"

"You want me to eat? I'll eat." She grabbed a strawberry from the basket and took a huge bite. "Happy how?" She chewed menacingly.

"Sweetheart, I'm just—just trying to help."

Ellie stomped to the pantry, found a fresh bag of Oreos, and ripped it open. She popped two in her mouth and stood in the dark pantry, chewing and shaking as she swallowed the crunchy, creamy mess.

"Are you still getting to your OA meetings?" Sara asked from the pantry doorway.

"Don't pull that program shit with me. Don't you dare toss a slogan at me or tell me I need a meeting."

"Honey, I'm just concerned about you, that's all. When you were—sick before, I didn't notice what was going on, and I don't want to make that same mistake again. If you're having a problem I want to help. If you were my sponsee I'd . . ."

"If I were your sponsee? *If I were your sponsee!* How about if I were your daughter, Mom? What would you say to me then? Huh?" Bits of Oreo flew out of her mouth, and tears streamed down her cheeks as she attacked. "What would you say to a daughter who had started throwing up again after twelve years of abstinence, huh? To a daughter who had fucked up her perfectly good marriage by having an affair with some WASPy heiress? What slogan would you toss at me then, huh? Let go and let God? Would that be it? Would it? Cuz I'm *not* some sponsee, Mom, or one of your fucking AA friends. I'm your daughter, Mom, remember?" She was leaning into her now, sobbing and screaming. "I'M YOUR DAUGHTER AND YOU'RE MY MOTHER! YOU ARE MY MOTHER!"

"You and Missy? What are you telling me?"

Ellie looked up to see Sara's silhouette in the pantry door. She wanted to throw her arms around her and hold on to her forever.

"I'm telling you that Missy and I are lovers." Ellie pushed past her,

walked to the fridge, and took out the milk. As she chugged from the carton, she stole a glance at her mother; she looked small and old. Ellie fought back a pang of sympathy and went in for the kill.

"What's the matter, Mom? She comes from such a nice family and she is a Smith girl, you know. I thought you'd be pleased." She closed up the milk and put it away. Sara stood silent and still in the pantry doorway as Ellie walked out of the kitchen.

In the quiet of the dark bathroom, Ellie wiped her eyes and blew her nose. She could see the smooth, squat form of her old friend out of the corner of her eye—right there, open and waiting. Her stomach heaved at the mere thought of it. She swallowed hard. She saw her mother's wrinkled and broken face in her mind, fell to her knees, closed her eyes, and opened her mouth.

"God grant me the serenity to accept the things I cannot change, the courage to change the things I can, and the wisdom to know the difference." The open mouth of the toilet bowl was calling her—hungry, begging to be fed.

"Help me, God, help me. I don't want to throw up, I don't. But I don't know if I can stop myself. Thy will not my will be done." She was pulling out all the stops; prayers she hadn't said or even thought of in years poured out of her. "God, I offer myself to thee to build with me and do with me as thou wilt. Relieve me of the bondage of self. Get me through this night, God, just tonight without throwing up."

Close the lid! a voice came loud and clear in her head. She reached over and flicked down the lid with the tip of her finger, then pulled her hand away quickly, as if the toilet were a flame. It fell with a clap.

Now get out, the voice continued. She got up and walked out of the bathroom. *Go!* The voice ordered. *Out!* She stood in the hallway; the silence of the house seemed to vibrate around her. *Go!* The voice ordered again.

She looked down at her bare feet. "Shoes. Where are my shoes?" she whispered to the dim hallway, then tiptoed to her purse on the window seat, grabbed it, and headed for the back room. She kept her eyes down, moving quickly. She expected to be caught at any minute. She unearthed her sandals from beneath the pile of clothes she'd left on the floor of the

back room before her run, tied her black cardigan around her waist, and opened the back door.

"Where are you going?" Her mother had appeared out of nowhere.

"Out." She stopped; the perfect indigo night stood waiting. Her mother was silent. Ellie couldn't look at her. "I won't be gone long." She waited for a reply, a rebuttal—nothing. Ellie closed the door behind her and slipped into the beautiful crisp California night.

Chapter Thirty-One

"Okay, God, I'm out! I'm out of that house and I didn't throw up!" Ellie said jubilantly, then found herself sprinting to her car. She headed down Portuguese Bend Road with no idea of where she was going. She gripped the wheel tightly, holding on to herself, to her abstinence.

"God, now what? Help me out here," she said as she passed through the gate, leaving Rolling Hills Estates behind.

No answer.

"God? Come in, God. What's next?"

Still nothing.

She crossed Palos Verdes Drive North and continued down the hill. The red and white sign of the Stop 'n Go glowed in the distance.

"Fuck!" Her palms began to sweat and she felt a pull in the chest at the sight of it. She could almost hear the hum of the fluorescent lights and see the familiar aisles of chips and cookies, the freezer full of ice cream.

It was only minutes from her house. Ellie had made countless trips to her twenty-four-hour supplier over the years, sometimes twice in one night.

"Help me, help me, help me," she whispered. The Stop 'n Go was now only one hundred yards away.

I could pull in and just get something to drink. Yes, that's what I'll do— she put on her blinker—I'll just get a couple of bottles of seltzer and bring them back to the house. She stepped on the brake.

Get to a meeting! The voice was back.

"A meeting!" she shouted. "Okay, God, but where?" Her hands relaxed on the wheel. She pulled the Lumina into the Mobil gas station just past the Stop 'n Go, parked in the corner of the lot, got out her cell phone, called information, and got the number for the local OA.

"I'm in Torrance and I need a meeting," she said simply when the OA volunteer answered the phone.

"Okay, let me see here." The woman spoke slowly with a hint of a Southern accent. Ellie could hear the rustling of pages.

Come on, lady, come on! Ellie screamed inside her head.

"Where did you say you are?"

"Rolling Hills Road and Crenshaw. I'm steps from a Stop 'n Go and I'm in big trouble," Ellie said slowly and quietly.

"Okay, honey, just take a deep breath and remember it's one minute at a time."

Don't give me slogans, Ellie thought, give me a meeting. She could see the red and white sign of the Stop 'n Go in the rearview mirror.

"Hello? Sweetheart, you still with me?"

Ellie was silent. She stared at the *end* button on her phone.

"Listen to me, sweet baby. If you always do what you've always done, you'll always get what you've always gotten."

The brilliance of the slogan and the sweet yet urgent sound of the woman's voice hit Ellie square in the chest.

"Talk to me, child. Are you still there?"

Ellie closed her eyes and took a deep breath. "Just barely."

"Bingo! There's an eight-thirty speaker meeting in Redondo Beach at the Presbyterian Church," her new friend told her.

"There is a God."

"Were you having some doubts?" the OA volunteer asked.

"Not really. She got me to you, didn't she?"

"It's on Pacific Coast Highway, just north of Aviation. So, get going, sweet baby, get going."

"Thank you." Ellie hit *end* on her phone and . . .

Ring!

She jumped, then pressed *send* as quickly as could be, hoping it was Peter.

"Hello?"

"Do you miss me?"

Ellie's heart dropped into her toes. "Missy?"

"Who were you expecting?" Her speech sounded slurred.

"Where are you?" Ellie dodged the question.

"I'm in Antigua, where you could've been if you hadn't been so ridiculous."

Ellie looked at her watch. How late is it there? she wondered.

"Didn't your mother tell you I called?" Missy asked.

"Yes."

"Why didn't you call me back? Don't you love me anymore?"

Ellie was speechless, her brain all cloudy. The Stop 'n Go sign seemed to have grown larger in the rearview mirror. She hadn't planned what she was going to say to Missy, how she was going to "break up" with her.

BEEP! Ellie's call-waiting sounded.

"Missy, I've gotta go, I have another call."

"I'll wait."

Ellie pressed *send*, her heart thumping like mad.

"Hi, it's me. Listen . . ."

"Lisa, not now!" She pressed *send* again. "Missy, . . ."

"Was that Peter? How is he?"

At the sound of Peter's name, Ellie magically found her resolve. She took a deep breath and sent up a quick prayer. "Missy, I can't see you or talk to you anymore. I don't know yet if Peter will even take me back, but it's over between us. This is not against you, but we never should've done what we did. I love Peter. I have never stopped loving him, and I just want to be back with him and my kids." There was a pause. "Missy, it's over."

"You're just figuring that out now?" Missy's voice sounded harsh.

"Figuring what out?"

"That it's over between us. I've been done with you for a long time."

"Then why are you calling me?"

"Well, you *did* leave me about five messages the other night and . . ."

Ellie could hear muffled talking in the background. Was that French? she wondered. She felt a tiny seed of jealousy somewhere. "Missy, who's there?"

"Well, you don't care, do you? Since it's over between us." There was more muffled talking and then laughter.

"Missy, don't ever call me again. Good-bye!" Ellie pressed *end* and then the power button, snapped her phone closed, and buried it in her purse. Then she backed out of her spot, put the car in gear, and watched the Stop 'n Go sign disappear in her rearview mirror as she headed north.

Hi, I'm Cynthia and I'm a recovering overeater, anorexic, bulimic—let's see, is there anything I've forgotten?" The packed house laughed at the sweet-faced blond woman at the front of the room. "Oh, yeah, and a recovering compulsive exerciser."

"Hi, Cynthia," Ellie responded with the group of suburban women as she settled into the last seat in the front row.

Cynthia's big brown eyes took in the smiling crowd that sat waiting for her story. "As many of you know, I've been in this program a long time. It's been over fifteen years since I walked into my first OA meeting. Fifteen years and I haven't run out of things to say." She tilted her head and shrugged her shoulders.

I think I like this woman, Ellie thought, relaxing a bit.

"But the reason tonight is so special is because it's my anniversary." The room erupted in applause. "Thank you. Today I'm one year back after a ten-month slip that nearly killed me."

A shiver ran through Ellie.

"One year ago today, I was rushed in an ambulance to South Bay Memorial." She stopped, took a deep breath, put her hand on her chest and patted herself gently.

The engine in Ellie's chest slowed to a quiet whir.

"But thanks to my Higher Power and the people in this program, I made it back." She smiled.

"First of all, are there any newcomers here tonight?" She scanned the crowd. A few hands sprung up. "Great, welcome. Anybody here who is not a newcomer but is having trouble staying abstinent?"

Ellie's arm shot up with a force that surprised her; Cynthia's big brown eyes locked with hers.

"I'm glad you're here," Cynthia told her quietly.

"Me, too," Ellie mouthed back silently. She closed her eyes and a perfect tear rolled down each cheek.

"When I first came in I heard someone in a meeting say, 'Stick around, your story'll get worse.' I didn't know what they meant. Now I do. I see now that the trouble started when I stopped going to meetings. I was an old-timer, for goodness sake. I didn't need meetings, right? After six months, I started to slip. Little things at first, like skipping a meal, then I started counting calories. Before I knew it I was weighing myself two—three times a day. I was going down an old, familiar—even comfortable—road and I couldn't get off.

"They say that this is a program of rigorous honesty. When I was dragged in here kicking and screaming, I had fifteen years of bingeing and purging under my belt. Rigorous honesty? Ha! I ate in secret, I binged in secret, and I lied about what I'd eaten and *if* I'd binged. I acted happy when I was suicidal. I acted on top of things when I was just holding on by a thread."

Cynthia's voice faded as all the lies Ellie had told over the last few months flew up in her face and took her breath away.

"About a year after I stopped going to meetings, I'm back to bingeing and purging six, seven times a day. This is far worse than any bottom I'd ever experienced before."

Ellie was clutching her metal folding chair with all her strength. Oh, God, don't let me go back there. I couldn't stand it!

"Then, one desperate morning, instead of sneaking off to buy more food and laxatives, I went to a meeting. I don't know why. Well, I do. I know *exactly* why. The night before, after a huge fight with my fourteen-year-old daughter—try being a good mother when you're in the thick of this disease. Anyway, after acting like Joan Crawford with my daughter, I had *finally* gotten on my knees and asked my Higher Power for help. And I realized as I was praying that I hadn't been on my knees since my early days in OA, when I was desperate and hopeless—desperate to just not throw up for *one* day.

"So, after that night, I start getting on my effing knees *every morning*, I'm back at meetings and I'm raising my hand, doin' the steps—*again*—but I can't stay abstinent, I just can't do it."

Don't tell me that! Ellie screamed inside her head.

"Thanks to OA, I had this fantastic life. And I had thrown it all away and now I couldn't get it back."

Ellie began to sob. A spiky-haired woman next to her handed her a tissue. She took it silently. Help me, God. Please help me, Ellie prayed as she sobbed into her hands. Cynthia's voice receded again as hopelessness swallowed Ellie whole.

But I'm here, she pleaded with God, I'm here and I didn't throw up. Isn't that enough? What more do I have to do? Anything! Just get me back my life.

"So, I'm in the hospital bed—"

Cynthia's voice slipped through a crack in Ellie's fear.

"—with the feeding tubes and the IV, praying like nobody's business, and in walks my sponsor." She smiled at the spiky-haired woman next to Ellie. "And she said, 'You haven't dealt with your family of origin.' Oh, brother, I thought. Then she told me, 'I finally got abstinent after I did a Fourth Step just on my father. I wrote down three pages of resentments that I didn't even know I had.' I said, 'C'mon, Janet, you know my dad, he's like a nonentity. I mean, he was barely even in my life when I was little. What the heck would I even have to be resentful about?' And she said, 'How 'bout the fact that he was barely in your life?'

"And I felt this clunk in my chest, like a puzzle piece falling into place, and I started to cry. And my sponsor hugged me—" Cynthia stopped and swallowed, eyes brimming "—and stroked my hair, which of course made me cry even harder." She rubbed her wet eyes with the palms of her hands and made a soft chuckle.

"So—" she took a deep breath and collected herself "—that day in the hospital I discovered that I'm not done yet." She sat back and gave the crowd a *can you believe that?* look. "I mean, fourteen years of meetings and slogans and literature. Shouldn't I be done?" she asked the room. "Apparently not.

"See, turns out my *family of origin* was a family of secrets and lies and chaos. The perfect training ground to become an expert bulimic. And when I was little, I had made this unspoken pact to protect the myth of my family. And that pact was so strong that I nearly lost everything in order to honor it. So, when I lost my abstinence and I was scared and desperate and lying and my life was in chaos—" she paused and leaned into the crowd "—I was home."

This bit of brilliance hit Ellie hard; she lifted her tear-stained face and waited.

"There was this part of me that couldn't stand this calm happy life that I had built, this part of me that only felt safe and comfortable when she was *in the chaos*. Does that make any sense?" she asked the room.

Yes! Yes! It makes perfect sense! Ellie thought and the engine in her chest stopped dead.

Chapter Thirty-Two

Number 5 Bridle Lane was dark and still when Ellie pushed the front door open. She stood in the foyer, wondering what to do next. She was bone tired, but filled with a new hope that energized her.

Is she already asleep? Ellie wondered as she put her purse on the window seat and eyed her mother's empty chair. She slipped off her sandals and padded down the hall to check on her children. As she rounded the last bend to her room she heard singing.

"In my room there hangs a picture
Jew-els cannot buy from me."

She stopped . . .

" 'Tis a picture of my Ahnika
She is the sweetest girl in the world."

It was the lullaby that her mother had sung to Angus at the birthday party all those months ago—the one her mother had told her was from her own childhood. She peeked into her room. Her chest expanded at the scene that was waiting for her.

Ahnika's cheek lay on Sara Fuller's shoulder, her eyes shut and her pink mouth in a sweet little pucker. Sara was stepping front then back—doing a slow and low cha-cha as she sang.

"And I love my little Ahnika
She is as sweet as sweet can be."

Once again, the words and melody hit Ellie somewhere deep in her body.

Thank you, God, she thought for the millionth time that night. Her mother's dance and the sweet song continued.

"In my room there hangs a picture . . ."

Ellie felt that she had traveled back in time, and that God was giving her a glimpse of her mother that she had long forgotten, a glimpse of whom her mother might have been before the secrets and lies and chaos, a mother who had sung to her sleeping daughter in the middle of the night while she did a slow motion cha-cha. And suddenly, magically, Ellie was filled with love a perfect, unsullied love that a baby must feel for its mother. A love free of hurt or disappointment, a love without a resentment in sight.

She watched, still as a stone, as the tears rolled down her cheeks, not wanting to break the spell, wishing that she could watch her mother and her daughter dance in the dim light of her bedroom forever.

Sara Fuller's navy blue loafers tapped lightly on the stone floor as she walked into the living room.

"Hi, Mom," Ellie said from the sofa. "You sang to me," she blurted out.

"What?"

"When I was little, you sang to me."

"Of course, I sang to you." She sounded angry. "What did you think, you were raised by wolves?"

"No, Mother, it's just . . ." She took a deep breath, trying to stay calm. "I didn't remember till just now. I saw you rocking Ahnika and singing that 'In My Room' song and I remembered."

"You used to call it 'In My Room' when you were little."

"I did?"

She nodded. "You'd say, Mommy squeeze my leg and sing 'In My Room.'"

"I did?"

"You did."

"How old was I?"

"Three, four."

"I don't remember."

"I do," Sara said simply. "You didn't always hate me."

"I don't hate you, Mom."

"Eleanor, please."

Eleanor? Uh-oh, Ellie thought, she must be *really* mad.

Sara strode across the living room to her easy chair and grabbed her crossword puzzle from the footstool.

"This evening's been trying enough. I don't need you to start lying to me now." She sat down, picked up her pen, and stared at her crossword puzzle.

This isn't going how I'd planned, Ellie thought, clenching her jaw.

During the car ride home from the meeting, filled with serenity and gratitude, Ellie had envisioned a perfect, heartfelt reconciliation with her mother. She had seen herself running into the house, bursting with apologies and insights. Then her mother—moved by the eloquence of Ellie's confessions—would melt into the softie that Ellie had always known she was gushing amends and self recriminations. It would be beautifully acted and scripted, accompanied by swelling violin music and ending in a warm embrace.

She's actually *doing* the puzzle, Ellie marveled.

"I know you're mad, Mom, and I—"

"I'm not mad, I'm irritated," she said, continuing to scribble.

"Jesus Christ, Mother!" Ellie ripped the newspaper out of her hand. "I'm trying to talk to you." All the insights and resolutions of less than an hour ago had vanished, and Ellie was right smack dab in the center of her fury. She was panting as she looked down at her mother. Sara met her gaze without a blink.

"Why are you so angry at me, Ellie? What is it that you want from me?"

Ellie wanted to tell her but couldn't. "Forget it." She turned to go. *I'm not done.* Cynthia's sweet voice sounded in Ellie's ear. She stopped short.

"I want you to be sorry," she mumbled into her chest.

"What?"

Ellie turned to face her mother. "I want you to be sorry."

"About what?"

"About what? About what! *About my entire fucking life!* About the fact that you never saw me or paid any attention to me or even seemed to care if I was around. When I was little, it was like I was invisible because you were so crazy about Daddy that you could never see past him to me. *He* was the center of your world. I was your daughter, your only daughter, but somehow I got left out of the picture. Then, after Daddy left, it was you and your martinis.

"I was stuffing myself and then going on all these crazy diets. I weighed 110 pounds and I went to a diet doctor at age fifteen because I thought I was fat. And you were too drunk to notice.

"Then, when you finally got sober, I thought 'Good, now I can *finally* have a mother. Now she'll finally see me, love me, want to spend some time with me.' But oh no! I didn't get any of you, not even for a second! AA got you and I got nothin' but 'Not tonight, sweetheart, I'm speaking at a meeting.'" Ellie did her dead-on Sara Fuller imitation as she spoke. "'Gee, I'm sorry I have to miss your recital. I know I said I'd come but I have a sponsee who's in trouble.'" Ellie's heart broke at the crushing disappointment of the memory—a memory she hadn't allowed herself to think of in over twenty years—but she continued on, the tears fighting with the anger as she spoke. "And I went to yet another performance *by myself* and danced the lead for other people's parents. I was still invisible, only now AA was upstaging me. I mean, for literally years you were at a meeting or on the phone with some other fucking drunk while your own daughter was bingeing and purging right under your nose, and you didn't have a clue because you were too busy fretting over some fucking drunk you'd just met at a meeting that morning.

"And even now, you come to New York, you meet Missy, and I see your eyes light up. I can see that *she's* the daughter you wish you'd had. You want her to take me shopping so I can dress like her. But I'm not her, Mother! And you know what? I don't even *want* to be her. This is me!" Ellie smacked her chest with both hands. "I'm an ex-dancer, comic, bulimic. I don't wear loafers or headbands or pleated pants. I didn't go to Smith or Madeira. I've never shopped at Talbot's, and I'm pretty sure I never will. Do you get that, Mother? I'm never going to shop at Talbot's! This is it! I'm forty years old, Mother, and you still don't have a clue who I am!"

The two women stared at each other in the now silent living room. Ellie was holding back tears and fighting the urge to say more. She waited.

"Oh, Ellie . . ." Sara began, shaking her head. "Don't you know that I'm sorry, sweetheart, don't you know?" She opened her arms and beckoned her daughter to her.

Without a thought, Ellie walked to her mother and climbed into her lap. She rested her head on her mother's shoulder, it felt sweetly familiar and her five-foot-five-inch frame fit magically onto her tiny mother's lap.

"I'm so sorry, sweetheart, I'm so, so sorry."

Ellie's anger melted and sobs leaped out of her, shaking her whole body, as her mother rocked her and gently patted her back.

"I'm sorry, sweetheart. I'm so, so sorry," Sara kept repeating softly to her sobbing daughter as she rocked her, patting her back gently and sweetly. "I'm sorry, sweetheart. I'm so, so sorry."

As Ellie's sobs eased, she wasn't sure, but she thought she could hear the mournful sounds of violin music playing somewhere.

Chapter Thirty-Three

Ellie had always loved the way the morning sun filtered through the trees and into the big kitchen at Number 5 Bridle Lane. A warm yellow light hung thick in the air. As she measured out the Bisquick, she savored every second that she had to herself on this miraculous morning. As she dumped the white powder into the crackled orange mixing bowl and it landed with a wispy thud, she felt suddenly as if all the mornings of her childhood were overlapping in this one morning—those easy mornings of long ago when her dad was still around and Ellie could bask in his charm. On those mornings her mother would rise with a sleepy smile on her face and kiss her daughter on the top of the head. And the scary mornings were there too, when the indictment was pending and everything in the house still looked the same, but nothing felt the same anymore. She could also feel the remnants of all those deathly mornings when Ellie got up to find Sara passed out in her chair or on the living room floor. Then all those desperate mornings of bingeing and purging, when the rising of the sun just signaled another day to get through without being caught in one of an endless string of lies and deceptions. All those mornings were with Ellie in the kitchen as she cracked eggs into the batter. And it was okay, it was just fine in fact, because all those mornings had brought her to this morning. This morning in March, when the thick yellow light hung around her as she melted the butter on the skillet and her children slept and she didn't hate her mother. She was making pancakes in the big kitchen of her childhood on this glorious morning and she did not hate her mother.

"Hi, sweetheart." Sara Fuller padded into the kitchen in her baby blue robe with matching leather slippers, her auburn pageboy perfectly in place.

She always looks like she just posed for a Sears catalog, Ellie thought, smiling.

"I'm making pancakes," Ellie told her as Jenny and Penny came clicking into the kitchen, yapping and squirming. "Morning, you two." She bent and patted them both hard on their graying rumps. "You guys in the mood for pancakes? Shall we do silver dollar ones like Dad used to?" she asked, pouring five small circles of batter onto the sizzling skillet.

"Sure, if you think it's okay?"

"I think it's okay, unless there's some ordinance against silver dollar pancakes in Palos Verdes that I don't know about."

"No, silly," Sara tsked at her daughter, "you having pancakes, is that on your—your diet, or whatever they call it?"

"Oh, yeah, it's fine. My food plan is I can have whatever I want. I'm just supposed to eat when I'm hungry and stop when I'm full. And for an anorexic/bulimic that is no small task. But guess what?"

"What?" Sara looked worried.

Ellie thrust both arms up over her head and announced, "I'm hungry! I woke up this morning and for the first time in months I was hungry! Ever since I slipped into this—thing with Missy, I haven't been hungry. Not once. I've been stuffed and I've been starved—" she stared blankly into the batter and puffed out a sad chuckle "—but mostly I've been numb. But today I woke up hungry.

"By the way, Mom, I'm going to need to go to a meeting every day while I'm here. Can you watch the kids?"

Sara pursed her lips at her. "What do you think, silly?"

"Okay, okay. But I just had to ask."

"No problem, sweetie."

"Thanks." Ellie flipped the small pancakes. Penny and Jenny were click-clicking around her feet, waiting.

"Calm down, you two. You're in on it, too. I'm making pancakes for all of us.

"Look at that. Perfect!" Ellie said, admiring her golden brown circles. "Remember when Daddy used to make these? He'd make like ten perfect little stacks of pancakes. We'd end up with about sixty pancakes for the three of us. Do you remember?"

"I remember." Sara grabbed Ellie and hugged her tight. "I love you, sweetheart."

"I love you, too, Mom."

Sara kissed her daughter on the cheek and didn't let go. Ellie felt suddenly awkward, her spatula flapping in the breeze.

"Mom?"

"Yes, sweetheart."

"The pancakes."

"Oh!" She released her quickly and Ellie lunged for the smoking griddle.

"No problem, no problem. I saved them," she said, sliding the golden discs onto a waiting platter.

"Thank God." Sara sat at the kitchen table with a thud. Jenny (or was it Penny) pawed at her robe, and Sara put the chubby dog on her lap, stroked its ears, and stared out the window as she spoke. "I laid awake all night thinking about everything that you said last night, and I have a few things I need to say to you. Do you mind?"

"No, Mom, it's fine. Go ahead."

"I just wanted to say that I'm so sorry that you lost me in so many ways over the years. I'm sorry that AA took me away from you. I never looked at it from your point of view. You see—and this is not an excuse, it's just— in those early years I was holding on to my sobriety by such a thread that I needed all those meetings and I thought, 'If I'm not sober, what good am I to her?' Every day that I stayed sober, I felt like I was making amends to you. I mean, I must've said 'I'm sorry' to you a million times during my drinking years. Once I stopped drinking, I thought another 'I'm sorry' would probably make you want to smack me."

"You've got a point there," Ellie said.

"So, instead, I was trying to *do* it differently. But it didn't work out that way, did it? Anyway, I'm sorry that AA just became another thing that kept us apart. And I'm sorry that I haven't told you enough how proud I am of you. An ex-dancer, bulimic, comic? Oh, my God, Ellie, you are so much more than that!" Sara turned and looked at her. "Look at you! You are this brave, strong woman. You have not only survived this s-h-i-t-t-y hand that you were dealt but you are thriving."

"Mom, I'm—"

Sara put up her hand. "Let me finish. And selfishly, I'm sorry that I missed really getting to know you, because I really think you're something. Yes, I have to admit that there is this part of me that wishes you were more . . ."

"More like you?"

"Yes, I guess that's it. Though, when I think about it, I don't know why I would want you to be more like me. I was in my mid-sixties by the time I finally felt comfortable in my own skin. And I spent years pining for a man who was . . . for goodness sake. After all these years I *still* don't know how to describe your father."

"A damn good pancake maker," Ellie said as she put the platter of perfectly stacked tiny pancakes on the table in front of her mother.

Sara smiled up at her daughter. "Yes, he was. And quite a good daughter maker as well."

Ellie kissed her mother on the cheek. "Thanks, Mom."

Jenny and Penny were click-clicking at her feet in anticipation of their treats.

"All right, you guys," Ellie said as she spatulaed up an entire stack of "silver dollars," put it on a plate and onto the floor. "Go for it, guys." The two stout dachshunds began to gobble wildly, their tails once again pummeling each other.

"Doesn't take much to make those two happy," she said as she dished out a healthy stack of pancakes for her mother and then a plate for herself.

"So what *about* your father?" Sara asked. Ellie's chest contracted.

"What about him?"

"Are you going to visit him while you're out here?"

"Why should I do that?"

"I don't know. Because he used to make you silver dollar pancakes?"

"Mother!" In all the years since her father's first stint in prison, Ellie's mother had never suggested such a thing. Ellie stood stock still, staring at her mother, a platter of pancakes in one hand, a spatula in the other.

"Just a thought," Sara said simply.

Now she's acting a little *too* much like a mother, God. Can you rein her in a little, please? Ellie headed to the pantry in search of the syrup, her elation of the morning ebbing just a tad. Then she saw the bright green Post-it with Missy's name and number on it sitting on the counter. (Ebb, ebb.) She snatched it off the counter, tore it into bits, and threw them in the garbage. There goes my appetite, she thought, heading for the pantry.

"You coming, sweetheart? Your wonderful pancakes are getting cold."

"Yes, I'm getting the syrup."

Fuck! Ellie stared at Aunt Jemima's smiling face on the pantry shelf. "Don't you have any *real* maple syrup, Mother?" she asked, stepping out of the pantry and holding up the hateful bottle.

"What's that in your hand?"

"They call this 'table syrup,' whatever that is. This stuff hasn't been anywhere near a maple tree, I'll tell you that much. Listen to these ingredients—" she read from the label "—high fructose corn syrup, corn syrup, caramel gum . . . Jesus!" She banged the bottle onto the table and fell into her chair. "Forget it! I don't even *want* any pancakes now." She pushed her plate away from her.

"Can't we make do with the Aunt Jemima for today?" Sara put her hand on Ellie's. She pulled it away, put her face in her hands, and started to cry.

"What have I done, Mom? What have I done?"

Sara skooched her chair next to Ellie's and put her arm around her. "You've gotten your self into a bit of a fix, haven't you?"

"Ha! A bit of a fix—that's a euphemism if I ever heard one. I've managed to ruin my marriage; I might even lose Ahnika and Angus. And I can't blame him after what I did to him."

Sara squeezed her daughter's shoulders. "I know one thing: The last time I saw him he was crazy about you. And I also know, from my own experience, that *A* doesn't necessarily mean *B*."

"What?"

"Well, I used to think, for instance, if *A*—your father got indicted, it would mean *B*—I couldn't love him anymore. If he really did those things that they said he did, then it would be over. But *A* happened. He got indicted and—guess what? I still loved him. He got indicted and all that that meant was—he got indicted. Or, I thought if, *A*—I stop drinking, then *B*—my life will work and everything will be okay. But I stopped drinking and all it meant was—I had stopped drinking. Don't get me wrong, things got a *lot* better after I stopped. But I still had an ex-husband in jail and an angry adolescent daughter and all the other things that were wrong in my life. You think, 'I've had an affair with Missy, so that must mean that Peter doesn't love me anymore.' But maybe you having an affair with Missy just means that you had an affair with Missy. Does that make any sense?" Sara asked, moving back to her spot and pouring syrup on her pancakes.

"Sort of. I'm still trying to wrap my brain around the fact that I'm discussing my lesbian affair with my mother." She shook her head and managed a smile.

"I'm trying to wrap *my* brain around the fact that you and I are discussing *anything* without having an argument." Sara handed the syrup to Ellie. "Can I interest you in some high fructose corn syrup?"

"That sounds delicious," she said, grabbing Aunt Jemima by the neck and pouring a thick golden lake next to her pancakes.

"How's Robbie?"

"How would I know? She stopped talking to me about a year ago. I know this sounds stupid, but sometimes I think this whole Missy thing never would've happened if Robbie and I were still friends."

"You have to let go, sweetheart."

"What do you mean?"

"Well, you have to move on from that time with Robbie, or you might miss what's right in front of you. When Daddy ended up in jail, I couldn't accept it, I couldn't let go. So I spent all this time, drinking and pining for him, and I missed out on what was right in front of me." Sara squeezed Ellie's hand. "You. Life is all about change, sweetie. One minute Angus is a tiny baby, the next minute he's walking. One minute you and I can't even have a civil conversation, the next minute we're chatting over pancakes with high fructose corn syrup."

"Okay, so things change. I'll buy that. But why can't I have a husband and kids *and* a best friend?"

"Maybe you can. But even if you and Robbie worked things out—"

"That'll never happen."

"The point is, whomever you're friends with now, it won't be the same as before Peter and the kids. You have a different life now. A better life."

"*Had! Had* a better life! I *know* it's different and I *know* it's better! And I know that I have totally fucked it up." Ellie put her face in her hands a started to cry.

"Maybe, maybe not." Sara put her arm around her daughter. "As Yogi Bear said, 'It ain't over till it's over.'"

Ellie started to laugh. "Yogi Berr-*a*. Not Yogi Bear. It's a quote from a baseball player, not a cartoon character."

"Well, how would *I* know that? It's your father's line, not mine."

"Thank God. Because you were sounding so goddamn wise it was starting to bug me."

Sara looked hurt.

"Mom, I was kidding." Ellie hugged her mother. "Clearly I should've called you a long time ago, and maybe I wouldn't be in this mess."

"Peter's not gone for good. I have a feeling."

"Why hasn't he called?"

"You could call him."

"And what would I say?" Ellie asked, wiping her face. "I don't have a clue what I could possibly say to him."

"How about 'I'm sorry'? I've heard that works wonders." Sara winked at her daughter as she stuck her fork into a triangle of dripping pancakes.

Ellie sawed at her stack of pancakes silently for a moment, then pointed her fork at her mother and said, "That's so crazy it just might work." She looked at her watch. "It's ten-thirty in New York. So . . ."

"So call him."

"Now?"

"What have you got to lose?"

Ellie loved her mother so much in that moment that she almost couldn't stand it. She leaped out of her chair and flung her arms around her neck. She couldn't remember another time in her life when she had had her mother as a pal, as an ally, as a—mother. It felt wonderful.

"Thanks, Mom, thanks."

"For what, sweetheart?"

"Just for being my mom."

"Glad to do it," Sara said, hugging her daughter. "Now, call that handsome husband of yours, for goodness sake!"

Ellie had the receiver in her hand in a heartbeat and was dialing, adrenaline raging through her. "So I just say 'Hi, honey, it's me. I'm sorry?' Is that right?"

"Just be honest with him, sweetheart. I don't know what he'll do, but I know there is a lot of power in the truth."

The phone rang once. She could picture Peter, sitting at his paperstrewn desk. The engine in her chest was back with a vengeance. A second ring—a third.

Where the hell is he? He's gone out and found someone else. It's too late. I've blown it. He's not fucking there!

"Moore Computer Consultants."

"Peter? It's me, Ellie. I'm sorry to bother you at work, but I just had to call and tell you how sorry I am, and how wrong I was, and that I love you, and that I want us to be together. And that you and the children are the most important things in the world to me, and if I could turn back the clock I would, and I'm so sorry that I hurt you, and I want to make it up to you." She finally took a breath and waited—and waited. "Peter? Are you still there?"

"I'm here." His voice seemed void of emotion.

"Are you going to say anything?"

"I'm not sure what to say."

"Well, you don't have to say anything. I just wanted to tell you that I had lost my abstinence, you know, and I finally went to a meeting last night, and I'm doing much better now. See, when I lost my abstinence, I lost my sanity and any clarity I might have had and— That's not an excuse it's just— I'm just trying to be honest because I haven't been very honest lately and I realize that I still have a lot of work to do. And I know I hurt you, and I am sorry, and I want us to work it out. Did I already say that? Did I already say I want us to work it out?" There was silence again. "Peter, please say something so I know you're still there."

314

"I'm still here, El. I'm just not sure what to say. I'm not sure how I feel."

"Of course, you're not. And if you don't have to say anything now, you don't."

"Good," he said. Was there a hint of anger in his voice? She waited—more silence.

"How are the kids?" he asked finally.

"They're fine. They're having a ball so far. We all swam in the pool till it was dark last night. They're still asleep. They'll probably sleep till noon." She switched the phone to her other ear and wiped her sweaty palm on her jeans.

"Peter, can I call you again? Would that be okay?" Silence *again*! She waited, listening to the sound of her thumping heart and his breathing. It took every ounce of faith and courage to wait and wait for an answer.

"No."

She moved the phone away from her mouth, covered her eyes, and puffed out tiny sobs.

"Let me call you."

"Sure," she said quickly. "If I'm not here, try the cell. I'll leave it on."

"Okay. If the kids really miss me, then you can call and I'll talk to them. Otherwise, let me call you."

"Okay."

"I gotta go, El. Bye."

"Bye, Peter. I love you."

"I gotta go." *Click*, and he was gone.

Chapter Thirty-Four

"Acceptance and forgiveness," Ellie said to the empty Lumina, quoting the speaker from her morning OA meeting and hoping that the mere words would fill her up with a little. "One isn't possible without the other, remember?"

True to her resolve, Ellie had made it to a meeting every day since her arrival in California. But unlike her first time getting abstinent there was no pink cloud, no easy click into staying clean. Every day of not bingeing felt like a struggle. All the while, through meetings and shares and slogans, a tiny voice in the back of her head kept asking her, What's the point? What's the point of meetings now that you've ruined your life? What's the point of not bingeing if you've lost Peter? What's the point of not throwing up if he's taking Ahnika and Angus? And like her first time counting days, Ellie cried her way through every meeting, but this time she knew why.

At this morning's meeting, when they had asked about newcomers, Ellie had raised her hand and told the group she was twelve days back. Everyone had applauded her success. It's good to be back, she had thought, feeling pretty darn serene.

But now, as she zoomed toward a reunion with the most enigmatic person in her life, serenity was nowhere to be seen.

It had been eight years since she'd spoken to her dad, eleven since she'd made the trip to see him. And in all that time he had only contacted her twice—gushing letters of congratulations after Ahnika's and Angus's births. She had never responded to those letters.

When she turned onto the access road to San Viejo Minimum Security Prison and saw the red tile roof of the main building in the distance, she began to dream of mixed nuts.

"God, I'm not really sure why the hell I'm here, except that my mother guilted me into this. So could you please just tell me what to say so I can get this over with and then get the fuck out?" She pulled up to the gatehouse. Both my parents live in gated communities, she thought. Who knew?

"Name, please," the guard called from his little house.

"Ellie Fuller," she called back. The boyish-looking guard was checking a list of names on a clipboard.

"Who are you visiting?"

"Paul Fuller."

"Really?" His face lit up.

Here goes, Ellie thought.

"You must be his daughter, the comedienne from New York City."

"Yeah, that's me," she said, blushing. Even though the description was fairly accurate, she suddenly felt as if she was going along with some con her father was perpetrating on this poor naïve boy.

"He talks about you all the time."

Didn't happen to mention the fact that we haven't spoken in eight years, did he? she wondered silently.

"You know how to get to the infirmary?"

Infirmary? The word hit Ellie in the chest with a thud. My father's sick? Paul Fuller sick? That's simply not possible. "No," she said, finally.

· · ·

The fluorescent lights, the greenish yellow walls, and the stillness of the room made everything feel surreal. Ellie looked down at the hand in hers. It wasn't familiar; covered with liver spots and in bad need of a manicure—surely this wasn't her father's hand. And the old man who was attached to this hand, sleeping propped up in the hospital bed, hooked up to oxygen by his nostrils—how could this be Paul Fuller? This man was pale and drawn, with gray matted hair. How could this be the handsome charming raconteur that was her father?

There's been some mistake, Ellie thought vaguely as she listened to his labored breathing. She studied his hand and tried to think of what she would say to him, but nothing came.

I never wrote him back, she thought over and over, I never wrote him back . . . Her brain felt thick and useless, as if it was packed with soggy cotton. She gave his hand a squeeze and closed her eyes, praying for clarity.

"I like the new hair."

She looked up. Her father's steel blue eyes were studying her, a boyish grin on his face.

"Thanks." It *is* him, she thought at the sound of his voice and the look on his now handsome face. She felt herself being bathed, instantly and completely, in a wash of forgiveness. The endless list of complaints and resentments and disappointments were suddenly and magically gone.

"Hi, Dad," she said softly as tears filled her eyes.

"Ellie Bellie Bella Bellou" he said, opening his arms to her.

"Oh, Daddy!" she said, tears spilling from her eyes. "The nurse said you have emphysema. Is that bad? Is it serious?"

"Oh, I think I'm gonna make it," he said, then coughed dramatically.

"Why didn't you write Mom and tell her? I didn't know you were sick."

"I'm fine," he whispered. "All I have to do is wheeze a few times and—boom—I'm in here in this comfy bed, room service, better food." He winked at her, smiling. "I just need a break from the daily grind every now and then."

"You're impossible!" she said, pushing him on the thigh.

"Well, you know what I always say; once a con man . . ."

"Always a con man." They finished the sentence together, grinning madly at each other.

She leaned over and put her head on his chest and hugged him. "I'm sorry, Daddy. I'm so sorry."

"What for, sweetheart?" he asked, patting her head. "What on earth are you sorry for?"

"For not visiting, for being so angry with you for so long, for not writing you back."

"Oh, stop it!" he said, giving her a little shake. "That's silly. You've got your own life, a husband and kids. You're off in the world now. You can't be bothered with me. I don't expect that, you silly girl. I did my job raising you, and now you're off in the world."

There was a catch in Ellie's chest. "You did your job raising me?"

"Yes. I don't expect . . ."

"Daddy, I was twelve years old when you were sent here for the first time. Twelve!"

"Well, I'd done all I could do. It was time for you to fend for yourself." He looked down and smoothed out the sheets across his stomach.

"Dad, what are you talking about?" She could feel disappointment swelling in her chest, pushing her breath aside.

"I'm talking about the fact that *my* father was gone when I was ten, eight—even younger—five years old, for Christ's sake!" His voice was stronger. "He was never around—always at the club, drinking with his buddies, and I spent my childhood comforting my mother and raising my little brother and sisters."

What could I have been thinking? Ellie wondered as she listened to him tell the same old story. What would have made me think that all this time in jail would have changed anything?

"I knew if *I* could do it, if I could survive *my* childhood, that you could do it, that you would be just fine. And I can see that you are." He grabbed her hand, gave it a squeeze, and flashed her his country club smile.

Her hand was limp in his. You can see that I'm fine? she thought. If you only knew. She felt defeated, trampled, sad beyond description.

"There's a young man here that I work with, he's a guard and he's . . ."

"What do you mean you work with him?"

"Well . . ." Paul grinned slyly. "We talk, he tells me about his feelings. He's been having a very hard time lately, you see. He had a horrendous childhood, poor kid—was put in a foster home when he was only three, separated from his siblings and . . ."

Oh, my God, Ellie realized, he's giving him therapy. Perfect! Only *my* father could read a few books about psychoanalysis while he's in *prison* and end up giving therapy to one of the guards. Perfect!

"So, we talk a couple of times a week and he tells . . ."

It's only gotten worse.

". . . Lately I've been helping him deal with his feelings toward his birth mother. . . ."

Ellie closed her eyes. Okay, God, help me out here. I've come all this way to see him and maybe work things out and now I just want to kill him. I just want to take a pillow and put it over his face and push down hard till he stops talking—forever. The thought of suffocating him calmed her a little. The fact that no one would suspect made the corner of her mouth curl up the tiniest bit.

"Are you still in analysis?" He was actually asking about *her*.

"Not now but I'm about to start again. In fact, that's why I'm here. I need to clear some things up with you." She was blurting it all out so he wouldn't interrupt. "Turns out, even with all these years of therapy and OA, that I'm not done yet."

"I guess we made a lot of mistakes with you." He squeezed her hand again. "But all parents do, don't they? Dennis, this young fellow I've been working with, he's a father himself and—"

"*Dad!*" she interrupted.

"For Christ's sake, Ellie, don't shout at me."

"I'm not shouting!" She was. "I just want you to listen to me. For once, could you just listen to me?" She pulled her hand out of his and stood up. "I've come all this way to talk to you—to talk about us! I don't want to hear about some—some—prison guard that I don't even know."

"Stop shouting at me, Ellie. I'm sick and I'm old."

"Are you sick or are you not, Dad? Which is it? Is it the real thing or just another one of your cons?" Ellie stared at her father, waiting. He looked down, studying his hands. The stillness of the room flooded in on her suddenly, her father's labored breathing the only sound.

Finally he spoke, slowly and without looking up. "I am sick, not *that* sick, but a little sick. The emphysema won't go away; it comes and goes and when it's here sometimes I need a little extra rest and oxygen.

Ellie resisted an urge to throw herself on his diminished lap. She waited.

"Now—" he looked up finally "—what did you want to say to me? I'm all ears."

She took a deep breath. "Well, I had a long ride up here to think about what I needed to say . . ." and I still don't have a clue, she thought ". . . and I know that we haven't seen each other in a long time . . . and I . . ." She stopped and put her head in her hands. No divine guidance was coming; her head was sloshing with fear and anger and confusion.

"Boy, this must really be something. It's not like my Ellie to be at a loss for words." He was smiling at her. All she could do was shrug her shoulders.

Acceptance and forgiveness, the words from the meeting rang in her head.

But I don't *feel* accepting and forgiving! she wanted to scream back. Then just tell the truth! a voice told her. Divine guidance, finally.

"Okay, here it is. All the way up here I've been trying to figure out you—us—" She walked to the end of the bed. "How I feel about you, where I can fit you in my life or my heart." She swallowed down a sob. "The facts are that after you were sent away, I was left alone with Mom, who was drunk from morning till night for literally years. Well, that really fucked me up. And the truth is, I've been furious with you since your second conviction." She turned to him. When she saw his wrinkled face and his frail frame under the crumpled sheets, she had to look away. "And the truth is . . . The truth is, I'm *still* mad at you." She closed her eyes and spoke quickly. "I know I shouldn't be. I know I'm a big girl and it's time for me to move on and all that crap, but I can't! I just can't! And I'm not gonna say I forgive you and not mean it. I'm not gonna give you some big kiss on the cheek and smile and pretend its all better—because it's not all better.

"And maybe it'll never be all better. Maybe I'll be standing over your grave, cursing you. I don't know. I hope not. I hope I can get to forgiveness before you're gone. But . . ." She shook her head and forced back tears. "I'm not there yet.

"So I guess this trip isn't going to be about some big cathartic scene where I forgive you and you're sorry and we weep and all that." She waited, hoping against hope that he would jump in with an I *am* sorry, El. But he didn't. "So . . . I guess what I *did* want to say is, even though I'm mad at you, there are still all these reasons that I'm glad you were my dad."

She turned to him, finally knowing why she had come. "I'm glad that you're my dad because you made silver dollar pancakes for me and Mommy when I was little." Her eyes welled with tears. "I'm glad that you're my dad because you could always make me laugh, and because, even though you've been gone for so much of my life, I've never doubted for a minute that you loved me. And I'm glad that I had a dad who listened to Ella Fitzgerald and Judy Garland and Tony Bennett. And a dad who can do the best Professor Harold Hill in the world, next to Robert Preston, of course. I love that you were always this big ham."

"I beg your pardon," he said, with mock indignation.

"Oh, c'mon, Dad. You know you were always a frustrated performer. Remember that time we whistled at the Waldorf?"

"I remember."

"That was my first trip to New York. We took a taxi to Sak's, and you bought me that outfit off the mannequin. Do you remember?"

"Like it was yesterday," he said, patting the empty space on the bed next to him.

She sat down on the bed and took his hand again. "I think of that day," she said.

"Do you?" he asked, putting his arm around her shoulders and giving her a squeeze.

"I think of that day a lot," she said, swinging her legs up onto the bed and leaning back onto his arm.

"Me, too," he said as he held her shoulders tightly.

"That was a good day, wasn't it?" she asked, tears sliding slowly down her cheeks.

"It was. You know what I think?" he asked.

"What?"

He leaned into her and whispered in her ear. "I think that just might have been the best day ever." Then he kissed her on the cheek and held her even more tightly. And father and daughter sat side by side in the small prison hospital bed, remembering a day long ago when they had whistled at the Waldorf.

Chapter Thirty-Five

Ellie lazed on the chaise longue in the shade of the olive tree while Angus, Ahnika, and Grammy played in the pool.

"Look! Mommy, look!"

"I'm watching, sweetie!"

Ahnika stood in the glaring afternoon sun, poised on the edge of the pool, inner tube on, with her Grammy standing in the shallow end, arms out stretched.

"Grammy, back up."

"Gamma," Angus called from his spot on the steps, his fifth new word since their arrival. Ellie's heart leaped and sank in one moment. Ahnika jumped into Sara's arms with a splash and a squeal.

"Good job, sweetie! That was great!" she called, and Ahnika scrambled out of the pool to do it all over again. "Mommy, watch!"

"I'm watching." And Ahnika jumped into her grandmother's arms *again*.

The last thirteen days in California had been an endless stream of bliss and torture. Blissful because of lazy, unstructured days, like this one, spent by the pool in the California sun just enjoying her children, something she hadn't done *really* since Bibi, Missy, and HBO had entered her life. And blissful because—since the evening of the violins—Ellie's relationship with her mother seemed magically transformed. Torture unfortunately followed every blissful moment. How could she have let all those months of Angus's and Ahnika's lives slip past her unnoticed? How many words had Angus learned when she was too busy with Missy and her bulimia to have noticed? Were these the last carefree days that she would spend with her children? Was she going back to New York to deal with divorce lawyers and custody battles? Had she *really* managed to fuck everything up?

Ring!

"I'll get it!" Ahnika yelled, scrambling out of the pool and running, dripping, into the kitchen.

"Careful, sweetie. Don't slip!" her grandmother called.

"Who is it?" Ellie could hear Ahnika ask. "Hi, Daddy! I can jump off the side of the pool."

"Dada," Angus said, beaming.

Ellie's eyes filled with tears for about the hundredth time since her arrival.

"Mommy! It's Daddy!"

Ellie hopped out of the lounge chair and rushed to the phone. This was Peter's second call in one day and she felt hopeful/full of dread, blissful/tortured.

"Bye, Daddy." Ahnika handed the dripping phone to Ellie, then raced back to her grandma and the pool.

"Peter?"

"Hi." The sound of his voice made her all swirly inside. "We got the letter from Calhoun."

"And?"

"She got in."

"Great! Well, Veronica always said we'd get our first choice. Are you happy?"

"Well, I'm glad about Calhoun. Aren't you?"

"Yes. I think it's the perfect school for her."

They were doing the "pretending everything's okay" thing. They had had several of these conversations since Ellie had made that first call to Peter at her mother's urging. They would chat, almost normally, about this and that, he would talk to Ahnika, and then they would say good-bye. The big tip-off that things weren't normal came at the end of each call.

"I love you," Ellie would say.

There would be a long pause, and then Peter would say, "Give the kids a hug for me." Then a click, and Ellie's empty chest would thump with regret and fear.

"Listen, El, I've been doing a lot of thinking."

"Yes?" she said, trying like hell to hear a hint about her fate in his tone.

"You're supposed to come back tomorrow."

"I know."

"And I think you should come home."

"Okay."

"I think that getting a divorce is a big step and I don't want to do that to the kids just yet."

"Just yet?"

"Yes. If we decide that's what we want, then—"

"I'm not going to decide I want that—ever," she broke in. "I can tell you that right now. I want you and the kids and our life back and I'm willing to do just about anything to get that."

"I know, El. You keep saying that, but you can't do the one thing that I really need you to do, can you? You can't take it back. You said you wished you could go back in time, and I believe you. But the problem is we can't do that. We can't make that it never happened. And no matter how many times I try to say that you are still you—you are still my wife and friend that I love—I can't believe that, because the Ellie that I knew and married would not have done what you did."

"But, Peter, she did."

"What do you mean?"

"I did it. But I'm still the woman that you married and loved. This is me on the other end of the phone. I haven't been body snatched; I'm still me. I know I did something that neither of us thought I was capable of doing. But what we have together and what we've shared, that weighs more than this, doesn't it?"

Silence.

"Peter, c'mon, I didn't chop the heads off of small woodland creatures. I had an affair. Maybe it seems worse because it was with a woman, I don't know but—people have affairs all the time and they forgive each other. A lot of the relationships survive. Look at Paul Newman and Joanne Woodward."

"Did Joanne have an affair?"

"I was talking about Paul."

"Did *he* have an affair?"

"Probably. I mean, c'mon, don't you think? The point is, they are still together and I want *us* to stay together. I've been doing a lot of thinking since I've been here and going to a meeting every day and I've had a lot of revelations about—"

"Ellie, look, we can debate the moral issue of this forever but the real question is—do I still love you? Because if I don't love you, do you still want to be married to me?"

"Well, do you, do you still love me? Jesus, Peter, don't torture me like this."

"*I don't know!*" he shouted into the phone. "I just don't know! I'm all mixed up! One minute it's yes, I love you desperately, completely, and the next minute I want to kill you. It's so hard having you and the kids so far away. I can't figure anything out without you here."

"So you want me to come back and we can go back to how it was and . . ."

"It can never go back to the way it was."

"Well, that's a positive attitude."

"Fuck you, Ellie. Fuck you and your sarcastic jokes! You're lucky I'm on the fucking phone with you and not at the divorce lawyer. You betrayed me in a way that can never be taken back."

"Peter, I'm sorry. I . . ."

"It's not the sex, forget about that. It's the emotional betrayal. I gave you everything, every part of me. I made myself vulnerable to you, then you took the insider's look at me and shared it with that fucking WASP cunt. Then you two lay in bed and critiqued me?"

"I never did that, Peter."

"I want us to be together, I do. I want to work it out, but the problem is, you can't give me back my dignity. No matter what you do, you can't do that."

"I never critiqued you, Peter, never."

"What about Missy?"

"Missy's a psycho and that's over. That is *completely* over."

"Did you tell *her* it was over?"

"Yes!" There was a long silence. "Peter, are you still there?"

"Just come home, Ellie. I can't promise you anything but I need you and the kids to come home."

Chapter Thirty-Six

I'm about to walk into a French movie, Ellie thought as her cab headed east through the park. But not the fun sexy part. Oh, no, that part's way over. This is the end of the movie when everyone in the theater is wriggling in their seats, wondering who's going to get shot—the heiress lover, the spurned husband, or the careless wife who broke his heart?

Well, at least I like my outfit, she thought, looking down at her cute yet sexy Betsey Johnson slip dress.

Just two days ago, Ellie had sat in Dr. Hubert's office, totally stumped.

"What do *you* want to wear to Ahnika's graduation?" she had asked Ellie. "Not what would *Peter* like you to wear, not what would your mother *hate*, but what would *you* feel great wearing?"

Ellie had bellowed, "I don't have a fucking clue!"

"Why not go shopping with a friend?"

"That's what got me into this mess; I don't *have* any friends!" Ellie had thought of Robbie and Missy and the total shambles of her life, and she had started to weep.

"I think what got you into this mess is a little more complicated than that."

"I know, I know," Ellie said as she blew her nose.

"Well, what do *you* think got you into this mess?"

"Believe me, I've been thinking and thinking about that. How could this have happened? How did I end up here? Why did I have an affair with a WASPy heiress when I love my husband and I'm not even gay?"

"And?"

"Well, I really think that it all goes back to meetings. When I stopped going to meetings, I lost my way; that's the only way that I can explain it. And now that I'm back in meetings, I can see just how lost I was. I'd completely lost sight of what's important."

"And what's important?" the doctor asked.

"Well, Peter and Ahnika and Angus, of course.

"What else?"

"At the risk of sounding like a fucking Moonie—God."

"Billions of people believe in God, Ellie."

"I know. But, believe me, when I walked into my first OA meeting, and they started talking about God and a Higher Power, I wanted to bolt. I wanted to say, 'Listen. I came here to stop throwing up, not to turn into some sort of religious fanatic.'"

"And what makes the meetings so powerful?"

She thought for a moment. "It's so magical. I don't know if I can explain it. I mean, here you are in a room full of people that have all said, 'My life doesn't work. I'm *so* desperate that I am willing to sit in a church basement full of strangers and say *Help me!*' I walk into a meeting feeling hopeless and scared, and I'm surrounded by other people who are—or who *have* been—hopeless and scared. And people talk—and I listen, and somehow—I'm healed. I don't know how the fuck it works. But it's got something to do with not doing it alone. Because during all this shit with Missy—when I had lost my abstinence and I was lying to everybody—I was *still* praying, but it didn't help because I was *alone*. All I know is that when God *and* meetings are in my life my head is *not* in the toilet. Without those two things I'm fucked!"

When Ellie had left Dr. Hubert's office that day, she had gone straight to Betsey Johnson and found the outfit of *her* dreams.

How's Peter going to handle this whole French film thing? Ellie wondered as the cab idled at a red light at Madison.

Since returning from her mother's, Ellie's life had sort of returned to normal—sort of. She was still being strung along by HBO, but Lisa, quite a bit mellower with a newborn, was only calling her once or twice a week. Her late night trysts on the sofa bed with Peter were no longer a part of her schedule. And no more treks to the dreaded East Side. No. Ellie had assigned Bibi to all drop-offs and pickups of Ahnika at Park Avenue Playgroup. And last, but certainly not least—no more Missy. Missy hadn't called, thank God, and Ellie hadn't had even the slightest urge to call Missy. Ellie hadn't even invited Missy to the small birthday party that they had had when Angus turned one. But despite Ellie's lack of desire for Missy, and Ellie's conviction to stay away from her, one question still haunted her: Who the heck is Missy Hanover, really?

As Ellie was paying the cab driver, a vivid image of Missy, all leggy and perfectly coifed, walking right up to Peter at the graduation and planting a big kiss right on his mouth, popped into Ellie's head. Oh, my God, she thought. Forget it! This graduation is going to be the end of my marriage, I'm sure of it.

She stepped out of the cab and onto Park Avenue, which was dotted with colorful tulips. She saw Bibi, with Angus and Ahnika in the double stroller, across the street and her spirits lifted a bit. "Hey, you guys!" She waved her arms and shouted, rushing to them. Ahnika and Angus beamed at her and squirmed in their seats.

"Mama! Mama!" Angus called.

"Mommy, it's graduation day!" Ahnika told her as Ellie plastered kisses all over their faces.

"Look how cute you two look!"

Ahnika, wearing a sleeveless navy blue linen dress with smocking, looked up at her mother shyly. Angus giggled. He looked adorable in a brand-new royal blue jumper from the Gap.

"Where's Ahnika?" Ellie said to Bibi.

"I'm right here, Mommy," she shouted from the stroller.

Ellie looked down and frowned. "No, you can't be my daughter. My daughter looks just like Darth Vader."

"Mommeee, stop it! It's me!" she said, laughing.

"Bibi, where in the world is Ahnika?"

Bibi smiled and shook her head. "I don't know where she is, but *this* little girl is awfully cute."

"You guys! *I'm* Ahnika!"

"You are! And you are the cutest girl in the whole world!" Ellie looked at her watch. We're right on schedule, she thought as she took the helm behind the double stroller. Her heart began to thump as the four of them headed to Park Avenue Playgroup for the last time.

The place was packed and everyone was seated when they arrived. Ellie saw Peter wave to her from an aisle seat near the back.

"Hi," he said with a tense smile when Ellie, Bibi, and Angus slipped into the folding chairs he had been holding for them.

I love you, Peter, I love you so much. I'm sorry I'm putting you through this, she wanted to say to him. But she just said "Hi," and gave him a *please don't hate me* smile.

"Welcome, families, friends, and caregivers!" Veronica Leeds, in her appliquéd apron and clanging bracelets, had appeared at the front of the room. "I love my job!" she began. "There's nothing else I'd rather do. But when you're dealing with a dozen two-and-a-half-year-olds, some groups are tougher than others. And, I'm telling you truthfully, I don't think I can remember a year when I've been so happy *every day* to come to work. This group here—" Veronica gestured to a row of kid-sized chairs that sat empty behind her "—has been a delight beyond description." She glanced at her coworkers on the sidelines. Lizzie Daniels and two other teachers were nodding enthusiastically.

Ellie suppressed an urge to grab Peter's hand.

"Every year at this time, I spend most of my waking hours fighting off tears, tears of pride as I watch my babies play and share and get along in ways that were impossible back in September. And tears of sorrow as I know I have to say good-bye to all these wonderful children." She reached into her apron pocket, pulled out a tissue, and dabbed the corner of her eyes. "Sorry," she told the crowd, then shook her head.

"Every September, I tell myself, '*This year*, I won't get too attached. *This year*, I'll remember that I only get them for a short time and then I have to give them back.'"

"But she cries every year!" Lizzie Daniels called from the sidelines.

"Oh, you!" Veronica said, dismissing Lizzie. Then she leaned into the audience and stage-whispered to the crowd. "I'll bet you five bucks she weeps before the day's over."

More laughter.

"Now, it's time for the fun. So, without further ado, I give you the graduating class of Park Avenue Playgroup for 2001." And with a wave of her arm, the commencement march began to play, the double doors at the back of the room opened, and every parent, sibling, and relative craned their necks to see the graduates emerge.

To Ellie's delight, Ahnika was first in line.

"She's first," Peter whispered, putting his hand on Ellie's knee.

She grabbed it; he didn't pull away. There was a tingling in her nostrils and a sudden lump in her throat.

As Ahnika marched through the doors wearing a white cardboard graduation hat, there was a group "Ah!" from the crowd. She stared at her black patent leather Mary Janes as she walked slowly up the center aisle.

Mason, in the Little Lord Fauntleroy outfit, was next in line, and Ellie's heart leaped at the sight of him. He was scanning the crowd, in search of Missy and Antonio, no doubt. He smiled and waved to someone. Ellie followed his gaze and her eyes fell on those incredible green ones of Antonio's.

Watch out, El, she thought, watch out. Her head tilted inexplicably to one side, then she gave him a Gidget-type smile—absent, she hoped, of anything sexual. He gave her an odd smile.

Was that a smirk? Ellie wondered. Is Antonio smirking at me? She saw an empty seat next to him. No Missy, that's weird. She looked away quickly and went back to watching Ahnika. All the graduates, in matching cardboard graduation hats, found their way to their seats as the commencement march came to an end.

Just watch Ahnika, Ellie. Just keep your eyes on Ahnika and act natural, she told herself. She smiled inanely as Lizzie Daniels led the graduates in a song about colors. She wasn't absorbing much of the little show that they were putting on; her mind was racing with fear and anxiety. She sneaked a look at Peter. He seems fine, she thought.

The rest of the show passed in a blur. A few more songs, a little speech from Lizzie Daniels, and then the giving of the diplomas. After Lizzie passed out the last diploma, Veronica led the graduates in a "hip, hip, hooray," and all the cardboard hats went flying, then all the kids scrambled to find their hats and their parents.

"Mommy! Daddy!" Ahnika came running toward them like a shot. "Didja like the colors song? Didja?"

Peter swooped her up and perched her on his hip. "I did, sweetheart. I loved it. But I think my favorite was the stand up, sit down song."

"Nahka!" Angus, still on Ellie's lap, was straining to get to his sister.

"Okay, handsome, okay." Ellie handed him to Peter.

"I like the stand up, sit down song, too, but nobody ever gets that right. We had to practice that *forever*," Ahnika said, rolling her eyes.

Ellie watched Peter holding his gorgeous children, smiling and nodding at Ahnika's chatter, and thought, Okay, the whole thing's over and there hasn't been a fistfight or a stabbing. She stayed glued to her seat, feeling invisible below the sea of voices and bodies. When the crowd thins a bit, I'll just stand, then we'll casually saunter to the exit and we're outta here.

"We have juice and coffee and cookies in the back!" Veronica yelled above the din.

"Cookies!" Ahnika said, then struggled out of her daddy's arms and headed to the back of the room. Angus, Peter, and Bibi followed suit.

Thank God Missy's not here, she thought as she began to rummage through her purse in an attempt to look busy.

She unzipped her makeup bag and fished out her lipstick. Did I mean *anything* to her? Ellie silently asked her reflection as she applied some Malt Shimmer. I really don't have a clue.

"Mommy!"

Ellie's heart stopped.

"Mason!" Missy's cultured voice carried over the hum of voices and hit Ellie in the side of the head.

Fuck! Ellie, lipstick still in hand, open purse on her lap, examined the folding chairs. Can I possibly crawl under all these chairs all the way to the back of the room and then out the door?

"Maman!" Camille's nasal voice broke the hum this time and Ellie *had* to look up.

Yes, there they were, just as Ellie had suspected; there, at the back of the room, stood Missy, with Marie-Claire by her side. The two had obviously just arrived—together.

Missy, looking effortlessly impeccable, as always, was holding Mason and smiling at the tale that he had to tell.

Ellie, feeling like a teenage girl who had just been dumped by some shitty guy that she was about to break up with anyway, went back to studying her reflection.

"Ellie, darling."

She jumped up. "Antonio!" Her purse crashed to the floor and its contents scattered beneath the row of chairs in front of her. "Shit," she said, looking down at the mess. "You startled me." Her heart was beating out of her chest.

"Come here, my little Ellie," Antonio said in a fatherly tone and enveloped her with his arms. "I have missed you," he whispered in her ear.

"Well, I've been busy with the show, the kids," she said as she gently broke out of his embrace, then got down on her knees to gather her things.

"Let me help you." Antonio pushed several folding chairs aside and joined Ellie on the floor.

"Don't take it personally," he whispered to her as he handed her a tampon.

"What?" she said, confused, staring at his offering.

"Don't take Missy's—defection personally. She can't help it."

"Oh," she said, snatching back her tampon, then grabbing her mascara and blush from the floor. I hope Peter can't see us down here.

"She can't help it. She's been this way as long as I've known her."

"Really?" She was trying to sound casual, hoping he'd continue.

"Marie-Claire is nothing special. She's so—so—obvious!"

"Obvious?"

"A French girl? What could be more cliché? Those French, all they think about is sex and wine, wine and sex. Where's the fun in that? Where's the challenge?"

Her gathering had stopped. She was frozen on all fours, waiting for the next piece of the puzzle to fall from Antonio's mouth, as the party buzzed on above them.

"And *I* was a challenge?"

"You were the best! Of all of them you were the best!" he told her in a grand whisper as he handed her her checkbook.

Of all of them? Ellie thought. Just how many were there?

"Is that according to you or Missy?" She prayed that she sounded light and playful.

"According to both of us. I always knew you would be. She wasn't sure about you at first, but I was. From the first moment I saw you at the cocktail party, with your leather skirt and crazy hair—" he tousled her hair like a big brother "—I knew you would be wonderful."

The puzzle was coming together, making a frightening picture in Ellie's mind.

"You two are so clever," she told him. "So, were you involved every step of the way?"

He seemed to puff up a bit. "Well, the sponge bath was *my* idea."

Every moment that Ellie had spent with Missy suddenly took on a different hue.

"So, that day with the sponge bath, you weren't really away on a business trip?"

"You're catching on."

She felt the blood drain from her face, but smiled coyly at him. "And New Year's, were you in on that, too?"

"New Year's was delicious, wasn't it, you two on the floor hiding from me? I loved it! I just wish I could've stayed and watched."

"Like at Mason's party?" Ellie was gripping her makeup bag for all she was worth.

Antonio just smiled, raised his eyebrows, then gently took her makeup bag from her, zipped it, and put it in her purse. "Just because Missy has moved on, doesn't mean that she did not love you."

Ellie slowly got back into her seat. "Oh, now it's love we're talking about. This game of yours is about love?"

"Not usually—but with you," Antonio said, sitting in the chair next to her. "She spent almost six months on you. She's usually done and gone in two."

"Well—" she leaned back in the chair and crossed her legs, trying to look relaxed "—I'm flattered." Faith Roberts's words of warning came back to her, *I heard a story about Missy that made my skin crawl.*

"She gets bored and needs someone new. Is that so horrible? In Argentina, many of the marriages are like this."

"You're kidding me!"

"No, only in my country it is the *man* who needs the variety—it is so macho, you know. And the wives, they just look the other way." He gazed across the room at his stunning wife. "I have met many women in my life, but never one like Missy. I love her, so I want her to be happy. If she needs variety, then . . ." He shrugged his shoulders. "But instead of looking the other way, I'm happy to get involved, to help her, even. Like I helped her with you." He pointed his finger like a gun at Ellie and gave her a playful wink.

Oh, my God, Ellie thought, wait till I tell Dr. Hubert *this*!

"My, my, my." Ellie fiddled with her hair and glanced quickly to check on Peter. He was pouring juice for Angus and Ahnika. "You two should be on *Oprah*. 'How to keep your marriage fresh,' or something like that. It's a very unique approach."

Antonio barked out one of his grand laughs. "We should be on *Oprah*! Oh, my little Ellie, you are the best!" And he wrapped his arms around her again. She froze. "I think of you, Ellie. I dream of you. Do you ever dream of me?"

Ellie, one eye on Peter, reached between Antonio's legs and began searching. He eased toward her and moaned in her ear. She wrapped her hand around his balls and gave them a little squeeze.

"Do you like that?" she asked in a deep whisper.

"Yes," he told her in a throaty voice.

She squeezed a little tighter. "And this? Do you like it?"

"Yes, Yes."

"How 'bout this?" She clamped down on his balls with every ounce of strength she had. Antonio stiffened and a slight groan escaped his lips.

"Don't make a sound!" she commanded in his ear.

"But, Ellie, you're . . ." He tried to pull away, she pulled back.

"Uh, uh, uh."

"You little whore," he said in a deadly whisper, then grabbed her wrist.

"Let go of me, Antonio, or I'll scream."

His grip loosened.

"If anyone looks this way, I'll stand up on my chair and tell all these fancy people the real story about you and your Missy."

He hesitated.

"Go ahead. Try me. I don't give a shit about these people. And I've got nothing to lose."

"You let go and I'll let go," he squeaked out.

"Not till I've said my piece." She looked him in the eyes. "How dare you use me to amuse your psychotic wife and then act like I should be flattered. You're as crazy as she is. The two of you came into my life and trashed it, then walked away and didn't give it a thought. If I'm lucky, if I grovel at my sweet husband's feet, *maybe* I can save my marriage. And you talk about it all like it was some game? If I thought it would work, I'd take out a full-page ad in *Town & Country*, warning people about the two of you.

"Now, if you'll excuse me, I have to get my family and get the hell out of here." Then she released his balls and was gone.

Chapter Thirty-Seven

You ready for the L.A. bigwigs?" Peter asked as he shoved his running shoes into his blue duffle bag.

"I guess so. I mean, these L.A. people are unbelievable," Ellie said, looking in her dresser mirror as she put on her lipstick. "It was way back in March when Lisa called and said I had to be ready to pitch to them in less than two weeks. And they've rescheduled and canceled so many times. I mean, at this point, I really don't even care."

"You don't?"

She thought for a moment. "No."

"Well, that's a pretty healthy attitude."

"You think?"

"Yeah," and he gave her a sweet smile.

It was the first time that the two of them had been alone together in their bedroom since she'd been back from California. She felt all sappy and weepy all of a sudden and fought off an urge to throw herself at his feet and start begging him to fuck her.

"Thanks for last week," she said finally.

"For what?" he asked.

"For going to the graduation and—I don't know. It was a difficult situation, to make a huge understatement."

"Well, I wasn't about to miss my baby girl's graduation. I'm not sure if I'm relieved or disappointed that I didn't get to punch anybody out," he said, fishing in his top drawer.

Peter punching out Missy, Ellie mused, now *that* I would've liked to see.

"I'm sorry I kicked and screamed about Ahnika going to Park Avenue Playgroup. She loved it. It really turned out to be a good place."

"Easy for you to say. That fucking place ruined my life." He threw a handful of socks into his bag.

"Peter, Park Avenue Playgroup didn't ruin your life, I did."

"It's that fucking Missy. That cunt."

"Peter, I'm not defending Missy—I'm not. But I have to take responsibility for what happened so it never happens again."

"What are you saying, Ellie? Are you saying that you would do something like this again? Because if that's the case, then . . ."

"No, Peter. I'm not saying that." She paused and searched her brain frantically for the right words. "But I have to ask myself—what's *my* part in all this? And my part in it is that I was a sitting duck for Missy. Why did she choose me? Why me, and not Faith or Libby? When she came along, I was teetering on the brink and somehow she knew it."

"Well, in that case, I'm really disappointed that I *didn't* punch her fucking lights out."

"Me, too." Their eyes were locked and there was silence suddenly. The look on Peter's face told Ellie that he wanted to kiss her. She stepped into him and—

"Mommy, why can't you come to the park with us?" Ahnika was suddenly standing in the doorway, one hand on her hip.

Ellie swooped Ahnika into her arms and gave her a squeeze. "Because Mommy has to work."

"With the big shots?" she asked.

"With the big shots."

"Then are we going to New Jersey?"

"Yep! Look!" Ellie gestured to the puffed-up suitcases on the bed. "I'm all packed and Daddy's almost done."

"Come on, sweetheart." Bibi came down the hall with Angus in one arm and eased Ahnika away from Ellie.

"Mama!" Angus reached out to her.

"Go to the playground, sweet boy. I'll see you soon," Ellie said, kissing his cheek.

"Let's go, you two. We're going to the Elephant playground so Mommy can work."

"Mama!"

Ellie's chest contracted as she watched Angus's face crumple into a sea of tears as the three of them marched down the hall away from her.

"Bibi! Wait for me. I'll walk out with you guys." She turned back to Peter, who was zipping up his duffel bag.

"Peter?"

"What?" He looked her in the eyes.

"I love you, y'know."

"I know." He held her gaze.

"See, I'm just hanging back, and giving you some room. When, and if, you're ready to love me again just let me know, give me some kind of sign. Y'know, whistle 'Dixie' or speak in Pig Latin or something and I'll be there. I'm just waiting, okay?"

"Okay." The two of them were silent for a moment. "Good luck today," he said, still holding her gaze.

"Thanks," she said, not wanting to leave.

"Mommy, come!"

"You better get going."

"Right," Ellie said, reluctantly backing out of the room.

Lisa Bienstock, looking slightly less chic and a little thick through the middle since becoming a mother, was chewing on a Stim-U-Dent and pacing back and forth in the large windowed HBO conference room. "Now, don't be nervous. You'll be great. It's a great idea and you're hysterical."

She's the one who's nervous, Ellie thought.

"Now, Michelle and Larry are great," Lisa said, still pacing. "They really are, but Michelle doesn't have the greatest people skills."

"So Michelle's a bitch?"

"No, not at all. In fact she's just back from a personality enhancement seminar, so I heard she's much more animated now."

"A personality enhancement seminar? You're kidding."

Lisa shook her head just as the conference room door opened. The two women exchanged an *oh, shit* look. Did they hear us, Ellie wondered as the omnipotent Larry and Michelle walked in.

Larry, tall and skinny with messy brown hair and a goatee, wore a green Telluride T-shirt, cargo shorts, and black suede Merrells. Oh, my God! It's a Shaggy from *Scooby Doo*, Ellie thought.

Michelle's jet black hair flowed down to the middle of her back. She wore lots of turquoise jewelry and a snug white T-shirt, and her generous hips were poured into a pair of faded Levi's.

Okay, so it's Cher and Shaggy, Ellie thought, could be worse.

"This is Ellie Fuller, the fabulously talented woman I've been telling you about," Lisa said, gesturing to Ellie.

"Hi, nice to meet . . ." Ellie walked toward them, her hand outstretched. Larry and Michelle both mumbled hellos, then slumped into two chairs at the conference table.

"She must be a *miracle worker* if she can make a show about *parenting* interesting enough for me to fly all the way to this stinkin' city."

"I guess you're not a dad," Ellie said, trying to keep it light.

"Not likely," he said, propping his feet up on a neighboring chair.

"Ellie?" Michelle/Cher was addressing her.

"Yeah?"

"I saw you do a set at Caroline's back in the nineties. You were brilliant," she said, moving as few facial muscles as possible.

"Thanks!" Ellie felt as if she'd just been sainted.

"Can we get started?" Larry asked. He had the disdainful expression of a teenager being forced to endure a lecture on responsibility.

"Yeah." Michelle checked her watch. "I have a massage at Bliss in forty-five minutes." Then she grabbed an extra chair and propped up her boot-clad feet as well.

And this is *after* personality enhancement?

"Oh-*kay!*" Lisa said, giving Ellie a *good luck* grin and taking a chair up front.

"Well, here we go!" Ellie moved the chair in front of her aside, then she stood at the head of the table CEO-style, placed her notes in front of her, took a deep breath, and . . .

"*Pregnant on Purpose* will have all the juicy 'girl' energy of *Sex and the City*, all the dish of *The View*, all the controversy and fun of *Politically Incorrect*, plus more star power than you can find at your local multiplex." She paused and surveyed her audience. Michelle's face was so impassive that Ellie wondered if perhaps she had gone suddenly deaf. And Larry, jaw slacked, sat fiddling with his goatee.

She opened with her conception monologue, then she gave them the format of the show, the topics. She gave them all her funniest anecdotes, all her best jokes . . . nothing. With each bit and story and joke, Ellie could feel her breath getting shallower, her heart rate increasing, and her whole body sweating.

What the fuck am I doing here? she wondered. She had rehearsed the pitch so many times and Larry and Michelle were so disinterested that Ellie's mind kept wandering. I wonder how long Bibi will keep the kids at the park. If this thing's over soon, maybe I can get there before they leave, she thought as she launched into her bit about a support group for kids who murder their parents. Well, they're zombies, but at least they're not chatting on their cell phones or writing in their Palm Pilots.

The end was in sight. Ellie took a deep breath, squared her shoulders, and called up her CEO persona once again.

"*Pregnant on Purpose* is a show that's got everything: humor, conflict, love, sacrifice—even sex. And it's a show that was custom-made for HBO because it's got balls and a heart at the same time. *Pregnant on Purpose* is a show that can't miss."

There was a beat.

"Lisa." Michelle called Lisa over. Lisa skooched her chair between Michelle's and Larry's, and the three of them huddled together speaking in hushed tones.

Brother! Ellie thought. She walked to the windowed wall and looked north to Central Park and waited.

"Of course. No. No problem. Great!" Lisa's overly enthusiastic voice rose above the others.

Ten minutes later the three of them were *still* whispering and Ellie was getting antsy.

"Listen, guys, I don't want to be a jerk but I'm supposed to be leaving for the shore in less than an hour."

"Yes, we all have busy lives, Ellie," Michelle said with a snotty smile.

"Ellie—" Larry this time "—we have a great idea for the show that we're sure you're going to love." He took his feet off the chair next to him and patted it. Ellie looked to Lisa, hoping to get some hint about her future in Lisa's expression, but she was examining her manicure. Ellie walked slowly to the seat next to Shaggy, sat down, and braced herself for the blow.

"Ellie—" Larry gave her an insipid smile "—Tracy Ullman is looking for a new vehicle, and we told her about your show. She loves *Pregnant on Purpose*, and she's agreed to host it."

All movement and sound stopped in the conference room. Lisa, Michelle, and Larry were watching Ellie like nurses in a psych ward with a violent schizophrenic on their hands. Ellie stood, gathered up her notes, and put her purse on her shoulder.

"I quit," she said simply.

"Come on, now. You'd still be head writer," Michelle said, sounding almost as if she had a personality. "You could probably even be a guest now and then. We'll get you double scale and . . ."

"I *might* get to be a guest on the show that *I* created? No, I don't think so." She walked to the door.

"Come on, Ellie! Don't be a spoilsport," Larry piped in. "Look, Tracy's a name, you're not. She's got a track record. It's nothing personal. That's just how it is in the real world."

Ellie whipped around and fired. "Larry, I *live* in the real world. As a matter of fact, I would bet that *my* world is quite a bit *more* real than yours. And nothing personal? It couldn't get much more personal; this is *my* idea and *my* show with *my* voice. Jesus! It's my fucking life! And I've worked like a dog on it and I'm not giving it away."

"But, Ellie, you could—" Lisa tried to speak.

"Uh-uh." Ellie put her hand up and wiggled her index finger at the trio. "No! I've been giving away parts of myself left and right lately and saying yes to things when my instincts were saying no and this is where it stops. Right now it's stopping!" She opened the conference room door, then looked over her shoulder and smiled at the dumbfounded group.

"Nothing personal." And out she went.

Chapter Thirty-Eight

Ellie was beaming as she racewalked toward home. As their building came into view, she could see Peter meticulously arranging suitcases, coolers, and floaties in the trunk of their blue Audi. Raffi was blaring from the car stereo, and Ahnika and Angus sat in their car seats, singing along.

"Well, what did the big shots say?" Peter asked.

"I quit."

"What?" He dropped a bag of linens into the open trunk. "You're kidding."

"No."

"Why? What'd they do?"

Ellie gave Peter the blow-by-blow as they packed and repacked the car, trying like hell to get a month's worth of stuff into the small trunk.

" 'Sorry, nothing personal,' I said, and I just walked out," Ellie said, finishing the story.

Peter's eyes were like saucers.

"But here's the big thing," she continued, "when I was pitching it to them and they were barely registering a pulse, I thought, what the hell am I doing here? And then, after I told them no, when I got in the elevator, I had this huge smile on my face, and I realized that I was relieved!"

"Relieved?"

"Yeah! When I was giving the kids a bath the other night and I thought, *this* is my gig. I don't need another gig right now. I wasn't looking to have my own show. After Angus was born, we figured it was a five-year stint, remember?" Peter nodded. "Okay, one year down. In four years, Angus'll be in kindergarten and Ahnika'll be in second grade, and then I'll get a little of my life back. But, in the meantime, mothering is my gig. And even though I was exhausted and disoriented and all that stuff, I was perfectly happy doing that—until Lisa Bienstock called and—and I just lost my way. I mean, it wasn't even *my* idea to pitch a show to HBO."

"That's true."

"I just didn't have the brains to say no." Just like with Missy, Ellie realized. It wasn't *my* idea to have an affair. I just didn't say no.

"So, Tracy Ullman, huh?"

"God does for us what we cannot do for ourselves."

"Man, you are like Twelve Step Barbie."

"Scary, isn't it?" Ellie laughed. "Yeah, Twelve Step Barbie; she comes with a folding chair and a meeting list. Then there's Bulimic Barbie, my evil twin; she comes with two pints of Häagen-Dazs, three bags of chips, a case of Diet Coke, and a toilet."

He smiled at her. "Who knew losing your deal with HBO would make you so peppy?"

Ellie shrugged and smiled, thinking—Well, I'm pretty fucking ecstatic that you're talking to me again. She wasn't sure, but it seemed as if he was acting like the old Peter; treating her the way he did before the whole Missy thing.

"Go! Go!" Angus called from the car.

"Mommy, Daddy, let's go!" Ahnika bellowed.

"Okay!" Peter and Ellie said simultaneously as they closed the trunk.

Peter got in the driver's seat as Ellie climbed over Angus's feet and wedged her ass in the small space between the two car seats in the back.

"Mommy, how many days till my birthday?" Ahnika asked as Peter pulled away from the curb.

"Sixteen, sweetie."

"Is that a lot?"

"Well, we started counting at 132 days. So, no, it's not a lot."

"For my party, are we going to the boardwalk and the rides?"

"We are!"

"Whoopee!"

"Oh, I almost forgot," Ellie said, "we need to stop at the Love Store, for diapers."

"No problem," Peter said, turning onto Seventy-second Street.

Ellie paid for her two packages of Huggies, grabbed her bag, and turned to go.

"What d'ya think? Does this color work?"

Ellie heard a familiar voice behind her. Oh, my God, oh, oh, my God! she thought and she turned to see Robbie Boots puckering her lips at the woman behind the makeup counter.

"Looks good," the woman said, without an ounce of conviction.

"I dunno." Robbie squinted at her reflection in a small mirror on the counter.

"It's too pink," Ellie said.

Robbie turned. Her face lit up. "I always go for the pink one, don't I?"

"You do."

"And I can't wear pink, can I?"

"No, you can't." Ellie was so happy to see her old friend that she wanted to wrap her arms around her and squeeze her for about ten minutes.

"I'm gonna pass," Robbie told the woman, handing back the lipstick.

"How are the kids?" Robbie asked, gesturing to the diapers.

"Still pooping," Ellie said, deadpan. Robbie chuckled. "Ahnika's toilet trained, of course."

"She's not!"

"She is! She's almost three."

"Wow! How's Peter?"

"Good, he's good." There was an awkward silence. "Where are you? Did you move?"

"Yes!" Robbie waved a diamond-clad hand in front of Ellie. "I moved in with my fiancé."

"My fiancé! Get out of town!" Ellie said, giving Robbie a playful shove.

"I know. Can you stand it?"

"That was kind of fast, wasn't it?"

"Yeah. Like you and Peter."

Is that a sheepish grin? Ellie wondered, studying her ex-best friend. "Well, that's fab! He's not a comic, is he?"

"Are you kidding? He's a civil rights lawyer."

"So he's like Gandhi."

"Basically." Robbie brushed her wavy red hair off of her forehead, looking suddenly dreamy. "He's perfect."

"Robbie, I'm so happy for you, really!"

"Hey! We're having a little engagement party." Robbie was rummaging in her beach bag of a purse. "Here." She thrust an invitation at Ellie. "It's next week."

Ellie took the invitation and read it. "At the Pierre? My, my!"

"Are you kidding? My father's so ecstatic that I met a nice guy and that I'm actually getting married before my last eggs drop, he would've rented out Buckingham Palace but it was booked. Between this party, the wedding, the reception . . . he's spending my entire inheritance on this fuckin' thing. Come! I want you and Peter to come, really! It's going to be a blast!"

"We're not going to be here. We're going to the shore."

"Ho, ho, ho! Get her!"

"Yeah, well, I just live the perfect life, never a bump in the road."

Robbie gave her a look.

"I'm kidding." Ellie suppressed an urge to spill the entire Aaron Spelling nightmare of the last few months.

"So, your life sucks?"

"Well, the jury's still out."

"Excuse me?"

"Let's just say I've had a *challenging* year. Yes, I think that's the euphemism for it."

Robbie furrowed her brow at her friend. "You okay?"

Ellie considered the question. "Yes. I am. I'm okay."

"Good. Are you writing?"

"I was. Remember Lisa Bienstock?"

"I heard she's at HBO now."

"She is. Well. I have a great Lisa Bienstock story but—" Ellie glanced out the glass door of the Love Store to the street and saw Peter, turned around in the driver's seat and fussing with Ahnika "—I'll have to tell you some other time. I should go. I left Peter alone in the car with the kids, he's double-parked, and—"

"Go! Go!" Robbie shooed her towards the door.

"Congratulations on your impending nuptials," Ellie said in an arch English accent.

"Thank you, dahling," Robbie said with the same upper crust accent. Then she put her hand on Ellie's shoulder.

"Ellie, I'm glad I ran into you because I've been thinking about you a lot lately. See, Allen and I got this puppy—Sydney—and he's *so fucking cute!* But he is *so much work!* And I keep thinking about you—while I'm scooping up his poop or lugging him to the vet or walking him at 6 A.M.— I keep thinking, my God! how did Ellie do it with two *kids* so close together! I—I mean, he's a puppy. I don't have to breastfeed him or change his diapers. Anyway, I've just been thinking about how—y'know— how after Angus was born, how I didn't cut you a fucking break. I mean, I just didn't get it. I didn't get how hard it was. And I guess—part of it was I didn't want things to change. Y'know, you and I had a pretty good gig and I wanted everything to stay the same. But—life goes on. I've got Allen now, and you and Peter are happy and—well—things change, right?"

Ellie thought of her mother's words and laughed. "Yep, things change." Ellie said, once again resisting the urge to tell Robbie how much she'd fucked up her life. Robbie pushed the door open and the two friends stepped out of the Love Store and into the bright June sun.

Robbie looked at her watch. "Oh, I'd better run. I'm taking the one-fifteen sculpt at Equinox. Get this butt in shape for my wedding." Robbie smacked her perfect ass.

"B.I.D.," Ellie said, smiling.

"*Some* things change, but my Body Image Distortion is eternal."

"It was good to see you," Ellie called.

"Good to see you, too," Robbie called over her shoulder as she headed west on Seventy-second Street. "Give Peter my best, will you?"

"Sure."

"That's my new number on the invitation. Call me!"

Wow, Ellie thought as Peter pulled the Audi onto the West Side Highway, Robbie Boots, the single woman's best friend, is having her engagement party at the Pierre! Things really *do* change.

"Was that Robbie you were talking to?" Peter asked as Ellie squeezed back into her spot.

"Yes! And guess what? She's engaged."

"Wow!"

"I know, isn't that wild?"

The floor space in the backseat was packed, leaving no place for Ellie to put her feet. In a desperate attempt to get comfortable, she kicked off her clogs, stretched her left leg between the two front seats, and rested her heel on the console next to Peter's elbow.

"Daddy, I wanna hear *Buzz Buzz*," Ahnika called.

"Okay." Peter ejected Raffi and put the *Buzz Buzz* tape in, then pulled into traffic.

"Someday, maybe, when you're both in college," Ellie said, "Mommy's actually going to sit in the front seat with Daddy." She caught Peter's eye in the rearview mirror. Is he smiling? she wondered as Laurie Birkner's voice filled the car.

Peter and Ahnika began to sing along, "Buzz buzz ba-buzz buzz . . ."

What's he thinking? Ellie wondered, staring at the back of his neck as they headed south on the West Side Highway. Is he dreading this vacation? Looking forward to it? She looked at Ahnika, on her left, singing at the top of her lungs, and Angus, on her right, squealing and bouncing along to the music. Then she gazed across the Hudson; the Palisades looked like a brochure for New Jersey, all green and gorgeous above the sparkling river. Thank you, God, she thought, for this day, for this moment right now.

When the song ended, Ahnika shouted "Again!"

"Okay!" Peter pushed the rewind button. Then, instead of putting his hand back on the steering wheel, he placed it squarely on Ellie's bare foot and gave it a squeeze. Then, clear as a bell, in the now silent car, as the tape rewound, Ellie's sweet husband began to whistle "Dixie."